# PRAISE FOR "THE BONE HUNGER" BY CARRIE RUBIN

"The reveal is a real shocker, and Rubin's winning lead is well-suited to sustain a series. This is just the ticket for Robin Cook fans."

*PUBLISHERS WEEKLY*

"The author's prose is sleek and organic, regarding both descriptions and punchy dialogue. But the most striking passages are from the killer's periodic narrative perspective —disturbing thoughts from a clearly tortured mind… An aptly crafted, riveting, and often unnerving mystery."

*KIRKUS REVIEWS*

"Rubin's ability to blend the investigative and medical thriller components into a wider-ranging exploration of Ben's psyche and his career and family challenges lends to a story that is gripping, involving, and hard to put down."

D. DONOVAN, SENIOR REVIEWER, *MIDWEST BOOK REVIEW*

D1484785

# PRAISE FOR "THE BONE CURSE" BY CARRIE RUBIN

"A tense, perceptive tale of an investigation into a terrifying threat."

—*KIRKUS REVIEWS*

"Realistic details of Ben's hospital clerkship as he and other med students diagnose patients help ground the story's paranormal elements. ... The novel's strength lies in the author's sensitive commentary on adult responsibilities and mental illness."

—*PUBLISHERS WEEKLY*

"*The Bone Curse* is a strong medical thriller—inclusive, skillfully written, and inviting."

—*FOREWORD REVIEWS*

"Take note medical thriller fans, the genre has a new contender, and her name is Carrie Rubin."

—LARRY BROOKS, *USA TODAY* BESTSELLING AUTHOR

"A teeth-grinding story of ancient curses and mystical remedies ... The Bone Curse will keep even the most skeptical reader awake long past midnight."

—ANDRA WATKINS, *NEW YORK TIMES* BESTSELLING AUTHOR OF *NOT WITHOUT MY FATHER*

# PRAISE FOR "EATING BULL" BY CARRIE RUBIN

"A solid thriller that manages to infuse one boy's coming-of-age with a whole lot of murder."

—KIRKUS REVIEWS

"A deftly crafted novel of suspense and a compelling read from beginning to end... Very highly recommended."

—MIDWEST BOOK REVIEW

"Each of Rubin's characters is carefully developed and believable."

—AKRON BEACON JOURNAL

"Rubin is a masterful storyteller who weaves her medical knowledge into a gripping thriller, diving head-first into a meaty subject that has been ignored for far too long."

—DIANNE GRAY, AWARD-WINNING AUSTRALIAN AUTHOR OF *SOUL'S CHILD* AND *THE EVERYTHING THEORY*

# PRAISE FOR "THE SENECA SCOURGE" BY CARRIE RUBIN

". . . fun, fast, original, and won't strain your emotions."

—SCIENCETHRILLERS.COM

"*The Seneca Scourge* by Carrie Rubin was impossible to put down."

—TRUDI LOPRETO FOR READERS FAVORITE

"I love, love, love, **LOVED** this book. 4 out of 4 stars...well written, well thought out, well planned, and just a great book altogether."

—ONLINE BOOK CLUB

"Rubin masterfully blends medical thriller, mystery, and sci-fi into a thoroughly enjoyable read."

—AUDREY KALMAN, AUTHOR OF *WHAT REMAINS UNSAID*

# THE BONE HUNGER

# THE BONE HUNGER

CARRIE RUBIN

INDIGO DOT PRESS

Indigo Dot Press
indigodotpress@gmail.com

First edition, 2020

Library of Congress Control Number: 2020907746

FIC031040  FICTION / Thrillers / Medical
FIC030000  FICTION / Thrillers / Suspense
FIC031000  FICTION / Thrillers / General

ISBN 978-1-7328541-4-7 (hardcover)
ISBN 978-1-7328541-5-4 (trade paperback)
ISBN 978-1-7328541-6-1 (ebook)

Cover design by Lance Buckley Design

*For Brenda, Dan, and Jo'Rinda*

# 1

I nside the wintry woodlands of Philadelphia's Wissahickon Valley Park, the mother of Benjamin Oris's child cried out, "Oh my God, is that a leg?"

From his crouched position on the deserted trail, Ben shot up, abandoning Sir Quincy mid-pet, the yellow Lab sniffing the rocky terrain for the promised but undelivered treat. Buffeted by the January wind whipping the trees and bellowing through the gorge, he spotted nothing but a Walmart bag swaying from a snow-covered branch and a discarded soda bottle jutting from a shrub.

"It's just plastic," he said, returning to Sir Quincy. He relinquished the bone-shaped biscuit and ruffled the dog's fur with his glove. "Don't worry, bud. We'll get you out of this cold soon. You, me, and Maxwell got a new train track to build."

"Not that." Sophia Diaz's fleeced mitten jabbed the air. "*That.* It's sticking out of those bushes. You don't have to be an orthopedic surgeon to know what a leg looks like, you know."

In the frigid air Ben could literally see her breath of sarcasm. He peered again in the direction she pointed and this time followed her mitten's trajectory beyond the connecting trail that led up to

Council Rock and the fifteen-foot Lenape warrior that perched there.

"I don't see any—" A fleshy mass protruded from a tangle of bushes and broken branches near the stump of a felled tree. "Jesus, that *is* a leg."

He hurried forward, Sir Quincy following along on his leash and Sophia's boots crunching the frozen ground behind them. With her bum knee, she shouldn't even be on this trail. Its bouldered and uneven terrain required cautious footwork, especially in winter. But despite the frosty weather, she'd been adamant about tagging along on his Sunday morning hike. "There's something I need to tell you," she'd said.

On the other side of the connecting trail, Ben held a protective arm in front of her, his puffer jacket an insufficient barrier against the elements. With the partially frozen creek rushing and lapping a short distance away, they stared at the prickly bushes near the oak's wide stump. From the mess of twigs and dead leaves, a bare foot up to its shin poked out. Like the rest of Mother Nature in the miles-long park, the leg wore a fresh dusting of snow.

Ben's core dropped another ten degrees. "Whoever it is, he—"

"Or she."

"—has been here since before it snowed." A quick scan of the trail confirmed no tracks but their own.

Sensing Sir Quincy's desire to explore their new find, Ben secured the leash around a nearby tree and offered another biscuit to keep him occupied. When he returned to Sophia, he grabbed her arm just in time. "Don't touch him."

"He could be hurt."

"He could be dangerous."

That gave Sophia pause. Her hand hovered in the air. In reality, Ben knew the owner of the limb was no danger to anyone. The foot didn't move. Didn't wiggle its toes. Didn't flex its ankle. And even under a thin veil of snow the shin's coloring was off. Though Ben couldn't see the rest of the body through the bushes, he knew whoever lay there was long gone.

"Is he dead?" she whispered.

"We better call 911." He zipped his coat as high as it would go. Doctor or not, finding a dead guy in the park was unnerving.

"Shouldn't we at least check to see if he's alive? What if he needs CPR?"

"He's beyond CPR. We shouldn't disturb the body in case it's a crime."

"You don't know that for sure." Sophia, a good Samaritan if there ever was one, crouched down and tapped the guy's foot with her mitten. "You okay? Hello?"

"Sophia, don't."

"Can you hear me?" She tugged the lifeless foot. "Are you—"

The leg popped free from the bushes.

No body followed.

Sophia stumbled backward, the limb still clutched in her hand. Like a slab of frozen meat, it dragged against the snowy ground, leaving a dirt-streaked trail behind it. She jerked her arm away, and all color drained from her face. From his tethered position, Sir Quincy barked.

Ben gaped at the morbid find. A chewed-up leg, severed about three inches above the knee, lay on the rocky path. *It can't be.*

After a beat, he realized Sophia was still on her bottom. He helped her up and then crept back to where the limb had dislodged. Carefully, he riffled through the mess of bushes, branches, and winter debris. Snow and dirt matted his gloves, and thorny bramble pricked his wrist in the gap below his coat sleeve, but no dead body materialized. Nothing farther up on the trail either. Only swaying trees and hilly, jagged terrain in every direction. Then again, had he expected otherwise?

Stepping back, he yanked his knit cap lower over his ears. "You okay, Sophe? You hurt your knee?"

She brushed snow off her ski pants. "I'm fine. Just a little startled." After retrieving her phone from the pocket of her parka, she plucked off one of her mittens with her teeth. While it dangled from her mouth like a limp rabbit, she fumbled with her screen.

Although Ben's shock was dissipating, his chill was not. Shivering in the blowing wind, he bent over and examined the severed limb, careful not to disturb it further. Its short journey with Sophia had shaken free most of the snow, and frozen strands of shredded tissue above the knee were now visible. Near the joint and below it, bites of various depths punctured the hairy shin. Some tore away the flesh, revealing bloodless muscle and bone beneath. Others were more superficial. The work of scavengers, most likely, grateful for a winter feed.

"No, we're on the Orange Trail," Sophia was saying. "Below the Tedyuscung Statue."

A flash of silver caught Ben's eye.

*Is that a...?*

He squatted for a better look.

*Oh God, it is.*

He drew closer, the frozen ground dampening the hem of his sweatpants. An implant. An orthopedic implant. The same kind he'd helped place during surgery nearly every day for the past two weeks. Through a quarter-sized opening on the side of the knee, where skin and muscle had been torn away, the device's smooth, metallic surface gleamed. Shaped like a horseshoe, only the implant's edge was visible now, the amputation too high above the knee to see the rest.

A hand on his shoulder made him jump. "They're on their way," Sophia said.

Realizing he'd been holding his breath, he exhaled and glanced up. Her lips were bluer than her scarf. Hoping to shield her from the wind, he started to rise, but when he moved, his running shoe shifted the leg. A tattoo on the lifeless calf popped into view.

Ben's stomach flipped, and his whole body tensed. He could no longer delude himself. From the moment Sophia had dislodged the limb, a part of him knew what he'd find.

As if sensing his master's angst, Sir Quincy's barking grew louder. Too upset to console the dog, he stared at the tattoo on the amputated limb. A cartoon roadrunner. One whose head, beak, and feathered tail were familiar, even after being chewed up by animals.

Slowly, he stepped back. He considered bolting. Considered being long gone when the police arrived. They didn't need him.

What was done was done. No need for him to get involved any further, right?

"Are you okay?" Sophia was studying him with concern. She seemed a mile away. All he could manage was an open-mouthed silence.

*I can't get caught up in weird shit again. Not with so much on the line.*

He'd lose the reputation he'd built. He'd lose his shot at the junior-resident research grant. He'd lose the respect of his superiors —and just when he and Dr. Lock were getting along so well. It had been over three years since a horrific, freakish thread of events had derailed his life, and though he'd moved on, there were those in his professional circle who hadn't forgotten. Would never forget, in fact. So no, he wouldn't survive another scandal.

But there he was, about to dive headfirst into one.

Because Benjamin Oris, second-year orthopedic surgery resident, knew whose severed leg it was.

# 2

Inside OR number four in the east wing of Montgomery Hospital, Dr. Kent Lock, dressed in full sterile garb that resembled a hazmat suit, bowed his head and steepled his gloves in front of his gown, its blue fabric rustling against the surgical drapes of the anesthetized patient. Although a Christian prayer in a diverse hospital seemed a little last-century to Ben, he kept the thought to himself. He didn't want his impatience—or his atheism—screwing up his first case with the man. Working with one of the best reconstructive surgeons in the country was a small price to pay for piety.

"Lord," the Nordic-looking attending began, "thank you for bringing this surgical team back together. If not for your good grace, all of us might have died in the crash."

With a lowered gaze, Ben glanced at the patient on the table, a sinewy sixty-one-year-old mail carrier awaiting a new knee. Having chosen general anesthesia over regional, the guy was hearing nothing but the prayers of Saint Propofol. In the sterile field, his only visible body part was his right leg, its knee joint flexed and covered with a clear incise drape. Beneath that sheer, sticky plastic, his scrubbed flesh glowed like a Betadine pumpkin.

"Thank you for our pilot's skill," Dr. Lock continued, "and for

Alaska's cushioning snow. Five days we froze and starved, but you didn't abandon us."

Across the table a throat cleared. It seemed to come from Angela Choi, mother of two and Lock's physician's assistant, or as he put it, his "right hand, left hand, and everything in between." Aside from the fact she too had been in the plane crash and used to work in a nursing home, Ben knew little about her.

"Thank you for keeping us safe. Thank you for getting Michael to the hospital in time. That he lost only a toe and not the whole foot is a miracle."

Michael Alvarez, the scrub nurse on Angela's left, whose sterile tray displayed the myriad metal and plastic pieces required for a joint replacement, whispered an *amen*. Like the others, he was in full aseptic garb, his gloves clasped in prayer at chest level, but whether his reverent posturing was out of sincerity or for show, Ben didn't know. Before Dr. Lock had arrived, the thirty-something nurse with closely cropped hair was boasting about his phalangeal sacrifice. If he was upset by his missing toe he hadn't shown it.

At the head of the bed, the anesthesiologist, Dr. Muti King, a slight man in his fifties with a reserved demeanor, quietly swiveled his stool to adjust the anesthetic drip. Ben hoped the movement would jar Dr. Lock away from the heavens (it didn't), but at the same time he understood the team's need for a devotional respite. Save for the patient and the circulating nurse, Ben was the only person in the room who hadn't been on the humanitarian mission four weeks earlier that had ended nose-first in the Alaskan tundra, halfway between Fairbanks and Fort Yukon. Aside from Dr. Lock, the other passengers in the OR who were on board were Dr. King, Angela, Michael, and Joel Smith, a med student with a Hollywood face and a cavalier attitude who had once wanted Ben dead and probably still did. A senior resident, Karen Dukakis, was another survivor of the crash, but given she wasn't a member of Dr. Lock's core team, she wasn't in the operating room with them that morning.

"We pray you'll look after the Alaskan natives who couldn't get their surgeries because of our accident. Keep them in good health until our return."

*Return? This guy's ballsy.*

"And finally, Lord, we thank you for giving us Dr. Oris for the next two months. From what I hear, he's a rising star among the second-year residents. May I do his education justice."

Ben felt himself blush, not only from the unexpected praise but from his disinterested mind-wandering during the prayer. Beneath his sterile attire he was already starting to sweat, but the full suits, complete with head cover and plastic face shields, were necessary to minimize the risk of infection, which could severely complicate a joint replacement.

"Amen," Dr. Lock said.

"Amen," Dr. King and Michael echoed.

Everyone straightened and rotated their spines, as if finally free to move. Having already performed the surgical safety checklist, they were ready to begin.

A smile crinkled the forty-year-old skin around Dr. Lock's eyes. He held out an open palm. "Scalpel please, Michael. Joseph Sampson here is expecting a new knee, and we always deliver."

As he cut through skin and soft tissue, the orthopedic surgeon narrated his actions to Ben and Joel, pausing occasionally to allow Angela to suction away pooling blood. "You'll be reconstructing hips and knees on your own by the time your rotation is done," he said to Ben. "But I need to see for myself that you're competent before I hand over the saw." He glanced across the table at Joel, who had to strain his neck to peer past Angela and Michael for a glimpse of the surgical field. "You'll mostly be watching. In my OR, med students take a back seat to residents."

Using small retractors, Dr. Lock spread the knee tissue apart. Skin and a scant amount of yellow fat bunched up behind the metal lips of the instruments. When the wound gaped widely, he indicated Ben take hold of the retractors. As Ben did so, the surgeon cauterized a bleeding vessel, and the charcoal scent of burned tissue charred the air.

"Wider," Lock ordered when Ben's hold on the retractors loosened. "That's better. Tell me what you see." The surgeon rotated the kneecap out of the way.

Ben studied the inner anatomy of the mail carrier's flexed joint. The pinkish-yellow surface of the femur yawned at a wide angle to the tibia below. "His cartilage is shot."

"Exactly. Looks like he's been bone-on-bone for a while. Tough old bird. Part of it's from a nasty joint infection he got as a child. The rest is from years of walking miles every day."

"I've never seen so much erosion of the tibial surface."

"Same here," Michael said. "That joint's begging for a replacement."

"Well, he's come to the right man for the job." Dr. Lock scraped the bone's surface with his metal probe. "Even if he had to wait eleven months to get on my table."

A whiff of ego lingered in the air. *Eau de surgeon*, Ben's friend Laurette would call it. "But not you," she'd add in her Caribbean accent. "You are different." He wasn't sure about that, but he appreciated her saying so.

Dr. Lock peered over his shoulder at Ben. "Speaking of poor joint surfaces, how's Sophia's knee doing?"

Ben's hold on the retractors loosened. He tried to keep the surprise out of his voice. "You know Sophia?"

Lock extended his hand toward Michael. "Alignment guide please." The scrub nurse slapped the guide onto the surgeon's palm. "She came looking for you in the residents' lounge last week. I was outside the door talking to your chief. He introduced me to her."

The way Dr. Lock said the word "chief" confirmed what Ben already knew: the reconstructive surgeon and the chief resident, Lenny Reynolds, were the feuding Hatfield and McCoy of the orthopedic surgery department. For that reason Ben had no intention of telling his new attending that he and the chief resident were good friends.

"I told Sophia that given the recent events, you wouldn't officially start with me until today. She knew about the plane crash— probably from you—and we had a nice chat." Dr. Lock stared up at the paneled ceiling. "She even prayed with me."

"Um..." This was more information than Ben could process.

"Is Sophia your baby mama?" Michael handed Dr. Lock the bone saw.

The surgeon gripped the tool and narrowed his eyes at the scrub nurse. "Ms. Diaz is the mother of Ben's child. Show a little respect."

*What the hell's happening here?* Like the team's airplane, Ben felt as if he'd just nosedived into a parallel universe. Blending his personal life with his professional one was something he avoided, especially in a room full of people.

Lock laughed. "Relax, Oris. You look like you just chopped off the patient's leg. I'm only asking about Sophia's knee because we're meeting up this week to talk about a replacement."

Meeting up? As in a clinic appointment? Or as in something else? Ben and Sophia shared custody of their toddler son, and although there was no romance between them, he needed to know if knee surgery was on her docket. His skin itched all over, but the sudden whir of the bone saw saved him from further conversation. He focused on keeping a firm grasp on the retractors while Dr. Lock molded the bone to fit the implant.

After several minutes of cutting, shaving, and pounding bone, the attending surgeon said, "There, that should do it." He straightened to full height, which was a good three inches taller than Ben's six feet. "Let's cement these suckers in place and get this guy one step closer to a pain-free mail route." After applying the cement, which looked like putty, Lock affixed the implants, first the tibial and femoral components and then the plastic spacer that fit in between. The implants differed a little in appearance from the few Ben had seen in med school. He knew each surgeon had their preference— including Lock's desire to use ones that had been customized to the patient—but he was still too startled by the mention of Sophia to ask about them.

Throughout the procedure, Lock, Michael, and Angela had made for a fluid team, the latter two ensuring a seamless juggling of the many implant parts and tools and offering their opinions when needed. When Ben mentioned as much, Lock said, "That's because I sent these two directly to the implant manufacturer for training. No need for device reps in my OR. Saves the hospital a lot of money." Finally, with all the pieces in place, the attending surgeon flexed and extended the knee, making sure the new joint was up to the task of human mobility.

As he did so, the patient's calf tattoo of a cartoon bird popped into view. During the pre-operative exam earlier, Ben had asked the man about it. The mail carrier had said, "Some days I gotta move so fast to finish my route, I feel like a damn roadrunner."

Ben had laughed. "Not sure how fast a tattoo will make you move, Mr. Sampson, but that new knee we're about to give you? That thing'll keep you running for years."

———————

With the sun making its pink-orange descent behind dense clouds, Ben started early evening rounds on 4 East and 4 West, the ortho-pedic wings of Montgomery hospital. Situated in the heart of downtown Philadelphia, the main hospital building was a dated structure whose interior decor consisted of lofty plants and a nine-story atrium topped off by a glass ceiling. Nestled around this central building (and covering three city blocks) was the rest of the medical complex, including specialty clinics, research facilities, and academic offices. Some edifices connected via glass-enclosed skywalks. Others required an outdoor trip across the street. Given it was early January, many blustery crossings were in Ben's near future, especially since the winter was proving to be an arctic beast.

Frigid weather or not, he was upbeat and efficient, checking in with the nurses and weaving his way through every patient room. The steady work suited him. Over the last year and a half of resi-dency, he'd grown as comfortable in scrubs and a doctor's coat as he was in jeans and a tool belt. His entire life he'd only wanted to be one of two things: a carpenter or an orthopedic surgeon. During his twenties he labored on jobs for the former to save money for school for the latter, making him a good five or six years older than his counterparts. But he'd eventually made it, and nowadays, when he wasn't hammering, sawing, or drilling wood, he was hammering, sawing, or drilling bone.

His last patient to see on 4 East was Joseph Sampson, the man they'd operated on earlier that day. Tucked inside a bland double room with walls the color of eggshells, the mail carrier was grumbling about his "saltless soup and mushy potatoes." Other than that he was stable with good pain control. The bed next to him was empty.

"Tell you what," Ben said. "You let us get you up walking later tonight, and I'll bring you a slice of pizza from the cafeteria. Think your stomach's up for pepperoni?"

Mr. Sampson snorted. "Is a sailor up for a shag?" He flipped the sheet off his legs and pointed to the compressive sleeves on his lower limbs. "These things are driving me crazy, doc."

"You need them to prevent blood clots. Trust me, you don't want a clot traveling to your lungs. And make sure you keep blowing into that." Ben pointed to the plastic spirometer on the patient's bedside table and pulled on a pair of gloves. "It'll keep your lungs open." He unwrapped the patient's knee dressing and examined the stitches and incision site. "Looks great."

"Looks like a train track on a grapefruit."

"We'll get that drain out in the next day or two and hopefully your urinary catheter by later tonight."

"You'll get no argument from me there."

Ben fist-bumped Mr. Sampson, told him to keep up the good work, and headed to the academic building across the street via a second-floor skywalk. Lenny was working late, and Ben wanted to stop by for a visit. He hadn't seen the chief resident since the guy had returned from vacation a few days earlier, and he had a question about the schedule.

Inside the Morrison building, paneled ceilings and wainscoted walls bearing faculty photographs replaced the colorless confines of the hospital ward. After two staircases and one long administrative hall, he entered Lenny's office, a room crammed with a desk, two file cabinets, and three bookcases. A smaller desk, more of a tiny table with a chair, was squeezed in between two of the bookcases.

The stocky chief tipped back his wheeled chair and swiveled toward Ben. "Well, if it isn't the spine king himself." He put down his energy drink and waved a report in the air. "I was just reading Dr. Miller's evaluation of you. Looks like you aced his rotation. Says your spinal fusion skills are—and I quote—'kickass'. You must've given Miller a blow job for that kind of praise."

"I gave him two."

Lenny erupted in laughter and tossed Ben a red-hot jawbreaker from the pocket of his white coat.

Ben popped the fiery treat into his mouth. "Your dentist must love you. And those things'll kill you." He pointed to Lenny's energy drink and sat down on the tiny desk. It currently belonged to Chip Owens, a fifth-year resident recently appointed to be next year's chief. Unlike most surgery residency programs, whose chief resident position was filled by several fifth-years throughout their final year, Montgomery Hospital offered a full-time position for a deserving candidate. Though that meant staying on for a sixth year, the job was considered an honor, and Lenny would soon start showing Chip the ropes. Since Chip was an asshole, sitting on his leather blotter seemed fitting.

"I'm addicted to these hot little bastards." Lenny tossed a jawbreaker into his own mouth. He seemed over-caffeinated, his speech a bit rushed. "Besides, the nurses love them. Still won't date me though. Maybe I should carry Godiva chocolates. Up my game."

"Why don't you try talking to them instead?"

"Spoken like a man who's never had trouble getting women."

"Those days are behind me. I'm a dad now." Being a father before he was an established surgeon had never been part of Ben's plan, but a one-night stand had forever changed his life—for the better. He smiled at Lenny and added, "Besides, don't sell yourself short."

"Yeah, 'cause there's so much demand for a chubby chemistry major with glasses. How's Maxwell doing, by the way?"

"Great." Ben flashed Lenny a few pictures of Maxwell on his phone. "And that's Sir Quincy next to him. I told you about him, didn't I? We got him from a rescue a couple months ago. Fully house-trained, obedient, cool dog all around. He goes where Maxwell goes, so Sophe and I take turns with him."

"Good-looking pooch. What's up with the name?"

"Maxwell named him after his favorite steam engine. Those toy trains cost more than a knee replacement, but he's obsessed with them."

"What three-year-old boy isn't? And Sophia?"

"She's good, I guess. Other than handing off Maxwell, we haven't had much time to talk lately. Same can't be said for her and Dr. Lock." Ben cracked his neck, an old habit hard to break. "Apparently they've become quite chummy. Normally I wouldn't care—I'd be happy for her, you know?—but my attending surgeon? That's too close to home."

"That's my bad. I introduced them outside the residents' lounge, and they got to talking about her knee." Lenny gambled against physics and tilted his chair back even more. "I didn't know she had a history of cancer."

"Yeah, lymphoma. Her cancer's long gone, but the steroids she took for it really messed up her joint."

"She need a replacement already? How old is she, anyway?"

Ben shrugged. "Maybe. She's thirty-four, same as me, but physical therapy hasn't helped. She works from home as a web designer, but she still has to run around on Maxwell. With my schedule, I don't know where I'd be without her."

"Well, Lock's certainly the best choice for the job. Even if he is an asshat."

Ben shifted the candy to the other side of his mouth. "What's your beef with the guy, anyway?"

Lenny's chair dropped from its tilt with a thud. "Hey, you got my key?"

"Shoot. Forgot to bring it. It's in my locker. And don't think I didn't notice you changed the subject."

"Ah, just keep it for the next time I'm on vacation. Thanks again for feeding my fish."

"No big deal. Maxwell liked visiting them, especially that bluish-orange one. Calls him 'Stripey'."

"*Stripey* is a candy basslet that cost me nine hundred bucks."

"Jeez, Len. Glad I didn't overfeed him and send him to an early grave. Now, again, what's up with you and Dr. Lock?"

Lenny sighed and rubbed his jaw. There was a slight tremor in his hand. "I don't know, man. Maybe it's that whole 'consistent team' crap he spouts. This is a teaching hospital for God's sake and he's one of the best reconstructive surgeons around. But even I—a chief resident—can't do a hip or knee replacement with him. I'm not part of the *team*." He shook his head. "What an arrogant prick."

"He lets junior residents rotate with him."

"That's because the hospital makes him. There's only so far his and his family's money can go. Still, the powers that be cater to his every whim. Guess that's what happens when you fund a pavilion and get it named after you."

Lenny was referring to The Lock Pavilion (funded by The Lock Foundation), a new hospital wing created for the delivery of pro bono surgeries to those who would otherwise go without, particularly children from third-world countries, whom the hospital flew in at no cost. While a host of surgeons performed everything from cleft lip and palate repair to correction of congenital heart defects, Dr. Lock performed most of the orthopedic surgeries. Money from The Lock Foundation also funded uninsured patients who couldn't afford joint replacements. Tough to place such a charitable surgeon in the "arrogant prick" category, or at least the "prick" part, especially one who prayed before every surgery, but it was clear to Ben that Lenny did. Still, it seemed more than that. It seemed personal.

"Lock's had a rough go of it lately," Ben said, coming to the attending's defense. "That crash had to mess him up. Everyone else on the plane too."

The chief resident crunched the remains of his mouth-burning candy. "Fair enough. Poor Karen's hardly eating anything, and she's skinny enough as it is. 'Course, as a senior resident, she's not on Saint Lock's *teeeam* either. Had to go to Alaska just to get a chance to operate with him. Guess he doesn't balk at an extra hand when it comes to his charitable work." Lenny's expression lightened. "Hey, Karen won the Conley Grant when she was a second-year, you know. She says you're one of the best junior residents she's worked with. I think you're a shoo-in for the award." He winked. "And I'm one of the people who votes. You'd get to co-author a paper with Chief Fisher and everything."

Ben raised his hands. "Let's not get ahead of ourselves. I'm barely holding everything together as it is." But man, he wanted that win. He'd been working on his proposal every spare second he got.

"You're holding up better than the rest of us."

The tone of Lenny's voice and the sudden slackness in his face made Ben worry something was wrong. "Hey, what's up? Something bothering you?"

Lenny glanced at his phone screen. "Oh crap, I've gotta be somewhere." He burst up and hustled out the door, his voice fading down the hallway. "Sorry, man. Talk to you later."

His abrupt departure practically left skid marks on the carpet. Ben hoped the guy was okay. Despite the recent vacation, he'd seemed agitated and stressed. Ben would have to take him out for a drink. See what was up. Lenny was a great doctor, one who treated new residents with respect and helped them whenever he could. As an intern, Ben had ordered ampicillin for a severely penicillin-allergic patient. Although no allergies were listed in the chart, Ben should have confirmed it with the patient. It was a stupid but potentially deadly oversight. Thankfully, Lenny had caught the error before the patient received the drug. Ben had expected to be berated. Ridiculed, even. But Lenny had done neither. Instead, he relayed a tale of one of his own intern mistakes and added, "In medicine, mistakes are our harshest but best teacher. We never forget a serious mistake and we never make it again."

Truer words were never spoken. From that moment on, the first thing Ben did with each new admission was confirm that a patient's allergies were listed in the chart. So yeah, he owed a lot to Lenny. And that included trying to find out what was wrong.

3

No matter what I do, I can't shake the cold. Inside, outside, I shiver. My skin is numb, and my bones are frosted over. My cold is everywhere.

I crank the heat, my cold is there. I swaddle myself in blankets, my cold is there. I run in place until sweat stings my eyes, my cold is there.

And I'm hungry. Always so hungry. Nothing satisfies the gnawing icicles that poke and pierce my stomach.

Nothing.

4

On Thursday afternoon, Ben strolled into Joseph Sampson's hospital room and found him flipping through TV stations with one hand and drumming the bedrail with the other. "Took you long enough," the guy said. "After three days in this prison, I'm ready to bolt."

"Did you honor our deal?"

"I did."

Ben crossed his arms, his white coat bunching up against his scrubs. "You walked the twenty feet to the nurse's station like we agreed on?"

"Almost. Halfway, anyway. That physical therapist is even bossier than you."

"Halfway isn't good enough to prevent blood clots. You'll be on a blood thinner for a bit, but you still have to walk and move that limb around. If you get worried you've gone too far, we have wheelchairs in the hallway and by the elevators." Ben had expected Mr. Sampson to be discharged the day before, but despite the guy's years of walking a mail route, he wasn't ambulating as much as he should be. It appeared to be hesitancy on his part—not unusual for someone with a new joint—because his incision site looked clean, and his vital signs and lab work showed no signs of infection.

"I will, doc. Scout's honor." Mr. Sampson pointed to a walker in the corner of the room, the drugstore tag still dangling from its central bar. "Got that stupid thing waiting and ready to go. Wife picked it up yesterday. Makes me feel like a damn geezer."

"Everybody starts out with a walker. You'll need to keep working with the physical therapist for a few weeks too, but you'll be back to pounding the pavement soon enough." At least Ben hoped so. Dr. Lock had made it clear he was annoyed by the delayed discharge. Having a post-op complication would only irritate him further. The renowned attending had a surgical reputation to protect. He also had a church date with Sophia tonight. Was that even a thing? She'd asked Ben to take Maxwell so she could attend. "Okay then," he said to Mr. Sampson. "I'll write your discharge orders. Once the nurse reviews everything with you, you'll be free to go."

"Good. My new roommate is driving me nuts with his yakking. Wife couldn't take it anymore. She left for a cup of coffee."

Ben glanced at the empty bed near the window, its sheets obviously slept in. "Where is your new bestie?"

"Getting an X-ray. Hope he gets trapped in the machine."

"Nice to see surgery hasn't removed your sunny disposition."

"Ha, good one, doc. You're all right, you know that?"

"One last thing. Use your pain meds judiciously, but don't be a hero. If you're hurting, you won't be walking, and we need you to walk. We'll give you Tylenol with oxycodone, but—"

"Yeah, yeah, your chief already went over everything. You guys are Pete and Repeat."

Ben's arm whacked the bedside table and knocked over a cup of water. He snatched a wad of paper towels from the bathroom to mop it up. "My chief? What do you mean, my chief?"

"Your chief. The chief resident. Am I speaking Chinese?"

"Are you sure it wasn't my senior resident, Karen Dukakis?"

"Not unless Karen's a chubby man."

So it was definitely Lenny. Chip Owens, the chief-resident-in-training, was a fitness freak and the opposite of chubby. "Did Dr. Reynolds say what he wanted?"

Mr. Sampson looked at Ben like he had a plastic urinal coming out of his nose. "You guys ever hear of communication? You're making my head hurt. All I know is your chief picked up my pain meds and blood thinner from the outpatient pharmacy so the wife didn't have to wait in line—which I have to admit was damn decent of him—and then told me how often to take 'em."

Confused, making sure he'd heard right, Ben restated slowly, "Dr. Reynolds picked up your oxycodone prescription?"

"Good grief, there's a parrot in here. The bottle's in my bag over there if you don't believe me."

From the flimsy armoire next to the bathroom, Ben fetched an Army-green canvas bag that smelled of sweat and spilled beer. When he handed it to Mr. Sampson, the mail carrier plucked out a brown pill bottle. "See?"

The label showed nothing out of the ordinary. Ben shook the pills inside. Plenty to get Mr. Sampson by.

"Your chief's a nice guy. Said he likes to help patients and residents out whenever he can. Even gave me and Chatty Carl over there a red ball of fire from his doctor's coat. The damn thing practically burned a hole through my cheek."

That part Ben believed. Both the candy and the helping hand. Lenny was nothing if not generous.

"Sheesh, doc, you look like a sheep that's just had its ass shaved."

Despite his ongoing confusion, Ben laughed. "You sound like my friend. She's always talking about goats."

"Then you need to set your sights higher, young man. Or give the poor girl a new topic."

Ben chuckled again and headed to the door. "Trust me, Laurette's a better catch than the two of us combined. As for you, we'll get you out of here as soon as we can."

When he left the room, his levity faded and his bewilderment returned. Helping hand or not, fetching a patient's meds from the outpatient pharmacy was weird. Even for Lenny.

# 5

The following Tuesday morning Ben, along with the rest of Dr. Lock's surgical team, waited inside OR number three for the man himself to arrive. At forty-five minutes past eight, he was uncharacteristically late. Save for Dr. Muti King, perched on his anesthesiologist's stool, and the circulating nurse, all the team members were scrubbed in and wearing their hazmat-like garb. Too bad for Ben, because when an itch on his nose refused to abate, a wiggle of his nostrils inside the face shield offered nothing but an extra whiff of plastic and synthetic fibers.

On the operating table lay Kim Templeton, a fifty-nine-year-old paralegal awaiting a new hip. A skiing accident ten years prior had shattered the old one, and despite repair at the time, she hadn't been pain-free since. Though she had opted for a spinal block instead of general anesthesia, Dr. King's sedating cocktail had lulled her to sleep. Her soft snoring threatened to do the same to Ben.

Across the table Michael Alvarez, the scrub nurse, was clearly getting bored. After fiddling with his tray of hip implant parts and pieces, he steadied his gaze on Joel, who stood a few feet from Ben. In an authoritative tone, he asked the med student, "What's the unhappy triad?"

Pimping—the peppering of questions at underlings—was usually done by attendings or residents. Apparently, Michael had missed the memo.

"Uh...unhappy triad?"

"The unhappy triad. Of the knee?" Michael raised his eyebrows and held out his gloved palms.

When Joel still didn't answer, the scrub nurse looked at Ben. "What exactly are you teaching your student? Methinks you're too easy on him."

Though Michael said this in a teasing fashion, the tension in the room climbed. He was right though. Ben *was* too easy on Joel, both because Joel's internist stepmother, Dr. Taka Smith, was a mentor to Ben and because Ben still felt responsible for the death of Joel's girlfriend over three years before.

Angela Choi, who was standing next to Michael on a small stool, seemed not to notice the friction in the air. Instead, the physician's assistant—or PA as they were called—seemed lost in her own thoughts, her forehead creased inside her headgear.

"The unhappy triad," the scrub nurse continued, "is when the ACL, MCL, and medial meniscus are all injured inside the knee. Two ligaments and a disc of cartilage all shot to hell. Happened to me playing ball. That's how I met Dr. Lock. He repaired my knee, got me interested in medicine, and I went back to school for my nursing degree. After all, I couldn't play in the minors any—"

"Where the hell is he, anyway?" Angela's outburst made everyone jump. Even the sleeping patient stirred. The PA clasped and unclasped her gloved hands. "I'm sorry. My nerves are frayed." She swallowed and then, more tentatively, said, "Aren't you guys having trouble adjusting?"

No need to spell out her meaning. Everyone knew she was referring to the Alaskan plane crash.

When no one answered, she lowered her head. "Maybe it's just me then. I keep dreaming about the wreckage site, how cold it was, how hungry we all were. My husband and kids are worried about me." Her voice caught, and she stopped talking. Ben's own throat grew tight, but he had no idea what to say. He'd neither been there himself, nor did he know her well enough to offer platitudes.

"Don't let us fool you, Angela," Dr. King said, perfectly aligning syringes on his anesthesiology table—a millimeter here, a millimeter there. From their past surgeries together, Ben knew that the man, although American, had moved back from London five years before. "We're all feeling the effects. Aren't we, Michael? Joel? We almost starved out there."

Both men nodded but said nothing.

"We should take advantage of the therapist the hospital made available to us. Even Karen, tough as she is, should talk to her." Dr. King glanced at the cardiac monitor and adjusted the patient's IV bag. "Although I like my cozy apartment—reminds me of the one I had as a resident in Madison—losing my house in the divorce and having my ex-wife take the kids back to England to care for her sick mother was awful enough. But then the crash? Believe me. Talking to the counselor is nothing to be ashamed of."

An introvert by nature, Ben was always surprised when others shared intimate details about themselves. Not to mention uncomfortable. Being the odd man out in the crisis didn't help matters either.

Michael started to say something, but his words got cut off by a commotion outside the operating room window. Dr. Lock had just stormed into the outer vestibule. From a container on the wall near the sink, he ripped out a scrub brush. Several more flew into the air behind it. Moments later Lenny rushed into the vestibule too. Looking like a mad scientist, he pointed a thick finger at the surgeon. "You're hiding something, I know it." His accusation reverberated through the glass.

Lock pumped soap onto his brush and, with a ferocity that threatened amputation, started scrubbing his fingertips and nails. He muttered something, but it was muted by the window. Like plants bending toward the sun, everyone, including Ben, leaned toward the drama in the outside room, hoping to catch the exchange. Fortunately, the patient kept dozing.

"Then why can't I scrub in?" Lenny's shout was muffle-free.

"Why're you keeping the senior residents out of your OR? Afraid we might see something? Is that it?"

The attending physician froze, the scrub brush suspended above his palm. A ruddy hue flushed his face, and for an instant he caught Ben's eye through the window. Before Ben could look away, Dr. Lock turned to the chief resident and barked, "You're delusional. I don't know what's going on with you, but get some help. Before I report you."

Lenny stammered a few seconds, his face bloated with a rage and belligerence Ben had never before seen from him. Finally, the chief resident pivoted and barreled out the vestibule door.

Behind the window, Dr. Lock took several deep breaths, his chest rising and falling beneath his scrub top. When he resumed washing, his anger seemed to dissolve with the suds. Five minutes later he entered the operating room with outstretched wet arms. After drying them with the sterile towel provided by the OR nurse and being assisted into his sterile attire and gloves, he shrugged and said, "Guess you can't fix crazy."

# 6

Wednesday evening Ben muddled through an on-call night from hell. While Montgomery's orthopedic program normally had a night-float position to ensure residents' work hours remained within guidelines, a recent shortage of bodies meant the program director—and Lenny—had to reshuffle things for a few weeks. One of the second-year residents was out on maternity leave, another was recovering from a disabling case of Guillain-Barré syndrome, and because of an organizational snafu, four residents were doing away-rotations when only two should have been. As a result, the rest of the orthopedic residents were covering old-school call, working both day and night, while still juggling their work hours so none of them exceeded their limit, either in the number of straight hours worked or in total hours for the week.

*No wonder Lenny is stressed.*

So for the past five hours, Ben had been up to his stethoscope in popped stitches, bed sores, joint infections, and other on-call disasters, not to mention a few trips to the emergency department to help out the ortho resident stationed there who'd been bombarded with fractures of fingers and toes and everything in between. Plus, he'd hit a snag in his research proposal for the Conley Grant. Twenty of the cases he thought he could use for his ACL-repair study didn't fit the study criteria. To make matters worse, Lenny wasn't returning his calls. Ben still didn't know what the shocking argument outside the OR the day before had been about. And he really wanted to see his kid. Sophia had offered to bring Maxwell in for a quick dinner in the cafeteria, but sadly, Ben hadn't had the time to spare.

Karen Dukakis was the senior resident on call with him, and although sometimes the seniors covered from home, tonight was not one of those nights. She even offered to answer the outpatient phone calls until Ben got caught up with his inpatient mayhem. As he typed an antibiotic order into the chart for room 422's wound cellulitis, the last pressing task on his list, she approached him at the counter. Her expression suggested the news wasn't good. She plopped down onto a chair next to him. All around them computer keys clicked, staff members buzzed by, and cabinets opened and closed as nurses fetched IV tubing and gauze pads from the supply closet across the hall.

"Uh oh, what now?" he said.

"You're not going to like it." She crossed her legs on the squeaky chair. Inside her scrubs, her lower limbs looked like twigs. Her pencil-thin arms were no meatier. How she managed to perform some of the more physical demands of orthopedic surgery, he didn't know. Trauma procedures and joint reconstructions required a fair amount of upper body strength. Her onyx hair hung in a limp ponytail, and dark shadows rimmed her eyes. He realized his rough call night was nothing compared to her ordeal with the plane crash, and he felt guilty for his earlier self-pity.

"What am I not going to like?"

"Your man Joseph Sampson is on his way to the ER. Just got off the phone with him."

"Oh shit. Why?"

"Says he's having pain."

"In his knee?"

Karen picked at a chewed-up cuticle. "Not sure. Tough to get information out of him. He spent the whole time grumbling about how long he had to wait for a doctor to call him back."

"Sounds like my guy."

"Said he wanted to see 'the doc with the big eyebrows.' When I told him he'd get his wish since you were on call, he grunted and said his wife would bring him in. He hung up before I could ask any more questions."

Ben sank back and rubbed his eyes. "We discharged him six days ago. He shouldn't still be having pain." *Did I miss something?* Dread formed a lump in his throat. There was a time a surge of acid reflux would have followed, but over the last few years he'd learned to better deal with life's unpredictability. His father, Willy, had always warned him he'd have to be less rigid in medicine. "Things happen, son. We can't control everything. The sooner you stop trying to, the better off you'll be."

"Probably just seeking more drugs," Karen was saying. "You know the type."

"Mr. Sampson isn't a drug-seeker. He's a pain in the ass, but he wouldn't come back to the hospital unless it was serious." Ben glanced at his watch and then at Karen's gaunt face. "I probably have about ten minutes. Want to go downstairs for a snack? The Quick Bite is still open."

Karen shook her head and made to leave but then slumped back down. "Hey, did you hear about Michael?"

"No, what?"

"His wife kicked him out."

"Wow, that's pretty harsh after what happened in Alaska."

"So is cheating on your wife."

Ben opened and then closed his mouth. He couldn't argue with that. But he also didn't want to be gossiping about the scrub nurse, so he shifted gears, even if it was a gear he wasn't sure he should be shifting. "You doing okay, Karen? If you ever want to talk, or, you know, just have someone to—"

She bolted up from her chair. "I'm fine. Good luck with Joseph Sampson. Page me if you need anything."

He was about to tell her he would when his cell phone buzzed in his scrub pocket. Seeing it was Laurette, his mood instantly boosted.

With a goodbye nod to Karen, he leaned back and greeted his best friend.

"What insect transmits *Leishmania?*" she immediately fired off, her accent as much French as it was Haitian.

"Come on, Bovo. You can do better than that. Too easy." The nickname stemmed from their first encounter in an epidemiology class over five years earlier, when his botched attempt at her last name came out *Bovo* instead of *Beauvais*. "It's the sand fly."

"Ah *bon*," she said, which he knew was the French word for *good*. "You still have some medical knowledge. I worried spending all that time fixing bones has made your brain soft." After Ben laughed, she added, "I'm sorry I have not texted much lately. I'm in Peru."

"Peru? What are you doing in Peru?"

"There is an outbreak. Very bizarre brain symptoms."

"But why are *you* there? You're finished with the EIS."

Laurette had graduated from the CDC's two-year Epidemic Intelligence Service training program over six months earlier, but after being awarded a prestigious fellowship in epidemiology, she'd decided to stay in Atlanta one more year. Considering she already had an RN degree and a master's degree in public health, the CDC training made her a powerful candidate for a position anywhere in the world. Her plan had always been to return to Haiti, but Philadelphia's public health department had recently offered her a position as assistant director of their epidemiology program. She coveted the position but wrestled with the guilt of letting her country down, which could certainly benefit from her skills. Although Ben knew what *he* wanted her to do, he didn't feel it was his place to ask her to stay. He couldn't live with himself if he crippled her choice for his own selfish wants.

"Derek requested I come since I had seen a similar case in Africa last year. My fellowship director agreed."

Ben straightened in his chair. "Derek?"

"Dr. Epps. Remember? He is the CDC psychiatrist I told you about." When Ben didn't answer, she said, "Are you there?"

"Yeah. Yeah, I'm here. Sorry. A nurse just asked me a question," he lied. "Sounds interesting."

"Derek thinks it's a parasite, and I agree. Together we—"

"Oh jeez, I'm sorry, I just got paged." This time he wasn't lying. His pager—a system the hospital still used for ease of communication, particularly during codes when a team of providers was needed en masse—notified him that Mr. Sampson was in the ER. "This night's been one headache after another. Can we talk later?"

"Of course. A goat always returns to its favorite shrub."

Ben imagined the smile on her lips as she spoke, along with a unilateral lift of her lovely brow. Regretfully, he ended the call. Then he stood and braced himself for Joseph Sampson, the cantankerous mail carrier with the roadrunner tattoo.

---

Every bed in the orthopedics pod of the emergency department was occupied, some with patients suffering new injuries, others with return customers like Joseph Sampson, who Ben found huffing and puffing—literally—behind curtain number three. His wife was seated next to his bed, a worried expression on her doughy face. Wendy, a nurse with a thick braid down to her waist, clipped an oxygen saturation probe onto the mail carrier's finger and, before exiting through the curtain gap, whispered to Ben, "Mr. Congeniality is all yours."

Ben approached the bed and peered down at the patient's knee, which the nurse had already freed from its dressing. "Wound looks good, Mr. Sampson. What's up?"

"The price of eggs. Sheesh, what the hell do you think is up?" The man's bravado slipped a notch, and his face sobered. A sheen of sweat dotted his brow. "I'm not doin' so well, doc. Having some trouble breathin'. Wife said I better call you guys."

Ben's visual examination of the man went from his knee to his chest and then to the machine recording his oxygen saturation. Ninety percent on room air. Not good enough. When Ben pulled down the top of Mr. Sampson's gown to listen to his lungs, he was distressed to find chest retractions: the mail carrier was using extra muscles to breathe. "Are you having any chest pain, Mr. Sampson?"

"Yeah. Just started. Can't seem to catch any air. But I ate Mexican tonight. Might just be my damn heartburn."

Or a pulmonary embolism, Ben thought. *Please don't be a pulmonary embolism.* "Have you been walking?"

A pause, then, "I won't lie to you, doc, not as much as I should be. Crazy, ain't it? I walk for a living, and now all I want to do is sit. But it hurts to walk."

"Are you taking your pain meds?" Ben tried to keep the fear out of his voice. When Mr. Sampson's breathing grew even more labored, Ben whipped open the curtain and waved the nurse back over.

"I'm taking them, I'm taking them, but they don't seem to do much. My knee, my calf, my whole damn leg hurts—" Mr. Sampson abruptly stopped talking. His hands flew to his chest, one over the other. His oxygen saturation dipped to the eighties and his pulse climbed even higher. "I can't, I can't…" he sputtered.

His wife jumped up from her chair. "What's wrong? What's wrong with my husband?"

"Wendy, I need you and the ED attending now," Ben called out. "And get someone to page respiratory therapy too. We might have a massive PE in here."

Oxygen saturation in the seventies now.

Ben dashed to the wall and grabbed the bag valve mask that hung there. Securing the mask part over the patient's nose and mouth, he supplied both breaths and oxygen to the quickly fading mail carrier. Across from him, Mrs. Sampson pressed her hands tightly over her abdomen, terror widening her eyes.

Despite the oxygen delivery, Mr. Sampson's pulse grew thready, his blood pressure nosedived, and his face paled to a sickly ash. Ben was now a hundred percent certain that a blood clot had traveled from the man's leg to his lungs, causing a pulmonary embolism— commonly referred to as a PE—where it lodged inside his pulmonary artery and blocked off the critical vessel. Not only would the clot restrict blood flow to his lungs, it would put the man at risk for sudden cardiac collapse.

Within seconds a full ED team was in the small space, but no matter what they did, no matter what medications they plunged into Mr. Sampson's IV, no matter how long they coded him with chest compressions and cardiac shocks and ventilation, the mail carrier did not wake up.

He did not resume breathing on his own. He did not maintain a heartbeat. He did not survive.

# 7

I'm so cold and hungry. Though others are next to me, I feel alone.

Even when I eat, I can't be satiated. I want more. I crave more. But I crave what I don't understand. The thoughts swirling around my brain are too horrible and inhuman to believe.

And yet I can't shake them. They're as much a part of me as this relentless cold, a cold so intense it feels as though my skeleton has frozen.

Can the others tell? Do they see my agitation and hunger?

No, I think I hide it well, or maybe they're too caught up in their own pain to recognize mine.

I'll shake this. I'll recover. There's really no other choice.

Because if I don't, I'm terrified of what I might do.

## 8

I nside Willy's Chocolate Chalet, which his father had owned for years, Ben installed the last of three new inventory shelves. Given it was Friday evening, the shop was now closed. Although sweet aromas emanated from every glass display case, inside of which lay chocolate truffles, cream-filled delights, and countless flavors of fudge, Ben's ongoing despondency over Joseph Sampson's death two days before had dampened his appetite.

Although his rational brain told him there was nothing more he could have done to prevent the mail carrier's death, the taint of culpability nonetheless seeped its way into his being. He felt it in the slump of his shoulders, the slackness of his jaw, the twisting of his gut. He'd hoped a little manual labor at the store would help him relax, but as he screwed a bracket into place with his combi-drill, his mind continued to play tricks on him. Over and over it watched the defibrillator shock Mr. Sampson's heart, the man's chest lifting off the bed with each jolt. Over and over it saw the cardiac tracing bottom out to the flat line of asystole. Over and over it flashed the anguish of Mrs. Sampson's cries as she hovered over her husband's dead body.

The day before, while Ben was making a much-needed run to

the coffee kiosk in the atrium, Lenny had finally returned his calls. After the chief resident apologized for his absence on the wards the past few days, which he blamed on administrative duties and scheduling nightmares, Ben relayed the details of Joseph Sampson's hospital course and subsequent emergency department visit, grateful to have a nonjudgmental ear to run the case by.

When he finished his summary, Lenny assured him Mr. Sampson's demise wasn't his fault. "You're beating yourself up for nothing. PEs happen, and you know as well as I do that a massive one can cause quick death. It's a shitty complication, but it happens. Maybe if the guy would've come in sooner, you'd have been able to prevent it, but he didn't."

Ben understood the truth of Lenny's words, but it didn't make Mr. Sampson's death easier to swallow. He had seen other patients die during his residency, but they hadn't been *his* patients. They hadn't been walking, breathing, talking people he'd been directly responsible for. Critically ill orthopedics patients were usually shipped off to the internal medicine ward or the ICU.

Ben had then asked Lenny about Mr. Sampson's outpatient pain meds. "Why'd you pick them up from the pharmacy, anyway?"

"Just trying to help my residents out. What's a chief resident for if not that?"

"Do you think there could've been something wrong with the prescription? Mr. Sampson complained the pills weren't helping enough and that's why he didn't want to walk. He—"

Lenny had cut Ben off. "Everyone responds differently, man. Quit torturing yourself. This won't be the first patient you'll lose." Then, before Ben could ask about Lenny's heated altercation outside the OR with Dr. Lock, the chief resident disconnected so quickly Ben was left staring at his phone.

And now he was staring at the inventory shelf he'd just installed for his dad, the cinnamon grains of its cherry wood swimming in and out of focus. An uncomfortable suspicion about Lenny took root in his gut, one he didn't want to entertain. Was the guy's odd behavior of late merely a result of his demanding position as chief resident or was there more at play? Competition in surgery could be fierce and—

"Looks great, Benny Boy."

Ben jumped, his arm banging the new shelf. It vibrated but held.

"Sorry, didn't mean to startle you. Thought you could use this." Willy held out a bottle of Philadelphia-brewed ale.

An older, stockier, shorter version of Ben, Willy shared his son's thick mane, only with more gray. That fullness came at a price though, because his eyebrows, like Ben's, bloomed to unruly, hirsute caterpillars if not regularly groomed. Willy liked to joke that his eyebrows kept people from staring at his big nose, which fortuitously Ben had not inherited. Their five o'clock shadows were similarly prominent.

After losing his lifelong partner Max—who, although not related by blood, was every bit Ben's other father—to colon cancer nearly seven years earlier, Willy had almost given up, but a grandson a few years later had revived him. Willy and Maxwell were inseparable. When Sophia or Ben needed help, Willy was there. The little boy loved spending time in the chocolate shop, watching his grandpa perform one confectionery miracle after another. What kid wouldn't? The latest additions were handmade, fair-trade candy dishes from Haiti, a partnership instigated by Laurette on one of her visits to her homeland and one Willy was thrilled to support. It was those dishes that had required the shelves.

"You okay, son?" Willy asked.

"Yeah, fine, but what about you? You said you had something you wanted to tell me?"

Willy lowered his gaze and stroked the stubble on his chin. "We better go back to my office and talk. And drink more alcohol. I'm worried after you hear this, you'll think I've lost my marbles."

Never a good start to a conversation, Ben thought.

There was a precedent for his worry: the last time Willy had taken Ben into his office to "talk," he'd dropped a bombshell by confessing his role in Max's death. In the last stages of cancer— nauseated from chemo, sick and feverish with skin and mouth sores, bones aching from metastases—Max had begged Willy to help him die. "Just a little extra morphine, my sweet Wills," he had pleaded. "I can't go on like this." After repeated refusals, Willy finally acquiesced, unable to bear the love of his life's ongoing suffering. The death raised no questions (Max was terminally ill and near hospice stage), but Willy had said it was the most excruciating thing he'd ever had to do, even though Max had assured him it would also be the most selfless. It wasn't until four years later that Willy had told Ben. He'd worried his science-minded son, who'd done everything he could to prolong Max's life, wouldn't approve. Truth be told, Ben still struggled to come to terms with it.

So, as he followed his father into the back room, where the tantalizing scents of fudge still lingered but the orderly tidiness did not, he wondered what tonight's bombshell would be.

Willy cleared a box of newly arrived Valentine's Days trinkets and stuffed teddy bears from a chair for Ben and then took a seat of his own behind the paper-strewn desk.

"So what is it?" Ben asked, steeling himself.

After a long swig of beer, his father sighed heavily and studied the sleeve of his checkered shirt. "She's talking to me."

"Who's talking to you?"

"Your mother."

Ben nearly spit out his Christmas Ale. "She woke up? How? What?" Harmony, Ben's mother, had been in a coma for the past three and a half years. A severe illness, one that had been linked to Ben, closed up her mind forever, and the once world-traveling, fire-haired woman was now wasting away in a long-term care facility.

His dad chuckled. "No, no, nothing like that." He tapped his temple. "She talks to me inside here."

That comment was equally unsettling. "Oh. Well, you spend a lot of time with her. It's only natural you're having imaginary conversations, right?"

"But that's just it, son. These aren't imaginary."

"Um…I'm not sure what you mean."

"Ha, that makes two of us. You know me, I can be a skeptic like you. That new-agey stuff was Max and Harmony's world, not mine." Willy ran his fingers over a framed photograph of a young and pregnant Harmony on the corner of his desk. "Your mother would swear ghosts were communicating with her, and I'd just give her a hug and say, 'better you than me.'"

It was true. Harmony could be flightier than a carrier pigeon, and she'd flitted in and out of Ben's life like one too, giving up all her parental rights. For years he'd harbored resentment. Wouldn't even call her *Mom*. But it took the awful events of three and a half years ago to make him see that everything she'd done over the years had been to protect him, both from the dangerous highs and massive lows of her severe bipolar disease and from secrets she'd never managed to disclose to him before she slipped into her coma. He'd assumed they had to do with her parents.

"But now…" Willy drained his beer and reached for another bottle in the small fridge behind his desk. "But now I'm wondering if she's getting the last laugh, because she's telling me things. I swear to God, Benny Boy, she's telling me things."

"The neurologist says Harmony will never wake up." Ben spoke softly, not sure how to proceed, delusional minds not his forte. "She can't be talking to you. Her situation is unusual, no doubt. She seems to have some higher function. But she's not capable of speech. She can't—"

"The first time was a month ago. I was sitting in her room, reading one of those No. 1 Ladies' Detective Agency books to her—you know how she always loved those stories—when out of the blue I hear, 'I miss you, Willy.'" His father raised a palm and cut off Ben's objection. "I know, I know, you think I just imagined it. I thought the same thing. Thought maybe I'd been around the chocolate fumes a little too long. But then, each time I visited, I *heard* something else. Just little things at first. Snippets here and there. Things like 'how's Ben?' or 'how's our grandbaby?'"

Was his father getting dementia? Was that it? But the man was only sixty-five years old and had shown no signs of mental illness, at least not since his depression over Max's death had lifted. He was as sharp as Ben's scalpel.

"And then…"

"And then what, Dad?"

"And then last week she said, 'The best thing we ever did was have Ben.'" His father tipped his bottle. "I certainly can't argue with that."

Ben smiled. His conception had happened during a night of partying when Harmony and Willy first met. She'd quickly learned of his desire to father a child as a gay man and, in her manic and inebriated state, decided to give him one right then and there. The stars were aligned enough that it worked. Or at least her fertility cycle was.

"But then last week she said something that scared me."

"And that was?"

Willy didn't respond right away. In the corner of the office, the air purifier hummed, and outside the store's front window, the sounds of South Street traffic passed steadily.

"Dad?"

"She said 'we have to protect him.'"

"Protect who?"

"I'm not sure, but I assume you, since you were the one we were 'talking' about. But I've visited her every day this week, and she's said nothing since." Willy thumped his head back against his chair. "Am I losing it? She can't be talking to me, can she? But then I think about what you went through a few years ago. I never thought that could happen either." He closed his hooded eyes. "Dear God, what's happening to me?"

Ben rose from his chair and pushed papers out of the way on his dad's desk, and then sat on top of it and faced him. "You're not losing it. I don't know what's going on, but you're not losing it." *Please don't let my father be losing it.* He was about to reassure the man once again when his phone rang. The caller was Karen, his senior resident.

"Dad, I have to take this, but then we'll figure this out, okay?"

Willy nodded, and Ben answered Karen's call. She wasted no time on small talk, and her bizarre words quickly pulled Ben's attention away from his father.

"Joseph Sampson's leg was hacked off in the morgue," she said bluntly. "Someone frickin' stole it."

9

On Saturday morning Sophia agreed to keep Maxwell a little longer so Ben could stop by the hospital. Although eager to have a full day with his son, he knew his mind wouldn't be in the right place without first finding out what had happened to Joseph Sampson's leg. He would need to pick up Maxwell by noon though. Sophia had plans. Ben wondered if those plans involved Dr. Lock.

After parking his black Mustang in the employee parking deck, he hurried through a frigid stairwell to access the skywalk leading to the main hospital. Although his car was thirteen years old and with his resident's salary he could afford a new one, he saw no need to waste money on an upgrade. Same went for his dingy apartment in Mrs. Sinclair's basement. Paying for Maxwell's needs took priority, including getting a head start on college savings so that Sophia could continue to work from home. When the weather was nice, he sometimes even still biked to the hospital.

Inside the nine-story atrium, he blew on his cold hands and hurried downstairs to the morgue. After Karen's disturbing call the night before, he'd paged Regina Jones, a second-year pathology resident and former med school classmate. She'd agreed to meet him this morning when things "calmed down a bit." True to her word, he found her scrolling through her phone inside a small break room just inside the morgue's entryway. Dressed in scrubs and a puffy bouffant cap to keep her hair away from the corpses, she looked up when he entered. "So you're the man who's come to see about a leg."

"Thanks for waiting for me." He took off his coat and draped it over a chair.

"No problem. It's the least I can do for the guy who got me through pharmacology class. It's not every day we get a missing leg around here. Our department head keeps waffling between outrage and shock. Was just reading the latest email from him now." She pocketed her phone and stood. "I started posting your patient last night. It could've waited for today's resident, or even for Monday, but I figured why pass up the opportunity? I hadn't done a post-mortem on a suspected massive PE yet."

Ben's stomach knotted, just as it did every time he thought about the mail carrier's demise. Which was constantly.

Regina pushed open the break room door and led Ben through the bowels of Montgomery Hospital, its basement walls devoid of any decorative warmth and its intermittent doorways leading to death in its most literal form. Over her shoulder she said, "Unfortunately, halfway through the autopsy we had three family members die in a car accident—two DOA and one in the ED. They were wheeled to the morgue, but because they're Jewish, relatives wanted the bodies for burial as soon as possible. We don't have much staff around here on a Friday night so things got really chaotic. I had to abandon Sampson's body mid-autopsy and tend to the accident victims." She stopped in front of a room marked by a painted number four. "Sampson's body was alone in here, and when I got back to him around two a.m., his leg was gone."

"That's so messed up." Ben rubbed a hand over the back of his neck. "Wait. Isn't there a security camera inside?"

Regina laughed. "Seriously? We can't even get the hospital to give us a working fridge in the break room. I've had icicles in my yogurt for months. The only security camera is the one in the hallway beyond the morgue entrance. Doubt it even captures who comes through the door. Besides, it's not like our patients will be up to any mischief." She snorted again, but Ben was too disturbed to laugh.

"What about a lock?"

His question was answered when Regina pushed open the autopsy room door with no more than a nudge of her shoulder. After following her inside, he was immediately glad he chose to work with the living. Two stainless steel tables equipped with drainage sinks and a collection of unpleasant-looking instruments filled the space. A tall scale to weigh plucked-out organs stood nearby. In the center of the room was a floor drain the size of a stop sign, and against the far wall, a massive sink punctuated a chrome countertop.

One of the tables was empty. The other held Joseph Sampson, wearing nothing but what Sophia and Dr. Lock's good Lord gave him. Minus half a leg.

Regina was slipping on a pair of gloves. If she noticed Ben's discomfort in the macabre setting, she gave no indication. "The cold rooms storing the bodies require a security badge to access, but the autopsy rooms are unlocked. Usually if there's a body in one, there's a pathologist or a pathologist's assistant working on it. Otherwise the cadaver would be in the cold room. Last night was an exception since I had to rush out to help with the other bodies."

"So what does hospital security do in a situation like this?"

"Don't know." Regina handed Ben gloves. "Our director said they'll notify the police, but how much time can they devote to something like this? The guy was already dead. My guess is it'll be more of an inside investigation. People are already assuming it was a prank."

"Pretty sick prank."

"No kidding." The path resident pulled a gown from a drawer beneath the stainless-steel table and gave it to Ben. "Just so you don't accidentally get anything on your street clothes."

Ben had no intention of touching Joseph Sampson's body, but he pulled the protective gown on over his sweatshirt and jeans none-theless. The gloves too. He stepped closer to the table and willed his mind into clinical mode, taking note of the purplish hue of lividity coloring the lower half of the mail carrier's body. He remembered enough from med school pathology class to know that was where the blood had pooled after death. His gaze traveled to the empty space below Mr. Sampson's right thigh, where the lower limb had been chopped off above the knee, and then to the Y incision in the man's chest, which had already been closed.

"What did you find in his lungs?" he asked.

"A pulmonary embolism, just as suspected."

"Dammit. I should've been the one to talk to him on the phone, not my senior resident. I could've asked more questions about what was going on. Could've insisted he come by ambulance."

Regina fluttered her lips. "You could have teleported him and he wouldn't have survived. The clot in his lungs was so big, Roto-Rooter couldn't clear it."

Though her words reassured him, the corpse of Joseph Sampson saw to it that his guilt remained. He leaned over and peered more closely at the hacked-off limb. Bits of quadriceps and hamstring muscles had dried up around the severed bone, and vessels showed rust-colored remnants from where the blood had once flowed.

Regina pointed to the sliced tissue. "Whoever did this obviously used an autopsy saw, but they didn't take their sweet time. The tissue's a mess. Then again, if I were stealing a leg, I wouldn't dawdle either."

After studying Sampson's body a while longer and realizing there was little else to learn from it, Ben said, "You want help getting the body in the cooler?"

"Nah, I'll take care of it. But you're the last ortho resident who wants to see him, right?" She led him back down the lifeless hallway. "You guys are turning up like roaches."

"What do you mean?"

"You didn't talk to them?"

"Talk to who?"

"One of your colleagues came in last night—it was before the leg went missing. Said he wanted to see the implant. The other one stopped by this morning, not long before you. Heard about the stolen leg and wanted to see the body."

Ben halted, his rubber soles squeaking on the tile. "Who were they?"

"I dunno. Some guy last night. Short, stocky, glasses. And some super-skinny woman this morning. Said she was on call with you the night the patient died."

So Lenny and Karen then.

"Why did my chief resident want to see the implant?"

"How would I know? He was kind of a weird dude." Regina resumed walking, and soon they were back in the break room, with its overly frosty fridge and rickety Formica table. "Maybe he was worried the hardware was related to the pulmonary embolism."

"But why would the implant be the problem? That makes no sense."

"Probably not, but maybe he was just being thorough. We have residents from all different departments come down to watch autopsies. That's nothing new. Why you getting so bothered about it?" When Ben didn't reply, she added, "He never got to see it though. I had to shoo him out when the car accident victims came in, and I hadn't gotten to the leg yet."

Regina pulled off her bouffant cap and grabbed a cup of water from the bubbling dispenser in the corner, while Ben tried to process what she'd just said. Paranoia quickly set in. Were Lenny and Karen's visits purely out of curiosity, or had the powers that be sent them to check on the autopsy to see if Ben was somehow at fault for the mail carrier's death? Did they think he did something wrong in the man's post-op care? Seemed unlikely, but neurosis over mistakes was an automatic response for any junior resident. Or had the two of them stopped by for some other reason entirely?

# 10

## BACK IN THE WISSAHICKON VALLEY PARK, JANUARY 20

Still disturbed by his and Sophia's discovery, Ben stared at Joseph Sampson's amputated leg on the snow-dusted park trail. Not even twenty-four hours had passed since he'd visited the mail carrier's body in the morgue. Two police officers—a man and a woman of similar height and build and both dressed in bulky, black coats—had responded to Sophia's 911 call. They squatted around the limb, their quiet conversation swallowed by the wind. Up above on their left was the rocky cliff of Council Rock, on their right was the creek, and in front and behind them stretched miles of wintry parkland.

Never had Ben felt so cold. His puffer jacket, thermal gloves, and knit cap might as well have been cotton undergarments. Sophia, too, was shivering uncontrollably, her parka zipped to her chin and her scarf wrapped around her face. With his arm around her, he tried to shield her from the cold as best he could, but what she really needed—what they both needed—was a hot cup of cocoa and a heated blanket. Even Sir Quincy, still tied to a nearby tree, looked miserable.

The ruddy-faced cop rose from his crouched position, the weapons on his belt shifting below the hem of his coat. After strolling over to give Sir Quincy a pat on the head, he said, "So, you're telling me you just happened to stumble upon the severed leg of your own patient?"

"Sounds incredible, I know, but it's true."

The other cop stood, brushed snow off the knees of her uniform pants, and approached them. "And you're sure this is his leg?"

"I'm not sure of anything, but I recognize that roadrunner tattoo and the orthopedic implant."

"Maybe not all that unusual of a tattoo," she said, "but throw in the recent knee surgery and the fact your guy's body was disturbed in the morgue, then yeah, it adds up."

"You said someone stole his leg. Run through that again for us, will ya?" The male cop's statement was more a command than a request, but to Sir Quincy he smiled and wiggled his eyebrows, as if the yellow lab were a small child to be entertained.

"I got a call from my senior resident on Friday night. She said someone took Mr. Sampson's leg from the morgue."

"How did she know?" the female partner asked. A burst of wind plastered strands of hair against her mouth, and she swiped them away.

Ben realized he'd never asked Karen how she first heard about the missing limb. He'd been so shocked by her phone call that he'd only asked what happened, to which she'd responded, "I have no frickin' clue." He still worried that her and Lenny's trip to the morgue to see Sampson's body had meant they suspected him of poor post-op care. Wouldn't get him any closer to the Conley Grant, that was for sure. To the cops, he said, "Maybe the pathologist called her. As my senior resident, her name was on Mr. Sampson's ED report too. The night he died."

"Hmm, I see." The male officer's tone suggested he didn't see.

"The patient died a few days ago," Ben said. "He suffered a massive PE—"

"A what?"

"A massive pulmonary embolism. That's a blood clot that travels to the lungs and blocks off the main artery."

"That's what the autopsy showed?" As the female cop asked the question, two members of the crime scene unit hiked toward them.

She nodded a greeting and pointed to the severed leg about fifteen feet away.

"Yes."

"So why did someone take his leg? Of course, we'll need to confirm it's his, but if it looks like a duck and quacks like a duck..."

"I don't know. Nobody does. Hospital security's looking into it, and from what I heard, they assume it was a prank by either an employee or students. But that's all I know. I'm in orthopedics, not pathology."

"And you have absolutely no idea who or why someone took it?" she repeated.

Ben splayed his gloved hands. "I have no clue. Maybe it *was* a prank."

The male officer plucked a Starbucks napkin from his jacket and honked his nose into it. "Yeah, see, I get that. Not the first time stunts like that have been pulled. But what I don't get is, how were *you* the one to find it? Your own patient. That seems kind of weird. Doesn't that seem kind of weird, Kramer?"

His partner nodded. "Yep. Seems kind of weird. You hike this path much?"

Before Ben could respond, Sophia, quiet up to this point aside from her chattering teeth, cut in. "I don't like what you're insinuating."

"We're not insinuating anything," the male cop said. "We're just asking questions. Why? Are you insinuating something?"

"No, I'm...I'm... Look, I'm cold, and we need to pick up our son from his grandpa's. Plus, Ben has to get to the hospital for a shift, and my knee is killing me."

"Not as bad as that guy's." The male officer snickered and pointed to Sampson's frosty, gray limb with its chewed-up muscles and tendons.

"My dog and I hike here a lot," Ben said, ignoring the joke, "especially on Sunday mornings if I have it off. Or else I run on the Forbidden Trail." He pointed past the creek to the wide, tree-lined path whose even surface was much more conducive to jogging than the craggy terrain of the Orange Trail. "But I—"

"This is a perfect place to leave a leg, wouldn't you say, Kramer?"

"I would," she answered, her expression unreadable.

Ben swallowed but said nothing. An old familiar burn took root in his throat. Given Mr. Sampson's death and hacked-off limb, not to mention Lenny's peculiar behavior and Willy's belief that a comatose woman was speaking to him, it wasn't much of a surprise that his acid nemesis had returned.

"Okay then," Kramer said, handing Ben a card. "We'll get a detective on the case. He or she will want to talk to you, but you be sure to call me if you learn anything before then. Got it?"

"Got it."

Her partner strolled toward the crime scene workers, his heavy shoes kicking up dirt on the snow-covered trail.

"Oh, and by the way," Kramer added before joining him. "Make sure you stick around Philly for a while."

And voilà, just like that, Ben was caught up in weird shit again.

11

Eight days later, behind the U-shaped workstation on the general medicine ward, Ben wrote up his recommendations for an elderly patient with pneumonia who'd fallen in her hospital room and injured her ankle.

Although not on the consulting service this month, he had agreed to see the patient when his med school mentor, Dr. Taka Smith, had personally requested him. It wasn't that long ago Ben had top billing on her shit list, having been wrongly blamed for her stepson Joel not getting into med school on his first try, but at some point the diminutive internist had deemed Ben worthy—much to Joel's irritation—and had even defended and protected Ben when he'd needed it most. She'd been a faithful advisor ever since, her only residual beef being that Ben had chosen a surgical field over internal medicine.

As he signed off on his electronic charting, the sound of clicking heels on hospital tile told him Dr. Smith had arrived. After taking a seat next to him, her Chanel-covered bottom barely consuming a third of the chair cushion, she said, "So, does Mrs. Freedman have a fracture? She knows better than to get out of bed on her own. She's already broken that ankle once."

"No, just a nasty sprain. Ice, wrap, elevate, you know the drill. But a follow-up bone-density scan would be a good idea. Her X-ray shows severe osteoporosis."

"That's why I thought it best to call you. Thanks for coming by so early on a Monday to see her." Her expression shifted to concern, and she wheeled her chair closer. "Heard you had quite the find a week ago."

"You and everyone else in the hospital."

"Well, as my father would say, it's very *okashii*. Strange." Dr. Smith's parents emigrated from Japan before she was born. The last name of Smith came from her neurosurgeon husband. "Are you okay?"

"I'm fi—"

"If you say you're fine, I'll make you consult on my patient in room 671. He's got an abscess on his butt."

Ben smiled. "No, really, I'm okay. Things seemed to have petered out, at least on my end. The news reports never mentioned my name. Guess the assumption is that it was a stupid prank."

"And you believe that?"

"The police have nothing else to offer." Last Monday Ben had asked Lenny about his trip to the morgue. The chief resident, distracted by an upcoming med student lecture he was preparing, shrugged it off, claiming it was his responsibility to check into any unexpected orthopedic deaths. Ben had translated that to mean: "I needed to make sure you didn't eff up with Mr. Sampson's care." Then Lenny had warned Ben to submit his research proposal for the Conley Grant soon. "Lots of good ones coming in, buddy. Don't want to get behind the competition." There was something weird in Lenny's tone, and if Ben hadn't known better, he'd have thought it was a veiled threat. After that, Ben let the discussion of Mr. Sampson go.

He tuned back into Dr. Smith. "Are they sure the leg belonged to your patient?" she asked.

"Same tattoo and a recent orthopedic implant, so yeah, but they'll run DNA to confirm it. That's about it though. After all, the patient died of a PE, not foul play. Still, I feel awful for his wife."

"Benjamin Oris, get that look of guilt off your face. You are not responsible for the man's pulmonary embolism."

He shrugged. Laurette had tried to tell him the same thing when he'd called her after finding the leg. The discovery itself and the police officers' suspicion of him had been equally disconcerting, and he'd needed to hear her voice.

"And Joel?" he asked Dr. Smith tentatively. "What does he think?" Her stepson was a subject the two of them didn't often discuss, but it wouldn't surprise Ben if Joel had incriminated him for Sampson's death *and* the severed leg.

Her hesitation confirmed Ben's suspicion. "Joel is still struggling from the plane crash. He acts like it doesn't bother him, but it does."

"Being stranded in the freezing cold with no food would bother anyone."

"I just hope it doesn't affect his work on your rotation. He's already not the strongest... Well, he's best suited for research, don't you think? Not every med student reacts on their feet as quickly as you did."

"With his master's degree in biochemistry, he'll be great at research." Ben left it at that.

His phone buzzed. A text from Angela Choi. Their first knee replacement of the morning would begin soon.

Dr. Smith rose. "I won't keep you, but it was wonderful to see you." She squeezed his shoulder. "Take care of yourself."

A disheveled intern rushed past the counter. Dr. Smith's affable disposition vanished, and as she strode toward the young man, her tone sharpened to a clip Ben remembered well. "Dr. Doyle, so glad you could find time in your precious schedule to pre-round on your patients today. And without a tie, no less. On my service, men will wear..." As her voice faded away, Ben smiled. She certainly hadn't lost her touch.

Seeing his mentor had done him good. Feeling more relaxed than he had in over a week, he made his way toward the OR. Maybe the whole thing with Joseph Sampson could finally be filed away under Over and Done.

As Ben wielded the surgical saw inside OR number six, he marveled at the complex but coordinated design of the human knee. Tendons connected bones to muscles to mobilize the joint. Ligaments anchored bone to bone to stabilize the anatomy. Crescent-shaped cartilaginous discs absorbed the shock of femur against tibia. And fluid-filled sacs and a synovial membrane lubricated the whole apparatus. All in all, it was an efficient gliding tool for ambulation, along with a host of more strenuous activities. But with its functional layout came risks: tendon strain, ligament rupture, cartilage tears, fluid accumulation. If luck was in the ether, injuries healed with time and rehab. If not, as the patient on Ben's operating table had learned, the surgeon stepped in.

With a final whirring shave, he cut away the last of Henry Paulson's damaged bone, leaving a clean femoral surface for the implant that would soon be placed. Paulson, a seventy-two-year-old retired teacher and avid marathoner, was deeply anesthetized, or as he'd put it pre-operatively: "Knock me all the way out. I don't want to see the OR. I don't want to smell the OR. I don't want to remember the OR." His wish for general anesthesia had been granted, and soon he'd be back to running marathons with no recollection of how it happened.

"Perfect," Dr. Lock said, examining Ben's work. "You sure you're only a second-year resident?"

Inside his headgear, Ben felt his face flush. For him, being allowed to perform a knee replacement surgery on his own—albeit with plenty of verbal guidance from Lock—was like reaching the top of Mount Everest. This was what he'd dreamed of. This was what he'd saved, studied, and drove a crappy car for. Everything else fell away, not the least of which was Joseph Sampson's severed limb. Inside the OR was where Ben felt most alive and in the moment.

"Hardware please, Michael," Dr. Lock said.

The scrub nurse handed the curved femoral shell to Ben. The metal implant glinted in the spotlight of the overhead lamp, and once again Ben noted its shinier sheen than some of the devices he'd seen back as a med student.

He was about to comment on it when Lock said, "Let's cement this baby in place, Oris. We don't have all day." As Ben did so, the attending murmured his approval. "Yep. Just like that. Perfect. Bone cement holds well, maybe twenty years or more, but patient age and activity level are going to determine when it's time for revision. Revision is more complex, of course. You've gotta clear out the hardware and cement. Takes longer than the initial surgery."

Ben worked on the tibial implant next and then positioned a plastic spacer between the two metal components. This would provide a smooth gliding surface. Finally he moved on to the plastic patella piece—the under-surface of the kneecap having already been trimmed and resurfaced—and while he fitted it, Dr. Lock fired a question at Joel. "What else might lead to revision, Smith?"

Though Ben was busy with the kneecap piece, he heard foot-shuffling from Joel, who was farthest from the surgical field. Ben had reviewed that very question with him the week before, had even given him an article to read, but the ensuing silence suggested the med student hadn't done so.

"Um...I think..."

"You think what?" Lock said briskly.

"Um...probably infection...and..."

"And...and..." Lock mimicked. "And what?"

To Ben's relief, Dr. King broke Joel's awkward stammering. "Vitals are looking good, Kent. Mr. Paulson is doing fine."

"Thanks, Muti." Dr. Lock chuckled. "And don't think I didn't notice your subtle save of my med student here. You're such a softie."

The anesthesiologist shifted on his stool near the patient's head. "I just don't think peppering questions at students or residents is an effective way of teaching. Some people don't think as well under pressure."

"Well then, they shouldn't be doctors, should they?" At Lock's snub, a blotchy redness crept into Joel's cheeks beneath his plastic face guard.

Hoping to temper the situation, Ben assumed a jovial tone, one that might rescue his med student without making an enemy of his attending surgeon. "Ah, I don't know about that. There are plenty of fields of medicine that require methodical thinkers, especially biochemistry whizzes like Joel."

"Exactly," Dr. King said. "Like my teenage son, who'll be a great researcher someday if he chooses that path." A sadness softened the anesthesiologist's face, and Ben realized it had to be torture being a continent away from his kids.

Seemingly oblivious to Dr. King's comment, Dr. Lock stared hard at Ben, making Ben worry he'd overstepped. Across the operating table, Angela suctioned a tiny bleeder, while Michael fiddled with a surgical hammer on the sterile tray. Though Ben waited for a sarcastic comment from the cocky—and recently separated—scrub nurse, none came.

Finally, the attending surgeon flicked his hand in the air. "You're loyal, Oris. I like that. Now, let's see if this baby works."

Ben returned his attention to the surgical field and flexed and rotated the metal joint he'd just built. When it appeared good to go, everyone except Joel cheered, even the taciturn Angela.

Pumped and energized, Ben sewed the knee incision back up. Though Lenny might balk at Dr. Lock's exclusion of senior residents from his team, there was no denying the guy was a great teacher to junior residents, at least when he wasn't berating med students. The whipped cream on top of the successful procedure was that Ben had made it through an entire surgery without anyone bringing up Joseph Sampson's severed leg.

"Well done," Lock said with an emphatic nod. "You're the first second-year resident on my team to complete an entire surgery without needing me to physically step in."

Ben's chest swelled, and while the introvert in him kept his outward display in check, he couldn't help a small grin.

"Let us pray," the attending said. Ben was too jazzed and too used to it by now to be uncomfortable with Lock's piety, but he'd no more bowed his head when the chair of orthopedic surgery, Dr. Isaiah Fisher, burst into the room.

"Kent, what the hell's going on?" the furious department head sputtered. "They just found another goddamn limb from one of your patients."

## 12

Not a single set of eyes was focused on the patient. Instead, every team member in the operating room stared at the fuming department head in stunned silence. Behind his face shield, Ben's gaping mouth had yet to close.

Dr. Fisher, a reedy man in his sixties who barked orders like he was still in the service, had been Montgomery's chair of orthopedic surgery for over a decade, the first African American to hold that title at the hospital. Prior to that he'd been an Army surgeon, serving his country well beyond the four years his free medical school ride had required. "Well? I need answers, Kent, and I need them now."

Like Joel had earlier, Dr. Lock started stammering, the surgical bootie now on the other foot. "I have no idea what you're talking about. Whose limb? Which patient? Where?" His questions fired out like shrapnel.

A machine on Ben's left blipped. Dr. King gave a small start and returned his focus to Henry Paulson, the patient, who was ready for recovery now that his surgery was complete. No one else moved. Near the wall, the circulating nurse gripped a clipboard in her hands. Joel was as stiff as a statue, and Michael and Angela still gawked over their shoulders at the chairman, who'd entered from the door behind them. A mask held over his nose and mouth was the extent of his sterile preparation.

"Kim Templeton. Part of her damn leg turned up in a park." He centered in on Ben. "Just like the one you found. That Joseph Sampson guy. You know something about this?"

"Me? No... I... It doesn't make any sense." Ben was too floored to ask how they knew it was Kim Templeton, the paralegal they'd performed a hip replacement on two weeks before, but Fisher answered him as if he had.

"At least the police assume it's her. Husband says she went missing."

Dr. Lock stepped back from the operating table and plucked off his headgear. "I don't understand."

"That makes two of us." Tufts of graying hair at Fisher's temples rose and fell in time with his bluster. "An upper thigh this time. Part of her pelvis too, hip implant and all. Jesus on toast, what a clusterfuck."

If Dr. Lock was offended by the chairman's word choice, he didn't show it. Instead, he rubbed his chin, a look of uncertainty on his face, maybe even fear. "I don't know what to say."

"Well, you better figure it out, because two detectives are here asking questions." Once again Fisher zeroed in on Ben, but this time he shot a finger his way as well. "And they're looking for you, Oris."

Ben finally closed his mouth. As soon as he did, it dried up like sandpaper.

---

Still wearing his surgical cap and scrubs, Ben sat at an oak table in a small consultation room just off the OR waiting room. Aside from a carpeted floor, its only embellishments were a fake fern in the corner and a framed black-and-white photograph of a covered bridge. For some bizarre reason, despite the winter month, cool air blew from a ceiling vent, making him wish he'd had time to grab his white coat from the residents' lounge. Across from him sat two detectives, their unblinking scrutiny heightening his chill.

The one on the right was Cal Becker, a trim, thirtyish book-worm type with blond hair, rimless glasses, and a well-fitted suit that smelled faintly of the same woodsy cologne Ben's other father Max used to wear. The detective on the left, Alex Patel, looked to be in his early fifties and, in his wrinkled khakis and tieless shirt, seemed less meticulous than his partner. Underneath his coffee-bean eyes, dark circles suggested insomnia was a way of life. A potbelly suggested exercise was not.

Ben had already met Detective Becker. The man had interviewed him the day after he and Sophia had stumbled upon Joseph Sampson's leg. A casual chat in the hospital cafeteria, fifteen minutes tops. After three phone interruptions and two text messages, the detective had dashed away, clearly having more pressing cases to deal with. Chopping off a morgue patient's leg and leaving it in the park might be gruesome, but its priority likely ranked fifty notches below rapes and murders, especially when there were no cameras inside the morgue to offer a list of suspects. Still, the guy had taken enough time to jot down Ben's cell number.

Becker's demeanor wasn't so breezy today though. After several beats of uncomfortable silence, punctuated only by the muffled voices of passersby beyond the closed door of the consultation room, he reached into his jacket and pulled out a notebook and pen. "What do you know about Kim Templeton?"

"You mean from a patient standpoint? Because I just heard about her leg being found. I don't know anything about that. Where was it? Are you sure it's hers?"

"We'll confirm with DNA," Becker said.

When nothing more was forthcoming, Ben continued. "We did Mrs. Templeton's hip replacement two weeks ago. January fifteenth, I think it was. Her joint had never healed right after a skiing accident a decade ago." Still nothing from the detectives. "I know she's married, no kids, and works as a paralegal, but that's about it."

"Everything go okay with the surgery?" Becker asked, jotting something in his notebook.

"Went great. She was getting around with a walker and able to use the bathroom on her own by post-op day two. Even went home a day early." Ben tried to keep his voice steady, but being interviewed by two cops made a person feel guilty whether they'd committed a crime or not. The fact he was the first one they'd talked to, aside from the orthopedics chairman, didn't help. "She's got a good support system at home, and her husband took time off to help her the first couple days."

Becker jotted more notes. Patel simply stared, his cracked winter hands resting on his belly. A tuft of hair poked out from a gap between the buttons of his shirt.

"I'm sorry," Ben said. "That's all I can tell you. Can you say where the leg was found?"

"Boxer's Trail. Fairmount Park. You ever jog there?" Only Patel's lips were moving.

"Sometimes, but I haven't lately."

"Where were you Saturday night between seven and eight p.m.?" Becker asked.

Ben's knee started bouncing. "Why?"

"Where were you?"

"Um…" Ben rubbed his neck and scoured his brain. "I was…" *Think, Benny Boy, think.* "Oh, wait." He exhaled in relief. "I was dropping my son back at his mother's place. His bedtime routine starts at eight, so I try to get him there by seven thirty."

"So that leaves you with a half hour unaccounted for," Patel said.

"Oh, come on." Annoyance tempered some of Ben's anxiety. "After I dropped him off, I talked to Sophia for a bit and then drove home. Probably not much before eight. Ask her."

"We will." Patel yawned as if the whole discussion bored him, but Ben sensed it did anything but. "Just seems kind of weird you find the first leg in a park, and barely a week later someone else you operated on ends up the same way."

"I wasn't the only one who operated on her."

"We'll be talking to everyone who was in the OR during her surgery." The overhead light glinted off Becker's lenses, making his eyes difficult to see. "We'll try to find out why two patients with recent orthopedic surgery were targeted. Maybe it's just a coincidence. The problem, of course, is that Joseph Sampson was already dead when his leg was stolen. From what we know, Kim Templeton was not." He let that sink in a moment. "Fortunately, her leg was discovered by a park worker early yesterday morning. If anyone else had found it, it might be on YouTube by now. And we'd like to keep this quiet for a while. That goes for this conversation as well."

Ben nodded. He had no problem with that. He didn't need his name dragged into it any further than it already was. "I wish I could help you more, but I'm as confused as everyone else. Poor Mr. Templeton. He must be beside himself."

Patel remained motionless, but Becker offered a sad smile and flipped to a new page in his notebook. "That's something else we wanted to ask you. Mr. Templeton said his wife had been acting strange ever since her surgery. Told him she felt like someone was watching her in her hospital room. According to her husband, the paranoia persisted at home, and then Saturday evening she disappeared. He'd stepped out to buy her more pudding—"

"Tapioca. Yum." Patel raised his eyebrows and licked his lips.

"—and then filled his tank at the gas station. When he got back his wife was gone. He called the police. Thirty-six hours later her leg was found. No body though. That's when we were brought in." Becker looked at Ben as if expecting a response.

"Are you saying she was murdered?" Although cool air no longer blasted out of the vent above Ben's head, his skin goosebumped all the same.

Patel scratched his scalp beneath his dark, oiled hair. "What, you think her leg just chopped itself off and trotted to the park?"

"Well jeez, that's...that's awful. Sorry. I don't mean to sound dumb. I'm just shocked. Really shocked."

Becker pressed his lips together. In understanding? In accusation? In confusion? Ben had no clue. "The limb shows postmortem findings, so yes, she was likely murdered. Did you know she thought someone was watching her?"

"No. Not at all. She never said anything to me about it, and the nurses never reported a problem."

"Maybe she was embarrassed." Becker adjusted his glasses. "Her husband chalked it up to the sedation and pain meds. Thought maybe she was having some lingering side effects from them once she got home. Is that possible?"

"Sure, it's possible." Ben was grateful to have something he could answer. "Plus, she'd been on an antidepressant before the surgery. She missed a few doses in the hospital until we restarted her home meds. Withdrawal from those can cause nightmares in some patients. Maybe that's all it was." He ran through her hospital stay in his mind, through their interactions together, both on rounds and the extra times he checked in on her, including once when he'd brought her the tapioca pudding from the cafeteria she liked so much. But she'd mentioned nothing about someone watching her. Had she told Karen about it? Or maybe Lenny when he'd filled in for them during an emergent surgery?

The same sinking feeling he'd had with Mr. Sampson returned. Had he missed something in Mrs. Templeton's post-op care? Was he indirectly responsible for her death as well?

"Does missing a few doses of your home meds also lead to getting your leg chopped off?" Patel's senseless question startled Ben out of his reverie.

"Of course not," he said, his face heating. "I have no idea what's going on. I feel sick about it. My whole team does. They've been through enough as it is." When Becker made a go-on gesture, Ben told them about the crash in Alaska back in December. The detective nodded—no doubt he'd have heard about it in the news—and asked which staff members were involved. Ben told them that too but mentioned there were a few other survivors on the small plane he didn't know, including the pilot and another nurse. But when Patel twirled his finger near his head and asked if any of the ones he *did* know were acting strange—"You know, going off the deep end. Cuckoo, cuckoo?"—Ben stopped talking. It seemed like a trap, and he didn't want to incriminate anyone. No one he knew would do this. No one. Finally, he decided on, "They seem like what you'd expect after surviving a plane crash: a bit of residual shock, not their usual selves, but certainly not people who'd kill one of our patients and stick her leg in a park." He could barely utter the ridiculous words.

Unexpectedly, Patel erupted in laughter, his droopy countenance springing to life. "Oh, Dr. Oris," he said, "if there's one thing I've learned on this job, it's that people are rarely who they seem."

---

As soon as Ben finished with the detectives, he headed straight to a call room to clear his head. Dr. Lock's second case of the morning was already well under way. No need to scrub in at this point. Inside the room, dust particles floated in the air, and the stale breath of slumber still lingered from the unmade lower bunk. Never one for small spaces, Ben felt like the walls were closing in on him.

Pacing back and forth, he texted Laurette to call him when she had a chance. Within seconds, she did. As per their game, her first words were a trivia question. "What virus ulcerates the skin after a bite from an infected goat or sheep?"

"Um…guess I'm not sure."

"What's wrong?"

As always, her sixth sense, even from as far away as Atlanta, unnerved him. There was a time he would have scoffed at such a notion, but after what the two of them had gone through together, he no longer did. "Is this a bad time? You busy?"

"Don't worry about me. The timing is perfect."

Ben doubted she would tell him otherwise. "They found another leg." He'd already told her about Joseph Sampson's limb so he knew she'd understand.

"What? Who did?"

"Some worker in Fairmount Park. It's from another one of my patients." He stopped pacing and leaned against the top mattress, the hospital-grade blanket scratching his bare arm. "I can't even believe it."

"*Mon Dieu.* How do they know it was your patient?"

"The hip implant was left in place and she's missing, so two plus two, you know? They'll confirm with DNA."

"My God," Laurette repeated, this time in English. "That's horrible."

"Guess who the cops came to first?"

"Oh, Ben, no."

"Yep. Yours truly. Do they really think I'd chop off my patient's leg and leave it in a park? That's insane." His shoe kicked a reflex hammer another resident must have dropped under the bed. He picked it up and squeezed it inside his palm until his skin blanched.

"They only questioned you because you were one of the surgeons."

"And because I found the first leg. Ding, ding, ding, give that man a prize."

"Maybe some gang kids are messing around. A weird initiation of sorts. Or some amateur cult, though that thought makes me shiver."

"But this patient..." Ben slouched down on the unmade bed. "This patient was murdered. She wasn't already dead like Sampson."

Silence from the other end. Then, "Are they sure? Maybe she died in an area hospital. Maybe delinquents broke into the morgue again, yes?"

"She seemed fine to her husband before she disappeared. Well, other than some paranoia, maybe medication-induced."

Someone interrupted Laurette. Ben heard a male voice through the line but couldn't make out what he said.

"I'm sorry, Ben, I must go. My meeting is about to start."

He checked his watch. "No, I'm the one who should be apologizing. You're busy, and here I am whining. Get back to your CDC business. But thanks, Bovo. It helps just to talk to you."

"You can always call me. Anytime. Who's the man who moved oceans to get me last-minute tickets to Haiti after my father's heart attack? Who's the man who sat by my Auntie Marie's side last year and helped her understand the 'gibberish' of her breast cancer doctors?"

He allowed a small smile. "Yeah, and she still doesn't like me much."

"And yet you held her hand and got her through it when my uncle and I couldn't be there ourselves. I will call later to make sure you're okay, yes?"

"I'll be fine." He tried to lighten the tone. "What's the answer, anyway."

"What answer?"

"To your infectious disease question."

"Ah, yes. It's the orf virus. Now you will never forget it should one of your patients stick his finger in a goat's mouth."

He laughed. "Seems unlikely in orthopedics." The levity felt good, but it didn't last long. As soon as they disconnected, he texted Lenny about Mrs. Templeton. Twice. No response, nor did the chief resident answer a call. Ben tried the guy's office instead. After three rings, Cheryl, the residency program secretary, picked up. Ben asked if Lenny was there.

"No, he didn't come in today. Out sick, I guess. At least I think that's what he mumbled when he called earlier. I had his office phone patched into mine for the day." The irritation in her voice was obvious.

Ben thanked her and hung up. Guess he wasn't the only one who'd noticed the chief resident's avoidant behavior of late. Over the past week, Ben had barely spoken to the guy. Lenny was never in his office, and most of Ben's texts went unanswered. In the residents' lounge the other day, Chip Owens, chief-in-training, was complaining about having to do too much of Lenny's job for him.

The incident with Joseph Sampson's narcotic prescription resurfaced in Ben's mind. How Lenny had picked up the meds. How the mail carrier had complained the pills didn't seem to help, that he'd been in too much pain at home to get up and walk, which put him at risk for a pulmonary embolism.

Ben sighed. Risk of losing the Conley Grant or not, risk of getting a shitty call schedule or not, risk of alienating his friend or not, it was time to confront the chief resident. Something was going on, and his gut told him it wasn't good. He opened up his phone contacts and called OR number four, where Dr. Lock would be finishing up his second case. When the circulating nurse picked up, Ben requested she let Dr. Lock know that he wouldn't be able to scrub in on the next surgery. "Tell him I'm sorry, but I forgot about an appointment." The excuse was flimsy, but to his relief, after the nurse relayed the message, Ben heard Lock holler in the background, "Do what you gotta do, Oris. Meet you after lunch for rounds."

No doubt Lock was as discombobulated over Mrs. Templeton's murder and body desecration as Ben was, so he likely didn't care whether Ben assisted in the next procedure or not, especially with the always efficient Angela and Michael by his side. Ben would take the opportunity to break away from the hospital and visit Lenny at home, whether the chief resident wanted him there or not. Although he worried the guy might be using drugs, it was too ludicrous to think he'd had something to do with Mr. Sampson and Mrs. Templeton's severed limbs. The mere idea was nuts.

But then the words of the shadowy-eyed detective came back to him: *If there's one thing I've learned on this job, it's that people are rarely who they seem.*

## 13

With his puffer coat zipped to his chin and his head lowered, Ben speed-walked the last block to Lenny's apartment complex, situated in downtown Philadelphia. Cold air bit through the thin fabric of his scrub bottoms, and humidity made icicles out of the tiny hairs in his nose (*why is this winter so effing cold?*), but at a distance of only eight blocks west from the hospital, walking was faster than retrieving his Mustang from the parking garage and driving through Philly's congested streets. Other than a few areas of slick concrete that required extra vigilance, the sidewalks were mostly cleared of snow and ice.

Outside a cream-brick building on Chestnut Street, where a queue of parked cars stretched as far as the eye could see, Ben pressed the buzzer for Lenny's unit. No response. He pressed it again. Nothing. While vehicles swished by on the narrow street and bundled-up pedestrians dashed into eateries, office buildings, and retail stores, he wondered how best to proceed. If Lenny really was home sick, he might need Ben's help. If he wasn't home, then where was he?

Determined to see the guy, Ben pulled off a glove and entered the four-digit security code Lenny had given him when he'd fed his fish. Ben still had the apartment key too, and as he entered the building, he dug his key ring out of his coat pocket.

Inside the vestibule, heat vents welcomed him. He took a moment to defrost his frozen limbs, and then unzipped his coat and stuffed his gloves and hat into his pocket. Like the apartment units themselves, the entryway was upscale, with crown molding, sconce lighting, and classy wooden mailbox clusters. Even the air freshener smelled swanky, a mixture of vanilla and spice. As a junior faculty member, Lenny made a nice nickel, and since he didn't have a child to support, it seemed only fair he got to enjoy the fruits of his orthopedic labor, at least until his twelve-month lease was up.

Ben climbed the stairs two at a time to the fourth floor. After several unanswered knocks, he used his key to open Lenny's door and stepped inside the seven-hundred-square-foot flat, whose posh interior with its open floor plan and glossy hardwood flooring made Ben's basement dwelling look like a hostel. Even with the lights turned off and the dreary weather outside, large windows in the living room offered plenty of natural light. A gray couch with patterned pillows sat empty. Across from it, Lenny's seventy-five-gallon fish tank bubbled and hummed. Vibrantly colorful sea life swam around in its depths.

"Lenny? It's Ben. You in here?" He crossed the short distance to the bedroom. "Just checking in on you. You didn't answer your—"

The chief resident sat on the edge of his unmade bed. He stared blankly in Ben's direction, his eyes red-rimmed and hollow, his stout —but definitely thinner—body naked except for a tattered pair of boxer briefs. Hair as thick as a chimp's covered his chest and belly.

Ben knelt in front of him. "Hey, what's wrong?" Lenny's pupils were small and the whites of his eyes bloodshot, but when Ben snapped his fingers in front of his glassy stare, the chief snapped to attention. He seemed more shell-shocked than high. "How bad is it, Len?" Ben raised his voice. "Huh? How long have you been using?"

Lenny blinked, his face pale. When he opened his mouth, it took a few beats for the words to come out. "I messed up," he croaked. His lips trembled, and he looked like he was about to cry. "I'm in trouble. Big trouble."

"Hey, hey." Ben sat next to him on the bed, ignoring the rank odor he emanated. "It's okay. I'll help you. Just tell me what you've been taking. Oxy? Percocet? Adderall when you need to be up, not down?"

"How did you…"

"How did I know? The real question is how did I not know sooner? I didn't even notice you'd lost weight." Ben, feeling like the world's shittiest friend, slipped off his coat and flipped it back on the unmade bed. "The next question is what do we do about it? How bad is it?"

Lenny lowered his head and rubbed his face with his meaty hands. If he realized he was dressed only in his underwear, he made no indication.

"Tell me. How bad is it?"

Nothing but silence from Lenny.

Ben's mouth went dry. "You took Joseph Sampson's pain meds, didn't you? Switched them with something less potent. What did Mr. Sampson actually get? Tylenol? Ibuprofen? Placebo? Have there been other patients you've stolen drugs from?"

Lenny's ongoing muteness was answer enough.

Ben shot up from the bed. "He died, Len! From a PE because he was in too much pain to get up and walk. His wife is now a widow." Ben balled his hands into fists, but when Lenny began to weep, his fury faded.

"I know, I know," Lenny sobbed. "I'm so sorry. I never meant for that to happen. It was wrong, so wrong."

A bathrobe hung on the door of the ensuite bathroom. Ben grabbed it and sat back down next to Lenny. "Here, put this on. Are you on anything now?"

"Not since last night."

"How bad are things? And tell me the truth."

The chief resident donned the robe and cinched the belt. He wiped his eyes. "It started with Adderall, you know? Just a little amphetamine kick to help me focus. Between my clinical work, my administrative duties, my research—not to mention trying to line up a job for next year—I can't keep up anymore." Like a wounded puppy, he tilted his head toward Ben. "I'm burning out, man. I just…I thought the Adderall would be all I needed, but then I got so stressed I started taking something to help me sleep. But I was keeping it under control." His eyes beseeched Ben. "I promise."

"Under control? A man might have died because of what you did. You need to get help. You need to report this to the program director, and you need to do it today." Ben wasn't sure whether sympathy or strong-arming was the best approach, so he decided on both. "I'll help you through this, but either you turn yourself in or I will."

"No, you don't understand." The veins on Lenny's neck bulged, and his face turned red. "It's so much worse than stealing patients' medications. I…I did something horrible. I…"

Trepidation pinched Ben's throat. "What did you do?" When Lenny didn't respond, he gritted his teeth. "What. Did. You. Do?"

"I was the one who cut off Joseph Sampson's leg," Lenny whispered.

"You…you…what…?" Ben could hardly spit out the words. Beyond the door, the fish tank gurgled. It might as well have been a hundred miles away. "Did you…did you kill…?"

"Did I kill Kim Templeton? Of course not. Are you crazy?" Lenny stood and started pacing. "I would never do something like that. Never. I only took Sampson's leg to prove something, but then when Dr. Fisher called me early this morning—told me that another limb had been found—I got so confused and scared I couldn't even face coming into work."

*Confused and scared? Make that two of us.* Ben pulled out his phone. "You've got five seconds to start explaining yourself or I'm calling Dr. Fisher. In fact, maybe it should be the police—"

"Wait," Lenny cried, holding up his hands. "I will. Just give me a minute, and I'll tell you everything." He started leaving the bedroom.

"Where are you going?"

"I need a drink first."

"Seriously?"

"Of water, for crying out loud. I'm not as bad off as you think."

"You just admitted to hacking off a leg and stealing it, so excuse me if I think you're *worse* off than I think."

Ben followed Lenny into the kitchen and eagerly guzzled his own glass of water. Then they retreated to the couch across from the fish tank. As Lenny began his bizarre tale, Ben watched a clownfish and dwarf angelfish vie for an underwater castle.

"Things started back when I was a second-year resident and one of Lock's star trainees." The bleary-eyed chief scratched a scab on his neck. "Back then, Lock and I really hit it off, just like the two of you are now. Our surgical styles meshed well, and he was a great teacher. Still is, though he's shut most of us out. And I know why too. I just need to prove it."

"Come on, Len. Not that 'consistent team' thing again."

"Mock me all you want, but there's more to it than you realize. You think his team approach is about having consistency in his reconstructive surgeries, about keeping the risk of his post-op infections down, because that's what he tells everyone, but it's not. It's about keeping more experienced surgeons from seeing what he's up to."

Ben shook his head. "The drugs are making you paranoid."

"Ha. If only it was that simple, but nope." Lenny twisted the terrycloth belt of his bathrobe into a tight spiral. "Back in my second year, one of our patients battled an awful staph infection after a knee replacement. The thing wouldn't clear up, and she ended up needing a complete revision. Dr. Lock bemoaned the fact there wasn't a better implant that would lower the risk of infection, something like a silver-coated implant. Silver's got anti-bacterial properties, you know." When Ben nodded, Lenny continued. "Lock told me research was in the works for one, but that no device had been approved yet because no one could figure out how to safely control the release of silver ions. So I started to give it some thought, started to put my chemistry knowledge to use. After playing around a bit, I came up with an idea for an implant that would do exactly what Dr. Lock wanted."

Ben had no idea where Lenny's story was going, and he knew he had to get back to the hospital soon before Dr. Lock grew suspicious, but he motioned for the chief resident to continue.

"At first, Lock seemed excited by my proposal, surprised even. But a couple weeks later he blew me off. Said he had looked into it by asking a friend who works R & D at a medical device company. The guy told him it couldn't be done. Well, that made me even more determined, so I continued pestering Lock about my plan until one day he shoved his soap-opera doctor's face into mine and ordered me to drop it. Told me I was just a second-year resident who should be concentrating on developing the surgical skills 'the good Lord' gave me instead of a failed product design."

"Sounds like Lock," Ben said.

"So I did. It's not like I didn't have enough to keep me busy. Like you, I was busting my balls for the Conley Research Grant—which I never got, mind you—but after that, things changed between Lock and me. He cut me out of his surgeries, didn't call me for consults, blew off my requests for research advice. I didn't know what was up his ass, and then, when I was a fourth-year resident, he came up with his 'consistent team' crap..." Lenny's voice trailed off, and although it appeared he had more to say, he simply stared at the expensive sea life darting around the plants and stones inside the fish tank.

"And what? What were—"

"Had he requested the same team for all his surgeries, the hospital bigwigs would've balked, even with the millions of dollars his family brings in, but he limited it to just his elective reconstructive cases, so they allowed it. They were even more on board when his post-op infection rate went down. Way down. So they encouraged him to keep his new approach going, and his research shifted to that. He's all about making a name for himself, you know." Lenny paused to take a breath and inhaled so deeply he wheezed. "But, given Montgomery's a teaching hospital, they made him take at least one resident. He agreed to a second-year trainee. A med student too, since they don't do much but stand there and look pretty. And he's been doing it that way ever since, completely locking me out of his joint replacements. Me, the chief resident."

He snorted and slouched down on the couch, as if his recount had fully spent him.

Ben felt like he'd learned nothing. So what? Lock was a rich surgeon who'd gotten his way. What else was new? As someone who'd been broke most of his life, Ben had seen that act play out many times before. But it's not like Lock was that much of an asshole. After all, he made humanitarian trips across the globe and considered church functions a date. "You're being paranoid again. It isn't just you, you know. He excludes all senior residents. And you can still scrub in for his other surgeries if you want."

Lenny's bloodshot eyes hardened. "And why's that, Mr. Ben? Huh? Why's it only his joint replacements he doesn't want us in on?"

Great. Not only was Lenny a drug addict, he was delusional too. And they hadn't even gotten to Sampson's severed leg yet. "Because that's what his research is in. Besides, Dr. King doesn't seem to have a problem with it."

"The anesthesiologist doesn't want to make waves. He likes working here. Doesn't want to go back to London, even though his kids are there." Lenny grunted. "Nope. There's more to it than Lock's research. I'm convinced he stole my silver-coated implant idea and that's why he doesn't want me in his OR." When he saw Ben's expression, his face sagged. "You don't believe me."

"It's just…far-fetched. Why wouldn't anyone else notice? How could he get it developed? If he really had an implant that cut the infection rate, he'd spread the word to other surgeons. Their patients could benefit from it as well. He wouldn't withhold such valuable information."

"He would if he stole the idea."

Ben pondered that. In a TV-miniseries way it made sense, but not in a real-world way. Then again, severed limbs were involved so… "Tell me what you did with Joseph Sampson."

Lenny scratched a thicket of chest hair through his gaping bathrobe but said nothing.

"Tell me, Len. Now. Or I'm calling the police."

"Okay, okay, give me a sec, will ya?" He took another deep

breath, this time less frenzied. "The only way I could know for sure if Dr. Lock stole my implant idea was to see one, but since I can't be in the OR with him, I had to look in the supply room."

"And?"

"Nothing but the same collection of brands that have always been there. Each surgeon has their own preference."

"Yeah, so that weakens your theory even more."

"But then I figured, duh, he wouldn't store the unapproved silver implants in there. He'd hide them someplace else. But where were they and how could I get to them? And then Joseph Sampson died."

"And you thought you'd finally get to see one up close and personal in the morgue."

"Yes. Figured I'd settle this once and for all. So I went to his autopsy to see the implant, but before the pathology resident could expose the knee for me, she got called away. And then..."

"And then what?" At this point, Ben's question was rhetorical, because he already knew *and then what.*

"You have to understand, I was high, high as the Eiffel Tower. And desperate. Don't you see how this is eating at me? Dr. Lock stole *my* design and now he's going to profit from it. Worse, he's going to get credit for it. My dream has always been to make a difference in medicine—not to win awards, not to get rich—but to really help people. I know that sounds cliché, but it's true. But I can't stand the idea of Saint Lock getting the credit for my achievement, so I slipped back inside the autopsy room Sampson was in, grabbed the saw, and cut off his limb above the knee. I had to act quickly, you know? Someone could've come in at any time."

"So you just stole it?" Ben could feel a vessel in his forehead throb. "Don't you realize how demented that is? How much trouble you could be in?"

"I needed to examine the implant." Lenny spoke so sharply a school of fish in the tank darted apart.

"What were you thinking? How were you planning to get rid of the leg, for God's sake?"

"I wasn't thinking, of course, I wasn't thinking! I was gorked out of my mind. I was frantic and hysterical and all I could think about was proving Dr. Lock was a cheat and a fraud and a liar. I wrapped the leg in a sheet and ducked out the emergency exit to avoid the entrance, but I was such a wreck when I got home that I swallowed some pills and passed out. The next morning, when I realized what I'd done, I panicked. Didn't even examine the implant because I'd cut too high to see it. Now that I was sober, I knew the only thing I had to do was get rid of it before someone realized it was me. Can you imagine? Police barge into my apartment and I'm digging around a severed leg with a steak knife? Even if I did manage to deduce the implant was mine, who would believe me? I mean, look what I did to get at it. I'd rather never know Lock's secret than face that." Lenny hung his head and stared at the floor, his hands shaking. "It was early Saturday morning, and I remembered you told me you hiked the Orange Trail on weekends. You said you liked to touch that statue up on Council Rock for good luck, that your girlfriend got you started on it."

Though Laurette wasn't technically Ben's girlfriend, now didn't seem the time to split hairs.

"So, figuring the trail would be pretty deserted in January—only diehards like you would hike it in this weather—I carried the leg in a duffel bag and dumped it in a spot you might see on your way to the statue. I knew the chances were slim, but hey, at that point, what did I have to lose? If you happened to be the one who stumbled upon it, you'd recognize the roadrunner tattoo. But even if you didn't and someone else found it, I figured I'd still be able to prove the implant was my design when forensics examined it."

Ben shook his head, trying to make sense of Lenny's actions. Welcome to Drug Use 101, he thought. "Your logic is so convoluted, I don't even know where to start, but thanks to your stupidity, the police are leaning on me. I'm the first person they came looking for this morning after they found Kim Templeton's limb. Thank God I've got an alibi for when she disappeared." He stared hard at Lenny. "I don't want to believe it—Jesus, I *can't* believe it—but you swear you didn't—"

"Kill Mrs. Templeton? Chop her leg off? Of course not." Lenny sat up so quickly he practically fell off the couch. His robe fell open, putting his ratty underwear back into play. "That's why I'm here instead of the hospital. I'm scared. I'm completely terrified. I have no idea who did it. *Why* they did it. But if the cops find out I took Sampson's leg, they'll think it was me." When Ben didn't respond, Lenny grabbed his arm. "You have to believe me. I swear I had nothing to do with Mrs. Templeton's death. Do you really think I could do that?"

Ben licked his lips, his mouth drying up all over again. "Regardless, you have to go to the police."

"I can't do that. I can't be pinned for murder. What I did to Sampson was horrible, but I'm not a murderer. You have to believe me."

"If not you, then who?"

"I don't know—and that scares the shit out of me. Maybe someone found out what I did with Sampson's leg and now they're framing me."

"That's ridiculous."

"You got a better idea?"

"So, what, you want me to lie to the police? Pretend I don't know anything about Mr. Sampson? You know how much trouble that could land me in? An accessory to your crime, even? I've got a kid, Lenny. I've got people who depend on me."

"Please. If our friendship has meant anything to you, please don't say anything to the police. Please."

Ben didn't need the chief resident to clarify. He read the subtext loud and clear. Lenny had always been there for him, during his intern year and beyond, helping him admit patients on chaotic float nights, bringing him hot meals when he hadn't eaten all day, even watching over Maxwell a couple times when Ben had gotten called back to the hospital. Lenny would walk the toddler through the children's area, with its noisy marble mazes and interactive gadgets, until Ben had finished his work.

Dr. Lock had hit the bullseye when he'd said Ben was loyal. In fact, he was probably loyal to a fault. But didn't this push the bounds of loyalty to the extreme?

"Dammit," he said. "I can't lie to the police."

"Not lie. Just…withhold the details for a while. Until I can figure this out."

Ben squeezed his forehead between his thumb and fingers. Could he really rat Lenny out? He believed him when he said he didn't kill Mrs. Templeton, but that didn't mean the police would. How would he live with himself if he were responsible for Lenny going to prison for a murder he didn't commit? Shouldn't he give him the benefit of the doubt? It wasn't that long ago Ben had needed people to do the same thing for him, back when his innocence was on the line and prison was a frighteningly real threat.

He shifted to the edge of the couch and exhaled a wave of anxiety and doubt. "Okay, I'll keep quiet for now—*Jesus, what am I doing?*—but only on one condition." *Please don't let this come back to bite me.*

"What? Anything."

"You admit your drug problem to the program director and to Dr. Fisher and then check into rehab for help. Immediately."

## 14

In front of the central workstation on 4 West, Dr. Lock gave Ben a good-natured slap on the back. "Strong work, Oris. You just saved this college kid from getting his knee drained. What made you think Crohn's arthritis instead of a septic joint, anyway? The ED docs missed it." The attending surgeon smoothed his light brown hair, now free of its surgical cap, and tossed the patient's local medical records onto the counter next to an abandoned IV fluid bag. To the ward clerk, who was nibbling her fruit-and-nut bar like a rabbit, he said, "Scan these into the kid's electronic record, please. And consult internal medicine. This isn't an orthopedic case."

Ben's mind was elsewhere. For one, he was desperate to learn more about Kim Templeton. The news of her discarded limb had put the entire surgical team on edge, and despite Dr. Lock's attempts at good spirits, Ben could sense he was similarly unnerved. Secondly, Lenny's earlier confession about stealing Sampson's leg was eating its way through his brain. Like a teenager, he kept checking his phone, waiting for the text that would confirm the chief resident had kept his end of the bargain and reported his drug use to their program director.

"Earth to Oris. What made you think of Crohn's?"

Ben realized he hadn't yet answered Lock's question. "Oh, sorry, just took a little extra history, that's all. They're swamped down in the ED."

"You're selling yourself short." Lock rounded the counter and took a seat behind a computer terminal next to Angela, who was scrolling through her phone and bouncing her knees up and down in a jittery fashion. "God not only gave you good hands, He made you a good thinker too.

Despite Ben's preoccupation, the compliment felt good, especially coming from an attending like Dr. Lock. Still, Lenny's earlier allegations against the man soured the attaboy a bit. It was difficult to reconcile the religious, humanitarian surgeon in front of him with the one inside Lenny's head: a thief and a fraud.

Dr. Lock signed off on his chart note and stood to leave. If he had any opinions on Mrs. Templeton's severed hip, he was keeping them to himself. "Thanks for finishing things up, Angela. I have a dinner date with a remarkable woman to get to."

Ben had a feeling that "remarkable woman" was Sophia. She'd mentioned she was dropping Maxwell off at Willy's tonight for a few hours since Ben was on call. Although he was happy she'd found someone—she hadn't dated much since Maxwell was born—he once again wished it wasn't in his own backyard. At least he now understood what she'd intended to tell him that day in the park when they'd found Sampson's limb: she was officially dating his attending.

After Dr. Lock left, Ben grabbed a stool from behind the counter and wheeled it toward Angela. She was no longer on her phone, having moved on to checking lab reports on the computer. He cleared his throat. "Have you learned anything new about Mrs. Templeton? I assume the detectives spoke to you?"

Her elbow banged the counter, and her expression darkened. "Why? What have you heard?"

"Sorry. Wasn't implying anything. I'm just confused, you know?"

She offered a nod in lieu of an answer, her straight hair catching in the collar of her white coat, and returned to the computer screen.

"Hey, Ben, ready to grab dinner?"

Unaware Karen was even there, Ben swiveled his stool in her direction. Dressed in the same blue scrubs as him, with her hair in a ponytail and her chewed fingernails drumming the laminate countertop, she said, "We better eat before the shit hits the fan. It's a full moon. The crazies will come in. Chopped off fingers, broken bones from superhero stunts, you name it, we'll get it."

He rounded the counter. "Not sure about your lunar predictions, but this day has been weird enough as it is. Let's not jinx things."

She tugged on the stethoscope around his neck. "Why do you always wear that?"

"Not everything is about bones."

"It is for me."

"Hey, do you know anything more about Mrs. Temple—"

She raised a hand. "No. Don't even go there. I won't be able to work with that on my mind."

Great, Ben thought. No one's willing to discuss the severed elephant in the room. He didn't blame the crash survivors for being skittish—who wouldn't be after their ordeal?—but the walking on glass around them was tiring. And where the heck was Lenny's text? They'd made a deal, dammit. "Okay then, boss," he said to Karen. "Let's go eat."

No sooner had he said goodbye to Angela and the ward clerk than Tara Sands, an ED nurse who had helped Ben navigate a number of difficult patients back when she worked ortho the previous year, approached the counter. As a single mom whose husband had left her with a mountain of debt and two high school daughters, she carried a heavy load.

She smiled warmly at Ben. "Oh good, you're on call. I was hoping to catch you. I finally have a little extra to pay you for patching up our roof last month. At least now if we get a heavy snowfall, it won't cave in on us." She pulled a check from the pocket of her patterned scrub top.

Ben waved her off. "Oh no, please don't worry about it. Didn't even take me an hour. Save it for Alice's tuition next year. You're gonna need it."

She replaced the check and gave him an unexpected hug. "An

hour, ha. You were up there in the cold for a good four at least." When she pulled away, she held onto his shoulders. "I mean it. Thank you."

He fiddled uncomfortably with his stethoscope. "We just wish we could get you back in the OR. We miss you, right, Karen?"

Karen gave a half-hearted nod and checked the clock above the workstation. For someone who hardly ate anything, she sure seemed to be in a hurry to get dinner. Or maybe she just needed to keep moving. Less time to think about plane crashes and severed legs that way.

"If all the surgeons were as nice as you, I'd still be there." She left it at that, but Ben knew what she meant. Like Lenny, she was annoyed by Dr. Lock's insistence that only certain people could scrub in on his reconstructive surgeries. In her case it was Michael who was the chosen scrub nurse. Although Tara didn't particularly care whether she worked with Lock or not, she'd told Ben it was the principle of the thing. As if no one else was good enough to make the privileged surgeon's team.

"Ben. Dinner. Now," Karen barked.

"Yes, ma'am." He saluted her, said goodbye to Tara, and followed his senior resident down the hall. He made it half a hallway before his phone buzzed. Lenny. *About time.*

As he trotted behind Karen he read the text: *All's good, man. Program director and ortho chair notified. Off to treatment, but as far as anyone else knows I'm helping a sick cousin with cancer. I know you'll protect me.*

Ben read the last sentence twice. Protect him? Did Lenny mean protect his secret about drug treatment or did he mean protect him from inquiring detectives?

The first he could do. The second, he wasn't so sure.

## 15

The first thing Ben did when he left the hospital post-call Tuesday morning was visit Kim Templeton's husband in their ranch-style home on the outskirts of Philly. Though Ben doubted Detectives Becker and Patel would approve of his house call to the bereaved husband of the recently murdered woman, he felt like he had to do something—anything—to figure out what happened to his patient.

Unfortunately, other than learning that Del Templeton was a heartbroken man with the body of a lumberjack and that Kim Templeton had been a wonderful dancer before her hip injury derailed her quickstep, Ben discovered nothing new, only confirmed what the police had already told him: that Mrs. Templeton had disappeared Saturday evening when her husband stepped out to buy her pudding, that she'd been paranoid someone was watching her (which they had attributed to her medication since Del had found no evidence of trespassers), and that her body still hadn't been found. After Mr. Templeton clarified for Ben there'd been no sign of a break-in or a struggle, he added that the outdoor camera he'd ordered as a safety net hadn't yet arrived before she disappeared. At that point, he pounded the table and broke down completely.

After comforting the man as best he could, Ben said goodbye and returned to his Mustang to go visit his mother. Forty minutes later he arrived at the Sethfield Long-Term Care Facility, fifteen miles from downtown Philadelphia in a small, working-class community. With its urine-colored brick and shutterless windows, the five-story complex wasn't pretty, but it at least offered good care to a comatose woman.

As always when he entered the flavorless room with its hospital-grade bed, chipped wooden dresser, and two plastic chairs, he hoped he and his dad had done enough to make the place homey. Max had been the one with the keen eye, not Willy or Ben. But Ben had installed lace curtains over the lone window and hung prints of shorelines and meadows on the walls. Willy had dotted the dresser with family photographs, Ben and Maxwell beaming from most of them. And together they regularly filled the ceramic vase on her nightstand with flowers. Judging by the sweet fragrance of Lily of the Valley in the air, Willy had brought in the most recent bouquet today, but although his coat was draped over one of the chairs, he wasn't in the room at the moment.

Still dressed in rumpled scrubs and his mind still pregnant with his conversation with Del Templeton, Ben slipped off his winter jacket and laid it on the other chair. He bent over and kissed Harmony's forehead, and then smoothed back her long auburn hair, the locks thinner and sprinkled with gray but still vibrant thanks to the stylist he hired to come weekly.

"Hey, Mom, it's Ben. Missed you. Maxwell's been asking when he can come see the Quiet Passenger again. Believe it or not, that's his new nickname for you. Must have something to do with his trains." Ben smiled at his son's obsession. Harmony would smile too. She'd raise her pale arms, gauzy dress flowing around her, and whoop, "Nothing quiet about me." Except, of course, when she was in the throes of depression.

At first Ben wasn't sure about his son seeing his grandmother in a coma, but Sophia had convinced him it was a good way to gently initiate him into the sad realities of life. Had Maxwell shown fear, they would have stopped his visits, but he seemed to enjoy sitting next to his grandma, showing her his trains and books, convinced she was equally enthralled. "She likes Sir Quincy the best, just like me, Daddy," he'd once told Ben.

Willy entered the room, breaking Ben's thoughts. His appearance was as usual: salt-and-pepper hair ruffled, eyelids hooded under untamed eyebrows, checkered shirt tucked into his jeans. "Oh good, you're here," he said to Ben. "I was getting worried. You didn't answer my voicemail." He gave Ben a quick hug. "I read about that leg in the paper. The article said the patient had hip surgery at your hospital. Is that true? Did you know her? Do they know who dumped it in the park?" He spoke so quickly Ben wasn't sure which point to tackle first.

He started with, "Sorry I didn't call you this morning. I visited the patient's husband after I left the hospital, and since your message said you'd be here, I figured I'd just stop by before going home to crash." With good-natured sarcasm, he added, "I would've texted you, but we both know how often you check those."

His father chuckled and took a seat. "You know I'm old school. Rough call night?"

"The usual. Managed two hours of shut-eye." Ben yawned and slumped down on his chair. "I'll take a nap before picking up Maxwell later. Didn't know Mrs. Templeton's leg made the papers though."

"Oh yeah. Splashed all over the front page: *Severed Leg Found in Fairmount Park*." Willy looked unsettled. "Do you think it's related to the one you found in the Wissahickon Valley?"

Although Mr. Sampson's leg hadn't been big news—maybe because Ben was the one who'd found it and didn't blab about it on social media or maybe because the police figured it was a hospital prank and not worth further exploring—he wasn't surprised Kim Templeton's was. A severed leg and a missing woman made for a hot story. He skirted his dad's question. "What else did the article say? Did it mention any names?" *Like my own?*

"No, I don't think so. Just said a woman who'd had recent hip surgery at Montgomery Hospital went missing and that her detached limb was found by a park employee. There were comments from her husband, her coworkers—I think the article said she worked in a law office—that sort of thing."

"Did it say anything about an orthopedic implant?"

"No. Why?"

"No reason." Lenny's insistence that Dr. Lock had stolen his implant idea poked at Ben's brain, but how it tied into Kim Templeton's severed limb—or if it even did—he didn't know.

"You okay, son?"

"I'm fine. What about you. Anymore...?" Ben wiggled his index finger Harmony's way, her breathing softly sonorous.

"You mean is your mother still talking to me?"

Ben nodded.

"If I say yes, will you have me committed?"

Ben knew Willy was joking, but he also understood his dad's response was an affirmative.

"Don't worry about me, Benny Boy. I'm all right." His father grew serious. "But your mom is still worried about you. Something about her parents too, I think."

At that moment, Harmony's hand slipped off the bed. Ben jumped at the weirdly timed movement. An occasional stirring from her was normal—sometimes her lips smacked or her fingers twitched or her expression darkened—but it startled him nonetheless. Although the doctors felt the movements were simply a reflex response, Harmony clearly had residual brain activity. Her EEGs suggested as much, which confused her primary care doctor and neurologists alike. Her coma was unlike others they'd seen. Regardless, whatever brain activity remained was not enough to wake her from her never-ending sleep.

As far as he knew, her parents had only visited her twice, once at the beginning when he'd tracked them down to tell them about their daughter's condition (which wasn't easy to do, having no clue who they were) and once a couple months ago. Both of them, who had to be in their mid-seventies if not older, were remarkably spry and well-kept. They were polite but reserved and said very little. Their aloofness hadn't surprised Ben. Willy, who'd never met the couple, had mentioned that Harmony tried to avoid them, and she herself had once hinted they were terrible people, particularly her father. At least they were footing the bill for her long-term care facility, beyond what Medicaid didn't cover.

"How's your landlady?" Willy asked. "Her vision still fading?"

It took Ben a moment to shift gears. "Poor Mrs. Sinclair. I'm worried she'll be blind within a year. The other day I smelled burning. I ran upstairs and saw she'd turned a burner to high instead of off. I'm not sure she'll be able to live alone much longer."

"At least she has you there."

"Sure, and I'll stay as long as she needs me, but I'm not around much. I helped her set up an alert system. If she gets in trouble, it'll go directly to 911. My cell too." Ben's phone buzzed in his pocket. "Speaking of…" When he saw the call was from his mentor, Dr. Smith, he frowned and said, "Sorry, Dad, gotta take this."

Outside in the quiet hallway, he listened to the internist's calm yet firm voice. At her mention of Detectives Becker and Patel, his muscles tensed.

"They're looking for you," she said. "They came to my office."

"Why would they do that?"

"Maybe because I'm your mentor. And because I helped you through your…your ordeal a few years back." She hesitated, as if unsure how to frame her next remark. "They asked me some questions about you."

"What kind of questions? Did—"

"Please, there isn't much time. They'll be headed to your apartment soon."

"My apartment?" Ben rubbed furiously at his temple, his confusion magnified by his fatigue. "Why?"

"I've asked my friend, Shala Lamb, to meet you there."

"Who's she?"

"She's one of the hospital lawyers."

His throat thickened. "Why do I need a lawyer?"

"There's been a new development with Mrs. Templeton's leg. An awful development." Again, she hesitated. "They think you might know something about it."

## 16

My hunger has grown so strong that the energy required to ignore it is exhausting. How long can I hide it? How long before someone figures it out?

Who could believe I'd do something like this? It's unimaginable...extreme. I've released souls before, it's true, but never this horrifically and never without moral grounds. But I can't seem to resist these urges.

Maybe it's not my fault. Maybe it wasn't me in command of my body or mouth. It was someone else. Some*thing* else. Something triggered by that first limb in the park. I was forced to follow my cravings, and now a power greater than me has flipped the cerebral switch of no return. I became an animal, a ravenous beast with a yawning jaw and razor-sharp teeth.

But I have to fight to regain control. Otherwise I risk losing everything.

Dear God, I'm repulsed by my actions. A part of me worries I won't be able to stop. Like taffy being pulled (and pulled and pulled), my craving will grow, and I'm scared the hunger will never be filled.

Because they all call to me. They thread their way into my psyche and call to me.

*I'm next*, they whisper. *I'm next.*

## 17

Feeling like he couldn't race home fast enough, where God only knew what the detectives were saying to Mrs. Sinclair, filling her mind with scary images of severed limbs and missing bodies, Ben squealed out of Sethfield's parking lot and sped back toward Philadelphia's city center. After rushing through yellow lights and honking at an SUV that was performing an illegal U-turn, he finally slowed down on Wallace Street, where his landlady's red-bricked row house was located. Hopefully he'd find a nearby parking spot, but it never failed: If he was in a hurry, spots were rarer than moon rocks. If he had time to spare, open spaces were plentiful.

Just when he worried he'd have to circle back around the block, he spotted Detectives Becker and Patel on Mrs. Sinclair's stoop. She was coatless and appeared trapped between them, each man gripping one of her arms.

Not caring about double-parking or blocking the right lane of an already narrow street, he slammed on the Mustang's brakes and bolted from the car. His shoes kicked up packed snow and dirtied the hem of his scrubs as he ran. "Hey, leave her alone."

The two detectives looked up in surprise.

When Ben reached the stoop, its icy concrete pebbled with winter salt, he said, "Edith, are you okay?"

"Oh heavens, don't worry about me, I'm fine. Just tripped over my doorstep. Can hardly see it anymore." She wiped her failing eyes as if to clear them. "These men grabbed my arms just in time. I'd have slipped down the stairs like a human toboggan if they hadn't. They're here to talk to you. Are they friends of yours?"

"Not quite," Ben said, hands still fisted by his sides.

"Got quite a temper there, don't ya, doc." Patel gazed up at the sun, which was making an afternoon appearance. The glare triggered a sneeze, but the detective caught it in the crook of his elbow, his shabby overcoat no worse for the wear.

Becker, more contemporary in his wool peacoat, released Mrs. Sinclair's arm. "We're detectives, ma'am. We didn't get a chance to introduce ourselves before you stumbled out."

"Detectives." Her expression shifted to alarm. "What's wrong? What do you want with Ben?"

"Let's get you back inside," Becker said. "That sweater's no match for twenty-degree weather."

Edith pulled her cardigan tighter against her shoulders, her thinning gray hair lifting in the wind. "Yes, well, yes…I guess." She looked back and forth between the detectives and Ben, as if unsure what to do. Whether she could clearly see any of them, Ben didn't know. "Should I send them down to your place?"

He scaled the stairs and grabbed her hand. Warm air from her still-open door wafted out. "That'd be fine. Sorry they startled you. It's nothing to worry about." He wished he could believe his own words.

When Ben started to help her back inside, Patel cleared his throat. Ben glanced back at him. "What?"

The detective lifted his lip in a lazy smirk and nodded toward the double-parked Mustang. "Better move that first. You'd hate to get a ticket." He winked. "Don't worry. We'll wait for you."

Ben didn't dislike many people, but he disliked Detective Patel. Was maybe even starting to loathe him. Although he understood the guy's attitude was merely a ploy to rattle him, it didn't make it less effective. Consider me rattled, Ben thought as he headed back to his car.

Just as he was climbing into the driver's seat, a woman dressed in a cashmere coat and knee-high boots came trotting down the snow-cleared sidewalk. Her dark hair billowed out from beneath a knit hat, and the decorative ball on top of it bounced with each step. She raised a gloved hand in the air. "Wait, wait, don't say anything yet, Dr. Oris." She sounded breathless, as if she'd had to park far away.

Patel looked amused. "And who might you be?"

"I'm Shala Lamb, one of the hospital attorneys."

A chuckle from the irritating detective. "So the doc needs a lawyer, does he?" He gave Becker a friendly slap on the back and entered the row house after Edith. "Guess we're talking to the right guy then."

----

Inside his basement apartment, Ben felt no warmer than he had on the stoop. Based on what Dr. Smith had told him over the phone forty-five minutes earlier, shit was about to hit him. "Can we just get this over with?" he asked the detectives.

Across the table Becker nodded, but Patel hadn't yet taken a seat. Instead, he wandered the short distance out of the kitchen, into the living room, and then into the single bedroom and bath-room. His self-guided tour was no skin off Ben's back. He had nothing to hide.

When the detective returned to the kitchen, he smoothed his coal-black mane and sat down. "Nice digs," he said.

It was no doubt a sarcastic jab, because although Ben had upgraded his furniture the year before and replaced Mrs. Sinclair's garish shag carpeting after a few months of earning an income as an intern, the humid cave dwelling was still a few tiles of peeling linoleum and chipped laminate away from "nice digs." But he'd childproofed the place as best he could and tried to make it a comfortable second home for Maxwell. "It's a regular penthouse suite," he replied.

Patel ran his fingertips over the butcher-block table and whistled. "You make this yourself? I understand you're quite the carpenter."

How the detective had discovered that piece of trivia Ben didn't know. "Yes. Last year."

"That's impressive workmanship. You make that wooden train track out in the living room too?"

"No."

Patel pointed to a corner of the kitchen where two bowls sat on the floor, one with a few pellets of dried dog food in it, the other half-full of water. "Where's the pooch?"

"With my son and his mother. She takes Sir Quincy when I'm on call."

The dark-eyed detective guffawed. "Sir Quincy. Great name. You've got quite the imagination, don't you, Dr. Oris?"

*What's this guy playing at?* "Didn't realize you came here to discuss toy trains and dogs."

"Yes, gentlemen," Shala Lamb spoke up. "Let's not waste any more of Dr. Oris's time. He's post-call, and I imagine he's had little sleep." Seated next to Ben, the lawyer's floral scent helped mask the funk of his day-old scrubs. "Ask him what you came to ask." She turned to Ben. "And don't answer anything I tell you not to."

He glanced at the attorney, her windblown hair smoothed by her fingers and her cashmere coat draped over the back of her chair. Although she looked every bit the experienced lawyer, Ben figured the discovery of severed limbs fell a few notches above her usual purview of malpractice threats and patient injuries. "But I haven't done anything," he said. *Is this really happening?*

Detective Becker adjusted his tie. "Relax. This is just routine. You cared for both Mrs. Templeton and Mr. Sampson in the hospital, so you might be able to shed some light for us."

"Shed some light on what?"

"There's been a new development with Mrs. Templeton."

"Okay," Ben said slowly, waiting for the bookwormish detective to clarify.

Patel answered instead. "Medical examiner found human bite marks on her leg."

Ben gaped at the slovenly detective. *Is he joking?* The man's flat expression suggested he wasn't.

From the inside of his coat pocket, Patel withdrew a manila envelope, pulled out a collection of photographs, and smacked them down. His thumped the top one, a five-by-seven image of Mrs. Templeton's severed upper leg and pelvis on top of an autopsy table. "Have a look." His tone was casual, as if he'd just told Ben to flip through a Sears catalog.

Ben slid the photographs closer and sifted through them, tentative at first, and then with more interest. Unlike Joseph Sampson's lower limb, which had been severed above the knee and left intact below it, Kim Templeton's upper thigh was severed above the hip and above the knee, thereby showing two areas of amputation. No shin or foot remained. He wondered why it had been done that way. Maybe a shorter limb was simply easier to discard? Also unlike Sampson's limb, which had been gnawed and chewed up by animals, particularly at the site of amputation, Kim Templeton's severed borders remained fairly smooth and surgical, the muscles, ligaments, and bones sheared with precision within the pinkish stumps of soft tissue. Purplish lividity colored the lateral aspect of the limb, and in two of the photographs, a flash of metal peeked out of the truncated flesh of the otherwise intact hip joint. Ben recognized that as the patient's recent implant. An implant he himself had helped place. When he spotted the bite marks, he grimaced.

"I see you've found what we're talking about," Patel said. "Pretty nasty, huh?"

"Those are...human bite marks?" Ben's finger hovered over reddish, curvilinear impressions on Mrs. Templeton's sickly flesh, most of them clustered on the lower part of the limb.

"According to the pathologist they are." Becker flipped open his small, black notebook.

Patel leaned forward and jabbed one of the photographs Ben had laid down. "You see how clean the edges are? Limb probably wasn't in the park long before it was discovered. Otherwise animals would've enjoyed a nice meal like they did on your other patient's leg. But these," Patel pointed to a pink bite mark, "these match a human's teeth, not an animal's."

Ben longed for a cup of hot coffee to warm the chill the images gave him. *This is Kim Templeton I'm looking at. Two weeks ago she was one of my hospital patients. Now she's a severed limb in a picture. Jesus.*

"None of them break the skin though," Patel continued. "It's as if the killer's heart wasn't really into it. Maybe he—or she, no need to be sexist, am I right?—was just messing around."

With a thick tongue, Ben asked, "Are the bites pre- or postmortem?"

"According to the pathologist some are premortem," Becker said.

"But the amputation was postmortem. Good thing for Mrs. Templeton, don't you think?" Patel's lips formed a grim line that stopped short of a smile.

Ben sat back, his scrub top stuck to his torso and his throat dry. Next to him Shala remained silent, probably wishing Dr. Smith had called a different hospital lawyer. "So...what are you saying?" Ben asked. "Somebody bit Mrs. Templeton while she was alive and then killed her before cutting off her leg?" He blinked at the detectives, his mouth hanging open. "Who would do that?"

"Who indeed." Detective Patel raised his eyebrows. "Who indeed."

Ben looked at Becker, hoping for a more helpful response. The sandy-haired detective scribbled something in his notebook, his penmanship a lefty's scrawl. "That's why we wanted to talk to you. We'll try to get DNA from the limb, from saliva left behind, but seeing as how the killer washed the limb down with bleach, that might be difficult, especially if the right kind was used."

"What the...? Bleach?" *This is insane.*

Patel's lazy gaze roved the kitchen and stopped at the sink. "Got any bleach around, doc?"

Ben rubbed his forehead so hard it hurt. "Who doesn't? Look, I don't know anything about the 'right kind' of bleach. Check my laundry detergent for all I care. I don't know why you're trying to incriminate me. I have an alibi for the time Mrs. Templeton disappeared. I already told you that, and Sophia said you confirmed it with her." He tossed his phone on the table. "Search my location history if you don't believe me." When neither detective reached for it, Ben felt a sliver of comfort. "Can't you look for fingerprints? Analyze the bite marks? Anything?"

"No prints—maybe the killer wore gloves—and it's not as easy as you think to analyze bite marks," Becker said. "But we'll try. Either way it'll take a while. We're hoping to keep the bite marks out of the news—no need to cause public hysteria—so we trust you to keep quiet. You're a doctor, you should be good at that, what with your oath of confidentiality and all. Got it?"

Ben stared at Becker, the lenses of his rimless glasses as polished as the rest of him. "Then why are you telling me about them? I don't think you'd give me all these details if you really thought I was guilty—"

"Okay, enough talk about bleach and bite marks." Shala folded her arms over her blouse, her no-nonsense nails tapping the silky fabric. "What do you want from Dr. Oris?"

"We want to know if there's anything else he can tell us." Becker glanced at Ben. "Anybody you know or work with who would—"

"Bite people? Christ, of course not."

"That's funny, you know why?" Patel's tone may have sounded jovial, but Ben knew it was anything but, and his smile held not a drop of warmth. The detective straightened the photographs and returned them to the manila envelope. "It's funny because we thought you, being into voodoo and all that, might be able to help us. After all, this is some weird, cultish stuff, isn't it?"

Ben's stomach flipped. *Oh. That's why you're here.*

"Whoa, whoa," Shala said. "Dr. Oris does not practice *voodoo*. Over three years ago, he suffered a neuropsychotic episode induced by an unknown pathogen."

Ben swiveled sideways and stared at the lawyer. The fact she had that comeback at the ready sickened him almost as much as the human bite marks on Mrs. Templeton's thigh. Had Shala foreseen this? Foreseen that the cops might bring up his past and therefore had reviewed his medical school records in preparation? Or had Dr. Smith mentioned it to her during their phone call? Either way, it looked bad for him. And in all honesty, he couldn't fault the detectives for going there. He would too in their place.

"Ben was extremely sick and got caught up in something strange," Shala said. "He was cleared of all involvement. It's behind him now. *Far* behind him."

"You gotta admit," Patel said, fingers scratching at something in his oiled hair. "That was some wild crap he got 'caught up in.' Blood sacrifice, possession." He glanced at Becker and pretended to shudder.

Becker twirled his pen between his thumb and index finger. "If Dr. Oris *does* know anything about this, now would be the time to speak up."

With his heart pounding, Ben's mind once again shot to Lenny. No way would the guy chomp on a limb for shits and giggles. He'd sworn to Ben he had nothing to do with Mrs. Templeton's limb, only Mr. Sampson's (who was human-bite-mark-free, thank you very much) and Ben had believed him. But should he?

He thought about Lenny's drug use. About his paranoia over Dr. Lock stealing his implant idea. And then he thought about how Lenny had always been there for him and how Ben had once been in desperate need of people's benefit of the doubt too.

No, he couldn't feed Lenny to the wolves. Not yet. He knew all too well how that felt. The last thing Ben wanted was for Lenny to be falsely blamed for murder and end up in prison just because Ben was too much of a self-serving wuss to protect him a bit longer. He needed more proof before making that kind of accusation. But if not Lenny, who?

"Who do you think would do this, doc?" Patel asked. When Ben didn't answer, just stared blankly at Sir Quincy's water bowl in the corner of the kitchen, Patel leaned his potbelly over the table and flicked Ben's forehead. "Dr. Oris? Hello, are you in there?"

Ben yanked his head back, his cheeks heating in anger. "That's your job to find out, isn't it? Not mine. No one I know would do this. No one I work with could ever do such a thing." He believed it too. He had to believe it. Because if he didn't, it meant he might be working with a killer.

## 18

S training pasta with blighted visual fields couldn't be easy, but upstairs in her kitchen, Edith Sinclair was giving it her best shot.

"Here, let me help you." Ben abandoned the pot of bubbling marinara on his landlady's stove and hurried to the sink, where clumps of limp spaghetti noodles fell from the strainer into the basin. Mrs. Sinclair's cat, Izzy, circled Ben's feet. Although the tabby had once been a regular visitor to Ben's basement apartment, Sir Quincy's presence had put an end to that.

Edith patted her gray curls, dampened by the steam, and covered her face with her hands. "I don't know how much more of this I can take. It's like someone took a black marker and scribbled out the center of my eyes. You must think I'm a foolish old woman."

After dumping what remained of the noodles into a ceramic bowl, Ben put an arm around her stooped shoulders. "Of course not," he soothed. "I don't think that at all. Macular degeneration's a bitch, no getting around it. I'm so sorry it's still progressing."

"Everything's starting to look crooked now too. Soon I'll be blind as a bat, and then what'll I do?"

Ben guided her to the glass table—a surprisingly contemporary find in the three-story row house that was otherwise stuck in the seventies—and helped her onto one of the padded chrome chairs. The dining set had been a gift from her deceased daughter, Kate. As if on cue, Ben's throat constricted. Another death he felt responsible for.

"I'll finish up," he told Edith, plucking a rogue noodle from his jeans. "Once the broccoli is done steaming we'll be set." To Maxwell, who was playing with a plastic train station Mrs. Sinclair kept on hand for him in her living room, he called out, "Dinner-time, buddy. Go wash your hands in Grammy's bathroom. Use the step stool so you can reach the soap."

"Okay, Daddy."

As always, hearing his son's tiny voice eased whatever ache he had.

"Is he staying over with you?" Mrs. Sinclair slowly raised a glass of wine to her lips, the burgundy liquid sloshing perilously close to the rim.

"Yep. I'll drop him back at Sophe's tomorrow morning before I head to the hospital. He's an early riser anyway. She needs to be off her feet tonight. She tripped yesterday, and her bum knee is swollen again."

"Oh, poor thing. The sooner she gets surgery the better."

Ben plopped the pot of marinara on a trivet harder than he'd intended.

"What, you don't want her to have surgery?"

"No, no, of course I do." He sponged the spilled sauce off the glass table with a paper towel and dumped it in the trash. "I just wish she'd consider having it someplace else."

"But I thought the surgeon you're working with is the best. Is his waiting list too long for her to get on?"

"No. I mean, yes, it's long, but he'll work her in somewhere." Dr. Lock had said as much to Ben the day before in the OR, after prat-tling on about Sophia's computer prowess and her delicious vege-tarian meals, both of which he'd apparently had time to sample.

Ben had used the attending surgeon's distraction over Sophia to his advantage though, taking extra time to examine the ortho-

pedic implant they were about to place in a patient's knee. In
sterile gloves, he had run his fingertips over the smooth surfaces of
the femoral component, flipping it this way and that, but other
than being a bit shinier than some of the other implants he'd
seen, he found nothing unusual about its design, nothing that
shouted its initial concept was stolen from a drug-addicted chief
resident.

When Ben once again inquired what it was about that particular
implant the surgeon preferred above the others, Dr. Lock had taken
the bone saw from Michael and said, "Keplen Biomedics makes a
great product. I've used their brand since residency, and now they
customize the implants to my patients, so the sizing is precise. Don't
fix what ain't broken, right?"

Ben couldn't argue with that. Nor could he dispute the fact that
the OR director, whom he'd tracked down afterward, had
confirmed that Lock had indeed been a loyal user of Keplen
Biomedics during the eight years he'd been at Montgomery, which
was before Lenny had even entered the scene.

With the evidence on Lock's side, Ben could hardly accuse the
attending physician—one whose recommendation would factor into
the Conley Grant decision, not to mention the rest of Ben's career
—of stealing a resident's implant design. So once again, he had to
assume Lenny's suspicions were unwarranted and paranoid.

Realizing he'd drifted off, he said, "Sorry, Edith, I missed what
you said. What was that again?" He filled Maxwell's plastic cup with
milk.

"I asked why you want Sophia to go somewhere else for her
surgery. I'd think you'd want her to have the best." As soon as she
said it, recognition dawned in her failing eyes. "Ah. You're worried
because of what happened to that patient."

At that moment Maxwell darted into the kitchen. He grabbed
Ben's leg and swung around his limb as if it were a tree trunk, his
head barely missing Ben's nether regions. "Whoa, buddy, watch out.
Daddy might want to have another one of you someday." To Mrs.
Sinclair, who was chuckling at the scene, Ben said, "I thought we
weren't going to talk about that." He made a side glance at Maxwell

who was scrambling into a booster seat secured to one of the chairs. A purple train was clutched in his fist.

"Of course. It's just…well, it's so awful. It's all over the news."

"Believe me, I know." So did Ben's colleagues. Ever since the detectives came sniffing around two days ago, everyone was on edge, not because they were worried about their safety but because the events were too bizarre to comprehend. At least none of them had been mentioned by name in the press, except for Michael, who'd spoken to a reporter about Mrs. Templeton before the hospital's PR team had been able to muzzle him.

"How are Willy and Sophia taking it?" Mrs. Sinclair asked. When Maxwell's head popped up at the sound of his grandpa and mother's names, she quickly added, "Last question, I promise."

Ben dumped the steamed broccoli into a serving dish and brought that and the noodles over. He served a small portion to Maxwell and shrugged. "Sophia thinks it's terrible, of course, but she says I'm overreacting to her having surgery at Montgomery. A man at her church got a knee replacement by a surgeon at Pepperton Orthopedics, and Sophia says he's worse off than he was before. She wants the best, which, of course, I want for her too. But…"

"And Willy?"

"My dad's more concerned. Hates to see me have to deal with something so strange again, but I'll be fine." He hoped that would seal off the subject, and it did, but Mrs. Sinclair's next topic caught him off guard.

"How's your lady friend?"

"My lady friend? You mean Laurette?" He ladled marinara sauce over Mrs. Sinclair's pasta and served her a side of broccoli.

"Will she be coming to visit soon?"

"I hope so."

"She's a good girl." When Ben didn't answer right away, she added, "I bet if I could see your face clearly, I'd find a nice pink blush."

"If I am blushing, it's only from my surprise to hear you speak so positively of her."

With her head lowered just inches from her plate, Mrs. Sinclair twirled spaghetti on her fork, squinted, and carefully brought the loaded utensil to her mouth. Once in place, she chewed, and her eyes returned to a relaxed state. "I think I was a bit too hard on her in the past."

A *bit* too hard? At one point Edith had banned Laurette from ever setting foot in her home again.

"Water under the bridge, I suppose," Edith continued. "Laurette was a real help to me when she visited over the holidays. Took me to my eye appointments, helped me get my questions answered, sat in the waiting room for over an hour with me. What was that doctor doing, anyway? Filing his taxes on all the income my impending blindness is giving him? Nobody sees an old lady, you know, but your friend helped make sure that they did." Mrs. Sinclair's voice caught, and she started wrestling with another tangle of spaghetti.

Ben said nothing. He'd seen his own colleagues brush off elderly patients during rounds, as if advanced age somehow precluded the ability to weigh in usefully on one's health. He vowed never to do the same. "Laurette is the best, no debate there."

Maxwell chimed in, his lips a Picasso painting of tomato sauce and broccoli buds. "Bovo tells me funny stories."

Ben laughed. "She does at that. Bovo and her goats."

"Well, my wonderful tenant," Edith said to Ben, "you may have a lifestyle that's too modern for me, but at least you surround yourself with good women."

"I'll drink to that." Ben raised his wine glass and clicked hers so she wouldn't have to search for his own. "Present company included." Instead of his plastic cup, Maxwell raised his train and giggled when Ben clicked it.

Mrs. Sinclair beamed, and Ben was pleased to see her happiness. She hadn't had too much of that lately. Thanks to a couple of severed legs, neither had Ben.

---

A few hours later Ben tucked Maxwell into his race-car bed. "Sorry, buddy, no trains." He grabbed a red caboose from Maxwell's left hand and a green passenger car from the right. "Don't want you to hurt yourself."

The three-year-old protested, but his whimpering soon died down to a yawn. Freshly bathed and smelling like cherry-blossom shampoo, he rubbed his eyes and sank deeper onto his pillow. Squeezed next to Ben's own double bed, what little space remained in the basement bedroom went to a dresser, a Craftsman tool chest, and a treadmill.

After kissing Maxwell's forehead, Ben tiptoed to the living room, powered up his laptop, and took a seat at the desk situated below a framed Pink Floyd poster. A few hospital cases needed reviewing, including a rare bone-tumor patient he and Joel had admitted that morning. Unfortunately, Joel had bungled the history, forcing Ben to wake the ailing patient back up and re-question him.

Clearing his head of severed limbs, sloth-eyed detectives, and subpar medical students, he cracked his knuckles and started to read. He'd barely perused two paragraphs on primary lymphoma of the bone when his phone buzzed on the desk beside him. With relief, he saw Laurette's name in the caller ID. He'd texted her after the police interrogation in his kitchen two days earlier and she'd called him right back, but he hadn't spoken to her since.

As usual, her trivia question came quickly. "I ate barracuda two hours ago," she said. "I now have vomiting, diarrhea, and stomach pain."

"Sucks for you."

"My teeth hurt, and I feel itchy and am tingling all over. I think maybe even my vision is blurry. What do I have?"

"Hmm." Ben leaned back in the chair, his toes digging into the plush carpet, his mind searching his infectious disease database. "This is a tough one." His hand hovered above the computer mouse.

"And don't Google it either."

"Ha, you know me too well." He combed his brain for all those weird diseases he'd learned in med school and then promptly forgot about. *Barracuda? Really?* "I give up. You got me. What do you have?"

"I have ciguatera."

"Cigua what? What organism causes that?"

"Not a bug per se. It's from a toxin in the barracuda."

"Cheater."

"Perhaps you should start doing crossword puzzles, my American friend. Might sharpen your brain. All that surgery has made it mushy." After Ben laughed, Laurette grew serious, and he imagined her high-arched eyebrows knitted in concern. "I called to make sure you are still okay."

"I'm fine, but yeah, it's not every day detectives accuse me of severing limbs as part of a twisted cult, or at least having knowledge of it." He caught her up on events since they'd last spoken which weren't much. He still hadn't told her about Lenny's confessing to cutting off Joseph Sampson's limb. Instead, he filled her in on the chief resident agreeing to go to rehab. "Everyone thinks he's taking two weeks off to help a cousin get through chemo."

"Two weeks for addiction?"

"I know, not optimal. It's one of those truncated programs that caters to busy professionals. Len joked about it being a speed rehab. But at least it's a start."

"You're a good friend to keep his secret."

"Stupid might be more like it. But the guy doesn't deserve to have his career tainted as long as he gets help. I told him I'd feed his fish while he's gone, but he's paying a new kid in his condo complex to do it. Didn't want me to have to stop in every day, which I have to admit is a relief. Things are a little crazy right now. Or a little *fou*, as you'd say."

"Can you at least contact him to see how he's doing?"

"He gave me the number of the center, but I guess we're supposed to wait before we call. Let them settle in first."

"So let me ask you something." Laurette's tone shifted to professional mode, a tone he recognized from her capstone presentation two and a half years before. He'd crashed her lecture—wouldn't have missed it for the world—and was as awed by her impassioned thesis on post-earthquake Haiti as the faculty members were. "How are the team members who suffered the Alaskan plane crash doing? Are they acting strange? Suffering post-traumatic stress? Seeing a therapist?"

"Whoa, what brought this on?" Ben stood and crossed to the couch, the fabric more comfortable on his back than the wooden desk chair. Another beneficiary of his resident's salary, the new sofa smelled far better than Mrs. Sinclair's ass-scented old one.

"Have they?"

"Well, Michael is still cocky, but sure, he's having a rough time. Mostly because his wife recently kicked him out. Angela—she's Lock's PA, remember—has never been that talkative, but she seems even more withdrawn since Alaska. With Joel, it's hard to tell. He hates me—always has, always will—so our interactions are distant and forced. How we managed to get stuck on the same rotation together is one of life's cruel twists. Dr. Lock still prays more than Sophia, which is saying a lot, but the guy's definitely more distracted and abrupt. Dr. King—he's the anesthesiologist, not sure if you've met him before—seems a little more OCD and anxious than usual, but I can't say I blame him. And Karen, well…"

"Well what?"

"Karen's a tough one to figure out. Yeah, she's weird since Alaska. Nice to me one minute, barking at me the next. Never seems to eat anything. Then again, she's always been skinny. Why are you asking all this?"

"Are they seeing a therapist?"

"Maybe. I guess the hospital arranged one for them. But why are you interested?"

"Do you remember the psychiatrist I told you about? Derek Epps?"

Ben picked up a throw pillow and tossed it against the opposite wall, where it narrowly missed his flat-screen TV. "The one you went to Peru with to investigate that recent breakout?"

"Yes, he's the one. He was wanting to know these things."

"You told him about this?" Ben couldn't help feeling a bit betrayed.

"Only in general. He was fascinated by the human teeth marks on the second limb."

"I told you that in confidence, Bovo. It's not public knowledge yet. I wasn't supposed to say anything."

"He respects confidentiality. The other night we…"

Ben didn't hear what came next. The word *night* drowned it out.

"In fact, Derek has been your way recently," she continued. "He's been helping the police investigate a murder in Trenton."

"As a psychiatrist?" If Laurette noticed the bite in his tone, she didn't let on.

"He's acting as a profiler of sorts. His knowledge in the unusual is vast. In fact, he'll be guest lecturing at Drexel University soon. Too bad you couldn't free up your schedule to hear him."

"Wow, isn't he quite the multitalented guy."

No response from Laurette.

"Sorry. Don't mean to be an ass. Guess I'm just tired and have a lot of work to do."

"It's all right. I will let you go now. Just wanted to hear your voice."

His shame over being so insolent deepened, and he apologized again. "You coming home to Philly any time soon? I miss your *tablet kokoye*." *And you.*

"I have a week of vacation in April. I will see you then, and I will fill your belly with your favorite Haitian coconut treat."

They disconnected on a better note, but the taste in Ben's mouth was still sour. He didn't know what bothered him more: the fact Laurette had talked to a complete stranger about the new mess he'd found himself in or that Laurette had told the guy at *night*, a word that conjured a whole host of images Ben preferred not to see.

# 19

At seven fifteen the following morning, the orthopedic surgery ward was already abuzz with activity. Dr. Lock's ensuing tantrum only added to the maelstrom.

"Is there nobody in this godforsaken place who can tell me what Mr. Martin's creatinine level is?" The attending surgeon glared in turn at each member of the rounding team, his jaw set and his neck veins engorged. If a horned helmet and wool cape suddenly replaced his scrubs and surgical cap, he'd look every bit the warring Nordic Viking.

Angela's fingertips tapped furiously over her tablet's screen. "Um, I don't see it here. Looks like it wasn't ordered."

"Oh for fuck's sake."

Ben had never before heard the pious attending swear, and judging by the stillness of the rest of the group, which included Joel, Karen, Angela, an intern, and a nurse, neither had they. Lock's gaze fell to the intern, a quiet but bright resident from the University of Wisconsin who'd made money during med school raising award-winning pigs. "Why isn't the lab order in the chart? Do you really want to give your patient a high dose of a renal-toxic antibiotic without knowing how well his kidney is functioning?"

Like Ben, the intern kept written notes on each of his patients rather than relying on his tablet alone. He flipped through them now, as if a miracle answer lay hidden within. The guy's anxiety was palpable, and Ben ached to rescue him, but the patient wasn't his own, and he knew little about the case.

"Guess I forgot," the intern finally said.

"You forgot." The surgeon's chiseled features hardened into cement. "You do know you're in a hospital now, don't you? Not back on Daddy's farm."

Ben started to interject—God knows he'd been in the intern's shoes himself—but Dr. Lock shifted to Karen before he could. "You're the senior resident on service. You should be following these things up."

"My bad. Won't happen again." A pro at handling attending outbursts, Karen appeared unruffled by Lock's temper. Though her thin face was still pasty, she looked a little more put together today.

"You better hope not." To Joel, Dr. Lock said, "And what about you? Didn't I tell you yesterday afternoon when we admitted the guy that we'd need to keep an eye on his kidneys?"

The coiffed med student nodded but said nothing, his usual lax demeanor absent.

Lock ripped off his surgical cap, his fury still aimed at Joel. "Why the hell should I be surprised? You've been worthless on this rotation. Absolutely worthless."

"Hey," Ben said, unable to keep quiet any longer. "It's been a trying time for everyone. I—"

"Stay out of it, Oris. Everybody knows you've been saving your med student's ass all month."

Ben didn't look at Joel, but he could feel the student's indignation and resentment burning off him from three feet away.

Dr. Lock appeared to be about to unleash another grievance but then caught his breath, exhaled heavily, and deflated like a balloon. "Ah, you're right, Oris. We've all been under extreme stress. I'm not being fair. Forgive me."

A major fender bender in college had given Ben less whiplash than Lock's abrupt emotional one-eighty just did, but he was relieved for the drop in temperature. Though many surgeons were known to be volatile, Lock was not usually one of them.

"Look," the attending said, "we've got an hour before our first surgery. Finish your work here, then meet me in the OR lounge in forty-five minutes. Angela, call Michael and Dr. King to meet us there too. I want everyone who was in Alaska to be there. You as well, Oris. You may not have been in the crash, but you're on my team. It's time for a group pep talk."

Three-quarters of an hour later, the summoned surgical team convened on leather sofas in the surgeons' lounge. Armed with coffee and pastries, they listened as Dr. Lock rehashed their recent traumatic ordeals, not just the crash in Alaska but the drama in Philadelphia too, where the past ten days had dished out two incomprehensible crimes on their former patients. (In Ben's case, one incomprehensible crime, since he was fully aware Lenny had stolen Mr. Sampson's leg.)

"In times like these it's easy to get distracted and let work slide." Dr. Lock steepled his hands and paced the carpeted floor in his Skecher slip-ons, the mesh ankle of one stained with dried blood, his surgical booty evidently failing to do its job. "What happened to Mrs. Templeton was brutal and horrific, but that's for the police to sort out. Our duty is to take care of our patients. Lives depend on us. We can't let our guard down." He likened their situation to that of the biblical Job, facing challenges and trials they didn't understand. "Job didn't lose faith, and neither can we. As my ex-wife used to say, being tested is good. Shows us our moxie." The attending paused, maybe for dramatic effect, maybe to find the right words. Swallows of coffee punctuated the silence. Meanwhile, Ben took the opportunity to ponder the fact that the devout surgeon was divorced.

Dr. King, two cushions down from Ben, broke the lull. "During a case with my chief resident yesterday, Dr. Fisher suggested we vary up our team a bit. Thought it might ease some of the tension in our group. I'd be happy to switch cases with the other anesthesiologists if you think it would help."

"Thank you, but no need for that, Muti," Dr. Lock said quickly.

"A move like that would be ill-advised. Our post-op infection rates are the lowest any orthopedic department has ever reported, and that's thanks to each and every one of you for adhering to my strict protocol."

Is it? Ben wondered.

"So is everybody with me? Do we stay a united team and give our elective reconstructive patients the best care in the world?"

Ben doubted such a question could be answered in the negative and still keep one's job—or land a coveted junior-resident-research grant—so like the others, he nodded and murmured his agreement.

Dr. Lock smiled, his teeth perfectly aligned and his features creased in an inviting fashion. With his charm and confident manner, Ben could see why Sophia was so smitten.

Per usual, the attending bowed his head to pray, asking those in the room who accepted God as their savior to join him. "And maybe even those of you who don't." He looked straight up at Ben, who dropped his head but kept his eyes open. He noted Joel and Karen doing the same. Sinners unite, he thought.

After the pep talk, of whose effectiveness Ben wasn't sure, most of the team left to prep for surgery. Ben lingered behind to pour another cup of coffee. His late-night studying after Laurette's phone call combined with Maxwell's early morning routine had left him bushed.

Karen sidled up to him. "Well, that was weird."

Ben handed her the coffee he'd just poured and served himself another. "This whole past month has been weird." He raised his sleeved cup toward hers in a toast. "But hey, it's February first. Maybe the earth'll fall back on its axis now."

They delicately clicked cups, steam rising from the surfaces. He was glad to see her lighten up a bit. He reached for another dough-nut, his third that morning.

"The police go after you too?" she asked.

"They did."

"I doubt anyone got it as bad as Michael though."

Ben paused mid-bite. "Why do you say that?"

Even though they were alone in the lounge, Karen stepped

closer and lowered her voice. "Did you know he had a girlfriend who was murdered?"

Ben choked on his doughnut. "What? How do you——"

"Back when he was nineteen, his ex-girlfriend was murdered. They'd been broken up for a month, but the police still considered him a suspect. An alibi cleared him, but they never found the killer."

The pastry lost its appeal. Ben placed it on a napkin on the counter. "You're just a wealth of information, aren't you."

"I swear to God, gossip has a way of finding me. All I want to do is keep my head down, finish my residency, and get a good job, but the nurses constantly feed me stuff in the dressing room. I can't unhear it."

"That tidbit's too juicy to unhear." Not to mention disquieting, Ben thought.

While they sipped their coffee in silence, the door opened, and a guy in scrubs shuffled in, his straw-colored hair cut in an unflattering bowl shape and his skin scarred from adolescent acne. He looked lost, and when he spotted Ben and Karen standing next to the coffee and pastry counter, he quickly apologized.

"Can I help you with something?" Ben asked.

The guy, whose name tag read *Lyle, RN*, shook his head. "Sorry. I'm still getting turned around in this place. Just started two weeks ago." He seemed nervous, and it was clear he felt out of place. "I'm trying to get to the recovery room. That's where I work."

Karen rolled her eyes at Ben. "After two weeks he's still lost?"

Ben ignored her. "No problem," he told the guy. He waved an arm at the tray of pastries. "Welcome to the surgeons' lounge, where an artery-clogging scone or doughnut is only a grab away. Help yourself before you leave. The recovery room is two hallways over. Go out the double doors to your right and follow the signs."

"Okay, thanks." The guy backed up to the door and hurried out, not bothering to take a pastry.

"Jeez, what's with that hair?" Karen said. "And what, no benzoyl peroxide in his youth?"

"Hey, mean girl, ease up. We don't know what his life is like." Ben deposited his partially eaten doughnut in the trash and headed to the door, coffee cup in hand. The college kid with the rare bone tumor was up first, and since he wasn't one of Lock's reconstructive patients, Karen would be scrubbing in. Given she was a fourth-year resident, Lock would likely let her take the lead. Impromptu prayers and the rare outburst aside, he was still a great teacher.

"Oh," Karen said as Ben held the door open for her. "I almost forgot. I was looking at next week's surgery schedule and saw a Sophia Diaz on for a knee replacement. Tuesday the fifth, I think it was. Isn't that your baby mama?"

Ben lost his grip on the door. It almost whacked Karen in the face before he grabbed it again. "What?" A million different thoughts—none of them good—collided in his brain. "How did she get a spot so quickly?"

"Guess there was a cancellation." Karen smiled, obviously seeing this as good news. "Lucky her."

# 20

I can't believe what I'm doing. I hate myself. As I bite into his flesh, I hate myself. Like a centaur, I have two parts. One half is a moral, decent human being who cares for people. The other is an insatiable beast who steals life. But I can't help it because when that beast half is hungry, it becomes my whole essence. It becomes *my* hunger. *My* thirst. *My* desire for flesh. I feel my whole body change, and if I looked in the mirror right now, a ravenous beast would gape back at me.

This is nothing like my past actions. Those were conscious, moral decisions. They were necessary. But this? This I don't recognize.

Some human part of me must still be there when the beast takes over, because when I bite into the man now, I stop the second I taste blood. Not because it repulses me (although it did the first time), and not because I don't crave it—dear God do I crave it—but because I can't bear the look in his eyes, the terror as he thrashes and pleads, even with the drug inside him.

So like the woman before him, I'll need to kill first and feast later. And like before, I have to get rid of the toxic limb. Once it's a good distance away from me, I'll be free of the crippling pain it causes.

I hid the last one too close. Just knowing it was there stabbed me like a sword. So I had to move it someplace else. Thanks to the first limb, the park made sense. It'll confuse the police.

Then again, do I want to confuse them? My actions speak otherwise, because even though I wear gloves and wipe away all traces of myself, why not bury it deep where no one can find it? Why not ensure no animal will ever dig it up? It's because even when the beast takes over, a human part of me still exists. If I'm caught, then the hideous transformation will end and peace will come to the families.

There's not much time left for this altruism though. The window is closing. The beast grows stronger every day, and I don't think I can fight it much longer. Tonight's kill will nourish me, get me through the next few days, allow me to hide the beast from those around me. But then the hunger will return, and it'll be so raw and agonizing that the only solution will be to kill again.

Even worse, I worry the beast part will grow too strong, and my human part will no longer give them a natural death first. I worry my teeth alone will become the fatal weapon.

## 21

Inside Sophia's two-bedroom apartment on Friday night, Ben tried to navigate the co-parenting boundaries with sensitivity and respect, but he sensed he was failing miserably. How do you tell a woman who's not your wife or girlfriend to not do something, even if you're strongly opposed to that something? At least if he and Sophia were married or dating, he'd have some leverage.

He gripped the top of a Windsor chair near the kitchen table and tried to keep the controlling undertones in his voice to a mini-mum. "You should've told me about your surgery. I had to hear about it from Karen this morning, and then I had to pretend I knew what in the hell she was talking about." Remembering Maxwell was in the living room, watching a cartoon with Sir Quincy by his side, Ben lowered his voice. "Especially when that surgery is in five days. I didn't even know your implant had been ordered yet."

"I can't keep going with a grapefruit for a knee. You of all people should know that." Sophia had been emptying the dish-washer when Ben had barged in a few minutes ago, and she returned to it now. Ceramic plates with rose-studded borders clanked together as she pulled them out.

"I do. I messed up my own knee a few years back, you know that. It's just—"

"The sooner I get this done, the better. I have some big projects coming up. Believe me, I'm not thrilled about it either."

"I know, but—"

"Don't worry about Maxwell. Rita and Willy will help out. It won't affect your schedule at all." Rita was Sophia's sister, and although the very religious Diaz family had practically disowned Sophia when she'd gotten pregnant out of wedlock—with an atheist to boot—the tough-veneered Rita had come around. An adorable nephew tended to have that effect.

"That's not fair. You know it's not about my schedule. But I don't want you having surgery now."

Sophia straightened, a saucepan clutched in her hand. He hoped she wasn't planning to thump him in the head with it. "Look, Ben, you're a great dad—the best—and helping me pay for this incredible apartment is beyond what I expect from you, but that doesn't mean you get to tell me what to do."

"I'm not trying to tell you what to do."

"Could've fooled me."

"Jesus, do I need to spell it out?" His holler broke Maxwell's TV stupor in the other room. Wide-eyed, the child stared at him. Ben forced a smile. "Sorry, bud. Go back to your show. Daddy's just tired." After a few beats, the toddler obliged, and soon cartoon trains were once again his world.

"Thanks for taking the Lord's name in vain in front of our son." Sophia put the pot away in a maple cabinet near the stove. Ben was relieved it was out of her hands.

"I know, I know, I'm sorry. I'm trying to have this conversation without mentioning you-know-what, especially with Maxwell so nearby, but I'm blowing it. What's going on with our patients has me scared, that's all. I'd fall off the deep end if something happened to you."

Sophia's expression softened. She tucked strands of chestnut hair behind her ear and limped toward him. "You could've just led with that, you know. You don't always have to be such a stoic." She hugged him, the lingering scent of vegetable lasagna emanating from her turtleneck sweater. When she pulled away, she held up two fingers. "Two. Two patients out of dozens of orthopedic patients a week. That's all there's been, and only one of them was murdered. The other one died of natural causes." She tapped her knee through her loose-fitting jeans. "I'll be fine. My legs will be fine. Neither of them will end up in a park."

They both glanced Maxwell's way, but the three-year-old remained engrossed in his show. Next to him, Sir Quincy's tail wagged back and forth, the dog seemingly as enthralled by the singing trains as Maxwell.

"Only ten more minutes, sweet cheeks," Sophia called out to him. "Then TV time is up."

"Okay, Mommy."

Sophia was about to start on the top rack of the dishwasher when Ben pulled out the chair he'd been gripping. "Here, let me finish. I should've offered sooner. Rest your knee."

"Don't mind if I do." She lowered to the seat and massaged her leg through her jeans. "But your super-somber face tells me you have something else on your mind. Spill it. And if it's about you scrubbing in on my surgery, don't worry. Kent said he'll keep you out of the OR during it."

Ben shelved an Avengers sippy cup. "It's not that."

"What is it then?"

Needing the extra oxygen for what he was about to propose, he inhaled deeply. "How about having the procedure done by a different surgeon."

"Seriously? Tell me you're joking. You've been singing Kent's praises since the beginning of your residency." She dropped her voice to a man's pitch and started mimicking Ben. "'Hope I get on his rotation. Can't wait to do surgery with the guy. Wonder if he'd agree to be my research adviser.' Need I go on? Plus, he says he'll wave any surgeon fees not covered by insurance."

"I get all that, but I'm not sure having him operate on you is…ethical."

"Ethical?" Sophia's tone took an edge. "In what way is it not ethical?"

"You know, with you guys, um…"

"Dating?" Her fingers tapped the tabletop. "We've gone to a few dinners and church functions together, that's all. Not all of us equate a night out with automatic sex, you know."

"Wow. Ouch. Didn't hear you complaining the night Maxwell was conceived."

"Touché. But you know I was celebrating my remission then. I was floating on air like I was invincible. I could've jumped off the Comcast Center, convinced God would catch me." She nodded toward Maxwell in the living room. "And in a way, I think he did."

They both fell silent. After Ben unloaded the remaining glasses, he sat down at the table next to her. "I'm just worried, that's all. Mrs. Templeton's murder has me scared."

"I need surgery, we both know that. Kent is the best, and instead of having to wait months and months, I got in last minute. Come on, how lucky is that?"

Ben doubted luck had anything to do with it. The sooner she had surgery, the sooner Dr. Lock could move out of the friend zone. "Sure, lucky, but things are different now. He's acting strange. The whole team's acting strange."

"They were in a plane crash. I'd be acting strange too." When Ben said nothing, only started picking at a fingernail, she put a hand on his thigh and added, "Everything will be fine, you'll see. Laurette would tell you the same thing. Hopefully she'll come visit soon. You're more relaxed when she's here."

Ben shrugged, but he couldn't deny it.

"Besides," Sophia said. "God didn't heal me from cancer and give me a beautiful little boy only to have me end up like Kim Templeton."

———

As a second-year ortho resident, Ben was guaranteed only one full day off a week. That made the current weekend away from the hospital a rare luxury, and he intended to take full advantage of it, starting with a late morning run on Forbidden Drive in the Wissahickon Valley Park. After his argument with Sophia the night before, he needed it.

Despite its ominous sounding name, there was nothing sinister about Forbidden Drive. Decades before, cars were banned from traversing it, and thus the moniker was created. As the widest and smoothest trail in the park, it was one of the easiest for running. Jogging from its northern tip to its southern netted him about seven-and-a-half miles. Sometimes, if he had the stamina, he'd drive to the park instead of taking the bus or an Uber, so he could double back for a fifteen-mile run in total. Not so this morning. Only two days into February and the month was proving to be every bit the arctic bastard that January had been.

Still, despite the wind whipping his insulated jacket and the frost making icebergs of his cheeks and icicles of his nose hair, he welcomed the runner's high. Inside the park, which was a nature oasis nestled within Philadelphia, the noise and chaos of urban life disappeared, not to mention the sights and smells. In their place came a rocky creek, sheltering trees, and jagged terrain through which multiple hiking trails coursed.

For Ben, no matter how much crap life dumped, nothing cleaned it up like a run. Even his worry over Sophia's surgery started to fade. Maybe she was right. Maybe Mrs. Templeton's awful demise was simply a fluke. No doubt the cops would find her killer soon.

And so with each stride he sprinted away severed limbs, skittish colleagues, drug-addicted chief residents, and fathers who heard comatose women speak to them inside their heads. By the time he reached the paved pathway that connected to Ridge Avenue on the south end of the trail, he was as close to zen as a tightly wound perfectionist like himself could get. Using the time it would take him to reach the Wissahickon Station to cool down before catching the bus back home, he slowed to a trot and then a walk.

At his reduced pace, his body temperature plummeted. He tugged his hat farther down over his ears and tucked his gloved fingers into his palms. A few feet ahead, a woman armed with shopping bags attempted to open a coffee shop's door. When Ben held the door open for her, the rich scent of cocoa beans hit him, and he ducked inside for a cup of his own.

Immediately, the warmth of the cozy shop and the chatter of customers seated at small tables filled him with the comfort of normalcy, a welcomed sensation given the events of the past two weeks. Taking his place in line, he made googly eyes at a pink-cheeked toddler in a stroller who shook her stuffed pony at him. She squealed in laughter and did it again. After a few rounds of googly eyes and pony shaking, the mother received her tea and lemon bread and pushed the child away. "Say goodbye to the nice man," she told her daughter.

Ben waved to the girl as she left and moved forward in the queue. A few copies of Saturday's *The Philadelphia Inquirer* remained on a stand near the cash register. When was the last time he'd relaxed in a coffee shop and read the paper? No rush. No hospital pages. No calls. Just a sweet, short respite before it was back to parenting and studying and working. Far too long, that was for sure. He could always catch the next bus. He and Maxwell weren't headed to Willy's until four.

After grabbing a paper, he placed his order with a heavily tattooed barista and shifted one step closer to the till. When he flipped the paper over to read the bottom headline, he froze. All craving for coffee and feeling of zen vanished. A swirling nausea and fear took their place.

At the bottom half of the paper, printed in big block letters, screamed the words: *ANOTHER SEVERED LIMB FOUND IN PHILADELPHIA PARK.*

## 22

The next morning, still reeling from Saturday's headline, Ben heard Sophia coming down Mrs. Sinclair's basement stairs before he saw her. With her bad knee, the mismatched thumps of her winter boots gave her away.

As soon as he opened the door, she sputtered, "I can't believe it. Did they really find another leg?" Her face was a tight mask of worry.

Ben scanned the stairwell. His son's absence piled on an additional layer of anxiety he didn't need. "Where's Maxwell?"

"I left him with Mrs. Sinclair."

"Not a good idea, Sophe. Her eyesight is getting really bad."

"Don't worry, he'll be fine. They're watching cartoons together. I'll crack the door a few inches so we'll hear them if anything happens."

"What about Sir Quincy? Edith's cat won't be digging his company."

"He's home in his crate." Sophia closed the door three-quarters of the way and plopped her tote bag on the floor. "I wanted to talk to you without Maxwell here, make sure you're okay."

"I'm…well, I'm better, but I'd be lying if I said I wasn't spooked."

"Who wouldn't be?" She shuddered and took a seat on the table chair closest to the open door. "It's awful. Just awful."

"Thanks for keeping Maxwell last night. As much as I wanted to spend the weekend with him, I wasn't exactly great father material."

"Of course. Completely understandable. Did you get a hold of your dad? After he saw the news yesterday, he called me. Said you weren't answering your phone."

Ben nodded. "I stopped by to see him last night."

"What about Laurette? Did you call her?"

"Yes, right after I called you."

Ben plucked a Philadelphia Eagles mug from the kitchen cabinet nearest the dented fridge and poured Sophia the coffee he'd just brewed. After she slipped out of her winter coat and boots, she wrapped her hands around the cup as if to siphon its heat.

"Then I grabbed an Uber and went straight to the hospital," he said, pouring his own cup. "Not sure what answers I expected to learn there, but I had to do something. I was crawling out of my skin."

"Who's leg is it? Were the police there? What about your colleagues?"

Ben started with the last question. "Karen was there. She was on call. And Dr. Lock was just leaving. He'd stayed late after rounds to work on a research paper." Ben paced a bit more and then set his mug on the butcher-block table and sat down. "If you think I was upset, you should've seen your new boyfriend. Frazzled would be an understatement. He dragged Karen and me to the surgeons' lounge."

"Was it another one of his patients?" The fear in Sophia's voice, albeit contained, was easily interpreted. She sipped coffee with one hand and rubbed her knee with the other.

"His *and* mine. Henry Paulson, a retired teacher. I replaced his knee joint last Monday. Lock let me do the entire operation. Paulson's recovery was so smooth we discharged him two days later." Ben closed his eyes. "He was a marathon runner."

"How do you know it was his?" From upstairs, Maxwell's laughter echoed through the vent in the ceiling. "I didn't see a name in the paper. Do they know what happened?"

"At first we didn't know anything. The three of us circled the surgeons' lounge like caged lions. Then Dr. Fisher came in—he's the orthopedics surgery chair—and said the police called him after the limb was found by a dog walker in Cobbs Creek Park earlier that morning, early enough to make the papers, anyway. They'd already received word from Paulson's daughter that he was missing, so again, they assume it's his leg, especially since the implant was left behind with it."

Sophia raised her eyebrows.

"Oh yeah," Ben said, "Someone cut the limb off just above the knee, implant and all." He took a sip of coffee, then another. "But although the police assume it's Henry Paulson's limb, they don't have his actual body. Just like Mrs. Templeton, the rest of him is missing."

"So there's a chance the two of them are still alive?"

"The amputations were done postmortem."

"Right. Today's paper mentioned that." Sophia's expression was a mixture of sadness and horror.

"Fisher told us that Mr. Paulson lives alone in the suburbs, but his daughter, who lives an hour away, had been staying with him to help out. She returned to her family on Friday but had planned to check back in on her dad on Saturday morning. When she got to his house, he wasn't there, so she called the police. As far as I know, they still don't have the body."

"How terrible. That means someone came for him Friday night."

Ben rubbed his neck. "There's more."

"What?"

"According to Dr. Fisher, the police said Mr. Paulson's daughter thought she saw someone outside her dad's kitchen window on Thursday night. Apparently she's no wallflower—a former soldier—so she went outside to look. Big yard with lots of trees and bushes, but she found no one. She figured maybe the frost on the glass made her see things that weren't there, and she chalked it up to having too much on her mind."

"So someone was spying on her dad? Didn't the other patient think that too?"

"Yeah. In the hospital and at home, but they blamed her symptoms on a medication reaction." Ben stared at Sophia's swollen knee through her yoga pants. "You can't have surgery with Lock, Sophe." When she didn't answer, he leaned forward. "Please." He grabbed both of her hands and squeezed. "Pick a different surgeon to place your implant. I have no idea what's going on and I'll do everything I can to find out, but in the meantime, please, please pick a different surgeon."

After a few seconds she pulled her hands away and nodded. "Okay. I'll switch doctors. But I'm staying with Montgomery Hospital. Even if I wanted it done by the Pepperton group—which I don't—they're out-of-network, and I could never afford them. Nor any of the other orthopedic groups."

"What if I take out a loan? Or—"

"No. No way. You've got enough student loan debt, and I don't want to take any money away from what you've saved so far for Maxwell's college."

"That's a long way off."

"I don't care. Montgomery will be fine." She lowered her voice. "It's only Kent's patients that are...you know. Why do you think that is?"

Unable to sit any longer, Ben stood and crossed to the sink to rinse out his coffee cup. With as jittery as he felt, more caffeine was the last thing he needed. "Lock thinks someone's setting him up."

"You mean framing him? Who would do that? And why in such a bizarre way?"

"Who knows? Lock is wondering about a former resident he booted from the program for incompetence five years ago. Said the guy couldn't get another residency after that, not even in primary care where they're desperate for bodies. Doesn't know where he ended up getting a job."

"Did he tell the police?"

"He did. They said they're going to look into it. I'm sure they'll take any lead they can get, but I'm equally sure they'll talk to all of us again too." The thought of facing Detective Patel and his unshakable slothlike eyes another time made Ben's stomach hurt. At least they couldn't pin the murders on Lenny. He was in rehab. Ben had tried to call him several times with a heads-up on the new limb, unsure whether or not the chief resident was following the news on the inside, but calls to Lenny's cell phone went unanswered. When Ben tried the rehab center directly—three different times—the tight-lipped receptionist offered nothing beyond, "Save for family emergencies, outside calls early in the treatment program are forbidden."

"Well, at least they might have a suspect then," Sophia was saying. "That's good, right?"

"Joel thinks I have something to do with it."

"You? That's crazy!"

"That's Joel. After Fisher left us, I stopped in the cafeteria for a slice of pizza. Hadn't eaten anything since before my run. Joel was there with some of his med student friends. Asked me if I was 'dabbling in voodoo' again."

"He's an idiot," Sophia said without hesitation, and for that Ben could have hugged her. "He's always been jealous of you and always will be. By the way, how's your dad with all this?"

"Worried. But more for you than me. He doesn't want the mother of his grandchild having surgery at Montgomery."

Before Sophia could respond, a human train chugged down the stairs. "Daddy, Daddy," a little voice sang out.

Ben stepped closer to Sophia. "So you'll reschedule with another surgeon, right?"

"I said I would."

"Tell me you promise."

"Yes, yes, I promise."

"Daddeeee," Maxwell sang in a teasing fashion, his face peering through the crack in the partially open door. "Someone's here to seeee youuuu."

Ben looked at Sophia. She raised her palms and shrugged, seemingly as clueless as him. He hadn't even heard a knock.

"And you're gonna be surpriiiised!"

Ben stiffened. A lump rose in his throat. A fan of surprises, he was not.

## 23

B en's apprehension over Maxwell's surprise quickly flipped to disbelief and excitement when he saw who was standing at the base of the stairwell. His baseline cool completely vanished. "Oh my God, Bovo, how…what are you doing here?"

With a red coat zipped to her chin and a cold blush pinkening her smooth brown skin, her smile lit up his dreary basement apartment, and when she embraced him in a bear hug, her citrusy perfume invoked a neurochemical release so heady and wonderfully familiar his knees weakened.

When she released him, he took in the sight of her. "I can't believe how long your hair is getting. Ponytail and everything."

She swished the strands back and forth. "Sometimes change is good, yes?"

"But the shorter curls were so fun to pull." He yanked her ponytail. "Guess this works too."

She laughed and removed her coat. Dressed in jeans, calf-length fashion boots, and a V-neck sweater, her lean muscles were readily apparent. As was often the case, her nail polish matched her sweater. Today's hue was plum.

"Speaking of hair, what bacteria causes—"

Maxwell cut Laurette's trivia question short. "Daddy, look, look! Bovo brought me a new train." The toddler thrust a russet coal truck encased in plastic up toward Ben. "His name is Coaley."

"Wow, he's really cool."

"Open it, open it."

"Here, sweetie," Sophia said, "let's find some scissors. We can let Daddy and Laurette catch up." She put an arm around Laurette and squeezed. "I'm so glad you're here." Before Laurette could respond, Maxwell grabbed Sophia's hand and dragged her into the kitchen.

"How *are* you here?" Ben took his friend's coat and draped it over the desk chair. From the kitchen, he heard Sophia say, "Careful, let Mommy do it. Coaley's almost free."

"She is a good mother, yes?"

"A very good mother."

"And you are worried about her?"

"That's putting it mildly."

"That's why I'm here. I could tell by the way you sounded on the phone yesterday you could use a friend."

"Hearing that another one of my patients was murdered is tearing me apart, no lie there, but how did you get time off?"

"I switched my April vacation to now. Easy. No problem. And my auntie and uncle are happy to have me stay with them again."

Gratitude washed over him. "Wow, I don't know what to say. Thank you. That's—"

Laurette clasped her hands together. "We must talk about everything, but first I need movement. That plane was too cramped, and I had a smelly man seated next to me. Fresh air will do me good. You too. You look like a goat who's just seen the sun die."

He smiled. "Gee, thanks. Whatever that means."

She mimed running in place. "Let's go jogging."

"Jogging? You just got here."

"Are you scared I will outrun you? It wouldn't be the first time."

"Ha, you're dreaming now, Ponytail Lady, but what will you run in? It's freezing outside."

"I have plenty of winter clothes at my auntie's. I used to live there, remember. Or has your soft surgical brain forgotten that?"

"But I ran yesterday, and I have Maxwell today."

"Now I'm just hearing excuses."

As if on cue, Maxwell came running into the living room. "It's okay, Daddy. Papa's making chocolate for Balantines Day, and Mommy said she'll take me to the store to watch." The boy was jumping up and down, Coaley clenched in his fist. Sophia was behind him.

"You sure?" Ben asked Sophia, glancing at her swollen knee in her yoga pants.

"I'll be fine. Maxwell can help Willy while I finish a design project in his office." She pointed to the tote bag she'd placed on the floor when she'd first arrived. "I've got my laptop with me." To Laurette, she said, "I'm so thrilled you came. You're just what the doctor ordered. And in this case, the doctor is an overworked resident with too much on his plate."

"Then it's settled," Laurette said. "Jogging we go."

"If you can keep up with me, that is."

Laurette glanced at her watch, its sleek silver band and Roman-numeral face new to Ben. "I'm confirming the date and time. I want to remember when I left you behind in my sneaker dust."

He lifted her wrist and studied the watch. "Whoa, fancy. Where did this come from?"

"Pretty, isn't it? It was a Christmas gift from my mother and father. Pure silver and so shiny." She waved her arms in a little dance, making Maxwell laugh. She picked him up and tickled his neck. "I will see *you* later. You can show me all your trains. But first, I will outrun your father."

---

Trailing Laurette on the Forbidden Trail so soon after his run there the day before left Ben with a sense of déjà vu. Same frigid temperature. Same snow-dusted canopy of oaks, maples, and poplars. Same wooden fence and partially frozen creek on his left. Unlike the day before, however, more souls braved the park on this Sunday afternoon, shivering alongside their dogs or trotting after their snow-suited children.

Laurette called over her shoulder to him. "You've lost your edge, old man." Her sneakers smacked the ground and trampled the thin snow on the crushed-stone trail. Decked in dark running clothes of tights, hat, gloves, scarf, and an insulated jacket zipped up to her neck, she looked every bit the woman who would have winter workout gear stored at her aunt's northern Philadelphia home.

He caught up to her. "I didn't know we'd be sprinting." The cold bit his face, and the wind flapped his jacket, but he was grateful for both the escape and the company. "Besides, who're you calling old? You've got two years on me."

"Don't remind me. I will be forty in four years. How is this possible?" She glanced his way, her ponytail swishing against her upper back.

"Well, you've got the stride of a twenty-year-old, that's for damn sure." Ben sidestepped a stick and a frozen puddle. With as casual a tone as he could muster in his hyperventilating state, he asked, "Have you decided whether you're taking the job at Philly's health department yet?" *Please take the job at Philly's health department.* "Heading up the epidemiology division is big doings."

"Assistant head. I would be working alongside a medical doctor, to be sure, but they feel my EIS training and my additional CDC fellowship would be an asset to the program."

"You'll be better trained than the doctor."

"Perhaps." Never one to be a braggart, Laurette moved on. "My auntie would like me to stay here. She says I need to quit hopping from place to place and settle down. Find a…"

Ben couldn't tell if it was the wind that had carried away Laurette's words or if she'd simply drifted off, but he got the gist of it. Back in Haiti in 2010, she had been engaged to be married. Three days before the wedding, the earthquake hit. Her fiancé was killed. She'd also been six weeks pregnant at the time, a fact she revealed to Ben only last year. She miscarried two weeks after the earthquake. She rarely spoke of either and had told no one else about the miscarriage, including her family.

"I would love the job here," she continued, her breaths choppy but not strained. "Very much so. But my training could help my country, and I don't want to betray them."

"You have a right to be happy and do what you want. Besides, there are plenty of people who need your help here in Philadelphia."

"Perhaps," she repeated.

After a few more minutes of running, their silence punctuated by a child's laughter from behind and a barking dog up ahead, they reached the stone bridge that crossed over to the Orange Trail and the connecting path that led up to Council Rock.

"Let's make our usual stop," Laurette said. "I want to see where you found the first leg."

"Wish I could say the same." As they crossed the bridge and neared the bushes and snowy bramble from which Joseph Sampson's bare limb had protruded, Ben's stomach tensed. He pointed to the spot. "It was there that Sophia saw it. I was back a few feet giving Sir Quincy a treat. At first, we thought the rest of the body was hidden by the bushes. Then we discovered there was no body."

Laurette squatted and studied the area for a few seconds. Then the two of them headed to the small trail that led to the statue of Tedyuscung up on Council Rock and climbed the stone steps to reach it. From his elevated perch the statue, dressed in tribal gear, headdress, and a light dusting of snow, crouched and surveyed the gorge below, his hand shielding his eyes from the sun, as if he were reflecting on the urban wilderness that had once been his hunting ground. Even in winter the view from the higher elevation was majestic. Come spring, new leaves would bring a verdant bloom to the hilly terrain, and by fall, the colorful foliage would humble all but the most blasé of hikers.

As was their ritual, they touched the fifteen-foot warrior's beige stone from behind. Even through gloves, its surface was cold. Given the abrupt hundred-foot drop in front of the statue to the rocky gorge below, their movements were cautious. No selfies with Tedyuscung, that was for sure, at least not from the front. Despite the bucking wind and the stinging cold, they took a moment to enjoy the panoramic view. Having the statue to themselves was an added bonus.

Laurette rubbed Tedyuscung's stone one more time. "Remember the struggles of others," she said softly. "They make our own struggles small by comparison." Then her voice returned to full pitch, and she asked for a recap of the discarded limbs.

"Sampson's was first," Ben said, "in that spot I showed you. Guess it was two weeks ago now. And then eight days later, Templeton's thigh popped up in Fairmount Park. Paulson's leg—three's the charm, right?—was discovered early yesterday morning in Cobbs Creek Park."

"Strange that all three were so readily found. Do you think the frozen ground made them too hard to bury?"

"Don't know." This was a partial lie. He *did* know that wasn't the case for Sampson's limb, since Lenny had confessed to leaving it there for someone to find.

"And all three had their implants in place?"

"Yes. Knees from the men and a hip from Mrs. Templeton."

"And the same team members operated on all three?"

"Yes."

An angry gust of wind interrupted their conversation. They reversed their tracks down the stone steps and returned to the connecting trail, where another brave runner was making his way up to the statue. Once they crossed the bridge and were back on Forbidden Drive, they resumed their rhythmic jogging.

"Three limbs, all with implants, all within two weeks' time," Laurette said, as if thinking through the details out loud. "Odd that the first one died of natural causes but the other two were killed. Presumably."

Despite their faster pace, Ben felt no warmer. He needed to come clean about Lenny's involvement in the first limb. It wasn't fair to withhold it. Not from her, anyway.

And so, contrite for keeping it to himself, he revealed Lenny's paranoia about Dr. Lock stealing his implant idea and taking Sampson's limb to prove it. Judging by Laurette's near stumble on the trodden trail and her wide-eyed expression, she was appropriately shocked. Ben quickly explained why he hadn't told her. "He swore me to secrecy, Bovo. He's been a good friend. I felt I owed it to him to keep quiet for now, at least until he sought treatment."

"But you could be aiding a killer!"

Ben looked around, making sure no one had heard her. "He's not a killer. I might be a clueless dolt about the rest of this shit-show, but I do know that. And you of all people should remember I was once in desperate need of the benefit of the doubt myself. I know what it's like to have my reputation unfairly threatened."

"Yes, my friend, I remember."

"Besides, he's in rehab now. Since last Tuesday, and Paulson's limb was found yesterday morning."

"And Lenny was not in Alaska, is that right?"

Ben studied her profile, but when his foot hit a rock he returned his gaze to the running trail. "No, he wasn't, but why does that matter? The police are focused on the team members, sure, since we're the ones who operated on these patients, but according to Fisher, Detective Becker told him they're looking at everyone who works orthopedics—nurses, orderlies, doctors. Could be an angel-of-death sort of thing. I don't envy them their long list of suspects, but I'm relieved there are others on it besides me."

"Hmm," was all Laurette said.

"It's just a shame that Templeton and Paulson's bodies haven't been found."

"If there even *are* bodies to be found."

Ben came to an abrupt stop. An eerie sensation danced down his spine. "What the hell's that supposed to mean?"

Laurette, realizing he was no longer at her side, jogged the short distance back to him.

"Let's finish and grab some coffee. I will tell you then."

With his nose running and his muscles frozen, coffee sounded like a little piece of heaven, but he couldn't wait. "No. Tell me now."

"Okay, but let's jog back to the car. It's too cold to stay still."

Ben obliged, and, with their sludgy blood once again circulating, they reversed course and Laurette continued. "You remember I told you about Derek? Dr. Epps, my psychiatrist friend, the one who was recently in Trenton to help with a murder?"

Ben managed a nod and a curt, "Yes."

"Well, as I told you, he has experience in dealing with bizarre psychiatric illnesses, illnesses that make people do things they wouldn't normally do."

"What, like chop peoples' legs off and bite them?"

A pause. "Perhaps."

For the second time, Ben halted. "What are you talking about?"

Laurette backtracked again, her chin buried deep in her scarf. "Derek says sometimes severe trauma can trigger unusual psychoses, and since several of your team members survived a plane crash that left them stranded in the tundra, he thinks this is a possibility here."

Ben stared at her, mouth open, breaths clouding the air.

"I fear I'm not explaining myself well. I'll let Derek explain it to you instead."

"He's *here*? With you?"

"Yes. And he has a theory you surely must hear."

## 24

Ben had expected Derek Epps to be good-looking. He had also expected the guy would be smart. But what he hadn't expected was a forensic psychiatrist so charming he'd managed to worm his way into an autopsy room at the medical examiner's office on a Sunday evening. At six-foot-two and muscular, he reminded Ben of one of those professional quarterbacks or basketball players whose appeal and charisma afforded them a seamless transition into television and movies. As a reserved introvert, Ben had neither of those traits.

At least Derek had allowed him and Laurette to tag along. Ben was desperate to find out what was happening to his patients, and given he had neither the skills nor resources of a detective, he was grateful for anything that might help him do so.

Although the ME's office was independent of the hospital morgues, the cold and chemical-scented drabness of its autopsy rooms was similar to Montgomery's. Same large floor drain, same industrial-sized sinks, same chrome countertops and cabinets, although of a better caliber. Central to all this was a stainless-steel table, but instead of an entire corpse, only Henry Paulson's severed leg lay on it. Stiff, hairy, and pale, its blood flow had long since ceased. Bluish varicosities twisted their way down the calf, and mangled nubs of toes protruded from the foot, their flesh and bones nibbled by predators. Though the incision was too high on the thigh to see the knee implant, its metal was visible through the pathologist's earlier incision. Once again Ben recognized the orthopedic device. He had placed it a week earlier.

Replaying the surgery in his mind, he half listened as Derek, psychiatrist extraordinaire, shot the breeze with the forensic pathology fellow on call, a bulldog of a guy named Mark who had apparently attended med school in Atlanta and had "the privilege" of rotating through Dr. Epps's service during his psych rotation. That probably explained the front row seat to the medical examiner's office on a weekend. Well, that and Derek's CDC credentials.

"Remember that psych patient who thought he was Jesus one day and Tonto the next?" the pathology fellow asked Derek. "Man, you're lucky you didn't die."

When Laurette raised an eyebrow, Derek clarified. "The man was psychotic and delusional, and he hated taking his medication. One day I was counseling him in the treatment room. We were sitting at a table, just the two of us, and I wasn't paying attention like I should've been. When I bent over to get a notepad out of my bag, he slipped some antipsychotic pills into my coffee without me realizing it. He must've spit out his morning dose, the nurse none the wiser. I ended up having an anaphylactic reaction."

Laurette put a hand on her sternum. "You were allergic to the pills?"

"Yep. Am to a lot of drugs."

"Oh, and what about the guy who stabbed his father thirty times and wrote you love poems about it?" Mark said.

"He kept me busy too."

Mark and Derek laughed, and after sharing a few more memories, as if a lifeless, severed limb wasn't displayed in front of them, they donned protective gloves. Ben and Laurette did the same and moved to the other side of the table, where a cool breeze from an overhead vent ruffled Ben's hair. Only the forensic pathology fellow wore a gown.

He pointed to the top of the limb. "As you can see, it's a clean cut. Surgical even. And these here?" He ran his gloved finger over a reddish oval imprint on the lower shin, one of several. "These are human bite marks. Some broke the skin, others didn't, which is different from the last limb we examined. None of those bites broke the skin."

"As if the killer was repulsed," Derek said, and Ben remembered Detective Patel saying something similar. Then again, who wouldn't be repulsed biting into human flesh?

"Maybe so," Mark said. "The forensic dentist has already examined the lesions and taken several pictures. You gotta act quick, because bite marks change on a deceased body over time. Still, bite-mark analysis is really complex. It's not so easy like they show on TV. You know: match the teeth to the bite, find the killer, call it a day sort of thing. And whoever did this wiped away all traces of salivary DNA. Probably used oxygen bleach and wore gloves."

Ben swallowed, trying to clear from his mind the image of Henry Paulson, his first solo knee-reconstruction patient, having his leg gnawed on by human teeth and wiped clean of evidence. The retired teacher and avid marathon runner would never cross the finish line again. Someone bit him. Someone killed him. Someone chopped off his leg.

Mark's gloved finger traced the air above the amputation site. "We were able to get a small amount of blood from a vessel to test for drugs, but from the lack of vital reaction—meaning no inflammatory response—you can see the amputation was postmortem."

"That's a relief," Derek said, his lips pressed together in a grim line.

"This purplish discoloration on the back of the limb is where the blood settled. Shows the limb was left calf-side down, at least during the time it took for the lividity to set in. Not like that tells us much. We need the body for a full autopsy."

Ben took a step back from the table. The cold steel against his jeans had felt too much like death.

"But these bite marks here?" Mark pointed again to the series of inflamed curvilinear imprints covering Paulson's lower shin, some leaving the skin intact, others breaking through. "This bruising? This dried blood around the areas of skin penetration? These bites appear to be premortem. The inflammatory reaction shows that."

The group contemplated this information in silence, ventilation fans whirring from opposite walls. Ben noticed something else too, something the pathology fellow hadn't commented on. All of the bites on Mr. Paulson's leg were a distance from the knee joint, just as the bite marks on Mrs. Templeton's thigh had been a ways from the hip joint.

He shook his head. Lenny may have a drug problem, but he wouldn't do this. He wouldn't bite into human flesh like a savage. There were far easier ways to prove Dr. Lock stole his implant idea, especially since Joseph Sampson's limb had been found and its implant could be studied. There was no need for others.

Lenny had finally returned Ben's call earlier that afternoon, just as Ben was stepping out of the shower after his run with Laurette. He'd apologized for not getting back sooner. "This is the first time the center let me look at my phone. Just saw your messages now." He'd paused before adding, "I'm doing okay. Some withdrawal symptoms, sure, but no need to worry about me." That's when Ben, who was still dripping from the shower, had told him the reason for his flurry of calls the day before was because another limb had been found. Lenny said he wasn't allowed internet access or news—the short rehab program demanded that a client's attention be focused solely on recovery—so he hadn't heard about Paulson's leg. The news had clearly shaken him, so much so that Ben had regretted telling him. But even in his shock, the chief resident was considerate enough to ask about Sophia's knee and seemed relieved when Ben said Sophia had agreed to reschedule with another surgeon. They had to end the call there though, because Lenny said a counselor was giving him the stink eye.

"…think you'll give a lecture at Montgomery?" Mark was asking Derek. "After all, you've got temporary staff privileges now. That would be cool."

Ben stared at Derek across the table. "You've been given privileges at the hospital? Why?" The question shot out more aggressively than he'd intended.

Derek smiled. (The dimples were a bit much, in Ben's opinion.) "I thought it would make things easier. While you went running with Laurette, I spoke to Dr. Fisher. I have some insights to share."

"Wow, don't you work fast."

Laurette chimed in. "As I told you while we were running, Derek has some ideas that might help with the case. A theory of sorts."

Mark perked up at that. "A theory? That's news to me. Care to share?"

"Sorry. I need more information from Ben and the police first." Derek deposited his gloves in a trash can near the autopsy table. "I don't want to put something out there I can't take back. But thank you for walking us through this. I promise, I'll pass the news on once I'm more confident." Derek went to shake Mark's hand, but when he realized the pathology fellow was still gloved, he elbow bumped him instead.

"Okay to get this leg back in the freezer then?"

"Yes, we're done." Derek extended his arm toward the door. "After you guys," he said to Laurette and Ben.

As the three retrieved their coats and weaved their way back to the front desk, Ben asked for more details about Derek's theory. It was only a matter of time before Detectives Becker and Patel came sniffing his way again, and he was desperate for any vine to cling to.

"We'll discuss it over pizza." Laurette glanced at Derek as he signed them out of the building. "No one eats pizza like Ben. Don't let his fit build fool you. When it comes to pizza, he's an endless hole."

Derek grinned, and they exited into the cold night air. "I think you mean a bottomless pit."

The two CDC personnel shared a smile that left Ben hollow. When they reached his Mustang, he yanked open the passenger-side door for Laurette, not caring if the psychiatrist had to squeeze into the back seat. "Maybe you should just tell me your theory now," he said.

"While we eat," Laurette repeated. "But when Derek tells you, don't roll your eyes and puff out your cheeks like you always do when you think something is *fou*."

"Well, this should be good." Ben started the car and cranked the heat. When he grabbed the gear shift to slide into reverse, Laurette rested her hand on his. "I'm serious, Ben. Despite…" She gave a slight glance toward the backseat, as if hesitant to say more. "Despite what we've been through, you still struggle to accept what falls outside of your black-and-white world.

---

A doughy odor scented the air of Rhonda's Italian Eatery, and breezy accordion music played from a speaker near the ceiling, its melody drowned out by scattered laughter and steady hums of conversation. From a padded booth in a back corner, Ben enjoyed none of it. He dropped his slice of meat-lover's pizza onto his plate and stared at Derek and Laurette across the checkered tablecloth. Struggling—but failing—to keep the sarcasm out of his voice, he tried to clarify what he'd just heard. "So, you're telling me there's a creature in Philadelphia who's eating humans. That's who's doing this?"

Laurette answered. "Yes, this is Derek's theory."

"It sounds ridiculous."

Laurette pushed the sleeves of her cable-knit sweater up toward her elbows and mumbled something in French. When Derek rested a hand on her forearm, just above her silver watch band, Ben wanted to smash a piece of pizza into his face.

"It's okay," the psychiatrist said to her. If he was offended by Ben's scoffing, he didn't show it. "I wouldn't believe it either if I hadn't seen some mind-blowing stuff over the years. But it's not really a creature exactly."

His appealing smile did little to win Ben over. Instead, a childish thought nagged at him: *Why did you sit next to him and not me?* But Ben had to admit, they made an attractive duo, Derek the Will Smith to Laurette's Jada Pinkett.

The psychiatrist leaned forward, his elbows on the table. A flaky patch of eczema blighted the back of one hand. "I know this sounds far-fetched, but maybe when you hear some of the other things I've dealt with, it'll be easier to accept. Laurette may have told you I recently helped with a homicide case in Trenton."

Ben nodded but said nothing. Instead, he finally took a bite of pizza. Although normally his favorite, it might as well have been shoe leather.

"It involved a sixty-year-old man who killed his wife because he was convinced an identical-looking impostor had replaced her," Derek said. "He thought this impostor was planning to murder his whole family. It's called Capgras Syndrome. The man also has early dementia, which no doubt fueled the illness. He's on trial for murder but remains convinced his wife is either dead—from the impostor's hands—or hidden away somewhere. I won't be surprised if his lawyer wins an insanity defense."

Having read something about the case, Ben shrugged. "Well, he didn't eat her, did he?"

Derek laughed. "No. No, he didn't." After a couple bites of pizza, he wiped his mouth with a napkin and continued. "I had another patient—this time near Atlanta—who killed his neighbor over a barking dog. Killed the dog too."

"Awful, but not weird," Ben said.

"Yeah, but the guy claimed it wasn't him who did it. It was his alien hand."

"Nice defense."

"Alien Hand Syndrome, it's called."

"Yeah, I got that." Ben took a drink of beer and swirled it around in his mouth.

"The man believed his hand was possessed by some foreign entity. Had a mind of its own, so to speak, and though he knew it was wrong to kill his neighbor, he couldn't prevent his hand from doing so. A stroke from a year ago probably contributed to his psychosis."

Despite Ben's determination to remain sullen, he couldn't help but grow interested in Derek's accounts. "Did the jury buy his mental illness?"

"No, he was found guilty." Derek flagged down their waiter, a bearded hipster in torn jeans and black glasses whose apathetic demeanor suggested he had better things to do than his job. "Another round for us, please. And you can give me the check."

After the waiter sauntered off, Ben, perturbed by Derek's offer to foot the bill, said, "I'm confused about your professional position. The CDC sends you to investigate these kinds of cases? I've never heard of that."

"I primarily work with the CDC on neuropsychiatric outbreaks, but since my main research is in psychosis as result of trauma or brain injury, I've also consulted across the country on a number of unusual homicide cases. I've done fellowships in both neuropsychiatry and forensic psychiatry."

*Of course you have.*

Laurette pushed her plate to the side, two slices of pizza apparently her limit. "Tell Ben about the woman who thought she was a cat."

"Did she meow so loud her neighbor killed her?" Ben asked.

Once again, despite Ben's sourness, the psychiatrist burst out laughing. "Actually, the killer was another cat," he joked.

Ben failed to suppress a small smile, and like a tectonic plate, his mood started shifting. Hating Derek was difficult.

When the fresh round of drinks was delivered, Derek handed the hipster waiter a five for being so prompt. The guy adjusted his black glasses and seemed both shocked and pleased. After he departed, the psychiatrist continued with his analysis. "Seriously though, lycanthropy is when a person believes they are an animal. Literally. This woman meowed, ate cat food, used a litter box." When Ben grimaced, the psychiatrist added, "Yeah, it was sad. I don't mean to make light. She really suffered, and although she didn't kill anyone—or even commit a crime—her family had to institutionalize her for treatment. That was back when I was a resident. I'm not sure what ever happened with her."

Another piece of pizza found its way to Derek's plate. Ben grabbed one too, and when he glanced up, he found Laurette smiling at him. A warmth crawled up his body. "So you really think what's happening in Philly is like that?" he asked. "The killer thinks he's an animal?"

Derek shook his head. "Not lycanthropy really. That condition doesn't normally involve violence. I'm wondering instead about something called Wendigo psychosis."

"Wendigo. Is that the name of the person who coined the illness?"

"No. The Wendigo stems from folklore among some Northern American natives. It's a cannibalistic, insatiable, murdering monster or spirit."

"Sounds lovely."

"Its literal form is a gaunt, horned creature with a long snout and sharp talons. Some believe a Wendigo develops from a human whose greed has transformed him or her into a flesh-eating monster." Derek raised a hand at Ben's derisive snort. "I know, I know, sounds preposterous."

"Hear him out," Laurette said.

"The Wendigo is associated with freezing temps and famine. As a result, it thrives in northern climates."

Ben watched a waitress at a nearby table unload a tray full of pasta meals. "Philly has some cold days, but we're not exactly the Arctic."

"I'm not saying Wendigos exist—of course they don't—I'm just giving you the folklore's background. The condition I'm wondering about is Wendigo *psychosis*."

"So some lunatic out there thinks he's a Wendigo?"

Derek frowned. "Something like that, but I don't like the word 'lunatic.' Psychiatric illness is no less real than physical illness. It deserves the same respect as diabetes or asthma. And as a doctor, I'm sure you know that most mentally ill people aren't violent. It's usually the sane ones we need to worry about."

Ben thought of his mother and her lifelong battle with bipolar disease. Chastised, he said, "You're right. I'm sorry."

"Don't sweat it. But yes, in Wendigo psychosis, a human becomes—or maybe it's better to say *feels* like they become—

possessed by a Wendigo spirit. They grow hungry, always hungry. Insatiable. Filled up only by human flesh."

"But why? Why would this develop?"

Laurette leaned forward, her sweater blotting a few drops of water on the tablecloth. "This is where you must listen closely. You must open your mind." She nodded to Derek to continue.

"The whys of someone slipping into a bizarre psychosis— Wendigo or otherwise—are not always understood. Oftentimes it's simply the result of their underlying psychiatric disorder. Other times it's substance abuse, or more rarely an infection. But some cases follow severe trauma, either physical or psychological. I think that's what may be going on here." As Derek's passion for the subject rose, so too did his hand gesturing. "You see, Wendigo psychosis has been described in people from cold climates, particularly those who've had to go without food for a long time. So long that they feel cannibalism is their only option. But their victims aren't random. They're not just anyone. They're people the" — Derek made air quotes with his fingers— "'Wendigo' has become very attached to, people they feel they have a strong, maybe even intimate, connection with."

Ben sat spellbound in his chair. The psychiatrist had his full attention now. "Jesus, are you saying—" His jaw clamped shut when the waiter came to clear their plates.

"Anything else for you guys?" Thanks to Derek's extra tip, the hipster's apathy had been replaced with enthusiasm. "Cheesecake? Tiramisu? Brownie sundae?"

Laurette cocked her head. "With whipped cream?"

"But of course," the waiter replied with a mock French accent.

"Then yes to the brownie sundae please."

The affectionate look Derek gave Laurette made Ben's insides twist, but when the waiter departed, their conversation steered back to the missing limbs. "So you're saying somebody is... You think someone is actually eating these people?"

"I don't know if they're *actually* eating the person. Judging by the tentative bite marks, I'd guess whoever's doing this is still confused about his or her urges."

"Some broke the skin though," Laurette said.

"True. With this last one, anyway." Derek rubbed a hand over his close-cropped hair. "I didn't see the first two limbs, but I was shown pictures of them. The first one had no human bite marks at all."

That's because Lenny took it, Ben thought, ignoring Laurette's pressing stare.

"The second had a few, mostly postmortem, but the third limb had several that were premortem. That tells me the individual is escalating, maybe feeling more sure of him or herself in taking on this cannibalistic identity."

After letting that sink in, Ben drew the natural conclusion. "So you think one of Dr. Lock's team members is doing this? Someone who was in the plane crash? After all, they were stranded in Alaska for five days without food." His mouth grew slack at the thought, and he had to take a drink of beer to make it work again. "Is that really possible? Could one of them have this…this Wendigo psychosis?"

"You'll find many psychiatrists who'd roll their eyes at the diagnosis, but it's been reported."

"And you?" Ben asked. "Do you believe it exists?"

"What can I say? I've seen psychotic people do extremely odd things. In fact, on a personal note, I was once stranded for hours in my car during a Midwestern blizzard—I'm originally from Minneapolis. No heat, no food, nothing but a whiteout on the rural road around me. When I was finally rescued by a friend, I was loopy for a good while." He shivered, as if reliving the experience. "Psychotic individuals need help to control their symptoms. It's an illness."

"It's murder."

"It is, of course it is, but it's also not quite that simple."

"Have you mentioned your theory to the police?"

"Not yet, but I've discussed it with your surgery chair, Dr. Fisher. He's the one who pushed for my temporary staff privileges."

"Ha, I can only imagine what Commander Fisher thought."

"Yeah, he wasn't too impressed with the idea, to say the least.

It's probably smart to sit on this a bit. At least until we figure out a few more things."

"The media would go nuts over a story like that." Ben's spine tingled unpleasantly as he imagined his own name being mixed up in the chaos. He lowered his voice. "And that would mean some-body on my team is a killer. It's tough to wrap my head around that."

The waiter breezed up to the table. "Voilà." A plate with a warm brownie smothered with melting ice cream, thick fronds of hot fudge, and a mountain of whipped cream materialized. Three spoons followed, along with fresh napkins. "Enjoy," the reformed hipster sang before darting away.

All three of them studied the dessert. None of them raced to pick up a spoon. At the thought of flesh-eating Wendigos, appetites seemed to have left the building.

## 25

On Monday morning, two days after Mr. Paulson's limb was found in Cobbs Creek Park, the operating room smelled like worry. Stress hormones radiated from Ben and his colleagues like drugstore cologne, and nervous glances flitted behind their protective face shields. As they surrounded the anesthetized patient on the table, a thirty-eight-year-old male scheduled for a knee osteotomy for painful arthritis, each of them no doubt wondered who among them was a killer. But as difficult as that notion was for Ben to entertain, the idea of one of the team members *eating* their victims was so far beyond comprehension that not even Derek's extensive and impressive track record as a forensic neuropsychiatrist could get Ben on board.

While Dr. Lock recited his pre-op prayer with an unusual lack of confidence, Michael straightened the tray's surgical tools too restlessly, Dr. King monitored patient vital signs too compulsively, and Joel plucked at his sterile gloves too noisily. Angela wasn't even there, making Ben wonder at her absence.

"Amen," Dr. Lock said, echoed by Dr. King and Michael. Then the surgeon studied the group in turn, starting with Joel on his right, then Ben and Michael on the other side of the table, and finally Dr.

King at the head of the patient and the circulating nurse beyond him. "Angela won't be joining us," he said. "She's decided to focus on pre- and post-op patient care, as well as our clinic. No surgeries."

The attending offered no further explanation, but none was needed. The OR was probably the last place any of them wanted to be. Murdered patients and severed limbs tended to have that effect, even on Ben who normally lived for performing surgery. From Karen, Ben knew Angela's family relied on her physician's assistant income, especially with her husband's meat shop flailing, and Ben doubted the PA could afford to take time off. Focusing only on before and after care was probably her next best option.

"It will be good for Angie to step away a bit," Dr. King said, checking the patient's blood pressure and adjusting an infusion setting. Ben imagined the anesthesiologist's next thought was: *Wish we could all do the same.*

"One other thing before we begin." Beneath his face guard, a vein in Dr. Lock's forehead swelled. "Dr. Fisher insists we rotate team members on our upcoming reconstructive surgeries. At least for a while. We won't be teaming up together as much in the next few weeks."

Michael stopped fiddling with the surgical tools on his tray. "But what about your research? Won't that ruin the study? Taint the results?"

"It sure as hell might, but apparently rigorous methods are no longer important. Guess our impressively low infection rate isn't either. Dammit." Dr. Lock's leg banged the table, and his newfound cursing continued to unsettle them all. "Fisher's just grasping at straws. With these two murders, he doesn't know what else to do. We've stopped scheduling new reconstructive cases, sure, but what about the people who've been on the schedule for months, desperate to get their pain fixed? Despite what they've read in the news, many are electing to proceed. They want relief, and they want it now. The old can't-happen-to-me syndrome. And who can blame them? Many of them rely on The Lock Foundation for funding. You think the private ortho docs are going to operate on them for free?" Lock exhaled slowly, as if trying to compose himself. "I guess by reshuffling our team, Fisher feels like he's doing even more."

Ben was relieved their patient was under general anesthesia. Hearing people talk about murders and severed legs was probably not high on the guy's bucket list.

"At least Karen'll be happy," Michael said, lifting the scalpel again. "She's been wanting to scrub in with you on a knee replacement since the…well, since Alaska."

Lock ignored him. "You ready, Oris? Let's switch places. I'll take over Angela's role and be your first-assist."

Ben nodded, changed sides with Lock without breaking sterile form, and received the scalpel from Michael. He had to give the attending surgeon credit. Letting him perform another procedure on his own when the whole team was rattled over the recent events was a bold move and a credit to Lock's mentoring skills.

The first few minutes of the surgery passed quietly, but soon the familiar routine seemed to put Dr. Lock back into confident-teacher mode. To Joel, he said, "The patient's pain is primarily on the medial side where his cartilage has worn down, so where should Ben make the bone cut?"

Ben looked up from the patient's gaping incision and stared hard at Joel, willing him to answer correctly. The two of them had reviewed that very issue an hour earlier, and Ben was not in the mood for an angry pimp session followed by more of Lock's rants about Joel's incompetence. It only made Ben look like a crappy teacher. He simply wanted to finish the surgery and survive the day. He'd been told Detectives Becker and Patel would be making another appearance, interviewing everyone from surgeons to nurses to orderlies, and he didn't relish another interrogation. Even cafeteria workers who delivered meal trays to 4 East and 4 West would be under scrutiny.

Fortunately, Joel answered Lock's question correctly. "Since his pain is on the inside of the knee, Ben should cut on the outside."

"And where exactly does he cut?"

"On the upper part of the tibia."

"Because?"

"Because removing a wedge of bone from the outside of the lower leg will shift the patient's weight-bearing toward the healthier outer cartilage, away from the damaged part."

Ben exhaled in relief. Dr. Lock raised an eyebrow at Joel. "Maybe there's hope for you yet, Smith." It was not said good-naturedly.

The rest of the procedure passed uneventfully. Just as Ben was about to remove the retractors and check the leg's new alignment for function, the operating door swung open. The reedy surgical chair, Dr. Fisher, marched into the room. Although he had a surgical mask in place, he remained gown-free.

"What are you doing here, Isaiah?" No politeness in Lock's tone.

"Just checking in. Seeing if you need me to scrub in for an extra hand. Heard your PA's taking a break from surgeries."

"We're fine. Oris is fully competent." Lock's words were clipped.

Without getting too close, Dr. Fisher studied the operating field, where the patient's off-white tibia bone remained exposed, surrounded by retracted skin and yellow fat darkened with cauter-ized blood vessels. The scent of sawed bone and singed flesh still clung in the air. Sweat trickled down Ben's back as the chair of surgery, the man who would have the final say on the Conley Junior Resident Research Grant, examined Ben's first solo osteotomy.

"Hmm, not bad, Oris, not bad," the militaristic chief said. "Now, if you could just keep the limbs you operate on attached to their bodies, we'd all appreciate it."

A snicker from Michael across the table.

"Something funny about dead patients, Alvarez?" Fisher snapped.

Michael shook his head.

"Didn't think so." The chairman fisted his hands. "Holy cheese on a shit cracker, what the hell is going on with these murders?"

No one answered.

"Look, I know we're all stressed, but we still need to do our jobs." Fisher's words echoed Lock's pep talk three days earlier, only with a sharper tone. "Too many people depend on us. So we need to stay focused on our patients. That's all that matters. They need to know they can come to Montgomery Hospital for their goddamn hip replacement and not end up in pieces." When no one responded again, Dr. Fisher said, "Is that understood?"

Everyone nodded, including the circulating nurse in the corner, whose expression suggested she might seek a transfer to dermatology.

"And speaking of patients, Oris, I see your son's mother is on my schedule for tomorrow."

At Fisher's words, both Lock and Ben jerked fully upright. "Tomorrow? I knew she was going to switch sur—" Ben cut himself off. Did Lock know yet about Sophia's plans to reschedule with a different surgeon? In case he didn't, he changed his wording. "With everything that's been going on, she said she was going to postpone it for a bit."

"Why in the world is she on *your* schedule?" The anger—hurt?—in Lock's eyes told Ben that Sophia had indeed not yet told him. "I'm the one operating on her knee. I'm the one who sized her implant."

Fisher responded to Ben first. "Thanks to the asshole who's mutilating our patients, I've had some cancellations, and probably just as well. But that left me with an opening tomorrow, and since her hardware is already here and she can barely walk on her own, Ms. Diaz got moved up." Dr. Fisher shifted to Lock. "And you shouldn't be operating on her anyway, Kent. She told my nurse you've been seeing each other. That's why she switched surgeons. What the hell were you thinking?"

The news seemed to relieve Dr. Lock, maybe because it preserved his hefty ego to think Sophia had canceled on him for that reason. No need for him to know Ben was the one who had instigated it. But what Ben hadn't planned on was her surgery happening so quickly.

At least Dr. Fisher would be her surgeon. That at least should keep her safe.

# 26

S tupid me, thinking I could control this. I could be discovered at any moment. Then they'll all see the hideous creature I've become. At least it would put an end to this hell.

And yet they don't see me. Even when I'm right in front of them, they don't see me, too distracted by their own thoughts and fears.

My actions are sickening. Repulsive. Brutal. I have to remind myself that in those moments it's not me. In those moments it's the ravenous monster who feeds on the ones I've tended to. Their flesh calls and their bones sing, and like sirens on an island they make me so heady and electrified with hunger I can't resist their pull.

I close my eyes and try to shut it out, but it's no use, because there's a new one waiting for me now. I snatched her from her home early this morning.

A sob catches in my throat. I wipe away my tears and grab the bone saw.

The monster wants to eat.

## 27

Early Tuesday morning inside Montgomery Hospital's surgical center, a packed registration area greeted Ben and Sophia. When it was her turn at one of the four check-in desks, each separated by plastic partitions, he held her aluminum crutches and helped her onto a chair in front of the desk. He took the other one, his scrubs fresh but his dark stubble in need of a shave.

The crutches, having been stored in Sophia's closest from a past injury, made their reappearance the night before when her swollen knee could no longer support her. She'd called Ben to come over, and upon seeing her inability to walk, he had quickly dropped Maxwell off at Willy's to spend the night and then returned to Sophia's in case she needed him. Laurette, too, had stopped by to keep them company and to catch them up on her Atlanta adventures. He could only wonder what she and Derek would be doing today.

He hated missing time with her—she'd only be in Philly for a week—but getting moved up on Fisher's schedule was a good thing for Sophia. Ben knew that. Given the pain she was in, there was no way she could wait any longer. Still, his own anxiety mirrored that of the other patients and families around him.

After a few questions and a lot of clicking on her keyboard, the desk clerk answered a phone call. While she spoke to the caller, Sophia turned to Ben. "I know what you're thinking. It's written all over your face."

"I'm not thinking anything."

"Ha, right, I've never known you *not* to be thinking about something. Always so serious. But don't worry. I'll be fine." She raised her fists in boxing mode, the long sleeves of her sweater covering her knuckles. "Nobody's gonna mess with me."

"They'd have to get through me first." Ben hadn't yet mentioned Derek's theory to Sophia. How does one tell the mother of his child there might be a psychotic killer roaming around Philadelphia pretending to be a mythical creature who eats people? "By the way, Laurette texted me this morning. Said to tell you good luck and that she's thinking about you."

"You need to make your move, mister. Before someone else scoops her up."

Ben said nothing.

"I know you think you'll hold her back if you tell her how you feel. You want her decision to move back here to be based on what she wants, not on some sense of obligation to you."

"I never said anything of the sort."

Sophia laughed. "Oh Ben, you think you're so hard to read. I've got news for you. You're easier to read than Maxwell's picture books. Stop thinking so much about it and just act already."

Ben stared at the clerk, hoping for rescue, but she mouthed an apology and continued her conversation on the phone. In the silence, Sophia's levity faded. Despite her overly long sweater, she rubbed her hands back and forth as if to warm them.

"Hey, you're going to be fine," Ben said.

"It's just scary, you know? Now with Maxwell I worry so much more. If something happened to me I'd—"

"Nothing is going to happen to you."

She nodded and exhaled slowly. "You sure it's okay you're missing rounds? I don't want to get you in trouble."

"Don't worry about me." He reached up and tweaked her ear.

"Karen's covering my patients until they take you back. Then I'll head to the ward. But Willy will be here when you wake up, after he drops Maxwell off with your sister."

"He should be at his store. Valentine's Day is coming up."

"His employees can make the chocolate for a few days. Besides, he won't be able to relax until he knows you're okay. And the fact he's even setting foot in a hospital again is good therapy for him. You know it's not his thing." Willy had agreed to keep both Sophia and Maxwell (and the ever-adaptable Sir Quincy) at his place until Sophia recovered enough to handle Maxwell on her own. Sophia's sister, Rita, would also pitch in. If Ben could've asked for the week off, he would've, but it was definitely not the time. Not only would his absence risk making him look even more suspicious to the cops, any further upheaval to the orthopedic service might be detrimental. They were already short-staffed as it was. For once he was actually relieved to be on call. Sophia would be admitted to his ward post-op, and he could check in on her frequently during the night.

The desk clerk finally hung up the phone. "I'm so sorry," she said. "Just a few more questions and we'll be finished."

Twenty minutes later Ben and Sophia were in the pre-surgical suite, the last stop for Ben before Sophia was wheeled away. He watched as a nurse inserted an IV above Sophia's wrist, finding the rare vessel that hadn't been damaged by her year of chemotherapy and blood draws. Shortly after, Dr. Amy Newton, anesthesiology chief resident, arrived to perform her pre-op assessment, and although Ben knew Dr. King was both more meticulous and personable than Dr. Newton—the two anesthesiologists often butted stethoscopes, a combination of clashing personalities and differing styles—Ben was relieved to have a different anesthesiologist than the one on Lock's team. As chief resident, Newton wouldn't need an attending by her side. The farther Sophia was from any of the team members, the better Ben would feel.

Finally, it was time to say goodbye. He hugged Sophia for a long time, Maxwell flashing in his mind. When he pulled away, he smiled the most reassuring smile he could muster. "You're going to do great. Pretty soon you'll be leaping and pirouetting like Baryshnikov."

From her gurney she gave a final wave before the nurse wheeled her around the corner. Ben stood there, praying to a God he didn't believe in that she'd be okay. *Don't you dare hurt one of your most devout followers.*

Back on 4 East he cracked his knuckles, rolled his neck, and redirected his mind to his work. He'd been excused from surgery for the day so he could keep an eye on Sophia. As a result, he'd hold down the ward duties for the other surgeons. He started by checking in with Karen to see if any issues had come up with his patients. He found her in the osteotomy patient's room, checking the guy's incision site. An empty breakfast tray was pushed to the side, but the smell of scrambled eggs and syrup still hung in the air.

When the bearded patient saw Ben, he grinned. "There's the doctor who fixed me up. Dr. Dukakis here says the site looks good. And look," the patient gently extended and flexed his knee a few degrees, "my leg still works."

"I'd be out of a job if it didn't."

Ben thanked Karen for picking up the slack while he checked Sophia into surgery, but as usual of late, she seemed distracted. Who among them wasn't? After she wrapped the wound with fresh dressing, she stood and instructed the patient on the plan for the day. Her tone was flat, her demeanor exhausted. Ben was about to tell her he'd take over from here when Chip Owens, next year's chief resident and the fifth-year filling in for Lenny while he was in rehab, popped his curly brown head into the room.

"Oris, need to talk to you."

"Almost finished. I'll—"

"Dukakis can take care of it. I don't have time to wait."

Ben gave the patient a *yikes* expression. He got a *someone's in trouble* look in return.

Barely had Ben closed the door when Chip was in his face. "Need you to lecture the med students on Legg-Calve-Perthes disease over the lunch hour." When Ben started to protest, thinking what little extra time he had needed to be devoted to Sophia, Chip cut him off. "Save it. Goddamn Lenny left me in a bind taking off like he did. The program director said something about a cousin getting chemo or some lame-ass excuse like that. Why the hell does Lenny need to be there for that? We need him here, dammit."

Though the central counter was buzzing with activity—residents charting, nurses darting back and forth with IV bags and doses of medication, students scrolling through online lab reports—a wide berth remained around Ben and Chip, and for good reason. When it came to chief residents, Chip was no Lenny Reynolds. No charm in his demands, no candy in his white coat pockets, no helping hand. Just an asshole whose time was more important than everyone else's. For that reason, most people feared him.

Ben wasn't most people. "Can't do it. Any other day would be fine, but my son's mom is having knee surgery today and I—"

Chip put his fingers to his lips and made a zip-it motion. "Go cry to someone else. You're doing this."

It'd been a long time since Ben had punched anyone—or wanted to—but at that moment it took real effort to not pop the square-faced senior resident in his coffee-stained teeth.

"I don't give a rat's diseased ass what you've got going on," Chip continued. "I've got a bone graft to do, two broken femurs to set, and a meeting with the residency director. And that's all before twelve thirty. That leaves me no time to explain avascular necrosis of the hip to snot-nosed med students." When Ben still didn't agree to it, Chip added, "And don't tell me you're not prepared. You presented the same topic at report two weeks ago."

Realizing he had no choice but to consent, Ben nodded. Chip clapped him on the back. "Now that's how a real surgeon acts." The senior resident walked away, his strut as confident as his ego. A trio of nurses steered clear.

The next couple hours flew by, Ben whizzing from room to room, attending to various duties and putting out metaphorical fires, some big, some small. As always when the work consumed him, he felt emboldened, reveling in the satisfaction that there was no other job he'd rather be doing.

Just as he was finishing a wound irrigation, his cell phone rang.

He whipped off his gloves, excused himself to the patient, and stepped outside the room. "Hey, Dad, she all done?"

"Yep. Did great too. I'm in the recovery room with her now."

A cement block of worry lifted off Ben's chest. "I'll be right over."

After giving a few orders to a young nurse and asking her input in return, he thanked her and told her to page him with any concerns. Then he hurried off down the hall, IV pumps beeping from at least two of the rooms.

In the far left corner of the Post-Anesthesia Care Unit, or PACU, Willy sat next to Sophia's bed. Half a dozen other beds in the large recovery room were similarly occupied. Some patients were awake. Others were asleep, including Sophia. Her arms lay free on top of the white blanket, IV tubing coiling from the left one. A bedside cardiac monitor traced her heart rhythm, and a probe on her fingertip measured her oxygen level. Her vitals blipped along stably, and for that Ben was grateful. You came through for me, he told her God.

"She's been going in and out," Willy said. "Still pretty groggy." Ben's concern must have shown, because his dad added, "Relax, Benny Boy, she's fine." Willy smoothed Sophia's hair and patted her arm, but despite his calm reassurances, Willy's tense posture told Ben his father still wasn't at ease in hospitals. After seeing Max wither away in one from colon cancer, and a few years later watching Harmony fall into a coma, hospitals had become Willy's worst nightmare. The fact he was there now swelled Ben's heart.

"That's a relief," Ben said. "Dr. Fisher's owly, but he's a great surgeon."

Confusion clouded Willy's hangdog face. "Dr. Fisher?" He shook his head slowly. "No, it wasn't a Dr. Fisher who operated on her."

"Wait, what?"

"That wasn't the surgeon's name. Oh, I'm blanking, what was it again...?"

While Willy racked his brain, Ben gripped the bed's safety rail, the sleeping Sophia oblivious to his mounting distress. "Are you sure?"

"Positive. It was a tall guy. Blondish-brown hair, nice smile, jaw like an actor's. He couldn't stop singing your praises as a resident, so I assumed he's the fellow you've been working with. You said he's the best."

"Was it…" Ben could barely voice the words. "Dr. Lock?"

"Yes, that's the one."

Ben's throat tightened. The recovery room began to spin. When the tile shook and rumbled beneath his feet, he was pretty sure the floor would swallow him whole.

## 28

Ben stood there dazed. All around the PACU, monitors blipped, electronic infusion pumps hummed, and the fumes of alcohol wipes and hand sanitizer cloyed the air. He didn't understand. The day before he'd heard straight from the chief horse's mouth that *he* would be operating on Sophia, not Dr. Lock. So why hadn't Dr. Fisher done the surgery as planned?

"What's wrong, son? You told me that Lock guy was the best." Willy leaned closer to Sophia's sleeping form. "Should I be worried?"

"Yes. I mean, no." *Get it together, Benny Boy.* "I mean, yes, he's an excellent surgeon."

"Then what's the problem? He said he did the whole procedure himself. Said Sophia was a VIP, and I could tell by the way he checked in on her he meant it."

Ben blinked at his father. Over the past few weeks, he'd relayed only the bare minimum to him about what was going on at Montgomery Hospital, beyond what Willy might have read in the newspaper. Not only did he want to avoid burdening his father with the gruesome news, he didn't want to worry him unnecessarily, especially during such a busy time of year for Willy's Chocolate Chalet.

Therefore, since Ben had mentioned nothing about mythical, cannibalistic creatures, Willy would not understand Ben's tight chest, thumping heart, and dry mouth. He would only be content knowing Sophia's knee had been rebuilt by the most skilled hands. Ben wondered who else had been in the OR. What other team members from the Alaskan plane crash?

Across the room a male nurse finished assessing one of his patients, an elderly woman who seemed to have trouble staying awake. After recording the woman's vital signs on a clipboard, the nurse headed their way. Ben practically accosted him.

"Why did Dr. Lock perform Sophia Diaz's surgery?"

The nurse raised his hands, including the one with the clipboard. "Whoa, don't know. I just take care of them post-op."

The odd cut to the man's straw-colored hair and his acne-scarred face triggered recognition in Ben. He glanced at the name tag on the blue scrub top. It was the new RN who'd wandered into the surgeon's lounge the week before while trying to find his way to the recovery room. The same guy to whom Karen had acted cruelly. "Lyle," Ben said. "Sorry. Good to see you again. It's just that Fisher was supposed to do Sophia's surgery, not Lock."

"I don't know anything about that." He looked past Ben to the PACU doorway. "Ask Dr. Lock yourself. He and his PA just walked in. Second time this morning." Lyle nodded toward Sophia. "She must be special."

The nurse took off, and Ben dashed toward the attending and Angela, who trailed behind, her fingers swiping her tablet's screen.

"Hey, Dr. Lock, can I talk to you? Alone?" Ben tried to keep the urgency out of his voice.

"What's up?" Worry creased the surgeon's face, and his gaze shot to Sophia. "Is something wrong? Is she having complications?" He started toward her. From Sophia's bedside, Willy watched both of them with a questioning expression.

Without thinking, Ben grabbed Lock's arm to stop him. "She's fine. No problems. I just need to talk to you alone."

The surgeon's lips formed a tight line of irritation, and he shook off Ben's grasp. He indicated to Angela that she go on ahead without him. Then, obliging Ben, he exited the swinging doors into the stark hallway. An empty gurney waited nearby. "What's with the big secrecy?"

"Why'd you perform Sophia's surgery instead of Fisher?" The question sounded more accusatory than Ben had planned.

"Isaiah had an emergency. One of his patients coded on the ward, so I stepped in. You questioning my abilities?"

"Of course not."

"Then what's the problem? You think she's going to lose a limb? Think she's going to end up…" Dr. Lock winced, as if unable to finish the sentence. Despite being a Protestant, he made the sign of the cross. When Ben didn't respond, the surgeon said, "Spit it out."

"So far it's only your patients who've been murdered."

"So you think I'm a killer, is that it? You accusing me of chopping off my patients' legs? Patients I've put my heart and soul into?" Lock bared his teeth. "Pretty stupid, Oris. Not the best way to score a research grant, that's for sure. Or even make it to your third year."

Ben swiftly tried to smooth things over. "I'm sorry, that's not what I meant at all. Things are just crazy, and I'm worried about Sophia."

"And I'm not? They're *my* patients." The attending surgeon fumed for a few more seconds, clenching and unclenching his fists. Then he exhaled slowly, his ire starting to fade. "I don't know how much Sophia has told you, but we've grown close. Very close."

"She hasn't gone into detail, no." With as good a mother as Sophia was, she would need to be very serious about someone before bringing him into Maxwell's world. Ben wondered if she had yet.

"You're a fine surgeon, Oris." Lock's composed demeanor returned, and he pushed open the recovery room doors to go back inside. "Don't blow it with insinuations like this."

While Lock and Angela checked on Sophia, who was now awake, Ben took a seat behind the PACU counter and logged into one of the available computer terminals. Before he joined the others, he wanted—needed—to find out who else was in the OR during her surgery. Given he'd be the on-call resident taking care of her, accessing her chart was not a HIPAA violation.

He wondered which one of Dr. Fisher's patients had coded. That wasn't common on the ortho ward, so he could see why Fisher would punt the surgery, but why did it have to be to the one surgeon Ben had not wanted? Tapping the mouse with more force than was necessary, he pulled up Sophia's records.

On the surgery report, Dr. Lock was listed as the operating surgeon, no surprise there, and Karen was his assisting resident. Ben supposed that had buoyed her crummy mood. As he already knew, Amy Newton was the anesthesiologist on record, but according to the nurse's note, Dr. King, her attending, had stepped in a few times as well. *Great.*

Ben next checked the scrub nurse. When he saw it was Michael, he cursed under his breath. Aside from Karen and the anesthesiologist, they hadn't exactly varied up the team. Although Michael seemed the least affected by the crash in Alaska, had even bragged about his amputated frostbitten toe, Ben didn't trust him. After all, the guy was a philanderer who'd been kicked out of the house by his wife, and according to Karen, he had an ex-girlfriend who'd been murdered.

Seeing that Dr. Lock and Angela were still at Sophia's side, engaging Willy in small talk, Ben kept searching through her OR notes. It appeared Joel had scrubbed in as well, but given his med student status and Lock's animosity toward him, he most likely stood there mutely. No way would Lock let Joel touch Sophia. And finally there was Asha, the circulating nurse, who was as quiet as she was small.

Ben pushed away from the computer and strolled toward Sophia and Willy. Lock, who was just leaving the unit, ignored him. Ben supposed he couldn't blame the guy. What surgeon wants a resident who accuses him of being a killer? Or at least hints at it.

Sophia would be fine. Of course she would. The list of suspects was huge, starting with the former incompetent resident whose career Dr. Lock had ended. Talk about ample motive to make Lock look like a murderer. Steal the career from the man who stole his, right? Ben wondered what kind of job the guy had finally found. Was it still in the medical field, just not as a doctor? He doubted his good friends, Detectives Becker and Patel, would tell him. And if not the former resident, then there were dozens of orthopedic nurses, several orderlies, and a whole host of ancillary staff members who could be the killer. Any number of them could hold a grudge against Lock.

Maybe the grudge wasn't even against Lock. Maybe the grudge was against Dr. King or Michael or Angela. They were all part of Dr. Lock's team. Or even Joel, though his time on the team was limited to his med student rotation.

Deep down, if Ben were being honest, a part of him was relieved Dr. Lock had performed Sophia's surgery. After all, he had the lowest infection rate. The last thing Sophia needed was a staph or strep infection in the joint. But whether it was because of Lock's skill and consistent-team approach or because of a stolen silver-coated implant idea, Ben didn't know. There was no evidence to suggest the latter. Ben had held the implants in his hands and had confirmed their brand with the OR director.

He raked his fingers over his face. Thinking about killer team members, stolen implants, and imaginary creatures who ate people was driving him batty. Instead of trying to solve a puzzle he didn't have the resources to solve, he should focus on his family and his patients and let the cops do the rest.

A glance at the clock revealed it was ten minutes before noon. He had a lecture to give over in the med school building. *Super.*

He returned to Sophia. "How you feeling, champ?"

"I'm okay," she said groggily. "My throat is still dry though."

On command, Willy snatched up the ice chips from the bedside tray table and offered her more.

"Are you in pain?" Ben asked.

"No."

"Then what's wrong? You look worried."

She opened her mouth to speak, closed it, then opened it again. "It wasn't…"

Ben squeezed her shoulder. "I know. It wasn't Dr. Fisher."

"He had an emergency."

"So I've been told."

"I'll be okay. Kent has lots of patients who are doing just fine."

Ben nodded. He chewed his lower lip. "I have to run off. Chip saddled me with a noon lecture. But I'll check on you later, okay? You'll probably be moved to the ward by the time I'm done. And I'll be here overnight so I can check in on you frequently."

"If I know you, you won't let me out of your sight."

## 29

For Ben, stepping away from the controlled—and sometimes claustrophobic—chaos of the hospital wards into the openness of the nine-story atrium was always a welcome respite. This evening's breather would be even better, because Laurette had agreed to join him for dinner, braving the questionable cuisine of the hospital cafeteria for some time with him on call.

Unlike the sterile blandness of the inpatient units, the atrium was full of color. Salmon tiles checkered the cafeteria floor, while tables and chairs in a rainbow of primary colors peppered its surface. Plant-studded dividers full of greenery and blooms separated the dining area from bordering hallways of administrative offices, and although the sky beyond the glass ceiling was darkening, the mood in the atrium's dining room was light. Laughter radiated from scattered patrons, and three kids played a boisterous game of *Sorry* at a corner table.

With no sign yet of Laurette, Ben grabbed a table near a large fern and slipped off his white coat, its pockets heavy with reflex hammers and other medical paraphernalia. Dressed in a fresh pair of scrubs, ones that didn't carry the scent of steady patient care and adrenaline, he watched the front door. Hopefully the intern covering the ward could manage things by herself for the next forty-five minutes or so. Uninterrupted time with Laurette would be nice.

He stretched out his legs and replayed the afternoon. Sophia's first day was going well. The usual pain-med requirements but nothing too bad. She'd be up walking soon. Along with Dr. Lock, Angela and Karen had kept a close eye on her while Ben was tied up with two motor vehicle accident patients, and Dr. Newton and Dr. King had stopped by to make sure there were no lingering anesthetic side effects. Even Michael had reassured Ben that his "baby mama" was doing well. Since the nurse's split from his wife, he'd been making frequent appearances on the surgical ward, hitting on the handful of single nurses and med students. Given that Michael's murdered ex-girlfriend was now common knowledge, Ben doubted victory was in reach for him.

Although grateful for the team's attentiveness, the thought, no matter how unlikely, that one of them might be a killer made Ben equally grateful that Rita and Willy had agreed to take turns staying with Sophia. Even though neither Kim Templeton nor Henry Paulson had disappeared from the hospital, Ben wasn't about to take that chance.

Just as Ben was starting to worry Laurette might not show, she strolled through the revolving door near the gift shop. Unfortunately, she wasn't alone. Derek Epps, psychiatrist extraordinaire with the charisma of a star athlete and the credentials of a Nobel Prize winner, was with her.

*Fantastic.*

They greeted each other, and when she unzipped her coat and hung it over a chair, Ben complimented her turquoise sweater. After a few more pleasantries, they made their way to the handful of buffet lines at the back of the dining hall and selected their meals— lasagna for Ben and Laurette, a deli sandwich for Derek. When they returned to their table and Laurette sat next to him instead of Derek, Ben had to resist a moment of childish satisfaction. A bit of small talk about Mrs. Sinclair ensued. She had called Ben earlier that afternoon to tell him how delighted she was Laurette had spent the morning with her, taking her to her eye appointment and running her around town for errands. Laurette then asked about Sophia, and Ben assured her she was doing well. "Her sister is with her right now."

At that point, Laurette got down to business. "If you are wondering why I brought Derek, it's because we have some updates for you."

"And what would they be?"

It was Derek who answered. "I met once again with Dr. Fisher, and also Dr. Beverly Rogers, the chair of psychiatry." He stuffed an escaped tomato back into his ham sandwich. "After hearing my theory, both would like me to spend time with each of the plane crash survivors."

"Seriously? They actually believe one of them's a Wendigo?"

"Of course they don't think one of them is an actual Wendigo. Neither do I." For the first time since Ben had met him, Derek looked perturbed. "It's a psychosis. The person only *believes* he or she is a cannibalistic creature."

Laurette pulled a napkin from the dispenser on the table. "As representatives of the CDC—unofficially, anyway—we have also been to see the detectives on the case."

"You spoke with Becker and Patel?"

"Is one a pensive librarian and the other a man in need of a good night's sleep?"

"Those are the ones," Ben said. "Wow, you had quite the busy day, what with Mrs. Sinclair and all. Bet Detective Patel thought you guys were full of crap."

An amused glint sparked in Derek's eyes. "Let's just say he didn't buy into it. Detective Becker either, although he seemed more willing to listen to the thoughts of a psychiatrist. But they're wondering if a vengeful former resident is behind it."

Better than one of my team members, Ben thought.

"And while I agree that's a much easier theory to swallow," Derek said, "they have no evidence, and parts of it don't make sense. How would the ousted resident have gotten the first limb from the morgue? And why would he suddenly switch to killing the victims? Seems like pretty brutal revenge."

Laurette elbowed Ben's side and fixed him with a laser-beam stare. "You must tell him about Lenny. Derek needs to know all the facts."

A momentary sting of betrayal nabbed him—he had told Laurette about Lenny in confidence—but he let it go. She was right. Of course she was. Despite his promise, Ben could no longer protect Lenny. How could a pattern be deduced when Derek and the police were missing a crucial piece of information?

Near their table, the kids playing *Sorry* packed up their game board and shuffled off. Once they were gone, Ben fessed up. He told Derek that the orthopedic chief resident was convinced Dr. Lock had stolen his implant idea, and to prove it, he cut off Sampson's leg in the morgue. But when he woke up the next morning from his drug bender, he'd panicked and ditched the leg in a park before he could examine the implant. "He was worried someone might have seen him take it and that police would be storming his apartment any second." If Derek was surprised or annoyed by Ben's hoarding of crucial information, he didn't show it. Nothing there but the neutral face of a psychiatrist. "But Lenny had nothing to do with the other two," Ben quickly added. "He's not a killer."

"A man who cuts off the limb of a corpse is obviously disturbed." Laurette spoke carefully, as if not wanting to pique Ben. "He might do things he wouldn't normally do."

"He's not a killer," Ben repeated, dropping his fork to his plate, where it clacked against the plastic surface.

Derek took a long time chewing a bite of sandwich, his psychiatric neutrality perhaps reaching its limit. "I wish you'd told me sooner," he finally said. "I've been trying to piece these three cases together but couldn't. Now I know why." He looked at Laurette with a whiff of irritation. "You should have told me."

"Hey, don't blame her."

"I'm sorry," she said. "You're right, but I couldn't betray Ben's confidence yet again. But he's telling you now. Nothing has changed. We have lost no time."

A few beats later, Derek's even keel returned. "I understand your predicament, but how are you so sure he's not involved with the other two cases?"

"Because he was in rehab when they happened. Besides, he has no motive beyond Mr. Sampson's limb."

Derek propped an arm over the back of the empty chair next to him. "You say the chief resident thinks your attending surgeon stole his implant idea. What if he lied to you about not getting a chance to examine the limb before he ditched it in the park? What if this is his way of getting revenge on Dr. Lock?"

Ben opened his mouth, closed it. His mind had no counterargument. Part of Sampson's implant *was* visible through the side of the limb, but Ben had assumed that was the work of animals.

"See, I'm trying to figure out why this disturbed individual would leave the limb with the implant behind. That's the part of my Wendigo psychosis theory that doesn't make sense. It fits better with someone trying to frame Dr. Lock for revenge."

"But surely you don't think the killer eats the rest of the body," Laurette said.

"Of course not. I'm not convinced he or she eats much more than a few bites. Psychotic or not, it's tough to override our basic human instincts, even if the killer is escalating. And if the person *is* escalating, let's hope the amputation stays postmortem with the next one." Silence, as they absorbed this. "But again, that's the part I don't understand. Why cut off the limb? Why not simply leave it intact with the rest of the body?"

"Maybe the killer wants to be found," Laurette suggested. "Leaving the implant inside might point the police in the right direction."

"Could be," Derek said. "Wouldn't be the first time a killer left clues, secretly hoping to be discovered so his carnage would end."

"Are you sure of your friend?" Laurette asked Ben. "Are you absolutely sure Lenny could not be doing this? He's on drugs. According to you he's a good man. So maybe he's horrified by what he's doing but is unable to stop. Maybe he needs someone to help him."

"I..." Ben thought of his jovial chief resident. He might be caught in the downward cycle of drugs, but a killer? The guy with the fiery jawbreakers in his pockets and the helping hand ever at the ready?

Derek rescued him by saying, "I agree, it doesn't all add up, especially since Lenny wasn't in Alaska. If he *is* the killer, then my theory is as off-base as that grumpy detective thinks it is." Derek leaned closer. "But here's what I do know. If I'm right and it's a case of Wendigo psychosis, then the killer will feel a deep attachment to the victims. Whether that's through being their surgeon, their nurse, their candy striper, I have no idea. Hopefully I'll know more once I meet with the Alaskan survivors."

"Mrs. Templeton did tell her husband she thought someone was watching her," Ben said. "And the detectives mentioned Paulson's daughter thought she saw someone outside his window."

"A person with Wendigo psychosis would definitely want to keep tabs on his or her victim, in whatever way possible."

Silence once again at the table, the topic too eerie for banter.

The chirp of Ben's pager broke it. The message indicated that his intern needed him to help with a dressing change that didn't look right.

"Gotta go." He stood, kissed Laurette on the cheek, and shook Derek's hand. A part of him was reluctant to leave them, worried about where they might go, what they might do.

Derek followed suit and picked up his tray. "Don't worry. We'll figure it out. What I dealt with in Trenton was no less strange."

"And once you do figure it out, what then? How do you stop a Wendigo?" Ben asked. "Therapy? Antipsychotic drugs?"

"Yes to both." Then Derek snorted a laugh. "But a silver stake might do the trick too. Anyone got one handy?"

Though the psychiatrist was clearly joking, his words made Ben drop his tray on the table. Heads turned at the clattering noise. "What did you say?"

"I was kidding."

Ben grabbed the psychiatrist's arm. "Tell me what you said." His temples throbbed, and a sick feeling swirled inside his gut.

Derek, seemingly startled by Ben's distress, replied, "I said silver. A silver stake. Wendigos are repelled by silver."

## 30

Located on the north side of the main floor, Montgomery Hospital's emergency department was only a short jaunt from the cafeteria, yet Ben couldn't get there fast enough. After Derek's bombshell revelation about Wendigos being repelled by silver, Ben had only one mission: to learn more about how a surgical implant gets from hospital point A to hospital point B. As a former scrub nurse, Tara Sands, the woman whose roof he patched up in December, should be able to tell him. Though his intern needed him up on 4 East, and two other pages awaited his attention, he couldn't focus on work until he knew the answer.

Because it might help him ID a killer.

If the implants did indeed contain silver, an element not yet routinely used in medical devices due to the safety concern of uncontrolled silver-ion release, that meant Lenny was telling the truth about Dr. Lock stealing his idea. Even more critical, it meant the killer, assuming Derek's Wendigo theory was true, would have to *know* the implants contained the mineral.

Before he'd dashed off like a madman, Ben had explained as much to Laurette and Derek, their nervous excitement initially matching his own.

"If it's true," the psychiatrist had marveled, as if he couldn't believe it himself, "then my theory might be spot-on."

Ben, anxious to get moving, had replied, "Maybe so, because the only person who would believe a silver-coated implant was lethal—"

"Would be someone who thought he or she was a Wendigo. Someone who knew the implants contained silver."

"And there are only two people who know about the silver." *And one of them just performed surgery on the mother of my child.*

"No," the psychiatrist had said, "you can't assume Dr. Lock and Dr. Reynolds are the only two who know. Anybody on the surgical team—or not on it, for that matter—could have found out. Even the former resident who's got an ax to grind. So the theory of revenge still holds up. The former resident. Your friend Lenny. Someone else." Derek's exuberance had faded. "We may be no closer than we were before."

With his pager buzzing, demanding he get back to work, Ben had bolted to the emergency department. The last thing he'd heard as he darted away was Derek telling Laurette they had to inform the police of the new information.

Ben imagined the police zeroing in on Lenny, carting him off to jail, to court, to prison, red-hot jawbreakers stuffed inside his orange jumper. The image nauseated him. Aside from Laurette and Sophia, Len was the only friend Ben had let into his inner circle.

*Sorry, buddy. I tried.*

When at last he burst through the ED doors, his pager trilled again. The pressure of needing to be in two places at once was akin to being drawn and quartered. Just a few more minutes was all he needed. A few minutes to talk to Tara. The three-to-eleven shift was her norm.

Moments later he found her, his relief more palpable than the protruding abdomen of the male patient she was examining. When she saw Ben she smiled and tucked her short hair behind her ears, the roots starting to gray. "Well, this is a nice sur—"

He pulled her to the other side of a partially drawn curtain.

"Whoa, dramatic much?" Her laughter faded when she saw he

wasn't joking around. "What's going on? Is it one of my daughters? Are they hurt?" Panic in her eyes now.

"No, no, I'm sorry. Didn't mean to freak you out. But I need to ask you something from your days as an ortho scrub nurse."

She scanned the bustling department. "Now? It's a zoo in here."

"It'll only take a moment. Please."

"Okaaay, what is it then?"

"Who brings the orthopedic implants into the OR?"

"What do you mean?"

"By the time the surgeons finish scrubbing in, the implants are already waiting for us in the operating room. I never gave it much thought. Just assumed the implants they ordered in clinic got delivered to the hospital, and when the patient's surgery day arrived, the circulating nurse or scrub nurse brought the devices into the OR."

"Sure, that's usually the case. We go to the supply room, find the patient's box on their surgeon's shelf, and bring it into the OR. Well, not every surgeon uses customized implants yet, but even then we keep a good supply of sizes. Then we document the brand, lot number, et cetera in the chart." She scrunched her face. "Well, that's *usually* how it goes, but not with your attending."

"What do you mean?"

She sighed. "Look, I don't want to speak badly about Dr. Lock. He's a good surgeon. A great one. Does all those humanitarian missions. Pro bono work here, too."

Ben sensed her hesitation. "But?"

"But, well, he's such a perfectionist, and not in a good way like Dr. King, who only wants to make sure his anesthesia is precise."

"How is Lock different?" Prickles of electricity danced down Ben's spine.

"When he decided to start studying the effects of using a consistent team in his reconstructive cases to decrease post-op complications, he kicked the rest of us scrub nurses to the curb. Only his personal scrub nurse was allowed to fetch the implants."

"So only Michael then?"

"Yes, and woe to the person who tried otherwise. Once, I was getting an implant from the supply room for Dr. Fisher, when I figured I'd save Michael the trip and bring back one of Dr. Lock's too. Michael was running late, and I'd seen the name of their first case on the board, so I figured I'd help him get started. But when I got back to the operating rooms, Lock freaked out on me, and not in just a 'me doctor, you nurse' sort of way. It was a full-out tantrum. Horrified everyone in the hallway. Guess I deviated from his research's 'consistency' requirements." Tara grimaced. "Just one more reason why I switched to the ER."

"I don't blame you. So Dr. Lock's implants come from the same supply room?"

"Yes. Why wouldn't they?"

"Just wondering." Ben's agitation remained. Based on Tara's information, Michael would need to be added to the list of people who might know about the silver-coated implants. This widened the suspect pool, and as Derek had suggested, any number of people could have discovered it on their own as well, including Angela.

A shout interrupted his thoughts.

"Tara, we need you over here!"

Ben thanked her, and she darted off. At the same time, his cell phone buzzed. Making his way to 4 East before the unsupervised intern killed someone in his absence, he answered the call.

As if he were running somewhere, a breathless Derek responded. "I called Detective Becker to tell him about the silver in the implant."

"And?"

"And he told me they found another severed leg. A knee this time."

Ben froze in the stairwell, his hand gripping the rail.

"It's from a woman. A younger woman from the looks of it."

Ben heard nothing else. He shoved his phone into his pocket and scaled the stairs like a cheetah in pursuit of prey.

*Sophia.*

# 31

Ben raced past the baffled intern leaning against 4 East's central counter and skidded toward room 434.

"Hey, I need your help with—"

"Be there in a minute," he called out to her. His behavior was irrational—the ward would've paged him had one of their patients gone missing—but he had to see Sophia with his own two eyes. Had to make sure she was still tucked in her bed, tethered to her IV pole, slurping her vegetable soup and meatless entrée.

With a shove to her partially open door, he burst into her room, startling all three of the occupants inside it. Only when he saw Sophia was one of them did he exhale a life raft's worth of air.

"Daddy!" Maxwell left Sophia's side and leaped into Ben's arms. He hugged the child close, the reflex hammer in his pocket pressing against his hip under the toddler's weight.

Willy rose from a vinyl chair, his unbuttoned shirt flapping open, a plain tee underneath. "Is everything okay? Maxwell really wanted to see his mom. The nurse said it would be okay for a few minutes." Willy massaged his hands. "Was I wrong to bring him?"

Still catching his breath, Ben lowered his son. "No, it's fine. Sorry to startle you."

Willy seemed to relax a bit and sat back down. Maxwell climbed up on his lap. Ben approached Sophia's bed, checked her IV fluid rate, and flipped up her blanket to examine her knee dressing and make sure it was dry. His actions were rushed, his pulse still thumping.

"Well, hello to you too, doctor. You might want to buy me dinner first." Sophia smirked. "Might want to work on your bedside manner too."

Ben covered her leg back up with the blanket and sat on the edge of the bed, careful not to pull the covering too tightly over her legs. He managed a smile. "Not gonna win doctor of the year, huh?"

She patted his hand, seemingly touched by his concern. "Relax, I'm doing great. Got a new knee, got my son, got my other dad, had my sister here too." She fished out the gold necklace beneath her hospital gown and raised its cross to her lips. "Got the big man Himself. And now I've got my doctor. What else could I want for?"

"Technically, Dr. Dukakis is your doctor. I'm just an on-call flyby."

"I don't like Dr. Dooki." Maxwell pulled at his sweatshirt, which showcased two smiling trains. "She's grumpy."

Ben raised an eyebrow at Willy.

"Dr. Dukakis stopped by just after we got here. Maxwell showed her the new train Laurette bought him, but I guess the doc's under-whelmed reaction wasn't what he hoped for." Willy added in Maxwell's ear, "She's a good doctor, Maxie. Just real busy. You can show her your train again next time."

As if unconvinced, Maxwell held up his new russet coal truck and sniffed.

"It's a great train car, buddy. Who wouldn't love it?" Ben reached over to inspect it in proper detail. "And Dr. Dukakis isn't so bad. Remember over Christmas when Sir Quincy got sick and we had to take him to the vet? How sad you were?" Maxwell nodded. "Well, Dr. Dukakis has had a sad time lately too."

Ben exchanged knowing glances with Willy and Sophia, both of whom were aware of Karen's involvement in the December plane crash. What they weren't aware of was that another severed limb had been found. Ben didn't know whose it was or where it had been discovered. In his panic over Sophia, he'd disconnected from Derek before he'd learned the details. But he had no intention of telling them until he knew more. Sophia needed to focus on her recovery, and Willy had enough to worry about.

"You sure you're okay, son? Busy night?"

Ben nodded. "I'm good. Gotta get back to work. My poor intern's probably busting an aneurysm waiting for me." To Sophia, he said, "Able to do any walking yet?"

"A little. Just to the bathroom. They took my catheter out."

"Good. Keep that up. Tomorrow the physical therapist will work with you. Take you down the hallway a few feet with your walker. There are wheelchairs in the ward and by the elevators if you feel you've gone too far."

"Don't worry," Willy answered for Sophia. "Rita and I will take good care of her. Between the two of us, we've got everything covered."

"Your dad's a saint," Sophia said. "One of the busiest times of the year for him, and he's here watching over me."

"Wouldn't have it any other way."

Sophia squeezed Willy's hand, their affection for each other obvious, and a nice warmth replaced some of Ben's chill. Despite the Catholic church's views on gay people, Sophia shared none of that philosophy. She'd also agreed, per Ben's request, to not "pile the religion" on Maxwell beyond weekly Sunday School classes and an occasional church picnic. So far, as co-parents with vastly different backgrounds, they'd made it work.

"Besides," Sophia was saying. "The sooner I'm out of here, the better. People are always poking at me, interrupting me, peeking at me." Maxwell giggled when Sophia covered her eyes and made a peek-a-boo motion with her hands.

Ben's pager buzzed yet again, maniacally it seemed to him.

He kissed Maxwell on the head, gently tugged Sophia's ear, and squeezed his dad's shoulder. "I'll see you all later. And remember, you stay at Willy's until it's safe to go home."

Sophia's smile faded. "Safe?"

"Until you're healed, I mean. No sense rushing things. No stairs to navigate at Willy's like at our apartments, and you won't have to be on your own with Maxwell."

"Of course."

She held Ben's gaze, and Ben realized she understood his subtext. Willy's countenance darkened as well. Only Maxwell remained oblivious, his coal truck scooting its way up the plaid squares on his grandpa's shirt.

# 32

The dark and freezing emptiness of the tundra is never far away. Over and over I replay the moment the horned creature hulked toward me as the others slept in our makeshift camp. Its glowing eyes and sharp talons were as hideous as its putrid stench.

I tried to run away. Got up and stumbled through the deep snow. But I was too weak and frozen to get far. It caught me and slipped into me. No, it *sliced* into me, sharp, evil, and disgusting. Who could believe a thing like that even exists?

The monster is never full. It only wants more. I try to resist until my insides are ready to burst, but where I could once go several days without giving in to its demands, I can now barely go one. It wants its fill.

The small part that's still me tries to be humane, of course, but the monster has squashed even that small kindness. With the last one, it started eating and sawing while her heart was still pounding. She screamed and fought so hard I wanted to die myself, but the monster craves living tissue and fresh bone marrow. It'll no longer let me wait. As before, I removed the part that could hurt us.

I never know who the monster will choose or which of the ones I've cared for will trigger its hunger. I only know their limb will contain that vile metal. It's like an inoculation of sorts. The monster wants me to build a tolerance to it so that someday it will no longer hurt us. But once the monster *does* decide who's next, that choice consumes me completely. I can hardly think of anything else.

And already the monster has chosen again. It calls for her, the one whose flesh is young and tender like the last one. Her marrow will taste sweeter than the ice and snow that planted this monster inside me.

I watch her sleep, the IV tubing and bandages not detracting from her peaceful rest. I lick my lips. My heart thuds in my chest. No…the monster's heart thuds. The monster lets me know she's the one.

She's the one.

## 33

Seated at a high-gloss table inside the conference room next to Dr. Isaiah Fisher's office, Ben was joined by the chairman himself, Derek, Detectives Becker and Patel, and Shala Lamb, the attorney who'd met Ben at his apartment the last time the cops had interrogated him. Her presence on this Wednesday afternoon could only mean bad things for him, so despite being up most of the night on call, his fatigue enveloping him like a dense fog, he was jittery and tense.

Absent from the table was Laurette, who, despite being a CDC disease detective and epidemiologist, had no official role in the investigation, and as such had not been asked to join. Too bad. Ben would've felt a whole lot better with her by his side.

Presently, Dr. Fisher, dressed in scrubs like Ben, was barking an order to someone on his cell phone while the rest of them waited. Ms. Lamb, her dark hair held perfectly in place by an invisible force, was scrolling on her own phone. Derek and Detective Becker were quietly talking, and Patel simply stared across the table at Ben, his shadow-rimmed eyes two dark pools of suspicion. His ability to look both menacing and apathetic at the same time was truly an applause-worthy skill.

Finally, Fisher disconnected. "Sorry. Damn insurance companies will be the death of me. Refusing to pay for an MRI, as if I order the things for shits and giggles. Now, what's this all about?"

A few swivels of chairs. A cough from Becker. And then, without warning or preliminary pleasantries, Detective Patel spiked an invisible ball at Ben's head. "So doc, seems you've left out some preeeety important bits of information about your chief resident. You know what we call that?" Patel winked, and Ben's pulse sped up in anxiety. "We call that obstruction. And if he turns out to be the killer? Well, we call that being an accessory to murder."

Clammy, sweaty, and stinking of his night on call, Ben sat rigid in his chair, his scrubs a thin barrier against its cool leather. From the end of the table, Dr. Fisher's narrowed gaze bore into him. "What the hell is he talking about, Oris? If you knew something about this shit-storm that could've stopped it, you'll be out on your ass by the end of this meeting."

Ben swallowed. An imaginary bulldozer demolished not only the Conley Grant but the rest of his residency and career. A jail cell took their place. Next to him, Shala Lamb was unhelpfully quiet, and at the other end of the table, Derek busied himself with some notes he'd jotted earlier.

Detective Becker studied Ben above his rimless glasses. "Why didn't you tell us Lenny Reynolds took the first limb?"

"What the fu—"

Shala Lamb cut Dr. Fisher off with a raised hand and a sharp tilt of her head.

"I...I should have. I'm sorry. I was just trying to protect my friend. He didn't kill those people."

"So you're a detective in your spare time now too?" Becker said. "The man's a drug addict. He chopped off a corpse's leg. And according to Dr. Epps, Dr. Reynolds is convinced his attending stole his implant idea."

"That's what we call *mo*tive," Patel added with his signature sarcasm.

Ben shook his head. "Len's in rehab. He couldn't have done this.

Besides, if he wanted to prove Dr. Lock stole his implant idea, he wouldn't start killing people. He'd have stopped at Sampson's leg."

Becker flipped through his notebook. "As you know, the lower leg of a woman was found last night in the Wissahickon Park, this time by a passerby who took it upon himself to photograph the severed limb and share it all over social media."

"Maybe you saw the nice YouTube video he posted before we got it taken down? Now *there's* something fun to watch with Grandma." Patel folded his hands on his belly. At the end of the table Dr. Fisher fumed.

"How is sarcasm going to help us here, detective?" Derek asked.

Shala nodded. "Agreed. Can we shelve the good-cop/bad-cop act and just get to the point please?"

Becker crossed his arms. "According to the medical examiner, the newest limb had probably been left there late Monday night or early Tuesday morning, likely hidden but dragged out by animals. There's a mixture of animal and human bite marks."

Quiet fell over the table.

"And if you think that's juicy news," Patel said. "Wait'll you hear this."

"Dr. Lenny Reynolds left rehab Friday afternoon," Becker said. "Just up and took off after five days. That means he was out during these last two murders, and, as you'll recall, he hadn't yet entered rehab before the first one."

"What? No. That can't be." Ben's gaze darted back and forth between the two detectives. "I talked to him on Sunday. He was at the center."

"He *told* you he was at the center," Becker said. "Doesn't mean he was."

Fisher bolted forward in his chair. "Why wasn't I notified of this?"

The detectives ignored the chairman. Instead, Becker asked Ben, "What do you know about Barbara Simmons?"

Ben scrambled to collect his thoughts, which were still focused on the impossible-to-believe notion that Lenny had fled rehab to pick up where he'd left off. *Have I enabled a killer?* "Um...who?"

"Barbara Simmons. The latest victim."

Blinking, Ben tried to place the woman. "Wait, I didn't operate on her. I was post-call and over my twenty-four-hour work limit." Despite his angst, a sprinkle of relief doused him. "Her surgery was last Tuesday. I stopped to see my mother at the Sethfield Long-Term Care Facility that afternoon. You can check the visitor's log." It was the same day Willy had told him Harmony was talking to him in his head and the day after Lenny had checked into rehab. "But from our rounds I remember she was in her early thirties and had severe knee damage from an old injury. Despite her young age, she needed a replacement, like Sophia."

"Who operated on her?"

"Dr. Lock, and since I couldn't be in the OR, Angela most likely assisted him. It'll be in the patient's chart."

His relief at not being in the OR for the latest victim's surgery must have shown, because Becker removed his glasses, hardened his pale eyes, and in an unexpectedly vicious tone that made it clear bad-cop/bad-cop was still on the table, said, "Don't get too confident, Dr. Oris. You withheld critical information and could be charged accordingly."

"So *are* you charging him?" Shala asked.

Patel smiled. "That depends on how helpful he is to us."

Becker clarified. "We've brought you here to tell us more about this implant situation. Are you suggesting Dr. Lock is using Dr. Reynolds's implant?"

"I'm not suggesting anything. That's what Lenny told me. But…" Ben's next words would only make Lenny look more suspicious, but there was no avoiding it. Ben wasn't keen on going to jail for obstruction, and if Lenny really was a killer, he wasn't about to defend the guy. Still, he felt like a sewer rat. "But what I don't understand is, if that were the case, that would've meant product design, testing, approval—all of that would've had to happen. How could no one else know about Dr. Lock's involvement in a new device?"

"Could he be using it under the radar?" Derek asked, not quite making eye contact with Ben, as if embarrassed for—or by— Laurette's poor decision-making friend.

"What do you mean?"

"Could Dr. Lock be using an implant that's not yet approved?"

Dr. Fisher pounded the table. "That's ridiculous. Would never happen on my watch. And now you're smearing a great surgeon's—"

"We need to consider all options," Becker said. A simmering anger still bubbled beneath the bookish detective's surface, making Ben see him in a whole new light. "The time interval is shrinking. Eight days passed between the discoveries of the first limb and the second. Five days between the second and third. Three days between the third and the fourth. Even if your friend is innocent and the first limb has nothing to do with the other three, the killer is clearly escalating."

"Jesus Christ," Fisher said, running his hands over his face. Next to Ben, the lawyer squeezed her pen until her knuckles blanched.

"That wouldn't be unusual for an individual with Wendigo psychosis," Derek said.

Patel scoffed, his sleepy eyes staring up at the ceiling.

"I know it sounds extreme, but the pieces fit. One," Derek raised an index finger to tick off the point, "the victims all had the same surgical team—except for Simmons, which, in my opinion, exonerates Ben."

*Thank God.*

Derek lifted a second finger. "The team members were all stranded in Alaska when their plane went down."

"Except for Karen," Ben said. "I mean, she was in Alaska, but she's not one of Lock's team members."

Derek mulled this over. "She should still stay on the list for now." He raised a third finger. "All of them have been suffering from posttraumatic stress disorder in some form or another. Any of them could slip into a psychosis that feeds on the cold and hunger they suffered, and as healthcare professionals, they would easily feel a powerful attachment to the victims."

Patel leaned forward, his act of indifference betrayed by sudden interest. "Is that what they told you in your sessions with them this morning?"

"You know I can't tell you that. It's privileged."

A muscle twitched in the detective's face. "Not if someone's life is at stake."

"I'm aware of the disclosure rules for psychiatry, thank you." Derek's tone was flat. "But while I can't tell you what the Alaskan survivors said, I will tell you that I can't pinpoint anyone as the killer. At least not yet. I need more time."

Patel grunted and settled back in his chair, his armor of apathy returning.

"So let's focus on what we have," Becker said. "Lenny Reynolds has motive to frame Dr. Lock and expose him for fraud."

"Killing people and hacking off their limbs is a messed-up way to do it." Dr. Fisher wiped his mouth in disgust.

"Agreed," Becker said. "But people do messed-up things when they're on drugs. Plus, Lenny left rehab, and no one knows where he is. That makes him suspect number one, and that's why you're not in jail this very second, Dr. Oris. If he reaches out to you—texts you, calls you, so much as whispers through the air to you—you need to tell us. Immediately."

Feeling disconnected from his body, Ben nodded. He simply couldn't believe it. Why hadn't Len called him? There had to be another reason he'd ditched rehab. Maybe he couldn't handle it. Maybe they caught him using. Maybe his damn fish missed him. But a killer? No way. "There are other people of interest though, right?" he asked weakly. "Dr. Lock, or someone out to get him, like that former resident?"

Dr. Fisher grunted. "Lock is no more a killer than I am."

"You've interviewed the fired resident, I assume?" Derek asked the detectives.

"On two occasions."

Becker left it at that, and Ben understood there was a limit to what they'd discuss openly.

Patel's hands were back on his belly. "Doc, run through this implant situation again."

Ben summarized what he knew, repeating what he'd told Derek and Laurette the night before and what the psychiatrist had obviously passed onto the detectives.

Becker looked up from the notes he was jotting. "So it wouldn't make sense for Dr. Lock to kill the victim and then leave evidence of his stolen implant for anyone to see."

"No," Derek said, "But you're thinking too rationally. Somebody with Wendigo psychosis wouldn't think rationally. They would only know they had to avoid silver, and that includes the implant. So they'd get rid of it." Derek smoothed his tie and then went back to gesticulating with his hands. "So whoever's doing this would have to know there's silver in the implant. That points to Dr. Lock, but it could also be somebody else on his team who discovered his use of the implant."

Patel stifled a burp. "I gotta tell you, doc, I think your theory is horse shit."

Derek's passive expression suggested he was no stranger to police skepticism. "You have a right to your opinion, detective, but I've already told you about some of the strange cases I've helped the authorities solve. Psychosis makes people do all kinds of things. Terrible things, even. And sometimes they're not even psychotic. After all, Dahmer ate his victims."

Patel waved a hand as if he still didn't buy it, but he turned to Fisher. "We need to see the implants Dr. Lock's been using. Compare them to the ones found on the victims."

Now it was Fisher's turn to scoff. "I've seen all the implants in the supply room. There's nothing unusual about them. They certainly don't kill people, for Christ's sake."

"Then you won't mind us looking around."

Like a slowly descending curtain, worry replaced Dr. Fisher's skepticism. He glanced at Shala, who seemed to remember why she was there.

"I'm sorry," she said, "but you'll need a warrant for that."

"Are you kidding me?" Though Patel's cheeks were flaccid, his eyes sparked anger. "You got something to hide?"

"I've got a department to run," Fisher barked. "Surgeries to perform. Patients—"

"About that," Becker said. "We'd like you to cancel all the upcoming joint replacement surgeries. I don't care whether patients want them or not."

"And where are the underinsured ones supposed to go, huh?" Fisher said. "The private ortho docs won't take them. The Lock Foundation covers patients who could otherwise never get an implant. You want us to leave them limping in pain indefinitely? Who knows how long this could go on? And what's going to happen if the public gets wind of this stupid theory that one of our doctors or nurses is a killer who eats people?" The chairman's eyes practically bulged out of his head. "Or the rumor that I've got a rogue doctor on my staff using unapproved implants? Do you know the lawsuits we'd face? We have to protect ourselves."

As lawyers often do, Shala put it more eloquently. "What Dr. Fisher is saying is that before you tarnish the sterling reputation of our orthopedics department or one of its finest surgeons, why don't you focus on your most likely suspects first: Dr. Lock's disgruntled former resident and Dr. Lenny Reynolds."

Be a lot easier for the hospital if it was a resident, Ben thought. A PR nightmare, sure, but less so than if it was an esteemed surgeon with a wing named after him.

"Oh, we'll get our warrant," Becker said, blinking behind his glasses. "In the meantime, the Philly PD will continue to do its best monitoring the parks and try to keep an eye on the patients who've been discharged, but I don't need to tell you how much manpower that would take. Impossible, really. Family members will need to be very watchful."

"And we'll have the ME check for silver in the cadavers' implants." Patel's gaze homed in on Ben. "Sure would've been nice to know about the possibility of a stolen implant from the start. We would've paid more attention to them. If you don't want to end up living the highlife with the other pretty boys in prison, your secrets end here, got it, voodoo man?"

Dr. Fisher joined the pile-on. "And if you learn anything else, you come straight to me, Oris. And here I thought you were one of the smart ones. Holy bastard on a birthday card, you're lucky I don't kick you out of the program right now."

Ben swallowed and nodded at both of them. He knew enough not to bite back. And yet, despite the worry for his own hide, he was far more fearful for Sophia. She still had at least one, if not two days left in the hospital. Plenty of time for some psycho Wendigo to get attached to her—if Derek's theory was correct.

Someone needed to take a closer look at those implants and fast.

But although the cops might need a warrant, Ben did not.

# 34

She won't be here much longer, and yet it might as well be a lifetime, because I'm not sure I can hold the beast at bay until she's discharged.

With so much fear and paranoia circulating around the place, the others pay me little attention. Still, suspicious glances are everywhere, everyone wondering who among us could do such unspeakable acts. Even I catch myself asking who it could be, before I realize, you idiot, it's *you*. It's you the monster chose. It's you the monster rendered cold and hungry and soulless.

I've visited her. We all have. It's only natural, so while I'm no more a suspect than the others, I still take a risk in stopping by. But avoiding her would be like avoiding breathing, or thinking, or simply being.

I stare at her while she sleeps, our connection strong. Like the others—maybe even more so than the others—we were meant to be joined together, fused through breath and oxygen, coupled through flesh and bone.

I'm scared I'll be unable to wait. The hunger is ferocious. And how will I get to her? He watches her so closely. Everyone watches her so closely.

But I'll find a way. I stay prepared at every moment, so I'll find a way.

The sooner the better.

The beast is hungry.

## 35

During the evening hours, the north wing of Montgomery Hospital's surgical center was the only one in use, a steady stream (sometimes smooth, sometimes chaotic) of emergent bowel obstructions, appendectomies, motor vehicle accidents, and gunshot wounds coming its way. The other three wings, which housed space for outpatient surgeries and scheduled elective ones, bore the night-time silence of ghost towns.

At ten p.m. on Wednesday night, several hours after his gut-twisting encounter with the detectives in Dr. Fisher's conference room, Ben trekked through the quiet and deserted east wing, empty backpack slung over his shoulder. Dressed in clean scrubs and his white coat, he hoped he looked fresher than he felt, but despite his fatigue, he needed to check out the implants in the supply room.

After his meeting with the detectives, he had called and then texted Lenny, the news of the guy's flight from rehab a complete gut-punch. When no response followed either attempt, Ben had trotted to Lenny's downtown condo to make sure the chief resident wasn't near death from a drug overdose. Why else would he have left rehab? But upon seeing a cop car parked outside the complex, Ben did a quick one-eighty and beelined back to the hospital. He'd been given strict instructions by Detectives Becker and Patel to notify them if he heard from Lenny. Going to the chief resident's place behind their backs would only make him look more suspicious. If Lenny was in bad straits up in his apartment, the police would've found him. No doubt they were staking out his place to await his return from wherever it was he was holed up.

So instead, after confirming with Rita that she would spend the night in Sophia's hospital room, Ben had retrieved his car from the parking garage and drove to Willy's, where dinner with his father, Maxwell, and Laurette had temporarily buoyed him. Their reassurances about Sophia's well-being and their skepticism of Ben's likelihood of being charged with a crime were welcomed comforts, regardless of whether or not they were true.

But that lightness was now gone, and although he wanted nothing more than to crash at his apartment, which thanks to his call night he hadn't set foot in for almost forty hours, he'd driven back to the hospital to get a look at the implants. He needed to study them away from Dr. Lock and preferably outside of a corpse's severed limb. What he'd find, he didn't know. Probably nothing. But he had to at least try. Sophia's life might depend on it, and if that seemed dramatic, so be it. He wasn't about to leave her safety to chance. Didn't even dare wait until the police had the most recent victim's implant analyzed. Who knew how long that might take? Thankfully, according to the nurse he'd just called, Sophia was resting peacefully, Rita still by her side. "Everybody loves her," the RN had assured him. "Don't you worry, Dr. Oris."

Easier said than done.

Outside the restricted section of the OR, he swiped his ID badge over the security panel and entered the dim hallway. The closer he got to the central area housing the supply room, the brighter the fluorescent lighting and the louder the noise from the north wing. A combination of footsteps, brief verbal exchanges, whooshing operating room doors, and blipping monitors reached his ears. Still, it wasn't nearly as chaotic as he would have liked. More activity meant less chance of being spotted snooping around.

Approaching his destination, he peered down the north hallway to his right. A nurse pushed open a door and disappeared into an operating room, outside of which a surgeon scrubbed her forearms and hummed a tune, seemingly oblivious to her surroundings. Even from Ben's distance, he could smell the antiseptic scent of the foaming suds, and like a Pavlovian response, he gripped an imaginary scalpel in his hand. Although no one else was in the corridor at the moment, the footsteps and voices he'd just heard, along with a second scrub sink showing discarded brushes and towels in its vicinity, suggested that at least one other operating room was in use.

As if he had every right to be there—and technically he did—he strolled up to the supply room door. He'd only been inside the place once, back as an intern when he'd accompanied a circulating nurse, wanting to learn his way around its shelves. He'd figured there might come a time he needed to fetch something for an attending, and he didn't want to look like an idiot. But if he had every right to be there, why were his shoulders so tense and his stomach so knotted?

Before he could swipe the door open, a female voice behind him made him jump.

"Don't tell me we have another one coming in."

He spun around, his heart in his throat. A nurse wearing a surgical bonnet and scrubs spattered with blood along the hemline stared at him expectantly. She was one of the scrub nurses, but Ben couldn't remember her name.

"Um, no, just…" He gripped the strap of his backpack. Would she be curious about why he carried it?

"Phew, because that last one was tough. The guy was a bleeder. Artery sprayed everywhere."

"Is he okay?"

"Yeah, he'll be all right." She tucked a strand of escaped auburn hair back into her bonnet. "So no new surgery then? Aren't you with ortho?"

Sweat beads blossomed on his brow. "I am, yeah, but uh…no surgery coming in that I know of. I'm just checking on some hardware for our upcoming cases. Make sure everything got delivered."

"Well, have fun with that." She paused, smiled a bit flirtatiously, and then departed.

Wasting no more time, Ben swiped his badge and entered the supply room, the light already on. Racked shelving divided the space into three aisles, with additional units on the walls. Packed with everything from surgical tools to sterile apparel to bandages, the place could've been nicknamed Hospital Depot. A quick scan revealed no security camera.

Vaguely remembering that the orthopedic hardware was in the back, he weaved his way past scalpels, saws, cauterizing equipment, intravenous lines, and enough needles and syringes to make a trypanophobic flee in fright. (Derek, psychiatry whiz kid, would no doubt know that meant fear of needles.)

On the back row of shelves he found what he was looking for. Boxes of implants. Plenty of them. Given Montgomery Hospital was large and supported several orthopedic surgeons, the shelves were fully stocked with the required hardware of various brands for upcoming surgeries. Hip, knee, spinal. Check, check, check. While all the devices were fairly similar, each attending surgeon would no doubt preach for an hour about why their choice was the best.

Ben dropped his backpack to the floor and zeroed in on Lock's pile, third shelf down. Several colorful packages labeled Keplen Biomedics sat waiting their turn to shine. Each package consisted of four separate, shirt-sized boxes secured together by an outer sleeve bearing the company's logo, bar code, Lock's name, the patient's name, date of birth, surgical date, and lot number.

Ben slipped all four plastic-wrapped boxes out of the cardboard sleeve. Each one held sterile contents, and if he opened them, he would render the equipment inside unusable for the upcoming surgery. The intended patient was listed as Harold Thompson, scheduled for a knee replacement in two days. No doubt Harry, if he was allowed to go through with his surgery, would be mightily pissed if his implant was tampered with, not to mention Dr. Lock. The procedure would have to be postponed until another customized implant came in.

He stared at the four boxes stacked in his hands. Did he dare?

Even if he only opened the box containing the actual metal implants, he'd have to get rid of the associated components in the other three boxes as well. Make it look like the implant order never arrived.

*Shit.*

Worth risking his job for? His future career?

But patients were dying.

*Shit.*

He re-sleeved Harold Thompson's boxes and replaced them at the front of the shelf. Then he reached to the very back and grabbed another implant package, this one a knee replacement for Susan Brown. Her February twenty-first surgical date would allow two weeks before its absence was discovered.

Glancing in the direction of the door, grateful it was evening and relieved he was tucked away in the back of the room, he pulled the collection of boxes from their sleeve and ripped open the one that contained Susan Brown's customized implants, along with several sizes of inserts. The other three boxes he left intact on the shelf.

When he lifted the femoral component out its felt compartment, he saw it was packaged in such a way that unsterile hands could open the outer plastic wrap at its edges and dump the inner sterile-wrapped device onto the tray table, at which point the scrub nurse could handle it.

Ben hesitated. He took another moment to weigh what he was about to do, his heart rate climbing with each passing second. Once he violated the sterile packaging, the expensive implant could no longer be used. He closed his eyes.

*Screw it. Sorry, Susan.*

He tore open the femoral component.

Once the cool metal implant was in his hand—*no going back now*—he rotated it around to examine it. Although there was nothing unusual about the device itself, it quickly became apparent that it was *not* the implant inside Dr. Lock's patients. Similar shape and similar weight, sure, but the ones Lock used, the one Ben himself had drilled into Henry Paulson's joint, were shinier than these. He held the implant closer to the ceiling lights. Definitely a duller sheen.

A slow dread crept up his spine. Although he didn't completely understand the meaning of his find, he knew it couldn't be good. Did the hip implants show the same thing? The only way he could know was to violate another implant kit, but he didn't think that would be wise. One missing package might be explained as an inventory error. Two would not.

He retrieved his backpack from the floor, opened Susan Brown's remaining three boxes, and dumped all the contents into the bag. As a unit, the four boxes would never fit inside his bag, at least not without looking like he was carrying around a breadbox. Then he mashed up the cardboard boxes with their interior felt compartments and stuffed them into the backpack. The bag was still bulky and awkward, but it was the best he could do without leaving any evidence behind. In two weeks, Mrs. Brown's surgery would come up—assuming the police didn't shut it down—and Dr. Lock would collapse a lung hollering about the missing implant, but no one would be the wiser about its true demise.

Slinging his stuffed backpack over his shoulder, he hurried out of the supply room, and, hoping not to run into the coy nurse again, dashed up two flights of stairs to the orthopedic residents' lounge on the fourth floor. He needed one more piece of the puzzle.

At this late hour the room was deserted. Bypassing the couch, the TV, the coffee pot, and the bathroom, he veered to one of the two computers on the back counter and logged into the hospital system, backpack lodged between his feet. After typing in Henry Paulson's name, he went straight for the nurse's op note. The implant was listed as a Keplen, just like the ones Ben had seen in the supply room.

Fingers picking up speed, he searched for Kim Templeton's chart, clicked it open, and once again focused on the op note. Keplen. A hip implant. Hastily, he started clicking open the charts of any reconstructive patients he could remember, patients Lock and he had operated on over the past four weeks. All of them showed the same brand of implant.

He leaned back against the chair. Every device was a Keplen, just as Lock had said. Just like the OR director had said. Just like the op notes said.

But the implants Ben and Lock had been placing inside patients were not the same Keplen implants that were inside the supply room (and now inside Ben's backpack).

An uneasy vise gripped his chest. Had Lock stolen the chief resident's silver-coated implant idea four years earlier and turned it into a finished product? Was he performing some kind of implant bait and switch? A sleight of hand that required a consistent-team approach to avoid being caught? That would explain why he only allowed junior residents in his OR. As newbies, they'd have seen fewer joint reconstructions and would be less likely to catch on.

Was the device even approved? Was the esteemed surgeon using it for his own gain, making Ben and everyone else in his OR an unknowing accomplice?

Ben's shock fused with anger. Something like that could end his *own* career—assuming the police or Fisher didn't take it away first.

*But hold on, Benny Boy.* If Lock was switching implants, then where were the unofficial ones? Not in the supply room, that was for sure. And who was doing the switching? Lock himself? An unwitting recruit? Tara had told Ben that Lock only allowed Michael to fetch his implants.

Grinding his teeth, he figured only one place made sense. Lock's office. But searching it would be far riskier than entering a freely accessible supply closet. If he got caught, it would be sayonara for Dr. Benjamin Oris. Then again, wouldn't holding the proof in his hands protect him?

## 36

If the darkened OR suites were a ghost town at night, the wainscoted lobby of the Morrison building, which was on the second floor given its access off the skywalk, was a graveyard. Home of the residency academic offices and research facilities, most of the staff were long gone for the day, although a few might be toiling on the lower levels in the research labs.

Slinking toward the stairwell, Ben passed photograph after photograph of past and present chairpersons, their distinguished eyes following his every move. It was after eleven p.m., and all he wanted was his mattress and eight hours of sleep, but despite his post-call exhaustion, his distress over the implant discrepancy he'd found in the supply room had rattled him awake. Well, that and the coffee he'd poured before he left the residents' lounge.

A few months earlier, Ben had visited Dr. Smith in her second-floor office. Like tonight, it was after hours, but Ben had needed the internist's advice on an ortho patient with congestive heart failure. During their discussion, she'd spilled cranberry juice on her beige carpet and scurried to the bathroom for wet paper towels to blot the fibers. "The janitor doesn't come until after ten," she'd said. "Don't want a stain to set in." Ben had thought little about it at the time, but the memory came back to him now, because the only way he'd have access to Dr. Lock's office was if the janitor had unlocked the door.

The thought of what he was about to do made his stomach lurch. His feet fought the ascent in the stairwell and resisted the walk down the surgery department's administrative hallway, which housed everything from Lenny's postage-stamp of an office to Dr. Fisher's oak-paneled suite.

Assuming the janitor started on the lower floors, Ben had hoped the guy would be on the third floor by now, but no such luck. The corridor was dark and the office doors closed. Lock's was three-quarters of the way down. After a furtive glance toward the elevator, which Ben assumed the janitor would use given his cleaning cart, he tried turning the handle on Lock's door. It didn't budge.

*Shit.*

It was a long shot, anyway. He wondered how much time it would take the janitor to vacuum, clean bathrooms, and empty trashcans on each floor. He had no clue. The guy could pop out of the elevator in a few minutes or a few hours. Or worse, maybe he'd already been there. In the shadowy hallway, it was difficult to discern if the carpet had been vacuumed or not. No scent of cleaning chemicals in the air though.

Realizing a wait was in his future, Ben slipped into the men's bathroom two doors down from Lock's office. If the janitor found him, he'd simply claim he was doing research downstairs but came up to see if the chief resident was in his office. In the meantime, two stalls, two sinks, and scuffed tiled flooring would be his companions. Given the full trash can with bits of paper towels spilling over it, the custodian hadn't yet arrived.

*Good.* But how long would he have to wait? Was this a fool's errand? Could he really prove Dr. Lock's duplicity by sneaking into his office? He wasn't exactly Dick Tracy.

Stepping up to the sink, he splashed cold water on his stubbled face. When he looked up at the mirror, bloodshot eyes stared back at him. What in the hell was he doing? He had to be back at the hospital in seven hours.

With a wad of paper towels, he dried his hands and face. Thirty minutes. He'd give it thirty minutes, and then he'd leave.

It took barely five. Down the hall the elevator bell pinged, and from outside the bathroom a whistling tune materialized, growing louder with each squeak of a rolling cart. Soon the rolling and whistling stopped, and keys jangled in their place. Start, stop, start, stop. Ben imagined the janitor making his way down the long hallway, opening each door ahead of time for more efficient cleaning. Although the bathroom wouldn't need unlocking, Ben prepped himself with his story regardless.

But the guy didn't come in, just kept jangling keys until that sound too disappeared, this time under the roar of a vacuum.

Ben peeked his head out of the bathroom. The custodian was nowhere in sight, but a cord extended out of the first office near the stairwell, signaling he was vacuuming inside. Three other doors on each side of the hallway separated that office from Lock's. It was now or never.

Despite the thunder of the vacuum, Ben tiptoed to the surgeon's office. Second thoughts over what he was about to do pummeled him, but he shoved them away. Once inside, he closed the door, but, figuring that might look suspicious should the janitor notice it, he opened it back up an inch. In the stillness he didn't dare turn on the light, but with only one window to let in the city glow, he could see very little. Grabbing his phone from his lab coat, he clicked on the flashlight. With as jacked up as his nerves were, it might as well have been a beacon.

At the back of the office, his phone lit up a rich mahogany desk and a plush leather chair behind it. Two more high-back chairs fronted it, the same ones Ben and Joel had sat in at the start of their rotation a month before. "You want to do well on my service?" the attending had said. "Then show up early, read everything I give you, and follow orders. Do that, and we'll get along fine."

Ben suspected that after tonight, he and Lock would never "get along fine" again. Swallowing his reservations, which formed a thick lump in his throat, he scanned the rest of the office with his phone's flashlight. A small fridge and a bookshelf were to the left and a wooden file cabinet with large, deep drawers to the right. Two additional bookshelves flanked it. If the implants were in Dr. Lock's office, they were either in his desk or the file cabinet.

The vacuum's tone shifted, first louder and then quieting again. The janitor had moved to a new room. With time ticking away, Ben got to work, starting with the desk, his phone light the only illumination.

The smaller drawers held typical desk paraphernalia: pens, notepads, stapler, paper clips. The largest drawer had a lock.

*Might be the bingo winner.*

But it opened freely, and on the inside were only files. Although curious what Lock might keep in them other than journal articles, it wasn't the time to find out. With the vacuum still humming down the corridor, he darted to the file cabinet. The top drawer was unlocked and contained more files. No surprise there. But the bottom two drawers didn't budge.

Locked.

The vacuum's tone grew louder, the custodian moving one room closer. Ben wiped the corners of his mouth with his thumb and forefinger, debating the consequences of picking the lock. It crossed a line he wasn't eager to cross. Had he really expected otherwise though? A nice pile of silver implants wrapped up in a bow for him on the desk?

Thinking of Sophia and knowing he couldn't waste another second debating, he hustled back to the desk, grabbed two paperclips, and straightened one end of each. It wasn't the first time he'd picked a file cabinet lock. After Max died, Ben had to go through his office papers, Willy too fragile to do it himself. One of the drawers had been locked and, unable to find the key, Ben had easily picked it, just as he had the cheap locks on his former apartments whenever he'd locked himself out. He hoped his attending surgeon's cabinet would be equally compliant.

Crouched down with the phone secured between his teeth, its light clumsily aimed at the keyhole, Ben used the two paperclips to shift the lock to the right on the bottom drawer. It proved as easy to pick as his late father's file cabinet. It would not go unnoticed though. Scratches around the keyhole and likely some internal damage were the cost of admittance.

Knowing the custodian might only be two rooms away, Ben whipped the drawer open and shined his light on the contents inside the drawer.

*Bingo.*

A large stack of implant boxes.

He lifted one out and noticed that unlike the implants in the supply room, there was only one box per patient, not four, but similar to those in the supply room, a label identified the patient's name, DOB, and surgery date.

With his heartbeat thumping his ribs, he removed more boxes, flipping through them until he found one in Susan Brown's name. The deep drawer held eight boxes, all knee implants. The hips were probably in the middle drawer. He put the others back, and, knowing he'd already tainted its counterpart in the supply room, he ripped open Susan Brown's implant box, sparing a quick glance over his shoulder at the slightly open door.

Inside the box, he found the femoral and tibial components of her knee device, each wrapped in an interior layer of sterile packaging like the ones in the supply room. But even through the plastic, with nothing but his phone's flashlight, he could tell their surfaces were shinier than those he'd seen earlier, not by much, but enough to stand out. Whether it was a silver coating that gave them their sheen or something else, he didn't know. What he *did* know was that this was the implant they'd been using, not the ones in the supply room.

With the box in his hand, he stood, his knees cracking from the crouched position. He exhaled slowly and imagined Michael retrieving the implant box from Lock's office, switching it with the one inside the Keplen Biomedics package, and then the unwitting circulating nurse dumping the twin implant onto the surgical tray, none the wiser. Or did Lock himself make the switch? More importantly, did this have anything to do with the murders? And if so, did it exonerate Lock as the killer, or did his bizarre behavior only shoot him to the top of the list?

Far too many questions, but no time to answer them, because the vacuum crescendoed and de-crescendoed again, and this time it was coming from the adjacent room. Spurring to action, Ben stuffed the implant box into his already full backpack and closed the cabinet drawer. Come morning, he'd call Dr. Fisher. Although he hated to involve Michael if he was an unwitting accomplice, he had no choice but to report it. He just prayed he wasn't wrong and that some simple explanation didn't exist.

*Shit.*

With a mouthful of uncertainty, he turned off his phone light and pivoted to leave. When he looked up, he drew in a sharp intake of breath. The door he'd left barely ajar a few minutes earlier was now opened all the way.

## 37

The overhead light in the office clicked on. In the doorframe stood Dr. Lock, tall, imposing, jaw rigid, eyes unreadable. His jeans and parka suggested an after-hours office run and not a night on call.

Several wordless seconds passed between them. Ben's heart thumped so loudly in his ears it almost drowned out the vacuum down the hall.

Releasing the door handle, Dr. Lock stepped forward. His gaze found the backpack hanging from Ben's shoulder. "And to think I thought you'd be the next rock-star resident." His tone was controlled and steely, the way a hitman might speak to his mark right before he blew him away. "One call to Fisher, and you're out of this program."

Ben gripped the strap of his backpack. "I'm sorry. But I…I had to know."

"Had to know what, exactly?"

"About the implants." Annoyed by his own kowtowing, Ben willed his nerves to chill out. "Do what you gotta do, but I think Fisher's going to want to hear from both of us. Why are you switching the devices?"

Down the hall the vacuum powered off, leaving the deafening buzz of sudden silence. This was followed by the sound of a cord dragging along the carpet. "Hello, is someone here?" a gravelly voice called out.

Dr. Lock leaned back into the hallway. "It's just me, Travis. Working in my office for a bit. No need to clean in here."

"You want me to get the trash—"

Lock closed the door on the janitor and strode closer to Ben. "Not that I have to explain myself to you, but ever heard of blinded studies?"

Ben's mouth opened, but nothing came out. Research methodology? That was what the device switcheroo was about?

"Yeah, that's right, you can close your trap now. Not quite worth losing your job over, was it?" Dr. Lock advanced another foot, shortening the distance between them. "Now hand over whatever you took from me and get your ass out of here before you screw up my research even more."

*He's lying.* "Lenny's worried you stole his implant design. Said you had it developed and are using it as your own." *Lenny, where the hell are you?*

Lock threw up his hands, the fabric of his parka swishing against itself. "What do I look like? An engineer? I hammer the things in, I don't make them."

Ben still wasn't convinced. Too many pieces of the puzzle were missing, and too many things were at stake if he backed down prematurely, starting with the next severed limb and ending with Sophia.

"Oh, come on," Lock said, reaching for the backpack. "You're going to take the word of a drug addict over mine? What, you didn't think I knew his secret? Please. Wasn't hard to figure out." He shook his head. "I really overestimated you, Oris."

"The police will have the implants analyzed, you know. Maybe they already have."

"So what? I have nothing to hide. It's all perfectly legit. It's not my fault Reynolds is weaving doped-up theories."

"Did you get the device approved? Within just a few years?" Ben wasn't sure of the logistics. Drugs took a long time from testing to approval. Was the same true for medical hardware?

"You don't know what you're talking about."

"Does Michael switch them for you?"

The attending surgeon's face flushed, and he spoke through clenched teeth, his earlier control gone. "Hand. Them. Over. And get out now. You're finished at Montgomery."

Despite Ben's determination to learn the truth and keep Sophia and the rest of the patients safe, the fear of losing his position and his career gave him serious pause. Between that and his extreme fatigue, his thinking grew muddled, and he struggled to know what to believe. What if Lock *was* doing blinded research? What if the new implant wasn't Lenny's idea at all but someone else's, and Lock had simply chosen to study it? Had Ben fallen into Lenny's conspiracy theory? A case of mass—or in this case, duo—hysteria?

But just as his hold on his backpack loosened, the words of a woman from a few years ago resurfaced in his mind, back when he was swirling in a storm of otherworldly uncertainty. "Be true to yourself," she had told him. And right now, the truest and most important thing was Sophia. He could risk a reprimand for falsely accusing Lock of fraud—dismissal from the program, even, although it would devastate him—but he could not risk trusting Lock if it meant losing the mother of his child.

His grip on the bag and the contents inside once again tightened. "I'm sorry. I mean no disrespect, but I have to take these to Fisher. If what you're saying is true, then I'll be the one strung up by the balls, not you."

Lock's face was still a cinnamon hue and his jaw jutted forward, but Ben detected worry in his eyes too. Outside the office the vacuum returned to life, quieter now with the door closed. "Give me the implants. I'll take them to Fisher myself." He held out his hand.

"I'm sorry. I have Sophia to consider. I can't risk—"

"You think I'm not worried about Sophia too? You don't think I've spent every spare minute by her side, watching her, making sure she's okay? Why do you think I'm here at this hour?"

Icy shards prickled Ben's skin. What was it Derek had said about

Wendigos? Something about their victims not being random, but rather people who the Wendigo had a strong, "even intimate," connection with?

Ben had to get out of there. And fast.

"I'm leaving now," he said. "And I'm taking these with me. If you really want what's best for Sophia, you'll understand." Without waiting for a response, he strode to the door. He never reached it. Instead, Dr. Lock grabbed him and shoved him against the wall. More shocked than injured, Ben floundered to keep hold of the backpack.

Lock exhaled hot, stale breath into Ben's face. "Last chance, Oris. Give me the implants and we'll forget this ever happened. You keep your mouth shut, my research stays pure. I keep my mouth shut, you stay in the program. Maybe even collect that pretty little research grant you're all creaming your jeans for."

*Humanitarian, philanthropic, devout Christian, my ass.*

Ben pressed the pilfered implants more tightly against his chest. "Sorry. Can't do it."

With all the playground battles Ben had fought as a kid, he should've seen it coming. But clairvoyance was murkier when the aggressor was an esteemed and respected surgeon, and never in a million years had Ben's rational mind expected Lock to grab his doctor's coat, yank him forward, and throw a punch at his face.

Ben ducked just in time, and Lock's fist hit the wall. A crunch and a holler followed, giving Ben the opportunity to sidestep his attending and scramble toward the door. Yanking it open, he sprinted down the hall and flew past the open-mouthed janitor holding a trash can.

Without looking back, he bolted down the stairs and through the lobby of the Morrison building, its photographed chairmen and women probably as stunned by his flight as the custodian. Hearing no footsteps behind him, he assumed Lock had stayed behind. As he raced back to the hospital and then to the parking deck, he could hardly believe what he'd just done.

The question was, what had he sabotaged by doing it?

## 38

Early the next morning Ben had no idea if he still had a job, but he roused himself out of bed at five thirty and dumped himself into the shower just the same. After a mug of strong coffee, he felt at least fifty percent human. The fifty percent that was zombie was still a groggy mess who needed far more than the five hours of sleep he'd nabbed. Thank God Maxwell was with Willy. Ben wasn't great father material right now. He glanced at the bulging backpack on the butcher-block table. *What have you done?* the implants inside seemed to cry.

Who should he call first? Dr. Fisher or Detective Becker? Although the cop might slap him with a B & E charge, staying quiet could lead to even more trouble. Since he hadn't been dragged out of bed and arrested during his brief but comatose slumber, he assumed Dr. Lock hadn't notified the police himself. Might be a weak assumption though. On the other hand, Lock calling Fisher seemed almost a certainty. Anything could be waiting for Ben at the hospital.

After unplugging his phone from the charger near the bed, he checked the screen for messages or calls that might have come in during his shower. Nothing. No pissed-off detectives. No threatening attending surgeons. No rehab-escaping chief residents. It'd been thirteen hours since Ben learned Lenny had jumped ship from rehab, but all of his text messages and phone calls to the guy remained unanswered. Nothing from Laurette either, but Ben hadn't yet confessed to her his theft of the implants. He'd simply raced out of the hospital, driven home, and collapsed.

Knowing he couldn't wander around his apartment in a stupor forever, he slipped his feet into his leather Eccos, pulled on his jacket, and emptied his backpack of the mashed-up boxes and implant accessories. He left only the metal devices inside, both those from the supply room and the ones from Lock's office.

When he reached for the doorknob, someone knocked. For a paralyzing moment, he thought the police had come for him after all.

"Ben, are you in there?" Mrs. Sinclair said from the other side. "I was hoping to catch you before you left. It's not like I can sleep anyway."

He exhaled in relief and opened the door. His landlady, wearing a terrycloth robe, stepped into his apartment, and, making a rare basement appearance, Izzy darted in behind her. The cat must have noticed Sir Quincy's absence over the past few days. Nonetheless, her slinking movements around Ben's kitchen remained cautious lest the canine interloper return.

"Is everything okay?" Ben asked.

Edith's hand fumbled for the light switch to the right of the entryway. "I can't see a thing. It's too dark in here for me."

He flipped it on for her. "Sorry. I was just about to leave."

"I won't keep you long." She shuffled the three-foot distance to his living room recliner and eased herself down, her vein-mapped legs extending from her robe like swizzle sticks. "Just let me sit a minute."

"You okay?" He squatted down next to her. The scents of cold cream and fabric softener greeted him. "Is it your eyes? Should I call your doctor? I could see if Laurette could take you again."

"I'll be fine. Just my usual morning dizziness. Standing makes it worse, especially when I can't see anything in front of me but that damn black dot." She honked her nose with a tissue from her pocket. "Getting old is just awful. I don't recommend it."

From his crouched position, he squeezed her forearm. "You know I'd make your vision perfect if I could. Sorry I haven't gotten to your cabinet yet. I'll fix it this weekend, promise." As if by the touch of a ghost, one of her kitchen cupboards kept opening, the hinges shot. She'd already walked into it once and cut her cheek.

"I know you will, dear. Don't know what I'd do without you." She patted the hand he'd placed on her forearm. "But that's not why I'm here. I wanted to make sure you got the note."

"What note?"

"The one I slipped under your door last night." She slowly scooted to the edge of the recliner, as if in her vertigo she feared tumbling off. "I hope it wasn't anything important, but the man who dropped it off seemed to think it was."

Ben was already on his feet, scouring the linoleum around the door. Inside his coat and still disoriented from lack of sleep, he felt like an overheated, malfunctioning robot, one whose warning button had just been pushed. "I don't understand. What man?"

"Last night, around eight, I think it was."

"Who was it?"

"I have no idea, but he seemed quite agitated when I told him you weren't home. Pleasant enough fellow, but he was sweating and he talked really fast. Asked me for some paper so he could leave you a note. I pointed to the notepad I keep by my phone in the kitchen. He was in such a hurry that with my eyes, it was easier to just let him get it himself."

"You let him into your house?"

"He said he worked with you. Flashed me his hospital ID badge, though of course I couldn't read it."

Every tiny hair on the back of Ben's neck pricked up. "What did he look like?"

"You're asking the blind bat?" She fluttered her lips. "He was taller than me, that's all I know."

Everyone's taller than you, Ben thought.

"Oh, and he had a baseball cap on, but I don't know about hair color. I suggested he call you, but he thrust the note at me and darted out the door faster than a cat in heat." Mrs. Sinclair started wringing her hands. "Oh no, is something wrong? I can't tell by your face, but I can see you pacing all over."

"I'm just looking for the note." He tried to keep the stress out of his voice.

"I tried to read it, you know, but of course I couldn't, not even with my magnifying glass. The scrawl is too messy." She seemed on the verge of crying. "I hope I didn't mess anything up for you."

Ben stopped his search and sank back down to put an arm around her. "Hey, you didn't mess anything up. It's not your fault he didn't call me."

In his awkward position, he shifted his foot, and when he did, a flash of white peeked out from under the recliner. It was the note. Either his landlady had slid it under the door with enough force to send it sailing under the chair or he'd inadvertently stepped on it and kicked it there himself.

He released Mrs. Sinclair and grabbed it. In shaky, scrawled penmanship, the note said: *I'm sorry. Tried to see you before I left. They'll blame me for everything, so I have to. I tried, I really did. Call me at this number if you want but not from your cell. They might track it. I hope you don't hate me for what I've done. For what I'm about to do.*

Ben's throat constricted. A dense fear washed over him.

"What's it say?" Edith asked. "What's wrong?"

The number to call was listed, but when Ben tried to read the signature, all he could make out was an *L*. The rest of the name was smudged. Mrs. Sinclair had said the visitor was sweating, but it was a drop of sweat in the worst place.

With wobbly legs, he stood. His landlady rose too, gripping the armrest for support, distress still etched on her face.

*L.* Had to be Lenny. Lock seemed unlikely to leave a note like this. But why hadn't Lenny called since he left rehab? And what had he done, aside from taking Sampson's limb? Worse, what was he *about* to do?

Sophia.

Bile rose in Ben's throat. Was she the *for what I'm about to do* part?

"Why aren't you saying anything? You're scaring me, Ben."

"I...I have to go. I have to make sure Sophia's okay."

He snatched up his backpack with the twin implants and guided Mrs. Sinclair out the door with him. Before he closed it all the way, Izzy shot through, making a quick escape.

If only Ben could do the same. But he had to get to the hospital. He had to make sure Sophia was still safe.

## 39

Despite Ben's mounting dread, nothing unusual awaited him up on 4 East. No program director to boot him out of his residency. No Dr. Lock to accuse him of being a breaking-and-entering thief. No Dr. Fisher to suspend him from surgeries until hell froze over. Nothing but a hospital unit coming to life, with overhead lights flicking on, kitchen staff rolling breakfast carts down the hall, and nurses rushing to finish last minute tasks before seven-o'clock shift change. Several of them greeted Ben. One at the counter, a stout woman named Nancy, told him Sophia had done well overnight and was still resting comfortably.

Although he'd already checked in on Sophia (she was sleeping) and said good morning to Rita who was resting on the convertible chair-bed, he thanked Nancy for the update. His relief over Sophia's smooth recovery was great, but any zen it gave him was canceled out by the stress of knowing he had two pilfered implants stuffed away in his locker. What would Lock do when he saw him?

An early morning call to Detective Becker, which Ben had made even though it could land him in the slammer, had as of yet gone unanswered. A call to Fisher would be next, but Ben would wait until he finished pre-rounds. Getting behind on his patients, of which there were plenty from his recent call night, would only guarantee Fisher's boot on his ass.

"Did Sophia need any pain meds overnight?" Ben asked Nancy.

"Oh, I didn't have her, actually. Just passing on what Lyle told me."

"Lyle?" What was the recovery room nurse doing on the ward?

His answer came swiftly. Lyle, dressed in the same light blue scrubs as Ben, strolled up to the counter and sat behind a computer terminal.

"Don't you work in the PACU?" Ben asked.

"I do."

"So why are you here?"

Nancy answered for him. "We haven't been as busy up here, you know, with some elective surgeries getting canceled…" The implication of her unspoken words was clear. "So our nursing supervisor has been cutting back on our overnight staff. But last night we got busy with some emergent admissions, so she called Lyle to come in."

"Put myself on the back-up list for extra hours," Lyle said. "Doesn't matter to me whether it's up here or in recovery—a paycheck's a paycheck. But I'll be relieved to get out of here in a few minutes. Long night."

An attending for one of Ben's patients surged through the double doors. Ben left the nurses and hustled to room 426 to check on the patient before the surgeon got there. For the next forty-five minutes, he completed the rest of his pre-rounds. Karen had yet to show up, and he wondered if she'd gotten tied up in an emergent surgery. Joel, too, was late. As his resident, Ben knew he'd have to reprimand the student when he saw him, but his heart wasn't into it. Too much else on his mind and no doubt on Joel's too.

Judging by the serious faces of the hospital staff and the absence of the usual chatter, Ben wasn't alone in his unease. Everyone seemed to be feeling the effects of the murders: A student nurse dropped a plastic wash basin, soapy water spilling everywhere. An intern ordered the wrong antibiotic for a patient. A family member refused to step out of her mother's room during a procedure. Said she needed to make sure her mom "remained in one piece."

Everyone was distracted. Everyone was on edge. No one had any answers.

At a quarter to eight there was still no sign of Dr. Lock (and therefore no indication that formal rounds with him would begin any time soon), but at least Ben had reached Dr. Fisher, who'd told him to stop by his office at eight o'clock sharp. "Show me what you need to show me, Oris," he'd said, cutting Ben off before he could explain his implant find, "but it better be quick. My schedule is jammed with press conferences and media handholding. That third murder elevated this shit-storm to a grade five tsunami. Apparently Barbara Simmons was an assistant producer at a local news station. Holy maggots on a mango."

Ben was tempted to add, *Just wait 'til you see what your prized Dr. Lock has been up to*, but Fisher had hung up before he could.

When he finished with his last patient, he checked on Sophia again. Her bed was empty and the shower was running. The chair-bed was back to being a chair, and Rita had left Ben a note on the cushion saying she'd slipped downstairs for breakfast while Sophia was showering but would be back before Ben needed to leave. *She likes to sit on the plastic bench in there under the hot water forever*, Rita's note said, the word *forever* underlined and followed by a smiley face. Ben figured he could spare another ten minutes on the ward to watch Sophia before he ran to Fisher's office. He returned to the counter and saw Karen had finally shown up.

"Good. Need to update you on a few patients," he said.

She looked up from a computer terminal, her hair pulled back and her complexion washed-out. The salmon sweater she wore over her scrubs did little to infuse her with color. "Where's Lock?" she asked.

"Good question."

"Well dammit, I've got surgery at eight thirty."

"Me too." *At least I think I do.*

The senior resident glanced up at the clock behind the counter and gritted her teeth. When Angela exited a patient room, her white coat buttoned up, its pockets full, Karen called out, "Where's your boss?"

Angela, who seemed lost in thought, jumped at the sharp inquiry and then shrugged. Ben tried to imagine the two women as Wendigos—or any of the team members, for that matter—chomping on human flesh and chopping off silver-contaminated limbs. He almost laughed out loud it was so absurd.

"How can you not know where he is?" Karen snapped at Angela. "Haven't you called him? And Ben, where's your useless med student? I need him to follow-up some labs for me. The ward blew up last night with new admissions."

"Of course I've called Dr. Lock." Some of Angela's spunk returned. "He hasn't answered, and he always answers, so don't think I'm not frustrated too. I've got orders I need approved. I spoke to Dr. King down in anesthesiology, and he hasn't heard from him either. This job's driving me crazy," she said through clenched teeth. "I'd go back to working in a nursing home if it paid better."

Karen shook her head in frustration and turned to Ben. "Guess we'll do our rounds without Lock. Just give me the abridged version on your guys' patients."

When Ben and Angela finished their abbreviated reports, Angela and Karen took off. Ben was about to see if Rita was back so he could race to Fisher's office when howling ensued down the hall. A second later a nurse flagged him down and yelled, "We need you in here. Now!"

He ran to room 425, where a patient was screaming that he couldn't feel his legs. He'd had a spinal abscess drained two days earlier. Although not Ben's patient, no other residents were around to step in, so after performing a neurological exam, he realized the man had indeed lost sensation in his lower limbs. Worried the abscess had reaccumulated—or something worse—Ben ordered a stat imaging study. While he was doing that, another calamity happened two doors down. A woman's cast was too tight, cutting off the circulation in her foot. While Ben was dealing with that problem, Fisher called to ask where the hell he was. It was now almost eight thirty, and not only had Ben missed his appointment with the chairman, he was late for his first surgery. Assuming Lock would allow him to scrub in.

Once the ortho tech arrived, Ben left him to finish applying the new cast. He hurried off toward the exit, stopping at Sophia's room one more time. Her bed remained empty. Thinking she was fixing her hair, he checked the bathroom, but that too was vacant. Discomfort tightened his throat. Where was she? Was she getting an X-ray? If so, who ordered it? And where was Rita?

He returned to the counter to ask Sophia's nurse, but as he did so, Rita came running down the corridor, her long cardigan flapping open against the guardrail. Full-figured with chestnut hair like her sister's, the woman wore a mask of fear. When she reached Ben, she grasped both of his arms and panted. "I can't find her, Ben. I can't find her anywhere. She was coming to meet me and I said no and—"

"Wait. Slow down. Tell me what happened." Ben hoped he looked calmer than he felt, but on the inside his stomach had just found his knees and his pounding heart threatened to set off a nearby alarm.

"I was downstairs getting breakfast." Rita still spoke rapidly. "Sophia was getting ready in the bathroom, but then she texted me and said since she needed to get some walking in, she'd just meet me in the cafeteria. Said she was sick of the ugliness of 4 East."

"Didn't you tell her to wait for you?"

"Of course I did, but I didn't see her text right away—maybe a couple minutes after she sent it—and when I texted her back to stay put, that I'd walk with her, she never returned my text. And now she's not in her room. She's not in the cafeteria either, I checked."

"Maybe you missed each other. Maybe she's in the elevator now. Maybe she tried to text you, but the signal was bad." Ben knew he was grasping at invisible threads, but this couldn't be happening. Sophia had been in their sights almost every freaking minute.

He spun around to Sophia's day nurse, a statuesque woman who'd been listening to the exchange, her eyes wide with concern. "Call security," Ben sputtered to her. At that moment his pager beeped a message. It was the OR, wondering when he and Dr. Lock would get there. "We're getting backed up!" the message shouted in all caps.

So no Sophia.

And no Dr. Lock.

A hot ball of dread ignited in Ben's gut. He sprinted off down the hall.

# 40

It must've been fate, because taking her was easy. As I drive back to work, I replay the scene in my mind, barely able to concentrate on the road.

I was looking into the morning delay, wondering what was holding things up, when just a few steps from the elevator there she was, in the small hallway between the restrooms and the elevator, dressed in a hospital robe over a hospital gown and pushing a walker, a purse slung over her shoulder. Thanks to my usual fore-sightedness, I'd been carrying my supplies in my pocket, never sure when or if the moment might come when I could take her with me. She was simply too closely watched. But the beast could barely wait an hour let alone a day or two until her discharge.

"Look at you, up and walking," I said, trying to camouflage the beast inside me. "I thought I'd check in again. See how you're doing."

"That's nice of you," she replied. "I'm headed to the cafeteria for breakfast with my sister. Can't take the ugliness of my room anymore. Or the runny eggs."

We both laughed. "Here, I'll go down with you. Safely deliver you to her." I grabbed one of the two folded wheelchairs leaning against the wall and pushed the down button on the elevator. My mind raced. Did an old hospital like Montgomery have cameras inside the elevators? Maybe. So might the corridors of the ward itself. But the two single bathrooms behind us or this connecting hallway? A quick scan of the ceiling said no.

"Oh, I won't need that," she said, pointing to the wheelchair, the elevator door dinging open.

"Just as a precaution." I smiled reassuringly. Despite my inner turmoil, the monster gave me outer strength. I glanced around and confirmed we were alone.

"I'll show *you*," she said, taking my words as a challenge. She gripped her walker and started for the elevator.

Before she reached it, I—or was it the monster?—grabbed her around the waist and yanked her and her walker inside one of the unisex bathrooms behind us.

"What are you—" She stumbled, fell against the sink, and slammed onto the floor, her cry cutting short. In her stunned state, I pulled the syringe from my pocket and uncapped it. I raised her gown and stabbed the needle into her thigh.

When she found her voice again—her knee must have been in so much pain—I clamped my hand over her mouth. The monster part of me was so excited that my human fear barely showed, but deep inside my core, it screamed. Before when I took souls, there was a moral reasoning, a call from a divine power. Now there's only greed and hunger and an insatiable monster.

Given the injection was intramuscular and not intravenous (her IV line had already been removed), subduing her took a few minutes, but thanks to her recent surgery and weakened state, it wasn't too difficult. With my hand still pressed over her mouth, muffling her protests, I pinned her against the floor tile until she fell asleep.

Once she did, I rose, cracked open the bathroom door, and, seeing no one in the small hallway, quickly grabbed the wheelchair by the elevator and pulled it into the bathroom. After I eased her onto it, I slung her walker over my forearm, and together we descended a flight and hurried through the skywalk that led to the parking deck. Thankfully my car wasn't far away. Although a sleeping patient in a wheelchair was no anomaly in a hospital, going outdoors without our coats on was. But soon the heat from my dash was blowing, and even though the human part of me recognized the horror of what the beast made me do, I couldn't help but smile. Everything was going perfectly.

We arrived at my place, and I removed her from my car, her slumberous breaths deep and full. As I eased her back onto the wheelchair, which had fit nicely inside my trunk, the monster could barely keep from devouring her flesh right there. The scent of her cucumber-melon shampoo, the feel of her cottony skin, the pulse of her beating heart. Our longing is not sexual—not at all. It's pure hunger. Lust for the flesh in its truest and most literal form. Dear God, was I salivating? But the time wasn't right, so I stood back up, away from her intoxicating aroma.

Then, before I could grab her purse from the seat and close the passenger door, something awful happened. I discovered I was no longer alone.

He was there, standing in the driveway, watching everything I was doing. In my hunger and anticipation, I hadn't even heard him arrive.

I was so confused. Why had he come to see me? What did he want?

For a moment we stood, open-mouthed, looking at each other, his eyes going back and forth between me and the slumped woman in the wheelchair. By now, without my coat, I was shivering violently.

With disbelief in his voice, he said, "It's you."

Even with the beast inside me, I panicked. Then the man panicked. When he rushed toward me, the beast acted. I was simply the marionette it controlled.

I reached into my car and pulled out one of the metal center punches I keep in the side compartment of each door, the kind that shatters a window for escape if you ever get trapped under water. I stepped away from the vehicle and plunged the pointy end of the tool into the man's neck, hardly even aware of what I was doing.

After I pulled it out—*thwuck*—I stabbed it in again—*thwack*. Right where I knew it would do the most harm.

His shock was as great as my own, but I had to kill him. I had no choice. We weren't done yet. The beast would have it no other way, not with the meal of flesh and bone so close at hand. So, despite my self-loathing, I killed the man in cold blood. Above all else, that should prove I'm no longer in control.

It took time for him to bleed out, and it made a mess on the ground, but we were far away from prying eyes, and the blood mostly splattered the snowy mulch, which was easy enough to kick around and conceal. Moving him, however, was no easy task. I dragged him as best I could to a spot where he couldn't be seen. It wasn't a permanent solution. He'd need to be better hidden. But at that moment I had to leave. She was starting to stir in the cold, and I needed to get her up to the safe room and back to sleep quickly. If she begged for her child, I might plunge that very center punch into my own neck before the beast could stop me.

I wheeled her toward the hiding place, the outdoor path uneven and bumpy. Despite her semi-alert state, settling her in took a Herculean strength I didn't know I possessed. Up until now, I'd left them groggy but awake for this part, my knife incentive enough for them to climb up the ladder with my help, especially in their dazed states. But without the monster's determination inside me, I doubt I would've gotten her inside. Twice her grip slipped and her body weight fell down on me. In the bitter cold, my hands shook and my legs wobbled perilously. Will the ice in my veins never thaw? But finally I settled her in, her whimpering growing louder, and once I sedated her again, I laid out the comfort items I had at the ready: food, water, soft music, a bucket, a thick blanket. At least the beast allowed me this much. There was no worry of escape. No one would see her. No one would hear her.

With one last look at her robust flesh and rich hair, the beast quivering with hunger, I crawled out, locked the door, and pocketed the key. We'd consume her tonight. She'd be one with us, part of us, her blood coursing through ours, her soul forever at peace. Just like the others before her.

The human part of me, the part that now ruminates about her while I drive, knows this will all come to an end. It has to. And for that I feel relief. It'll finally be over. Maybe knowing that I welcome the end will make others judge me less harshly. My actions are beyond comprehension, yes, but maybe they'll see it's not me who controls them. It's the beast. Like the opioid to the addict, the mouse to the lion, the chum to the shark, this horned and putrid monster must consume human flesh and bone. And though our feeding will have to wait, just knowing she's there keeps our hunger at bay, at least long enough for me to play my other role, because if I fail, our most prized catch will be for nothing.

So for now, I'll return to the person they think I am. I'll continue to play the part and hope I play it well. Because I'm trying. Dear God, I'm trying.

## 41

With growing panic, Ben scoured every nook of the hospital where Sophia might have gone: cafeteria, gift shop, patient library, pediatric ward. He even checked the oncology floor. It wouldn't be the first time she'd stopped in to visit the cancer patients. Her heart was huge, and as a cancer survivor herself, she was always first in line at her church to help others navigate its wicked terrain. Brought them meals, drove them to appointments, helped the women fix whatever hair they had left after chemo.

His gait grew unsteady, and on the way out of the oncology ward he had to grab the corridor's wooden guardrail for support. Was she in the hands of a killer at this very moment? A psychotic and unstable maniac who severed limbs and dined on human flesh? He doubled over, unable to breathe at the thought.

"Ben? Are you okay?"

Somebody grabbed his arm and helped him upright. His eyes recognized Dr. Smith before his brain did.

"What's wrong? Are you sick?" Dressed in a wool suit, her white coat starched to its usual stiffness, his mentor guided him down the hallway into an empty waiting room around the corner. Once he was seated on a padded chair with thin armrests, she fetched him a cup of water from a gurgling dispenser across the room. "Here, drink this."

Not having consumed anything since his early morning coffee over three hours before, he guzzled it. He crinkled the paper cup in his hand and rested his head against the wall. "Sophia's missing. I can't find her anywhere."

Dr. Smith inhaled sharply. "Oh Ben, no. Has security been notified?"

"Yes. The police too, including the detectives on the case." He leaned forward, his elbows on his knees. "I saw her when I came in this morning. Her sister was with her. We've tried not to leave her alone, you know? But when I checked back she was in the shower, so her sister ran down for a quick bite to eat. And then…and then I got so busy, and Sophia just slipped out for a minute, and now it's my fault, and—"

"This is *not* your fault. You did everything you could."

"If I had just checked on her more. If I had just gone back a few more times, she—"

"Stop." Dr. Smith rubbed his back, an act that would have been unthinkable when he was a med student on her service, the two of them circling each other like matador and bull. "For all you know, she's probably still in the hospital, unaware people are looking for her."

Ben doubted his mentor really believed that. "I feel like my hands are tied," he said. "I don't know where to go. I asked another resident to cover my patients, but I'm not sure what to do next."

"How can I help? Tell me what you need from me. I could take Maxwell. I have an administrative day."

"Thanks, but my dad has that covered. I called him. Told him not to let Maxwell out of his sight." A noose tightened around Ben's neck and squeezed his throat closed.

"The police will find her."

He hoped that was true, but they didn't know any more than he did. After realizing Sophia was missing, in addition to calling Willy, Ben had immediately called Laurette. She promised to call Derek right away, as well as Detectives Becker and Patel. She would also check Sophia's apartment in the unlikely chance Sophia had checked out against medical advice. Ben countered that she would never do that, but then Laurette reminded him she'd done that very thing once before, back when Maxwell was born, and it gave him momentary hope. While they were still on the line, he texted her a picture of Lenny's note—at least he assumed it was from Lenny—and told her to show it to the detectives. Ben still couldn't imagine Lenny as a killer, nor could he imagine him hurting Sophia, but he was long past protecting the guy now. Twice from a hospital phone he'd tried calling the number written on the note but had received no answer either time.

"Who do you think…" Dr. Smith hesitated, as if not sure she should ask.

"Who do I think took her? I have no idea. But I haven't seen the saintly and revered Dr. Lock all morning. No one has." Ben's tone was biting.

"You can't possibly think he's the killer."

The back of Ben's head thumped the wall. "I don't know what to think." Figuring the news would get out soon enough, he told her about the implants he'd found in Lock's office and Lenny's theory that the surgeon had stolen his idea. "I still haven't told Fisher about them. He needs to know. Detective Becker too. But all I can think of right now is Sophia. I've been too busy looking for her." The image of Maxwell crying for his mother popped into his mind, and an involuntary moan escaped his lips.

"Don't worry. I'll take care of it for you." As if eager to have a task to perform, Dr. Smith sat ramrod straight. If she was concerned about Ben's unscrupulous manner in snatching the implants, she kept it to herself. "I'll let Dr. Fisher know about them, and he can notify the detectives. You just focus on Sophia."

"Really? You'd do that? I don't want to get you in trouble too."

"Please, if Dr. Lock really is conducting unapproved research with an unapproved medical device, your little B & E will be nothing but a sneeze in a hurricane."

Ben allowed a small smile. Dr. Smith did not take ethics violations in research lightly. "One stinky plum in the bunch gives us all a bad name," she'd once told him.

"Where are the implants?" she asked.

"In my backpack inside my locker in the orthopedics residents' lounge. Do you know where that is?" When she nodded, Ben texted her his locker number and padlock combination. "I can't thank you enough. Really. I'm sorry to involve you. I owe you big time."

"Owe me? Quite the opposite. I'm afraid Joel would fail this clerkship if not for you." She grimaced. "And if Dr. Lock is a killer on top of a fraud, this whole hospital will owe you."

With that, she squeezed Ben's shoulder and, like a tiny version of The Flash, dashed out of the oncology waiting room, the heels of her designer pumps clicking on the hospital tile.

In her absence, Ben's despondency and feeling of powerlessness returned. With fisted hands, he pounded his thighs through his scrubs. He had to do something. Anything. There must be someplace else he could look.

Lenny's condo came to mind. Although yesterday the surveillance car outside had kept Ben away, today was a different day. Sophia was missing. If he was caught entering (he still had Len's keys from his stint feeding his fish), he'd simply say he was checking up on a friend.

After all, if he was going to look for a needle in a haystack, he might as well start with the haystack that belonged to the guy who'd chopped off the first limb.

---

Ben had barely unlocked the door to Lenny's apartment when he heard, "Well, well, well, look who's here."

He didn't need to see the source to recognize the voice. Leaning over to Laurette, who'd met him outside the condo complex moments before, he whispered, "That's Detective Patel. Fan-fuck-ing-tastic."

Like an unarmed man, he advanced slowly over the kitchen's glossy hardwood floor and raised the key high in the air so Patel could see it. "I have a key. Just wanted to check in on Lenny. See if he's here."

"That makes three of us." Detective Becker emerged from the bedroom and joined Patel in the small but upscale living room. Thanks to its expansive windows, the unit was awash in winter sunlight, but despite the panoramic scene beyond the glass, the rust-bricked building across the street did little to enhance the view. Both Becker and Patel's coats were unbuttoned and their suits visible, but as usual, Becker's tailored jacket whistled Nordstrom where Patel's corduroy blazer screamed Walmart. When Becker saw Laurette next to Ben, he said, "Make that four."

"Laurette's my friend. She's an epidemiologist with the CD—"

"We know who she is." The bespectacled Becker stepped forward to shake Laurette's hand. The same greeting was not extended to Ben. "Thanks for calling us this morning," he said to her. "We just got here ourselves. Between Dr. Reynolds's snatching of the first limb and that photo of the note you texted me, we got our search warrant." Becker lasered his eyes in on Ben. "If only we'd known about his involvement in all this before late yesterday afternoon, we'd have gotten one sooner."

"I'm sorry, I really am. I effed up big time." Ben didn't think he could feel more guilt over Sophia's abduction than he already did, but he was wrong.

Patel hitched up his pants. With his bowling ball of a belly, they slid right back down. "You shouldn't be in here, doc, but hey, since you are, you wouldn't happen to know where your chiefy is, would ya?" His tone was about as sincere as a poker bluff. "Did he send you here to pick up a few things?"

"Are you kidding me?" Ben shoved the key back into his coat pocket. "I told you yesterday I was done protecting him, and I meant it. Why do you think I asked Laurette to call you? I'm not positive the note is from Lenny, but he seems the best bet."

Finally noticing the apartment's disarray, Ben let his angst simmer and meandered a few feet into the small condo, the detectives' eyes on him the whole time. Styrofoam takeout containers with congealed brown goo and ripped-opened bags of chips and pretzels littered the kitchen island, their crumbs dotting the granite surface and the hardwood floor below. In addition to the spoiling food, an unpleasant scent of body odor and weed tinged the air. A bong on the desk in the living room explained the latter. Covering the rest of the desk were a laptop and a mess of scattered papers. Clothes lay sprawled on the end of the sofa, and a glance in the bedroom revealed tangled bedsheets on the unmade bed. Even worse, Ben realized, was Lenny's prized fish tank. Most of the tropical fish still darted and zipped around the colorful rocks and plants, but the water was cloudy and several smaller fish lay belly up on the surface, including the expensive candy basslet Maxwell had nicknamed "Stripey." Clearly, Len had camped out here for a while after his flight from rehab, but the fact he'd neglected his fish spoke volumes about his mental state.

"Oh, I'm sorry," Patel said, interrupting Ben's thoughts. "Are we in your way? Should we come back later to finish our search?" His tone sharpened. "You need to leave. Now. Why do you have Reynolds's key, anyway?"

"He gave it to me so I could feed his fish when he went on vacation."

Patel glanced at the cloudy tank with its belly-up sea life and snorted. "Looks like you did a shitty job."

That was it. Ben lost it. He spun around and faced the guy. "Why do you have to be such an asshole? The mother of my child is missing. My friend could be the killer, and if that's true, I might have helped him by keeping my fucking mouth shut for too long. How do you think that makes me feel, huh? Do you think anything you say can make me feel any worse? Just book me for obstruction already and be done with it. Or maybe you thought I'd lead you to him, that's why you haven't already? And why aren't you out looking for Sophia? Why aren't you doing your jobs?" Ben flicked his hands in the air as if done with the whole thing and lowered to the couch. "Is this all right? Am I allowed to sit down?" He buried his face in his hands and rubbed furiously at his temples, craving this all to be over. He wanted to pick up his son, play trains with him, take him and Sophia to an animated movie. Instead he was going to have to tell him that his mommy disappeared from the hospital.

Laurette strolled over and sat down beside him. "It's okay, my friend. We will find her."

Patel clapped his hands. "Bravo. You done? Any more tantrums?" He pulled on a pair of gloves. "Not that we owe you any explanation, but we *are* doing our jobs. You think we're magic? Think we know exactly where to find her? We've got our guys looking into every possible suspect. Keeping an eye on every goddamn park. Driving around the block of every recently discharged orthopedics patient. You think we haven't tailed suspects? You think we haven't checked out alibis? Just because a couple of them are flimsy doesn't mean we can arrest someone without proof. And news flash: we can't be everywhere at once. We chose *here*, because, to quote you, your buddy Len is the best bet. Satisfied, doc? We gonna get five stars from you on the rate-a-cop app?"

Ben pressed his nails into his palms and bit the inside of his cheek. It pissed him off that the insomnia-eyed dickwad made sense.

"By the way," Becker said in his usual neutral manner, sunlight glinting off his glasses, "we need that note if you've got it."

Ben blinked at him and then nodded in understanding. He reached into his coat pocket and retrieved the note Lenny had left for him. Without a word, Becker held open a plastic bag, and Ben dropped the piece of paper inside. "My landlady touched it too," Ben said, in case it was important.

Patel grabbed some papers off the strewn desk and held them up to Ben. "Since you've crashed this party, we might as well put you to use. What do you make of this?"

Ben studied the top sheet, the humming and bubbling fish tank the only sound in the small condo beyond the city traffic. Despite his rising body temperature, he made no effort to remove his coat. When he realized what he was looking at, he sat up fully. "It's a sketch of an orthopedic implant." Without touching the paper, he pointed to various spots on the drawing. "That's the femoral component, that's the tibial tray, and this here is the plastic spacer that goes between the two to make up the joint." Ben indicated Patel flip to the next piece of paper. More sketches and diagrams, along with scrawled notes that looked to be the same handwriting as the note Ben had received. "Looks like a formula or something. And see there? I'm no engineer or chemist, but I know what *Ag* means."

"It's the symbol for silver," Becker said.

The four of them pondered the finding in silence, its suggestion obvious.

"*Mon Dieu*," Laurette finally said, removing her crimson coat and placing it on the couch beside her, away from Lenny's strewn sweatpants. "Is this proof Dr. Lock stole Lenny's implant idea? Was your chief resident telling the truth all along?"

"Looks like it." From his seated position, Ben scrutinized the sketches in Patel's gloved hands. "But how could we prove when they were drawn? What if Len only did it recently? After all," Ben waved an arm at the disarray around them, "he's clearly in a messed-up state since he left rehab."

Becker rifled around the rest of the papers on the desk. "Looks like a lot of research articles and industry papers on implants and— Oh wait, this might help." He lifted a sheet of printer paper, perused it, and then flipped it forward so Ben, who was now standing, could read it.

"Looks like a detailed write-up of his idea," Ben said.

Becker pointed to the upper left corner. "A dated account."

Ben's pulse sped up. Sure enough. A date was listed on the printed Word document. Just over four years earlier. "Jeez, that *was* before Lock, patron saint of reconstructive surgery, started his consistent-team approach and research."

"We'll need to confirm it with Dr. Reynolds's computer, of course." Becker stared at the closed laptop sitting amid the papers. "Make sure he didn't just type it up that way to make it look suspicious."

"But if the date is accurate, it's proof Len presented the idea to Dr. Lock when he was a second-year resident. And with the implants I found in Lock's office last night—"

"Excuse me?" Patel said, his lip curling.

*Shit.* "I swear I wasn't trying to hide it from you. I *did* try to call you this morning," Ben said to Becker. "And you should be getting a call from the surgery chair or my mentor about it any minute. Everything's just happening too fast, and I can't keep up." He closed his eyes. "I just want to find Sophia."

"We do too," Becker said, his tone soft, making his words believable. "Now tell us about these implants you found."

Ben filled them in on his illicit trip to Lock's office, finding implants that differed from the ones in the supply room, their heated confrontation, and Lock's punch that landed on the wall. He could tell they were pissed, but not as much as he thought they'd be. Probably figured he'd just made their job easier, no search warrant needed. In his mind he could hear Patel say, *He's the one who'll hang for it, no skin off our teeth.*

When he finished, Laurette said, "But why would a man like Dr. Lock, with all his prestige and money, risk his career by stealing someone else's idea?"

Patel stifled a sneeze. "Oh missy, what I wouldn't give for your optimism. You'll grow cynical soon enough."

"I can make you a list longer than Interstate 80 of the successful men who've done stupid stuff," Becker said, in way of answering Laurette's question. "But the more important things to ask are: One, where is Dr. Reynolds? Clearly he caught us watching his place yesterday and ran. Maybe even before then. And two, where is Dr. Lock? Did Ben's discovery spook him into hiding or is something else at play?" Becker's questions made it evident they'd heard about Lock's no-show at the hospital that morning.

"And three," Patel finished for his partner. "Did one do away with the other to keep his mouth shut?"

"No," Laurette said, her frustration obvious. "The *most* important questions to be asking are who is killing these patients and where is Sophia? I understand the note Ben gave you makes Lenny look guilty, and maybe all this" —she crossed to the desk and waved her hands above the mess of papers on the desk— "makes Dr. Lock look guilty too, but Derek believes the killer is someone else who survived the Alaskan plane crash. He believes the only reason the implants are involved is because they contain silver and Wendigos are repulsed by the metal. Like a benign tumor discovered during an MRI for something else, Dr. Lock's fraudulent behavior is simply an incidental finding."

Becker scratched his cheek with the back of his hand. "We're aware of Dr. Epps's theory, yes."

"But you don't believe it?" Laurette asked. "You are black and white men like Ben, no shades of in-between gray?"

"Look," Becker said. "We're open to anything. These killings, their apparent relationship to the implants, the missing bodies, the brutality of it…"

Becker glanced at Ben, as if worried he went too far. Like a cannon ball to the gut, Ben's feeling of powerlessness over Sophia's disappearance returned tenfold. *Dear God, what's happening to her right now?*

"What I'm trying to say," Becker continued, pushing up his glasses, "is that none of this makes any sense."

"And that, my medical friends, is the only thing I'm certain of." Patel patted his stomach and for once looked equally chagrined.

"While we appreciate Dr. Epps's help," Becker said, "all the Alaskan survivors beyond Dr. Lock are at the hospital and accounted for. When you notified us of Ms. Diaz's disappearance, we sent additional units to Montgomery—we already had a couple of our guys routinely checking in—and they confirmed the staff members are there."

"Maybe the killer took Sophia and then returned," Laurette said.

"We've sent units to their homes too."

Before Ben could add anything, his phone rang in his pocket, startling them all. After Sophia went missing, he'd turned on the ringer to make sure he'd hear every call.

The screen showed a text from Karen: *Get your ass back to the hospital. Pronto.*

He couldn't type fast enough: *Is Sophia there?*

No response followed.

# 42

Sometime around noon, Ben was back in the hospital's nine-story atrium. Though they drove separately from Lenny's apartment—Laurette in her aunt's Ford Focus and Ben in his Mustang—he was so anxious to get to 4 East and see if there was news about Sophia that he barely remembered the trip.

When Laurette caught up to him near the gift shop, she opened a dark-chocolate and almond bar and thrust it at him. "Here, this was in my purse. You must eat something today."

Ben grabbed it and took a huge bite but tasted nothing. In a garbled mouthful, he said, "I'll text you if I learn anything."

"Same. I'm meeting Derek in the cafeteria. If he has any news, I will call you right away. He's been interviewing the Alaskan survivors again. And I will also keep in touch with Willy and Rita. They are desperate for updates, I'm sure."

Before darting off to the ward, Ben gave Laurette a quick hug, her citrus scent a comfort of its own. "Thanks, Bovo. If you weren't here I'd be going crazy."

"We will find her."

As Ben galloped up three flights of stairs, he prayed she was right.

Up on 4 East, Karen, dressed in scrubs and a white coat, stomped at the central counter like a bull. When she saw Ben, she snapped, "What took you so long?"

Nurses glanced their way but, as if embarrassed for Ben, quickly went back to their tasks. Joel sat behind the counter near the ward clerk. Ben was about to berate him for not showing up for rounds this morning—the med student could've been one more set of eyes to watch Sophia while Ben was running around putting out patient fires like a wind-up toy on Ritalin—but Joel's expression was sympathetic, a first ever, at least toward Ben, so he let it go.

To Karen, he said, "Why'd you text me so urgently? Is it Sophia? Has she been found?" He wiped a drop of sweat from his brow.

"No. Sorry." Karen's tone was blunt. "I know you're worried about her, and I feel bad for you, but this whole thing is disrupting everyone's life. I'm sick and tired of cops pulling me away from my work to question me about stuff I know nothing about. And enough with the visiting shrink, already. I'm trying to manage patients here, and because of you, I'm a resident short."

Ben clenched his fists. If she were a man, he'd have to force himself to hold back a punch. "Gee. Sorry for the inconvenience. Guess it's my bad the mother of my kid has gone missing and all those annoying police are trying to find her."

Karen dropped her attack stance and tightened her ponytail with both hands. "I don't mean it like that. It's just…well shit, that CDC shrink is asking things like are we tempted by human flesh? Are we uncontrollably hungry? What exactly is going on?"

"You think if I had the answer I'd be standing here taking your crap?"

"Yeah, well, none of this happened until you found that first leg. And now your friend is missing. People are starting to point fingers your way."

"Why'd you call me back, Karen? I'm in no state to see patients."

"Fisher told me to. He's on a rampage."

"What does he want?" Ben was pretty sure he knew.

"You. In his office. Stopped by the ward twenty minutes ago looking for you. Said he's been—and I quote—'shoveling shit' for the past hour. Said you'll know what it's about."

Less than five minutes later Ben was in the Morrison building, where the academic faces of past generations once again eyeballed him from their framed perches on the wainscoted walls. Barely had he stepped into the stately anteroom of Fisher's office suite when he heard a booming voice yell, "Oris, get your ass in here." How the chief had already spotted him, he didn't know, but he was grateful Fisher's secretary wasn't at her sentinel position to experience the earthquake.

Like in most physician offices, diplomas and other awards decorated one wall. Another wall showcased shelves of books and memorabilia, in Fisher's case of the military kind. A dark-wood desk fronted by two leather chairs consumed much of the room, and underfoot was a circular Persian rug. Fisher, dressed in a no-frills suit, paced its circumference, which was probably how he'd spotted Ben so quickly.

From the corner of his desk, the chairman seized the two femoral components Ben had stolen—one from the supply closet and one from Lock's file cabinet—twelve hours before. "Goddammit, Oris, goddammit," he fumed. "Imagine my surprise when some tiny little internist in fancy shoes brought these to me."

"I didn't have a choice. I asked Dr. Smith to—"

"Shut up." Fisher dropped the implants back on the desk and marched forward. A finger almost stabbed Ben's face. "You broke into your attending's office? Didn't even think to come to me first?" Warm breath blasted Ben's face.

"I didn't break into the office. The janitor was about to clean it. It was late, and it didn't seem right to call you when I had no idea what I'd find."

"And what, the implants just magically flew into your arms?"

Ben hesitated. "They were locked in his file cabinet." When Fisher didn't respond, just stood there crunching his jaw back and forth, Ben added, "I'm not trying to keep anything from you, sir. That's why I had Dr. Smith bring them over. It's like I have a million pieces of glass slicing through my head right now, you know? I can only focus on the sharpest, and that's finding the mother of my child."

His words seemed to have an effect. Dr. Fisher's ballistic tone flattened into understanding. "I'm sorry about that, Oris, I really am." He waved his arm toward one of the leather chairs. "Sit down."

Ben sat, every cell of his body desperate to be out hunting for Sophia, even though he had no idea where else to look. With each ticking second, his blood pressure rose. He could only hope the cops had a lead. He checked his phone in case the beep of a text message had gotten swallowed by Fisher's bellowing, but the screen was blank.

The chairman sank down behind the desk. After rubbing both hands over his face and under his glasses, he righted the spectacles and sighed. "It's not just that you didn't tell me about your little late-night escapade. It's that you also told the detectives working this goddamn clusterfuck of a case."

"They already called you?" Ben was relieved. Becker and Patel really were on the ball. "I had to tell them. Those implants might lead back to Sophia."

Fisher made a guttural sound. "Maybe, maybe not. They're sending someone to get them. Apparently they're 'evidence.' What a clusterfuck," he repeated. "Four tours in the Middle East, and never have I battled anything like this. Not only am I in the middle of a PR nightmare with these killings, now I have to deal with the possibility that one of our top surgeons is conducting fraudulent research."

If the chief expected sympathy from Ben, he got none.

As if reading Ben's mind, Fisher said, "I don't mean to make light of Ms. Diaz, son, but goddamn it, I keep learning everything after the fact, including about your chief resident hacking off a corpse's leg. You should've told me."

"Believe me, I should've done a lot of things differently."

The chairman's hot air cooled even more, as if realizing he couldn't beat Ben up any more than Ben had already beaten himself up. "Hindsight, Oris, hindsight. Guess we've all been there."

"So you think Lock's doing unapproved research?" Ben pointed to the shinier implant near Fisher's pen holder. "That's the implant I've been placing in patients with him. I recognize its sheen." He pointed to the slightly duller one. "And that's the one from the supply room. As you can see, it's different. Not by much—same shape and all—but by shine."

Fisher flipped the shinier implant back and forth, scrutinizing it closely. He sighed again. "Good goose-shit almighty, what's he been up to? If it was approved research, as chair I'd damn well know about it. And what do these devices have to do with the murders?"

"Dr. Epps thinks the silver in them repels the Wendigo, and that's why he—or she—abandons the limb."

"Do you hear yourself, for Christ's sake? That's hogwash."

Ben raised his hands. "I'm just telling you what the psychiatrist said. He's apparently seen enough sick stuff to know what he's talking about. As for Dr. Lock, I think he's been pawning Lenny's implants off as his own. How else can his infection rate be so low? The silver-coating prevents bacterial growth. That's why senior residents aren't allowed in on his reconstructive cases. They might notice the different implant. Once Lenny was gone from the program and Lock's results were enough to publish, he was probably going to unveil his masterpiece to the orthopedic world."

"Those are stiff accusations. Why in the hell would he do that?" Fisher's question echoed Laurette's back at Lenny's condo.

"Research? Recognition? Fame? Money from the implants for his foundation once his success rate is published? Everyone will want them. The cops found documents in Lenny's apartment that prove the design belongs to him." Ben stood, unable to sit any longer. "Look, I feel like a trapped rat. I can't just sit here hoping Sophia will show up." He started pacing the fancy rug. "What if it's even worse? What if Dr. Lock's responsible for everything? What if he's got Sophia as we speak?"

"Whoa, now hold on. As I said before, being an unscrupulous researcher is very different from being a killer. I'm already close to suspending you. My hands are tied and your program director agrees. Don't make it worse by accusing your boss of murder."

"Yeah, then where is he? Why is he the only one besides Lenny unaccounted for?"

As if he'd been standing outside the door, waiting for the perfect time to enter, Dr. Lock stormed into the office.

But it wasn't only his weird timing that shocked Ben. It was his fat lip, bruised cheek, and bandaged hand. Not to mention the sling on the other arm.

"Suspend him?" Dr. Lock's complexion flushed blood-red. "How about arrest him? That asshole assaulted me last night."

## 43

B en eyed Lock's fat lip and bruised cheek, knowing he'd given him neither one. "That's a lie and you know it." He pivoted to Dr. Fisher. "I never touched him. He took a swing at me and hit the wall instead. How his face and arm got banged up I have no idea." A horrible thought surfaced, and he charged toward Lock. "Did Sophia give you those? Where is she?" He grabbed the sling on Lock's arm and jerked it.

"Get away from him!"

Fisher's command snapped Ben back to a semblance of composure. After a beat, he stepped away from his preceptor. The surgical chairman stood behind his desk, palms pressed firmly against the blotter protecting its surface. Dr. Lock remained just inside the doorway, chinos and button-down shirt replacing his usual scrubs.

When Fisher seemed convinced Ben would behave, he ordered them both to sit down. "No one's ripping anybody apart in my office or elsewhere."

Ben's skin prickled with heat and impatience, but he took a seat. Lock and Fisher did the same. The chairman removed his glasses and rubbed his tie over the lenses. "Jesus Christ on a skateboard, I'd rather be back in Iraq."

"Oris needs to go, Isaiah. He's danger—"

"Kent, what the hell is this?" Dr. Fisher held up the implant from Lock's file cabinet. "And why was it hidden away in your office under the same patient name as the one in the supply room?"

Without hesitation but with plenty of passion, Dr. Lock explained how he was doing a blinded study. "And Oris has just screwed it up." He shifted toward Ben. "Do you realize the damage you've done? The patients who could've benefited from my research? Not to mention the damage you did to me last night."

Ben squeezed the leather armrests. "I never laid a hand on you. And how's it a blinded study if you know which implant the patient is getting?"

"I don't have to explain my methods to you."

"Then explain them to me," Fisher roared.

"It's a new implant, Isaiah. One that reduces the risk of post-op infection. It'll put this hospital on the map."

Ben scoffed. "An implant that was Lenny Reynolds's idea."

"That true, Kent? You steal the kid's idea back when he was a second-year resident?"

"Of course not." The attending looked so aggrieved Ben almost believed him. Almost.

"Oris here says he saw proof that Reynolds came up with the idea. Design sketches. Equations."

Lock faltered for a moment. He rubbed his bruised cheek and winced as he shifted his arm. "I don't know what to say about that. I suppose it's possible that Reynolds first planted the seed in my mind, but I don't recall any specifics. Besides, I'm no engineer. I hired someone to design it based on my desire to create an implant with antibacterial properties. I'm sorry for what Dr. Reynolds is going through, I really am. Drugs can do a number on the brain. But he's creating a fantasy if he thinks he designed the implants."

Fisher held the twin devices, one in each hand. He flipped them back and forth, seemingly unsure what to believe. Even Ben's confidence in Lock's duplicity wavered. Had he gotten it wrong? Was this just another fallacy in Lenny's downward spiral?

Lock raised his bandaged hand. "Come on, Isaiah. We've

known each other how long? Do you really think I'd risk everything by stealing someone's idea and passing it off as my own?" He nudged his head Ben's way. "Good surgeon or not, Oris needs to go. I feel for what he's going through with Sophia. I'm hurting for her too. But we can't have someone that unstable" —he pointed to his bruised face— "and volatile in our program. Given it's rough for him right now, I'll forget about pressing assault charges, but he has to be suspended or—"

"You telling me these implants are FDA approved then? Gone through all the proper channels?" Fisher dropped the metal devices back onto his desk where they clunked heavily against the wood.

"Of course." Lock looked affronted. "It's a predicate device, only minor differences from previously approved implants, so it didn't need the same testing as a new Class III application. Was reclassified as a Class II."

Ben didn't know enough about FDA approval processes to know if Lock's words were bullshit or not, especially if the implants truly contained silver and were unlike others before them. And if it was bullshit, that meant Lock's engineer was in on the fraud. Lenny had mentioned the surgeon had a friend who worked R & D. There had to be others in on in too.

Given Fisher's expression, he wasn't sure what to believe either, but Lock's explanation sounded reasonable enough, and that made Ben sweat even more. Outside the room the secretary's phone rang, just as it had been doing repeatedly throughout their heated exchange. After four rings, it went to voicemail, the woman not yet back from her late lunch.

Dr. Lock leaned forward, "Look. Maybe I could have gone about this better, not kept it so secret, but I simply wanted the cleanest research. I'm sure you understand that. But I didn't steal the idea, and for God's sake, I didn't have anything to do with Sophia." To Ben he said, "Regardless of what you think of me, I wouldn't hurt her. I've been praying for her ever since Angela told me she was gone."

"Then where have you been all day?" Ben asked.

He again pointed to his injuries. "Clearly not performing surgery, thanks to you."

Ben's pulse throbbed with fury. "I never touched you and you know it."

"You need help, Oris. Anger management even. Maybe if you spent less time making up stories and more time taking care of the mother of your child, she wouldn't be missing."

Ben burst up and threw himself on the attending surgeon. Like a flash, Fisher bolted around the desk and pulled Ben off of him. Graying temples or not, the reedy military man was as strong as ever. "Goddammit, stop it." Once Ben regained self-control, tugging his scrub top back in place, Fisher released him. "Kent's right, son. My hands are tied. Between this and you breaking into his office, not to mention assaulting—"

"I never touched the guy," Ben said, his voice so thick with frustration it might as well have been tree sap.

"And who am I supposed to believe, huh?" Fisher seemed to be crawling out of his skin as much as Ben. "I have no choice. I've got to suspend you until we get this sorted out."

"Screw it," Ben said, making to leave. "Do what you gotta do. I've got bigger worries right now."

Voices approached from the anteroom. "...see if the chairman knows where the guy is." Ben recognized the voice as Detective Becker's, and moments later the professorial cop entered Dr. Fisher's office, followed by Patel. They stopped short when they saw Lock. His presence seemed to get a rise even out of the languid Patel.

The sleepy-eyed detective snapped his fingers. "Guess it's our lucky day."

Becker reached inside his coat and plucked handcuffs from the pocket of his suit jacket. He ordered Dr. Lock to stand.

"What's going on?" Lock's gaze darted back and forth between the two men. He pointed to Ben. "He's the one who attacked *me*."

Noticing the sling on Lock's arm, Becker replaced the cuffs and said, "Dr. Kent Lock, you're under arrest for the abduction of Sophia Diaz. You have the right..."

Stunned, Ben watched as Becker led the attending surgeon out of the office, Dr. Fisher braying in the background, demanding to know what was going on.

Patel grabbed the implants from Fisher's desk. Before he followed his partner and the still-protesting Dr. Lock, he looked at Ben and said, "Maybe you're not so dumb after all, doc. We found Diaz's purse in the holy man's office."

## 44

With an agonizing sense of powerlessness, Ben wandered out of the Morrison building into the glass-enclosed skywalk that led to the main hospital. Down below, traffic crept cautiously on the icy street, and bundled-up pedestrians trampled the snowy sidewalks to get to their destinations. He longed to be among them, cold but worry-free, on his way to pick up Maxwell for an afternoon of sledding followed by hot chocolate and picture books. Instead he was trying to process the news that his attending surgeon might have abducted Sophia.

If that was the case, he would pummel the guy into oblivion.

Patel must have sensed Ben's ire, because after he'd mentioned they found Sophia's purse in Lock's office, he preemptively held Ben back from charging the guy, and when Ben had demanded Fisher give him Lock's address so he could see if Sophia was there, Detective Patel had pushed him against the wall with impressive strength. "You're not going anywhere," he'd said. "We've already got a warrant to search his house. If we find you anywhere near it, I'll lock you up myself." The detective's eyes had practically bored a hole into Ben's skull.

Ben had grumbled and bucked but eventually backed off. He

had to do something though. Anything. He was rational enough to know that if Sophia was at Lock's place, the police would find her. His efforts were better spent elsewhere. But where? He'd already tried Lenny's apartment. If only he knew where to find the guy.

So many things didn't make sense. If Lock was the killer, like the police now suspected, why would he discard limbs with his own implants inside them? It was too incriminating. Even if Derek's bizarre Wendigo theory was correct, and Lock was simply irrational and subconsciously spreading breadcrumbs his own way, how could he implant the silver-coated devices during surgery yet not tolerate them during his (and here Ben's thoughts faltered, because he could hardly fathom the idea that Sophia could be next) cannibalistic murders?

God, he'd failed her. In the worst, most horrific way possible, he'd failed her.

As he stepped into the main hospital building, his heart weighted with guilt and pain, his phone pinged. A text from Laurette. Derek wanted to meet with them in the cafeteria at four thirty. The psychiatrist was almost finished with a second set of interviews with the Alaskan survivors, minus Dr. Lock. His last session was with Joel.

That meant Ben, newly suspended from his residency, had a couple hours to kill. The police were handling Lock. Ben had no idea where Lenny was. Laurette was keeping Willy and Rita informed, and Maxwell was safe in their shared caregiving, still blissfully unaware his mother was missing. Maybe the best way for Ben to spend the time was to talk to the Alaskan survivors himself. He'd already spoken to the sullen Karen and didn't relish another round with her, but a quick trip to 4 East revealed she was still taking care of patients. Before she spotted him, he ducked back out and made his way down to the OR.

In the stairwell he ran into Angela. She was on her way up, probably to 4 East where Ben had just left. She gave a little "oh" of surprise and started to hurry past him.

He grabbed the sleeve of her white coat. "Wait." She stopped but avoided eye contact. "Do you have any news of Sophia?" When she didn't respond, he added, "Please, you're Dr. Lock's right-hand woman. You must know something about what's going on."

Her cheeks flushed. "What I know is you assaulted Kent. You stole implants from his office. You ruined his research. And now you've framed him for Sophia's abduction. Do you know how badly I need this job? How badly I need the money? Not to mention I was going to be co-author on his paper."

Given her knowledge of what had happened, Ben could only assume Lock had been allowed to call her. Or maybe it was Fisher who had called, wanting Lock's PA to be aware of the situation so she could manage his patients with a new surgeon.

"Only one of those things you accused me of is true," Ben said. "I did take the implants, but only to clear Lenny's name."

She scoffed. "Lenny Reynolds. Talk about an unstable person. You believe him over a respected surgeon like Kent? One whose career you likely just ended?" Shaking, she pivoted and ran up the stairs, leaving Ben in the wake of her fury.

Once inside the restricted corridors of the operating rooms, he started with the east wing, where the majority of orthopedic surgeries took place. Given the emptiness of the yet-to-be-cleaned rooms and the number of staff milling around in the hallway chatting, masks hanging loosely from their necks, things were winding down for the afternoon. No one stared at him as if he didn't belong, so word about his suspension hadn't yet reached them. Why would it? Fisher had enough on his plate. A few nodded in his direction, and the ones who knew him offered condolences about Sophia.

Outside a room where a patient was being wheeled out, her surgery complete, Ben found a scrub nurse who often worked with Dr. Fisher. "Have you seen Dr. King or Michael?" he asked.

She pointed vaguely to the right. "They're in the north wing. OR seven. Some combined neurosurg and ortho case about to begin." Ben thanked her and headed that way. He found Michael scrubbing in at the sink, but before he could talk to him, Dr. King exited the operating room across the hallway, and he and Ben nearly collided.

"Oh," the anesthesiologist said, his forehead creased. "Didn't expect you here." Whether because of Ben's suspension or because Sophia was missing, Ben didn't know.

At that moment OR number seven's circulating nurse popped her head out of the room. Her powder blue surgical bonnet barely contained a thick head of hair. "Hurry up, Alvarez. Dr. Owens is waiting on you."

"Tell Chip to hold his high horses."

"Yeah, right," she said, lowering her voice. "I'll leave that to you. He's already pissed at you for getting here late today and throwing off his schedule. Don't need him pissed at me too." She disappeared back into the room.

Michael glanced at Ben. "So thrilled I get to scrub in with your acting chief resident. He's an asshole. We need Lenny back."

Ben had no argument there. "Why were you late this morning?"

Before Michael could answer Ben's question, Dr. King said, "I'm sorry to hear about Sophia." As an anesthesiologist, the doctor didn't have to do a sterile scrub, but as obsessive about things as he was, he always performed a thorough wash before entering each room. He seemed as out of sorts as Karen and Angela had been, and when his unsterile hand reached for the soap and touched Michael's, the scrub nurse groaned. "Dammit, Muti, now I have to start all over again."

Michael tossed the scrub brush he was using into the trash and grabbed another. After opening the package, he rubbed at his flesh like it was covered in acid. Though Michael could be outspoken and crass, Ben had never heard him be disrespectful to the attendings before.

"Sorry," Dr. King said. "But don't bite my head off. It's not like they'll start without you."

"Easy for you to say. You have residents and nurse anesthetists to help you. There's only one of me."

Dr. King ignored him and reached for a towel. Before he slipped into the operating room, he said to Ben, "Good luck. I hope you find her."

After Dr. King left, Michael said, "This is all so effed-up. Cops tailing me, asking me my 'whereabouts,' some special shrink trying to get in our heads. I'm sick of it all." With hands raised to keep them sterile, he opened the OR door with his butt and stormed inside, the door whooshing shut behind him.

Ben left the OR wings, having no more information than he'd had when he entered. Everybody was stressed. Everybody was upset. Everybody was angry. And why wouldn't they be? Their department was falling apart.

But which of them might have Sophia?

———

Inside the hospital cafeteria, Laurette was cutting up an apple, the last of her small meal. Ben's own plate, with its turkey and swiss sandwich, had gone untouched. He was too preoccupied with getting Derek to spill the goods about his conversations with the team members to eat.

The psychiatrist took a drink of his fountain soda and jabbed at the ice with his straw. "You know I can't tell you the specifics."

"Sophia's life is at stake." Ben's desperation drew stares from nearby diners, who, given the late afternoon hour, were thankfully few.

"You don't think I know that?" Derek's retort carried its own emotion, and for the first time Ben realized the forensic psychiatrist's own stake in the matter. Not only might another life be lost if his bizarre theory proved wrong, he'd risk looking like a fool.

"Sorry. I know you're trying to help. It's just…to sit here and listen to you say you think the police have the wrong man, that Lock isn't the killer, even though they found Sophia's purse in his office, well, that scares the shit out of me because it means we're back to square one."

"It also means someone is framing Dr. Lock," Laurette said.

Silence fell over the table. Without conscious awareness, Ben raised the sandwich and took a bite. Robotically, he chewed. Hospital visitors roamed the corridors around the open dining area, and in front of the gift shop two children begged their mother for a toy. Ben thought of his own son. He hadn't seen Maxwell since his dinner with Willy and Laurette the evening before. It seemed like a lifetime ago. He tried to take comfort from the fact Laurette had stopped by the chocolate store earlier and found both Willy and Maxwell absorbed in making Valentine's Day treats. Though she said Willy had looked frazzled—the trifecta of Valentine's Day prep, grandparenting duties, and a missing Sophia would do that to Ben's dad—she'd said Maxwell seemed as content as could be, with store employees taking turns letting him help them and keeping him otherwise occupied. Knowing his son remained in happy and blissful ignorance over his mother's fate consoled Ben somewhat, but it wouldn't be long before the toddler started asking when they could visit Mommy in the hospital again.

A hand enveloped his own, and Laurette's tawny gaze caught his. "Do not lose hope, Ben."

He squeezed her hand, and for a moment it was just the two of them at the table. "Thank you for everything you've done. Checking in on my family. Mrs. Sinclair and Sir Quincy too. That's a huge relief to me."

Derek broke their connection. "Listen, what I *can* tell you is that although I talked to all the team members today aside from Dr. Lock, after he was arrested the police lost interest in anything I had to say. They figure they've got their man. I can also tell you that none of them—Michael, Angela, Karen, Joel, or Dr. King—seems to be doing well. Paranoia, flippancy, outrage, mockery. You name it, I got it from them, and they all want me to leave them the hell alone."

"But you still believe one of them could be involved?"

"I do."

"Well then, we must visit everyone's home," Laurette said. "See if Sophia is at one of them."

"The police have already done that," Derek said.

Ben was already on his feet. "Then we'll do it again. It'll be dark soon. Where do they live?" When Derek didn't answer, Ben said, "Come on, you've been inside their medical charts. You're the only one who can access them."

"I haven't been inside anyone's chart. These people never asked for my help. I sought them out. I've taken notes, sure, but I haven't snooped around their medical files. That would be unethical."

"Yeah, so is dismembering patients and eating them."

"Shh, keep your voice down." With a gesture, Laurette encouraged Ben to retake his seat. "Please, Derek, you must have asked them about their home lives. Who do we start with?"

"I don't know." The psychiatrist's expression was sincere. "Angela lives with her husband and kids in a multi-unit brownstone with two other tenants. Karen, Michael, and Joel live in apartments, Michael having been kicked out of his house after——" Derek abruptly cut himself off, apparently realizing he was about to reveal something he deemed confidential.

"After his wife kicked him out for cheating," Ben finished for him. "It's common knowledge."

Derek looked relieved.

"And Dr. King?" Laurette asked.

"He's in an apartment too." Derek glanced at Ben, maybe wondering how much of the anesthesiologist's life was also common knowledge.

Ben picked at his sandwich. "Dr. King and his wife are separated. No wait," he mentally shuffled through the conversations he'd heard during surgeries and from other OR gossip. "Michael is the one who's separated. King is divorced. His ex-wife got the house, so he lives in an apartment near the hospital."

"So none of these places would be easy to keep someone." Laurette's shoulders slumped.

"Not even if the person was drugged by the Wendigo. The effects would wear off by now. Probably."

"Quit saying 'Wendigo' as if it's a real thing," Ben snapped.

"Okay, the psychotic individual."

"How about 'killer' or 'murderer' or 'deranged lunatic'? Because that's what this asshole is."

Derek ignored Ben's outburst. "The psychotic individual is discarding the limb with the implant in place. Whether this is to get a personal distance from the perceived toxic silver or a way to call attention to himself—because he or she certainly can't want this—I don't know. Maybe it's both. But no bodies have been found. That tells me whoever is doing it has access to a remote area, or at least an area with a big yard where bodies could be hid."

"That makes sense," Laurette said. "You couldn't keep dead bodies in an apartment. They would stink."

At that moment a teenage girl walked by their table, her eyes growing comically wide at Laurette's words. In another time and place, Ben and Laurette would have laughed. Not now.

Once the girl was out of earshot, Derek and Laurette expanded on location possibilities. Ben tuned them out. He couldn't sit there a second longer. Even if it was futile and even if the police had already done so, he would drive to each of the team members' apartments. Assuming they were patients of the Montgomery Hospital system, he'd get their addresses from their electronic health records, HIPAA rules be damned. He was already booted from the program. What was one more infraction? And if their addresses weren't in the system, he'd hound HR or try Google.

And then, like sometimes happens when a brain is thinking one thing but something else pops in, it hit Ben. Like a bowling ball to the skull, it hit him. It was Derek's mention of a remote area that had triggered the connection. Why hadn't he connected the dots earlier?

He bolted up from the table, his chair clattering to the tile floor behind him. "Jesus, I know where she is. I know who the killer is."

# 45

As I warm myself in front of the fire and rub my hands together for that ever-elusive heat, I realize I've never had a day as hard as this one, not even when I had that trouble at my old job. They never proved it was me, and those souls I released are in a much better place. Their pain was obvious, and yet we kept saving them with our medical advances.

Still, since then, I've tried to anchor myself, tried to balance that tightrope separating right from wrong and lawful from unlawful. I stopped my altruistic acts and kept the souls intact.

But it's so easy to slip from reality. Life changes. You face one struggle after another. You lose all that's precious to you. When that happens, your weaknesses become exposed, and a terrible evil seeps its way through the cracks of your armor and steals your control.

My emotional state was already on a tenuous foothold before the crash, but then the cold and hunger crippled me completely. Now there's nothing but insatiable hunger. So while I survived that past trouble by leaving no evidence behind and moving away, I know I won't escape clean this time. The monster's—and therefore my own —disgusting hunger controls my fate.

All those questions from the police today. Worse, meeting with that psychiatrist. He's very good at getting inside the mind. The police were easier. They're trained to follow the evidence, and so I—or maybe the monster—planted her purse in Dr. Lock's office, unlocked during the daytime. I didn't enjoy doing it. This is my horror to suffer, not the surgeon's. But the monster insisted we keep the police off our scent.

Dr. Lock is a good and pious man, but he has his faults. Arrogance, for one. Zest for reverence and glory, for another, even if it means doing unethical things to get there. I found out about his implants a while ago. Deduced they were coated with silver. It wasn't hard after overhearing his exchange with that resident a few years back. Too trusting for his own good, that poor Lenny Reynolds was.

At first I was upset to be drawn unawares into Dr. Lock's fraud. After all, these were my patients too. But then I realized other people's secrets can be good to have.

The police are convinced they have their man, at least for now, but that psychiatrist is a different story. His insight is startling and his manner so genuine that I almost confessed to him. The creature wouldn't allow it though. Not after we killed a man for mere convenience this morning, and not with our next meal awaiting our return.

The creature assures me I've done well. No one will find us here. As we exit the house and step outside—because the two of us are one now, aren't we?—we let the difficulties of the day roll off us. Although in my weaker moments in the real world I might want to escape this evil hold, once we're here, once we're this close to her, we only want to feed. We refuse to ever go hungry again.

I hope she's been comfortable. Though she can't escape the windowless shack up in the tree, the creature made me bind her wrists with a plastic tie anyway. Even if she did manage to break the chain lock on the door—which she couldn't—she'd never get down without a ladder. Between her knee surgery two days ago and her bound hands, that twelve-foot drop would make walking impossible. But with her hands bound in front of her rather than in back, she can at least eat the food and drink I left for her and raise her hospital gown to relieve herself in the bucket I placed in the corner. And, of course, I left a thick blanket. She would need it in this weather.

The drug will have worn off by now, but it couldn't be helped. My day was too long. Hopefully the calming music I left behind for her will be a comfort.

When we enter, she'll show fear. They all do. But once her flesh becomes ours, she'll feel the relief we do. In that sense we're doing her a favor, and this at least brings the human part of *me* some comfort.

With a flashlight in hand and doses of medication in my pocket, we go to her now. Though the monster enjoys the fight, I don't, so before each feed I inject a heavy dose and make them as comfortable as I can. My other hand carries the bone saw. It's an unpalatable and horrific act for sure, but we have to get rid of the part that can kill us. Though we're building up immunity with our exposure—and I've had plenty of that in the hospital—we'd never survive a direct touch. Not yet, anyway. So until then, we have to get rid of it. When it's gone, we can suck at the marrow of the bone that's left.

As we make our way over the hidden path that leads to the shack, snowy dirt and twigs crunch beneath our boots. We try to ignore the bitter cold that makes cloudy puffs of air out of our breath every time we exhale. It worsens our hunger, which in turn makes me lose control in ways that scare me.

In the growing darkness we spot the structure and feel momentary pride. I designed it so well a few years back. We grab the ladder three trees away and position it against the small shack door. We climb up, unlock the padlock with the key, and crawl inside, careful not to hit our head on the tree that anchors it from inside.

The only light in the small space comes from bits of descending sun streaming through cracks in the wall. The acrid scent of urine hits us, and we're careful not to kick over the bucket. We see a figure crouched in the corner. She's not moving. Is she asleep? Or is she wearing the ear buds and listening to the music I left her?

We hear her whimper. Not asleep then. Her name is Sophia, but we don't like to refer to them by name. No need. Soon they become us.

"Please," she says, "these binds are too tight. It hurts, and I can barely feel my fingers."

We shine our flashlight on her. She blinks away in discomfort, but her eyes soon adjust. I whisk away the blanket on top of her, nothing but her hospital gown and robe beneath, and examine her wrists. They're bleeding—some areas crusted, others fresh. Though her pain gives me no happiness, the sight of her blood makes the creature salivate. Our mouth drops open, and at first I can't even speak. I try to quell my hunger, but the creature resists. Would it hurt to cut her binds? She can't get away. She has no weapon. And soon she'll be us. I'd rather consume her in a peaceful state than a pained one.

"I'll cut them," I tell her, "but first I need to give you a little more medicine." I withdraw a syringe.

"No, please, let me pee again first. And have another drink of water."

We can't help feeling irritated. Couldn't she have done this while we were gone? But I take a deep breath and remind myself she couldn't know when we'd return. Plus, fear makes our basic needs more vital. At least she's not crying for her son.

We place the autopsy bone saw on the floor and move closer to her. She trembles at the sight, and I say, "See? This is why we need to give you more drugs. It's my gift to you."

We plant the flashlight, beam up, on the wooden floor and pull the steel knife from my pocket. I bend down to cut her binds. "How's your knee?" I'm eager to show her that a human part of me still remains.

Before she answers, something sharp stabs our neck.

We cry out in pain and press our fingers to our neck. The flashlight falls over and spins around on the floor. Luckily, we feel no gushing from the wound, only a light bleed. She must have just grazed us, but with what? What weapon can she possibly have? In our panic, we drop the knife, and before we can grab it in the whirling light, something even sharper stabs the left side of our chest. It's our own knife. We fall back, stunned, and she pushes past us with a scream. She whips open the tiny door and struggles to descend the ladder. When my human form finally recovers enough to crawl to the door, we see her land on the frozen ground. She tries to grab the ladder and knock it over, but we grasp it in time. We're stronger than her, thank God, but my human form not by much. She gives up and, dressed in only the hospital clothes and slippers she came with, hobbles away on her still-recovering knee into the dusk, the surrounding woods making her invisible to anyone but Mother Nature herself.

The creature dips below the surface of my mind long enough for me to assess my injury. The knife is sticking out of the upper left chest of my winter jacket near my shoulder. My flashlight reveals the blade is only partially buried and should be okay to remove. When I pluck it out, I hold back my own cry.

Making my way out the small door, I descend the ladder, grimacing from the shoulder pain. My neck bleeds lightly, and when I reach the ground, I put a hand to it again. Then I feel something in my hair. With my flashlight, I see it's a sharp piece of bark. Clever woman. She managed to pry bark from the tree in the shack and stab me with it. Or maybe not so clever. Did she think it would kill us?

The creature surfaces again. We have to hurry. Despite her new knee, which must be extraordinarily painful to run on, she is disappearing farther into the woods. But we have two good knees and a flashlight, and we run toward her now.

She starts to scream, and as she hollers and shouts for help, we wonder if it could carry beyond the twelve acres of land. Any respect my human part felt over her clever attempt at escape vanishes. In its place comes a new emotion. An emotion almost as deep as our insatiable hunger and the relief her flesh and bones will bring us.

I—we—feel absolute fury.

## 46

Derek stood up from the cafeteria table and planted himself in Ben's path. "You're making a mistake going there by yourself. Let's call the police and have them investigate. Besides, what if you're wrong? It'll be another bullet in your career."

Ben righted the chair he'd knocked over in his haste to leave. "I don't care. If Sophia is there and I didn't try to find her, I'll never forgive myself." With his winter coat still in the residents' lounge, his white doctor's coat would have to do. There was no time to waste.

Laurette slipped on her jacket and grabbed her purse. "I'm coming with you. I will call the police on the way."

"No." Ben's firmness invited curious looks from hospital diners, their numbers growing as the dinner hour neared. "I've put your life in danger before, and I will *not* do it again."

He darted away before she could argue. Over his shoulder he yelled, "Just call the police and tell them to head there. They'll get there faster. Then call Detectives Becker and Patel."

Racing through the parking garage to his Mustang, barely noticing the cold despite his lack of outerwear, he pulled out his phone. If he couldn't find the address on Google, he'd have to go back inside and access the guy's medical record. But as Google so often does, it delivered. A house in a northwest Philadelphia suburb. People had no idea how much of their life was online.

Inside his car he entered the address in Google Maps, propped his phone in the dashboard holder, and let the female voice guide his way. As he drove northwest through Philadelphia to the suburbs beyond, icy streets and a Mustang's crappy winter handling dictated his speed. Soon homes grew bigger, yards more expansive, and wooded areas denser. In his frozen state, his teeth literally clacked against each other, his scrubs and doctor's coat no match for the car's old heater.

He prayed he was right. As Derek had inferred, wrongly incriminating another hospital attending would do Ben's career no favors, but it made the most sense. Divorced? Check. Ex-wife gets the suburban home? Check. Ex-wife and kids away in London for the year? Check.

If Ben recalled correctly, her departure had something to do with an ailing mother. But what if there was more to the story? What if his wife had left for other reasons? What if she thought her husband was falling off the deep end? And why exactly had he left his previous job in London before coming to Montgomery Hospital? Lenny had once hinted there might be more to the story, but Ben, never a gossip magnet like Karen, hadn't pushed further.

And who among the team had the most access to drugs? Drugs that could incapacitate a victim so he could…

Ben couldn't finish the thought. Wouldn't. He had to get to Sophia. He'd always let reason and logic guide him, but he'd learned from Laurette that sometimes the gut knew best.

At that moment Harmony's voice resounded in his brain: *Trust your instincts, son.* Her melodic speech was so oddly clear it was as if she were right there with him, but he had no time to ponder it further, because his GPS guidance indicated he'd reached the desired street, a rural, meandering, tree-lined road. Though the heater had kicked in, his shaking only worsened.

He slowed down. With the rush-hour traffic, the drive had taken nearly forty-five minutes, and darkness had since fallen. From that point on, an occasional streetlamp or a home's outdoor lighting was the only illumination. Each house was tucked back from the winding road, the elegant architecture an alternating mix of stucco, brick, and Tudor-style design. Acres of wooded land separated each residence, and although their immaculate, snow-covered yards were mostly barren of life, intermittent crops of evergreens made for a picturesque scene, even at night.

Long distances between homes. Lots of trees. Plenty of darkness.

Perfect place to hide someone.

*You have reached your destination*, the GPS guidance announced. Ben didn't need it. Up on the right, in a U-shaped driveway, a police car's swirling lights signaled he was in the right place.

*Thank God. Just don't let them be too late.*

Ben slowed the Mustang and drove onto the driveway.

He'd reached Dr. Muti King's home.

# 47

E venly spaced lampposts and in-ground lighting illuminated Dr. King's house, an elegant two-story structure of stucco and stone. The front door was closed, and the anesthesiologist was nowhere in sight. Two police officers were climbing back into their patrol car. One spoke into the radio attached to his shirt. The beam of their headlights revealed a dense, wintry woodland beyond.

"Wait," Ben called, flying out of his vehicle and trotting up the U-shaped drive toward the officers. The frigid air bit through his thin garments and stung his flesh, but he hardly noticed.

A brawny cop paused inside the driver's side door and then stood back up. One hand remained on the gun jutting from underneath his coat. "Sir, stand back."

Ben skidded to a stop and almost slipped on the icy pavement. His words rushed out. "I'm Ben Oris, my friend is the one who called you, it's my son's mother who's missing." The wind whipped his white coat against his scrubs.

The cop raised his hand an inch or two above the butt of his gun, but his fingers remained in position. "Sorry to hear that. But she's not here."

"Did you check the whole house?"

"Yep."

"The garage?"

"Yep."

"The backyard too?" Each of Ben's breaths, which were fast and shallow, released a visible cloud of air.

"Uh, yeah. Not my first rodeo, you know. Inside. Outside. The homeowner was very cooperative. No one—and not much else either—in there but him. Said he's getting the place ready to sell."

"What about the perimeter? Did you look all around the woods?"

"This is at least a ten-acre lot if not more, so no, we didn't 'look all around the woods.' But we covered a good area around the house. I think you're barking up the wrong tree with this guy."

Inside the patrol car, the radio sparked to life. A screeching flow of police speak requested a unit for something. The cop's partner yelled out, "That's us, Chuck. We're closest."

Chuck lowered his bulky body back behind the wheel. To Ben, he said, "Trust me, there's no one else here. Besides, we've been informed a suspect is already in custody. Let the detectives do their work."

"But—"

"Get back in your car, please. We'll drive away after you."

Ben stood rooted to the driveway, nose running, teeth chattering, wind howling around his ears. Then, realizing arguing wouldn't earn him anything but a ride in the back of the patrol car, he jogged to his idling Mustang, put it in reverse, and backed out of the U-shaped drive. Winding down the rural road, he saw the patrol car pull out of Dr. King's driveway and follow him.

*Shit. I have to get back there.*

After a mile and a half, the patrol car turned off on an intersecting road. Whether to respond to their call or because they were finally convinced Ben was heeding their order to leave, he wasn't sure. Didn't matter. After a few minutes, he made a U-turn on the deserted street and headed back to Dr. King's house. This time he stopped his Mustang the equivalent of two city blocks away, parking it as far over on the shoulder as he could to avoid having a passing vehicle clip it. Before he turned off the engine, he got out and swung around to the trunk to retrieve the emergency flashlight he stored there. Its beam was better than his phone's. He only wished he had an emergency coat as well. At least there was an old sweatshirt and a pair of gloves. He pulled both on and returned to the car, warming back up and readying himself for what he was about to do.

Once again, his mother's voice came to him. *Trust your instincts.*

He nodded as if she were there and turned off the car. At the same time, his phone rang in his pocket. Laurette.

"The police didn't find anything," he said as soon as he answered, plucking off a glove to make it easier. "They told me King willingly let them look inside and outside the house."

"Then she's not there. He's not the one."

"It's a huge lot off Evergreen Hills Road. No way could they search it all. And why would they? There's only two of them, and they think the suspect is in jail."

"Are they still there?"

"No, but I'm going back."

"Please, Ben. Don't go alone. Let me call the police. I will convince them to come back."

"There isn't time. I can't wait any longer, and there's no way I'm leaving before checking more of the grounds." He paused. "I'm trusting my gut here, Bovo. Isn't that what you always tell me to do? If Lock was the killer, wouldn't they have Sophia by now?" He pulled his phone away and checked the time on the screen. "Christ, it's already after seven. She's been missing for almost twelve hours." A swallow of grief choked off his words. "And it's dark," he managed to add.

"I understand. Just be careful."

Ben assured her he would and disconnected. He gloved back up, stepped out of the car, and headed toward the house, white coat flapping around his thighs beneath his sweatshirt like a fashion experiment gone wrong.

When the anesthesiologist's driveway came into view, Ben beelined to the woods. He wanted to avoid being seen. The last thing he needed was Dr. King calling the police on *him*. He noticed that in his absence, the outside lights had been turned off. Not even a porch light remained. Why would King leave the front of the home in absolute darkness if he wasn't up to something?

Waiting until he felt he was deep enough in the sea of snowy trees for his flashlight not to be seen from the house, he flicked it on. Shivering, he wandered deeper into the woods, the frozen ground a mixture of light snow, scattered twigs, and leafy debris that crunched beneath his shoes with each step. Beyond his quick breaths and the blowing wind, it was the only sound within the eerie, dark landscape. He tried not to let the size of the yard deflate him. He couldn't search it all, at least not quickly, so as abhorrent as it was, he climbed inside the killer's mindset. If he were going to hide a body—*please not Sophia's, please not Sophia's*—where would he do it? In the back of the house most likely. Even though the woods flanked the house from the sides and the rear, the camouflage was better back there. A bonus would be getting a peek in one of King's windows.

After walking what he assumed was a decent amount past the side of the house, he veered right and headed toward the back. A faint light shone through a window, illuminating a small swatch of stone patio. Ben quickly turned his flashlight off, hoping he hadn't been spotted. Were it July and not February, the trees would offer better protection.

With an eye on the house, he crept parallel to it, but he was too far away from its faint light to see effectively. He stuffed the flashlight in the pocket of his white coat and used his phone's light instead, dimming it to what he hoped would avoid detection.

He kept wandering, zigzagging the ground back and forth, but always keeping a parallel direction to the back of the house. He moved slowly at first, kicking at this or that, but as the cold bit and his frustration grew, he stepped up the pace. What was he thinking? Dr. King could have buried the bodies five acres away. And how would this help him find Sophia? If she wasn't in the house or garage as the police claimed, there must be a storage shed somewhere. That was what he should be looking for. But what if there was a hidden place *inside* the house? Did the cops search every room? Every closet? The attic? Instead of wasting his time in the yard, hoping to find some clue, he should try getting into the house.

But how?

With his despair mounting, his steps growing more aimless, and his blood freezing to slush in his veins, he reevaluated the whole "trust your instinct" thing. He should have listened to his head instead. That was where he worked best. He was getting no—

His foot struck something hard. He tripped and nearly fell, his heart rate shooting into the stratosphere. When he regained his balance, he shined his phone's light onto whatever had thwarted him. Still too dark. He turned up the screen's beam. More. More.

"Oh Jesus!" This time he did stumble back, falling on his tailbone.

Near the toes of his wet shoes lay an ashen and stiff corpse. Frozen blood covered the man's neck and coat, and more drops stippled his face all the way up to his dark hairline. His mouth was open in surprise, and beneath his dislodged, black-framed glasses his eyelashes were speckled with frost. His face wore a mask of terror.

Lenny.

At first Ben could only blink in disbelief, unable to process the improbability of his good friend and ally lying dead in Dr. King's backyard. It was absolutely incompatible with the Muti King he knew. Standing up slowly on wobbly legs, he brought his gloved hand to his lips and then his forehead. Only then did he realize it was the hand holding the phone, the screen light dancing all over in the dark.

He tried to shut it off, but his trembling fingers wouldn't cooperate. He ripped the glove off with his teeth and floundered over the screen, first shutting off the flashlight and then entering his passcode to call 911.

He made it through a 9 and a 1 before something crashed into his skull.

Staggering but not tripping, he stumbled a few feet forward. He rubbed the back of his head, his thoughts and vision blurry from the blow. Before he could see what—or who—was behind him, a needle slid into his neck.

In an effort to fight back, he spun around. Head forward, he lunged into the assailant, but between the head injury and the injection that was starting to take effect, his effort was weak. The figure stepped away, and just as Ben cleared his vision enough to get a look at the shadowy form of Dr. King, something swung out at him and clobbered his skull again.

He went down, down onto the frozen earth, his own coldness disappearing into a warmth of blackness where he heard a faraway voice say, "You shouldn't have come here."

Ben blinked his eyes open one last time, his phone light shining toward the back of the house. Someone he knew was running toward him.

Find Sophia, he tried to scream to the man, but no sound came. He gave up the fight and closed his eyes.

## 48

They aren't supposed to be here. Why are they here? The resident is unconscious on the snowy ground. The psychiatrist is coming closer. I hope he didn't see my attack. Maybe the cell phone flashlight was too faint to witness it. Has he called the police? Did the resident?

I think the answer to these last two is no, but what if I'm wrong? How can I kill them if the cops are on their way? There's no proof yet I killed the others. No bodies have been found, and my fake alibis are weak but unprovable. Plus, I easily fooled the police a short time ago. Pulled on a turtleneck sweater to hide my neck wound and avoided wincing in pain from the cut on my chest. So I might still be able to talk my way out of this. But not if these two men are found dead.

As if I'm a dog about to bolt, the psychiatrist advances slowly toward me, his gloved hands outstretched in a reassuring manner. Dressed in the same L.L.Bean coat and jeans he wore when he cornered me in the hospital this afternoon, he speaks smoothly and calmly. "I'll help you. Together we'll get through this. Just drop the weapon." His voice carries above the howling wind, and it's so silky and confident I almost believe him.

My mind is in a million pieces. I'm not sure what to do. I don't enjoy such senseless murder. I'm freezing cold and starving, and I feel like the beast has abandoned me. Left me to deal with this all on my own. I squeeze my hands around the tire iron that knocked out the resident and bite the inside of my lip until it bleeds. I have to stay sharp. I have to think clearly.

The psychiatrist comes even closer. I can't overpower him on my own. He's bigger, younger, and stronger and won't be easy to catch like the gimpy-kneed woman was. She was brave to try an escape. Her effort was so impressive I almost wanted her to make it. But once I caught up to her in the woods, I dragged her back to the shack and made her climb the ladder. "If you don't, I'll go after your son," I said. A bluff, of course, but she didn't know that. She climbed, sobbing the whole time, the pain in her knee obviously unbearable. Once inside, I sedated her again.

Also unlike the resident, I can't take the psychiatrist by surprise with the tire iron. So I play the game he wants. I toss the weapon far behind me. I confess. I sob. I beg for help and get down on my knees, the snow too thin to cushion me from the prickly bramble. And honestly, none of it's a lie. If he defeats me, I'll feel relief. Terror as well, of course. Terror over what will be my fate, terror over how to relieve my vicious and unrelenting hunger if I'm put away, terror over what effect my actions will have on my children. But relief nonetheless.

Still, I have to fight. *We* have to fight. Ah, the beast didn't abandon me after all. He's surfacing. He'll help me. Our hunger for her flesh and bones is too strong.

So when the psychiatrist extends his hand to me—to us—and helps us up, we reach into our coat pocket, wiggle our fingers out of our glove, and uncap the second syringe I'd reserved for the resident. Just as before, we stab it into the man's neck, which is the only skin exposed except for his face. Even his scalp is covered by a knit cap. He cries out in shock, and his lips form such a perfect wide *O* it's almost funny.

He falls more quickly than we expected. Hitting a blood vessel— even the large ones in the neck—with a blind stab is unlikely, espe-

cially here in the woods with the wind blowing all around us and the
only light coming from the cloud-covered moon and the resident's
phone on the frozen ground. But the beast has made me omnipo-
tent. The psychiatrist is already asleep.

With my chest still throbbing from the woman's earlier attack on
me, we drag his body closer to the chief resident, who we killed this
morning. The beast will want me to kill both of these men too. Bury
them back with the rest. But until we know whether we've been
identified by the police or not, shouldn't we wait? With the drug I
gave them, they'll sleep for a while. And why would the police
suspect me, anyway? It was easy to slip the woman out of the
hospital this morning, sight unseen. My chief resident oversaw the
anesthesiology patients in my absence. She grumbled, of course, at
being asked to do extra work, but I told her I had a difficult case on
another wing. After I tucked the woman away in the shack, I
returned to the hospital, no one the wiser. Beyond the resident and
the psychiatrist, no one suspects me, and if they *had* called the police
before I sedated them, wouldn't there be sirens by now?

A pain erupts in my head, and I squeeze my temples with my
palms. So many competing thoughts. The beast fades in and out,
and I'm not sure what's what. *Kill them now. Eat. Kill them later. Feast.
You're a caregiver. Devour. You're a monster.*

And then, in my delirium, the perfect solution comes to me. We
have to keep the resident alive for now. We'll feast and then we'll
frame him for the murders. The police might already suspect him.
We'll make it look like he took his own life, unable to keep going on
his horrific path. I almost envy him for that. If asked, I'll say he
must've discovered my former home was vacant and used it for his
killings. Of course, that means we'll no longer be able to feed here,
but then I'll either leave my job or kill myself. Either option is
imaginable.

But first, we have to kill the psychiatrist. The beast will have it
no other way. With a heavy but ravenous heart, I fish his phone,
wallet, and keys out of his jeans pocket. My gloves are back on, and
my thick finger accidentally presses the flashlight button. The beam
lights up the man's face, and I startle at what I see. His lips and

eyelids are swollen. A blotchy rash blooms on his neck. A bluish tint stains his lips. I crouch down next to him and hear a wheeze above the wind. I'm a doctor. I know what's happening. He's having an allergic reaction. Probably to the sedative. Without help, he won't get enough oxygen.

I dig in his pockets again and find what I'm looking for. An epinephrine pen. Although my natural instinct is to give it to him, the beast would never allow it. I slip the life-saving medicine into my coat. The psychiatrist's fate is sealed without further help from me. At least there's that.

"I'm sorry," I say. I repeat the words I said to the resident: "You shouldn't have come here."

Now we have to drag the resident into the house and tie him up. Can we do it? We're crazed with hunger. We're shivering too, but no longer from the cold. We're shivering in fervent anticipation of our feed. "We're coming," I call out to her in the shack that's a good distance away. "Don't worry, we'll all be one soon. Then you'll feel nothing but relief."

We pocket the resident's phone and drag his sleeping body toward the house, his sweatshirt and white coat riding up his spine. His keys and flashlight fall out, and we take those as well. He shouldn't be dressed so lightly in this weather.

Saliva pools in our mouth at the thought of our upcoming meal, and we lick our lips in anticipation. Still, the human part of me feels sadness. What would my son think if he knew the treehouse we'd built was now a deadly lair? Thinking these things brings me pain.

My wife took them away. My son. My daughter. Flew them back to her rich family in England.

"Let them stay with me," I cried when she revealed her plans.

"Are you serious?" she said. "Leave them with someone like you? You need help, Muti. Why won't you get it?" She looked angry and terrified at the same time. Though she couldn't be sure nor could she prove it, I know she suspected me of setting free those sickly souls in London, though probably not the one in Madison. What tipped her off, I'm not sure—women can be oddly intuitive—but her suspicions didn't develop until after we'd settled back in the

States in Philadelphia. "And don't even think about staying in this house after we leave," she'd told me as she kicked me out. "It's my money that bought it, and it's me who'll sell it."

So a year ago I tearfully said goodbye to my children and moved into an apartment. My kids never understood the reason, but they looked relieved nonetheless. Their expressions of barely concealed happiness ripped through my heart. So what if I was a demanding father? So what if I expected perfection from them and others? Didn't I give them my time? My love? My scrutiny?

Come summer, when school let out, she kept her word and moved them back to London. She listed the house a few months later. Little does she know I'm the one who bought it, using a business name I created. It took my retirement money and every penny I've saved over the years.

Still, it was too much on me. I tried to live here but couldn't. Too many painful memories. Nothing but furniture left anyway. No plants, no framed pictures, no knickknacks. None of the little things that make a house a home. My wife donated everything but the furniture—which she included for the new homeowner—to the mission downtown. So I tell everyone at work that I love my little apartment so close to the hospital. It's all a single man needs.

The plane crash in December was the final sledgehammer to my heart. I should've never made that humanitarian trip to Alaska, but I thought it would help take my mind off my family. Service to others, isn't that what they say heals our emotional wounds? But it didn't. It broke me. Huddling together with the others in the shattered remains of the aircraft, nothing but forced starvation and stabbing cold. It cracked me open and invited the ravenous, insatiable beast in. I doubt I'll ever be whole again.

On the patio, the beast returns and breaks my thoughts. We drop the resident's heavy legs and rub our head. Our brain is back in a million pieces. Feeding will help. Blood and flesh and bone. This is all we know, and it's what we focus on now.

After opening the sliding door, we drag the resident into the house, through the kitchen, and up the stairs to the master bedroom, flipping on lights as we go. His head, matted by congealed blood where we struck him, thumps each step, and this triggers sympathy in the man still inside us.

We dump him next to the heavy oak bed. Despite being outside, we're sweating from our exertion. Even at fifty-three, we're still trim and active, but we're weak from hunger, and this is hard work. It's been a long day of postponement and sacrifice, but it'll be over soon.

We run to the car in the garage, but all we can find is twine. We used the last of the plastic wrist ties on the woman after we carried her back to the clubhouse. It'll have to do.

Back in the bedroom that I used to share with my wife, where the kids once joined us for morning cuddles and breakfast in bed, we tie the resident's arms and legs around the bed's oak post by wrapping the twine around his wrists and ankles several times. He's still sedated and hopefully will remain so, because we used the extra dose of medication on the psychiatrist. His head lolls back and I gently reposition it so that it leans comfortably on the side of the bed, proof that a human part of us is still there. His blood stains the mattress, and the beast inside me roars with impatience.

We scuffle back downstairs, our legs shaking and our stomach raw with hunger.

The time has come. At last, we can feed. She'll become us, and we'll become her, and the resident will shoulder the blame.

## 49

A sliver of consciousness flitted into Ben's mind. Without remembering why, he tried to run, but his feet felt trapped in molasses. Maybe he was dreaming.

His arms encircled something. His legs too. Nausea plagued his core. Images and thoughts swam in and out of his mind. Fuzzy, incoherent, nonsensical.

And then one rose above the rest in its clarity: *she needs you.*

Like injured butterfly wings, his eyelids slowly fluttered open. Blurry, dizzying darkness all around him. No, a wedge of light on the carpet to his left. Coming from under the door.

He was in a room. Whose room?

His eyes threatened to close again, and he snapped them back open.

*Sophia. Find Sophia.*

With each mental bob closer to the surface, he started to move parts of his body. Throbbing head, numb fingers, legs as one unit. Softness against his face but hardness against his limbs. The smell of cushion and wood.

A bed post. He was tied to a bedpost.

How had he gotten there? The last thing he remembered was driving to Muti King's house and searching his back woods.

Oh no. Lenny. He'd found Lenny. Dead. Then he recalled pain. A blow to the skull. Maybe two. But how had he gotten in here?

With his alertness improving, he flexed his fingers to regain circulation. Realizing his wrists were bound around the bedpost, he shifted his arms and was relieved to find space to move. The diameter of the post couldn't be more than six or seven inches. Leaning his torso toward it, wincing at the pain in his head, he strained to get his mouth to the binding. Though he couldn't see it in the dark, the fibers felt rough and thin between his teeth. Was it twine? He bit into the bunched-up strands, and like an animal he gnawed, each motion of his jaw a lightning bolt of pain in his skull. He kept going, wriggling his wrists back and forth, the fibers loosening around them.

Sophia, get to Sophia, his brain echoed over and over again, and soon the chant synced in time to his chewing. When one strand snapped, he started on another. A front tooth chipped. He spit the enamel fragment out and kept going, trying to use more of his molars. Two strands, three strands, four, the slack around his wrists growing with each broken segment of twine, the skin of his forearms raw from rubbing against the bedpost as he worked. Finally, after what could have been hours or minutes, his wrists broke free. He pulled back from the bedpost with a satisfied grunt, his tongue working the surface of the chipped tooth. With his hands free, he tugged at the binding around his ankles. Unraveling the knot, he tossed the twine to the side, grabbed the bedpost, and clumsily stood.

Leaning against the bed for support, he lifted his sweatshirt and floundered around the pockets of his white coat and scrubs. His phone and flashlight were gone. Keys too. He realized the gloves he'd been wearing had been confiscated as well. He hobbled toward the wedge of light beneath the door, but his wooziness threatened to topple him. What drug had King given him? In his clearing state, he remembered an injection in the neck.

He flipped on the light. An elegant master bedroom with

unadorned furniture greeted him. Though Ben doubted King would lock him and Sophia up together, he searched the ensuite bathroom and empty walk-in closets to be sure. No Sophia.

Still staggering, he left the bedroom and, illuminated by a light from the great room below, lumbered through the upstairs corridor, his strength returning. How much time had passed? He looked at his watch, the hands uselessly blurring together.

He searched the two remaining rooms and a Jack-and-Jill bathroom. No Sophia. He shuffled down the steps and searched the entire main floor, flipping on lights as he went—great room, dining room, living room, kitchen. No Sophia. No landline phone either and nothing but paper plates and plastic silverware in the kitchen. Not a goddamn knife to be found.

Aware of the seconds ticking by, his panic grew. He flew out the side door by the laundry room and searched the garage. Empty shelves, a lawn mower, and an unlocked gray BMW. No Sophia. Not in the vehicle's trunk either, thank God. Still nothing to use as a weapon though, not in the garage itself nor the car or trunk. Given the absent tire iron, Ben had to assume it was what King had used to whack him in the skull. At least he found a big flashlight. He switched it on, saw a full beam, and turned it back off.

Next came the unfinished basement. Nothing but a furnace, a water heater, and more empty shelves. Despite the furniture in the main house, the place hardly looked lived in. What had the cop said? King was getting the place ready to list? Ben wondered if that was even true.

He ran back upstairs, his breaths heavy, his desperation growing. Where was she? King must be hiding her outside.

In the dark woods.

In the cold.

Pulling open the sliding door that separated the kitchen from the outdoor patio, he ran back into the woods. The cold was immediate, but he welcomed it. It cleared his mind even more. Using the flashlight from the BMW's trunk and the footprints in the snow to guide him, he returned to the spot where he'd found Lenny. Although the area was more than a hundred feet into the woods, the back of the house was still visible, especially with all the lights Ben had turned on. The thought of seeing his dead friend on the trampled ground again turned his stomach, but if there was a chance King had left Lenny his phone, he had to take it.

When he got there, his friend's ghostly death mask was no less horrible the second time around. Swallowing his sorrow, he bent over and rifled through Lenny's pockets—coat, jeans, fleece sweater —every pocket he could find. No phone. No keys. He wondered where Lenny's car was. He'd seen no other vehicles in the driveway when he'd arrived, and only the BMW, which wasn't Lenny's car, was in the garage. King must've already ditched it.

"Why'd you come here, buddy?" he asked mournfully. He wondered how Lenny knew King was at his old house and not at his apartment. And what had he meant in his note about forgiving him for what he was about to do?

No time to speculate. He had to find Sophia. But other than the blowing wind, there was nothing but an eerie night silence around him. Where did he even begin?

Glacial air penetrated his thin layers, and his shivering and teeth chattering quickly returned. As much as it disturbed him to do so, he removed Lenny's coat, stiff in places where the chief resident's blood had frozen, and put it on over his sweatshirt and doctor's coat. He grabbed his friend's thin gloves too. His actions would mess up the crime-scene analysis, but there was no time to worry about that. He'd be no good to Sophia if he froze to death. The temperature was in the teens, and with the windchill, even colder. At least there wasn't a lot of snow. He shined the flashlight around and started shuffling forward. He didn't care if King saw the beam. *Come and get me, you bastard. I'll—*

He stopped short. The flashlight caught something about six feet from Lenny. Another body. Derek.

"Oh Jesus no." Ben rushed to the psychiatrist, simultaneously praying he wasn't too late and wondering what the guy was doing there. Then he remembered seeing him before he was knocked unconscious.

He dropped to his knees and shook the psychiatrist's shoulders.

"Derek. Derek." No response. He shined the light over the guy's face with one hand and, after plucking off a glove with his teeth, felt his ice-cold neck for a pulse with the other. Light pulsations blipped against his fingertips. Still alive. He checked Derek's pupils. Pinpoint in size, suggesting, like Ben, he'd been drugged. But there was more to the story: swollen lips and eyelids, scattered welts blotting his face and neck, bluish lips. Ben remembered back at the ME's office Derek had mentioned being allergic to several drugs.

Feverishly, he checked Derek's coat and jean pockets for an EpiPen. Nothing. Would he even carry one if he was only allergic to certain drugs? Ben fished around again, but no phone or keys either.

"Fuck!" He needed to look for Sophia, but he couldn't leave the guy out there to freeze to death.

Doing the best he could with no phone to call for an ambulance and no car keys to drive Derek out of there, he heaved the psychiatrist over his shoulder and carried him back to the house. Twice Ben's legs buckled, and twice he almost fell, both from Derek's weight and from his own drugged muscles, but eventually he made it onto the patio and through the sliding door into the kitchen. He placed the psychiatrist on a checkered coach in the great room. He checked his pulse again. Still thready but at least there. Without the wind to mask the noise, a wheeze could be heard, and under the recessed lighting, Derek's facial swelling and hives looked even more horrific.

Ben stood back up. "Ah man, I'm sorry, but I gotta find Sophia."

Feeling like a piece of shit but not knowing what else to do, he pivoted and ran back outside. Waving the flashlight back and forth, he ran as fast as his wobbly legs would take him, heading deeper into the woods.

Barely a minute into his search, a sound stopped him short. He tripped over a branch and landed on his knees.

A cry. A muffled cry from somewhere off to his right. He was sure of it. He doddered his way to a stand, legs weak, head still foggy, and started in that direction, slow at first and then picking up speed. He whipped around the trees, flashlight bobbing, shoulders whacking branches, sprigs scraping his face.

Then, in the dark woods, a piercing scream split the air, an agonizing, awful scream like someone in pain.

He ran faster—*no, God, no*—sprinting toward the direction of the shrieks. Moisture hit his face, and his eyes blurred, and he realized it was his own tears.

And then the screaming quieted, but what Ben heard next made every hair on his head stand up.

"Stop! *Mon Dieu*, I am begging you!"

*Oh no, oh no, oh no.*

Laurette was there too. She must have come after she'd failed to hear back from Derek. Worse, she'd discovered where Dr. King was before Ben had.

He sprinted even faster.

## 50

Ignoring the cold stinging his cheeks and the frozen branches scratching his face, Ben rushed through the woods in the direction of Laurette's cries. To his enormous relief, the awful screaming had stopped, but what harm King might have already done he refused to imagine. Thanks to the adrenaline surging through him, his strength had fully returned, and the pounding in his head had weakened to a dull throb

A faint light appeared. He switched off Dr. King's flashlight to confirm it. Yes, there was definitely a light ahead. Turning his own back on, he sprinted toward the illumination, snowy twigs and branches flying out from beneath his shoes. Strangely, sounds of a struggle seemed to be coming from above.

"Why are you here?" a male voice cried. It was King's, but with a crazed tone Ben had never before heard from the reserved man.

With his heart pounding like a jackhammer and his breaths heaving in his ears, he ran toward the commotion.

Laurette screamed.

"I'm coming," Ben yelled. "Don't you fucking hurt them, King. I'll kill you myself!" He tried to run faster, but this far out in the woods, the trees were denser, some with naked branches, others with sharp pine needles. They poked his face, scratched through his scrub bottoms, and tore through Lenny's coat. Laurette's cries and Dr. King's eerie snarling seemed so close now—the light too—and yet he couldn't locate them.

Then he spotted the source of the beam. About twenty feet away, lying against the base of a thick tree, was a search flashlight on its side. When Ben saw what its beam illuminated, he stuttered to a stop. A bone saw, blood smeared on its blade.

He recoiled in horror, and sickness walloped him. Had King used that on Sophia? On Laurette? Was he too late? The idea was impossibly excruciating to contemplate.

Finding his feet again, he rushed toward the abandoned search flashlight and bone saw and found a ladder leaning against the tree. A glance up revealed a large shack, its tiny door open, dim light spilling from the inside. Growls and cries and the thudding of bodies hitting wood carried down from it. Was Laurette the one who'd tossed out the bloody bone saw? Hopefully before lasting damage was done?

After stuffing the flashlight in one of his coat pockets—beam pointed upward—Ben scaled the wooden ladder faster than a spider monkey. When he reached the small door, he flew more than crawled through its opening.

On his hands and knees, he looked around the well-built fort, illuminated dimly by a flashlight in the corner as well as the one in his pocket. About the size of a large bathroom, the shack was transected in the middle by the oak tree. A partially hidden body lay behind the tree, and in the left corner, on top of Laurette, was Dr. King.

Ben lunged toward him and gripped the back of his jacket. He heaved King to the side of the shack, where the anesthesiologist thumped off the wall and landed on his back. Though startled, in the shadowy light, King looked about as far from a man as possible. Crazed eyes, a matted nest of dark hair, snarling lips smeared with blood, mangled flesh dangling from his chin.

So beastly was the anesthesiologist's appearance that for a moment Ben could only blink in shock. But when the transformed

Dr. King started to rise, Ben snapped back into action and tackled him against the treehouse's wall.

He punched him once, twice, three times and felt more than heard the crunch of King's nose, the man's blood warming the thin fabric of Ben's pilfered gloves. "Bovo," Ben cried out, "are you okay?" He tried to locate her in the treehouse while also subduing King against the wall, but everything was too much of a blur. "Check on Sophia. Call—"

Something stabbed Ben's left forearm. He yelped. Pain shot up his shoulder, and his fingers tingled with electricity. A small blade protruded from his arm. Dr. King pulled it out, but before he could stab again, Ben grabbed King's wrist and tried to pry the knife from his hand. The anesthesiologist was stronger than Ben would have imagined. Not only did his small frame look the part of a beast, it *played* the part of a beast.

From behind, over Ben's shoulder, he heard Laurette sob, "Oh *Mon Dieu*. Oh, Sophia, Sophia."

Ben's stomach twisted in terror. "What have you done?" he shrieked to King. Rolling with him on the floor, smacking against the tree in the center of the shack, he tried to wrench the knife away from the crazed man, who was still howling and keening like a monster. Two more pokes stabbed through Lenny's coat into Ben's arm and more swung at his torso. Though Ben had at least thirty pounds on the anesthesiologist, he couldn't overtake him.

An idea came to him. *Ludicrous. It'll never work.* But he had to try. If he didn't do something, he'd soon have King's blade in his neck. "Laurette, give me your silver watch. Your watch!"

Laurette was speaking to a 911 operator. He worried she hadn't heard—or understood—but in the next instant she cried, "Here," and something flew across the wooden floor toward him.

With his stabbed arm feeling like shredded meat, Ben finally managed to get on top of King and, with his knee, pinned down the hand holding the knife. Then he leaned over and grabbed Laurette's watch. Feeling like a gullible idiot but praying Derek's theory was right, he held it against King's bloody face.

For a second nothing happened. Even Laurette's conversation with the 911 operator fell quiet.

And then, as if Ben had stabbed the knife through the anesthesiologist's eye rather than placed a silver watch against his cheek, King screamed, a scream so inhuman it pierced every cell of Ben's body and rattled his core. So intense was it, he had to fight the urge to release the howling man. "It's killing me," King cried. "It's killing me!"

Ben pressed it deeper into the man's flesh, unable to fathom that King's psyche was so damaged he actually believed the silver could kill him. But apparently he did, because the anesthesiologist gave up the fight and fell limp. He started muttering, then blubbering, and then sobbing incoherently.

Ben stared at him in the dim light, the man's face no longer the hideous mask of a monster but instead the visage of a confused, sick, and tragic man. Still, adrenaline coursed through Ben's arteries, and he remained pressed on top of King, unconvinced the fight truly might be over.

After Laurette described their location to the 911 operator, Ben panted, "Is she dead? Is she dead?" In his breathless state, his own voice sounded like a madman's.

No answer from Laurette. She must have still been on the line with the operator, because he heard her say, "Just hurry, please."

Though Ben continued to press the silver watch into King's face, he eased up on his body and finally pried the knife out of the man's hand, where it had been wedged beneath Ben's knee. The coat Ben wore was shredded from the blade and bloody in several places but mostly the left arm. Blood ran down his wrist and into his glove. King's coat, too, was stained with dried blood, especially near the shoulder. Had Sophia gotten in a lick before he'd restrained her?

"Laurette," he called out again, looking over his shoulder to the far wall. Sophia's unmoving body was partially visible behind the tree. "Is she okay?" Hot tears sprang to his eyes. "Is she dead? Please tell me she's not dead."

A pause. Then a pained, "Not yet. But I fear she will be soon. It's very bad, Ben."

Ben stared at the defeated, bloody-faced, broken-nosed anesthesiologist beneath him. Every molecule of his earlier fear shifted to fury. He sat up, his thighs still pinning King down. He raised the knife with his injured arm. The other one kept its hold on the watch against King's face. "What did you do?" Ben's words sprayed through gritted teeth.

More sobbing from King.

Ben edged the knife closer. He imagined burying the small blade into King's chest. Or slicing it across his neck. Imagined him writhing in pain and fear just like his victims had done.

"Don't do it," Laurette pleaded, as always sensing his mood.

After several raging breaths, he squeezed his eyes tightly together and held the knife across his body toward her. "Come watch him so I can check on Sophia." Though Laurette was a nurse before she pursued a career in public health and had tended to many wounds after Haiti's deadly earthquake, Ben couldn't even begin to breathe normally until he checked on Sophia.

Sirens in the distance, soft at first but growing.

As Laurette crawled toward him, shivering, her icy breath visible in the flashlight's beam, he realized her coat was gone and her left leg dragged behind her. Had King stabbed her as well?

"Just kill me," the man pleaded beneath Ben, his voice breaking.

When Laurette reached him, Ben pressed his frozen face against hers for a moment. Then he handed her the knife and the watch, which she continued to hold against King's face. "If he makes one move, one tiny move, I'll be right back here, but I have to check on Sophia. If she…if I don't get to say goodbye…I'll…I'll…"

"Go to her," Laurette said. "I can keep him down."

The sirens were very close now.

With battered and bruised limbs, Ben stood in a slouched position, careful not to hit his head on the low ceiling, and shuffled a few feet to the corner for the flashlight, his own having fallen out of his coat pocket during the struggle. He dropped to the cold wooden floor next to Sophia, where she lay limply beneath a blanket, her eyes closed, her breathing barely detectable. Swallowing his despair, he lifted the blanket and saw she was still dressed in her hospital gown. On her leg was Laurette's coat, and underneath that Laurette's belt, cinched above the knee to help stanch the bleeding. Even with the jacket's natural crimson color, Ben could tell it was saturated with blood. He flipped back the edge of it to check the wound and then mopped the hemorrhaging area with the corner of the blanket for a better look. A sob caught in his throat.

The bone saw had sliced all the way through Sophia's skin and muscles and partially through her femur, almost detaching it. Even with Laurette's belt as a tourniquet, the wound above the knee was so deep and wide in circumference that only immediate surgery would help save the limb. If even that.

With agony burning his insides and snot dripping from his nose, he placed two fingers to her neck. A faint pulse was palpable. "Oh Sophia. Sweet Sophia." Images of Sophia, Maxwell, and himself swirled through his mind. The three of them at the park, Sophia pushing a laughing Maxwell on the swing. The three of them at the toy store, Maxwell meticulously studying every train as if it were a precious stone. The three of them watching a cartoon on one of Ben's rare weekends off.

The sirens wailed near the house now.

Ben buried his face next to Sophia's, keeping pressure on her ghastly wound as best he could. "Stay with us, Sophe," he croaked. "Maxwell needs you. I need you. Stay with us." He lifted his head and to King sputtered, "Why? Why would you do such a thing?"

"She is a part of us now." The anesthesiologist spoke softly, and Ben had to strain to hear him. "We could no more deny ourselves her flesh than we could deny our own beating heart." Tears streamed down King's face, the silver watch still pressed against his cheek. "Please," he said to Laurette. "Just kill me." When Laurette didn't move, he pleaded more loudly. "Please. Kill me. Otherwise I fear I'll never stop."

Laurette raised the knife.

She stabbed its blade down.

51

The knife plunged into the treehouse floor, splintering the baseboard and sending wood shards flying. So shocked was Ben that Laurette had brought the knife down that it took a second for him to realize she hadn't really killed King. He almost wished she had. As he held pressure on Sophia's massive leg wound, all while trying to keep the blanket over her frozen body and checking her pulse frequently in case he needed to start CPR, he figured King didn't deserve any charity. Using the bloody sleeve of Lenny's coat, he wiped his eyes and nose.

"Please, just kill me," the anesthesiologist pleaded again.

Running footsteps and a blend of voices materialized in the distance.

Without letting up on the silver watch against King's face, Laurette leaned as far back toward the door as she could. "We're up here!" she cried out. "Up here in the treehouse."

Ben still didn't know the extent of Laurette's injuries, but he remembered her dragging her leg when they'd swapped places a few minutes before. "Did he hurt you?" he asked. He imagined her discovering King in the act of severing Sophia's limb and—using the element of surprise—prying the bone saw away from him and hurling it out the shack's door, where Ben had found it shortly after. It skewered his chest to think she had to witness such horror. "Did he hurt you?" he repeated.

Voices closer now. "Call out again so we can find you," one of them yelled.

"Up here, in the tree. Hurry!" To Ben, Laurette said, "He cut my leg I think, but don't worry, I am fine."

"There, over there, I see a light," a man's voice shouted outside the treehouse.

"Yes, we're up here!"

Ben pushed aside the blanket and lifted Laurette's coat to recheck Sophia's wound. Still too much hemorrhaging from the transected blood vessels. He tightened the belt tourniquet as much as he could, but it seemed to constrict no further. Saving her lower leg was a luxury at this point. All that mattered was slowing the blood loss. The wooden floor around him was sticky with congealing blood, some of it crystallizing in the cold. But the frigid temperature could work in their favor. In Sophia's case, a cold trauma patient might be better than a warm one.

With the cinching of the belt, Sophia stirred. Ben quickly covered her back up and tapped her shoulder. "Sophia. Sophe. Can you hear me?"

Her eyes fluttered open for a second and then closed.

"Stay with me, Sophe. Please." Ben pressed his face close to hers.

Her lips moved.

"What? What did you say? I can't hear you."

"Let me go," she whispered. "No tubes. If...that..."

Heavy shoes thudded on the ladder. Ben wiped his eyes again and then his forehead. How was he sweating when he felt like a human ice sculpture? "Stay with me, Sophe. Don't go. Think of Maxwell." A sob choked him.

Someone fell into the shack. From behind the tree Ben caught a glimpse of a police uniform. A bright flashlight lit up the space. "You can back away now, ma'am," an authoritative voice said. "We've got him."

Sophia was whispering again. Ben placed his ear against her mouth. "I didn't catch that. Say it again. Keep talking, that's good."

"No. Tubes," she repeated with great effort, her eyes briefly fluttering open and catching Ben's. He stroked her cheek. "Just...let me...go..."

"Oh, Sophe, I can't do that."

"Maxwell...our gift from God...take care of…"

His tears fell on her face. "You gotta stay with us. You—"

Somebody pulled him back. An EMT with a spinal board held awkwardly in his arms crouched in the confined space. "Let us get a look, sir."

More feet clomped up the ladder. Another paramedic spilled in, while a policewoman remained on the ladder. She swept the shack with her flashlight. "Whoa, too many people in here. Clear out."

It took Ben a second to realize she was talking to him, and it suddenly dawned on him how claustrophobic the treehouse was. In his panic over subduing King and tending to Sophia, he'd failed to fully appreciate it. But now his breathing grew tight, and a woozy dizziness washed over him.

"We got her now," the paramedic said to Ben, not unkindly.

"I'm a doctor," he croaked.

"You can come in the ambulance with us, but let us do our job now."

Ben, trying to process the chaos, stroked Sophia's face and started to scoot out of the way. He stopped. "Wait. There's another man who needs help inside the house. Derek Epps. He had an allergic reaction. Maybe to a drug this monster gave him."

"On it." The policewoman descended the ladder, and when she reached the ground Ben heard her call for another ambulance.

Ben scooted back against the wooden wall and let the EMTs access Sophia. Both men—one seasoned, the other young—tried to maneuver the spinal board behind the tree so they could load Sophia onto it. In the opposite corner a policeman was cuffing Dr. King. Laurette wiggled herself out the door and onto the ladder. With the now-ample light, Ben saw her face and hands were streaked with blood, and she grimaced as she started to descend.

Once she was out, the cop nodded at Ben. "Now you." A cuffed Dr. King was sitting by the man's feet, the watch no longer on his face. The viciousness he'd earlier displayed was gone.

Ben gave one final glance at Sophia while the two paramedics surrounding her in the tight space debated the best course of action. Try to get her down the ladder to expedite things? Or should they get a chopper, remove the roof of the treehouse, and collect her that way? To Ben's surprise, they already had an IV in her arm, fluid running in. That they had managed to find a vein in her cold, clamped-down state was a testament to their skill. Sophia would say it was just one of God's little miracles.

*Oh Sophe. Don't leave us.*

They decided immediacy was in order and opted for the ladder, which Ben now descended, his injured arm making his left grip weak. When he reached the ground, he found Laurette wrapped up in a blanket, two male cops asking her questions. He hurried to her and hugged her around the blanket, allowing her to lean on him for support, still unsure how badly her leg had been injured.

"Thank you," he whispered. "You saved Sophia's life."

"And you saved mine."

Dr. King came next, escorted away by the officer who'd cuffed him. His weeping apologies and sobs went ignored. One of the EMTs stuck his head out of the treehouse and pointed to the bigger of the two officers talking to Laurette. "Gonna need your help getting her down," he said. After making sure Laurette was okay, Ben darted back to the ladder to assist as well.

For the next several minutes, the two paramedics, the cop, and Ben worked on getting Sophia out of the treehouse and onto the ground. Strapped to the spinal board, more for ease of carrying her down than out of worry about a spinal cord injury, Sophia's eyes were closed. She seemed oblivious to her jostling descent, and Ben suspected she had slipped back into unconsciousness. Her chestnut hair whipped around in the wind, blowing into the face of the younger EMT closest to her head who was descending the ladder in an awkward sideways position, one arm gripping the ladder, the other the board.

When they got her on the snowy and trampled ground, the two EMTs jogged with her through the wooded terrain toward the front where an ambulance awaited. Ben started to follow but then worried about leaving Laurette. He wasn't sure if he was even *allowed* to leave. As if reading his mind, she said, "Go. Stay with Sophia. I'm fine." She looked at the officers. "He can answer your questions later, yes? He's a doctor and the father of her child. He should go with her."

One of the cops nodded, and although Ben knew he couldn't offer any more medical care than the competent paramedics, he darted off.

Dr. King's U-shaped driveway was a circus of flashing lights. Inside the ambulance, the EMTs got Sophia situated. As Ben crawled in behind them, his muscles frozen and his joints stiff from his brawl with King, one of the EMTs said, "Shit, we're losing her. No pulse."

The next few minutes were a blur, the ambulance speeding and flashing and wailing down a jumble of streets to the hospital. Ben wanted to be doing something, anything, and as one of the paramedics charged the automated external defibrillator and readied the life-saving medicines, and the other managed Sophia's airway, he took over chest compressions, her chest rising and falling beneath his bruised and frozen fingers.

"Don't die on us, Sophe, don't you die on us." He choked out the words. "We need you." Maxwell flashed in his mind, followed by Willy. For the first time Ben realized how truly agonizing it must have been for his father to let Max go. How much courage and self-lessness it must have taken him to help his life partner leave this world.

# 52

Six days later, Ben sat alone in Sophia's hospital room, his shock and grief as great as when he'd found her in Dr. King's tree-house. Although the *blip blip* of her cardiac monitor and the breathy pops of her ventilator gave the illusion of life, her brain was dead and gone. Her leg too. Too much blood loss. Too many cardiac codes over the past week.

Gone. Gone. Gone.

A zillion gut-wrenching, self-hating, torturous thoughts cycled through his brain, just as they had all week:

*If only I'd figured out it was Dr. King ten minutes earlier.*

*If only I'd driven to his place faster.*

*If only I hadn't spent the extra time searching his house after I got myself free.*

*If only I'd carried Derek in faster.*

*If only I'd started looking farther from the house instead of closer to it.*

*If only, if only, if only, if only, if only, if only. If. Fucking. Only.*

He leaned forward in the lime-green chair by her bed and squeezed his head in his hands. Maybe if he squeezed hard enough, he'd crush his brain into pieces. Crush the continuous loop of tormenting thoughts, the worst of which was the constant replay of the moment he had to tell his three-year-old son that Mommy would never wake up. Thank God Willy had been there to help him.

He choked off a sob. Soon Sophia's family would come, and with the help of the hospital staff, they would take her off life support. It would have happened sooner, but Ben was the holdout. He with the medical degree, he who understood there was no coming back from brain death, he who could interpret the EEG and scans, needed an extra day to accept it.

"Oh my dear daughter," Sophia's weeping mother had said, her husband speechless at her side, the same parents who'd shunned her when she got pregnant out of wedlock.

The choice was theirs to make. Ben and Sophia weren't married. He had no legal say. They had even declined organ donation (if any of her organs were even still viable) because they deemed it unnatural, and sadly, Sophia had no living will in place. But to their credit, they'd given him time to accept reality, his mind diving in and out of the obsessive what-ifs and the endless aching to turn back the clock. Although he couldn't imagine his son losing his mother, he knew Sophia's faith made her believe that she and Maxwell would be together again. That Maxwell would thrive under His divine grace. That death was a mere blip on the road to eternity.

How Ben longed for that kind of faith.

The time had come. He had to accept it. She was never coming back. One: evidence of coma with complete lack of responsiveness. Two: absence of brainstem reflexes. Three: absence of respiratory drive, confirmed by an apnea test.

Check, check, check. Sophia was three for three. Everything had been further supported by an EEG, cerebral angiography, and a nuclear scan. Given her young age, two physicians—an ICU attending and a neurologist—had evaluated her, and yesterday both had declared her brain dead.

And yet her heart beat. A ventilator filled her lungs with air. An intravenous line pumped her full of fluids. It seemed impossible to believe.

He was grateful to Rita, Sophia's sister. Over the past few years she had swallowed her animosity toward him, and she now promised him he wouldn't be alone. She'd even stood up for him the day before when Sophia's mother had repetitively wailed that Sophia's death was God's will, a phrase that made Ben want to rip off his own skin. God's will to take a young mother away? Bullshit.

When Sophia's mother had then promised they'd raise Maxwell to be a disciple of God, one whose path would share none of the moral lapses of his mother, Ben couldn't take it anymore. He'd burst up from his chair and was about to unleash, when Rita pushed away from the vent by the window and eased him back onto his seat. To her parents she'd said, "Maxwell is not our child. He's Ben's, and Ben will raise him how he sees fit." When her mother started to protest, Rita cut her off. "If we want to remain in Maxwell's life, we'll do it according to Ben's wishes and comfort level." Then she'd knelt down next to him and grasped his uninjured forearm. "I hope you'll allow us that." He had swallowed and blinked and nodded, grateful for another ally in the single-dad club he was about to join.

Plus, he had Laurette. She'd gotten him through this last week, extending her vacation to be with him, keeping Maxwell entertained, helping with Mrs. Sinclair.

He stood and approached Sophia's bed, her hair too rich and her skin too supple to belong to a dead woman, and yet her brown eyes, the ones she'd given to their son, were closed now and forever more.

He squatted and grabbed her hand, warm in his own but with not a whisper of movement or recognition. "Oh Sophia, I'm so sorry. So sorry," he repeated over and over until his mouth dried up and his eyes grew moist.

Someone's hands squeezed his shoulder. It was Rita. Her parents were near the door. "It'll happen soon," she said softly.

He wiped his eyes. "I'll give your family some time with her alone, and then I'll come back for…" He didn't finish. Couldn't.

Rita nodded, and Ben left the room, offering a solemn nod of support to her parents. Now was not the time to hold a grudge.

In a waiting room at the end of the hall he found Laurette. Although greatly relieved to see her there, he wasn't surprised. She would know he needed her, their bond eerily strong, which she believed stemmed from the force that had brought them together over five years before.

"Maxwell is with your father at his house," she said.

He sagged onto the chair next to her, its fabric stained with coffee. "That's good. Thank you. I already brought him in to say goodbye. Not sure how much he understood though." He steeled his jaw, holding back another set of waterworks. Never in his life had he been a crier. So much for that.

"It will happen soon now, yes?"

He glanced at the clock. "In forty minutes. Her family is saying their final goodbyes first, and then the staff will turn off her life support."

"You did everything you could, my friend."

"I did nothing."

"That's not true. You saved Derek's life. You saved my life." She pointed to her thigh. He knew beneath her jeans was a bandaged wound from Dr. King's knife. One of her cheekbones bore the greenish-yellow stain of week-old bruising, and although the swelling of her lower lip had resolved, a healing cut remained. Contusions probably lurked beneath her wool sweater too, just like they did under his own shirt. Stitched up stab wounds in his arm too, and his tongue kept probing the chipped tooth he'd sustained while chewing through Dr. King's twine. "You also saved future lives," she said. "The police thought it was Dr. Lock. Or Lenny. It could have taken another murder for them to shift their focus, if not more."

Poor Lenny. Derek—who was back in Atlanta and doing well after his allergic reaction—believed the chief resident's taking of the first leg might have been what triggered Muti King's bizarre Wendigo psychosis, or at least unleashed what was already building. Hearing about a severed leg with an implant—an implant King knew contained silver—might have set the murderous ball rolling. Although Derek had held several sessions with King in the jail after his arrest and as usual wouldn't reveal their conversations, Ben figured he was helping them out by revealing this "theory." Likely it wasn't a theory. Likely it was King's actual confession to Derek. Regardless, that night up in the treehouse, the anesthesiologist had looked every bit a monstrous Wendigo to Ben and not merely a man in psychosis.

But that was for the police to sort out. Ben was just sorry Lenny's name had gotten dragged into it. The newspapers and social media were having an orgasmic time with it all and didn't seem to care if their facts were correct or not. Lenny's parents lived two hours away, and when Ben had left Sophia's side to attend the chief resident's funeral, a somber event that broke what was left of Ben's heart, he'd set the record straight for Mr. and Mrs. Reynolds, assuring them that their kind-hearted son was not a weird, limb-stealing sociopath. He was merely a man who'd tumbled into the irrational and sad clutches of addiction.

"I failed Len," Ben said to Laurette, his voice soft.

"You could not have known he sent you an email that morning. The mother of your child went missing. Who checks their email on such a day?" Laurette rose and crossed over to the counter against the wall. Three large thermoses sat near the sink. She filled a paper cup from the one marked *Hot Water* and selected a tea bag.

She was right, of course, but it didn't dissolve Ben's guilt. A few days after the horrific night at Dr. King's, while the neurologist was running one of Sophia's tests to help confirm brain death, Ben had finally checked his email on his phone, trying to get his mind on something else for one goddamn minute. Instead of distraction, he found an email sent by Lenny early on the morning Sophia went missing. It was several hours after he'd left the note with Mrs. Sinclair. Maybe he'd been too paranoid to send it from his phone or computer before then but finally decided what the hell.

The email was another apology and not much more coherent than the scrawled note. In it, Lenny said he couldn't hack rehab, was too weak, and that he was going to find Dr. King for more drugs. Said a while back he'd learned something about the anesthesiologist's time in Madison, which was where King had worked prior to moving to London with his British wife. Apparently, King had left Wisconsin after an unexpected patient death. Nothing was proven, but Len said he figured it might be enough to lord over the anesthesiologist and get what he needed: more drugs and an escape. Between his substance abuse and taking Sampson's leg, he'd ruined his career, and worse, everyone thought he was a killer. He begged Ben to forgive him but felt he had no other option. From the email's tone, Ben imagined Lenny was ready to end it all.

From that message, Ben and the detectives had surmised that when Lenny went to blackmail the anesthesiologist, he discovered King had abducted Sophia. King killed Lenny (the chief resident's blood was found in the snowy mulch in King's driveway) and left the body in the woods to deal with later. How Lenny knew King would be at his old house—and in the morning, no less, when he'd normally be at work—Ben wasn't sure. Maybe he saw King getting in his car and leaving the hospital and then followed him, not realizing Sophia was in there too.

After interviews with various anesthesiology residents, Detectives Becker and Patel suspected King had slipped out of the hospital for a couple hours during the time Sophia went missing. The anesthesiologist had told his chief resident, Dr. Newton, that he had a case in a different surgical wing, but that lie was quickly debunked.

From that, the detectives deduced King had drugged Sophia, abducted her, taken her to his former house (which the news reports claimed King had bought after his wife listed it), and left her there until he could return that night. And according to the grapevine, King had since confessed some of it.

"So are you back in the program yet? It's strange to see you in jeans and a sweatshirt instead of surgical scrubs." Laurette handed him the cup of tea, her mauve fingernails a contrast to the white paper. "This one contains lavender," she said. "To help soothe you."

It took him a second to switch mental tracks. "Thanks. Yeah, the program director called me this morning. Said he'd needed time to review things but that Dr. Fisher had recommended my suspension be lifted and my record wiped clean, so to speak. That is, if I don't end up in jail for obstruction. I hired myself a lawyer just in case."

"In light of everything, I don't think that will happen. At least I hope not. And you deserve that research grant. You will win, I'm sure of it."

"Dr. Smith also put in a positive word for me."

"She's grateful for the help you've given her stepson. Will Joel pass the rotation, do you think?"

"With everything that's happened the past couple months, they're not going to hold him back. But I doubt he'll end up a surgeon."

"Perhaps that's for the best."

Ben allowed a small smile at Laurette's elegant dig. "Dr. Fisher —and the police—had the implants analyzed. Definitely silver-coated and based on Lenny's design, so Lock's got some explaining to do." Ben cracked his neck, old habits dying hard. "Sorry if I'm repeating myself. Just helps to take my mind off things, you know?"

"Of course. But what I don't know is what will happen to Dr. Lock. And what about his physician's assistant and scrub nurse? Did they know the implant was based on a stolen idea?"

"According to Karen, who always seems to have the inside scoop, neither of them knew, but it appears Lock offered them financial incentive—payment for being his research assistants—and the opportunity to co-author his paper when he eventually published the results." Ben kept talking, anything to get his mind off what was about to happen to Sophia. "I'm guessing it was more like payment for silence, but there's no way to prove that. And it's clear Angela needed the extra dough. Michael probably too. I wouldn't be surprised if either one of them had figured it out, especially Michael since he's the one who made the implant switcheroo."

"Will Dr. Lock lose his medical license? What he did was wrong, of course, very wrong, but he's done much good too, yes?"

"I'm not sure. Between his humanitarian work and his founda-tion, Montgomery will probably try to spin it. But he paid someone at Keplen—probably a few someones—to keep quiet, and that's not going to smell right to the public, nor should it. Plus, he stole Lenny's idea, even though he vehemently claims otherwise, and he likely physically harmed himself to make it look like I roughed him up. That's a pretty devious mind." Ben took his first sip of the lavender tea, but it offered no soothing. "I'm gonna do my best to redeem Lenny's name. Make sure people don't only remember him as the drug-addicted chief resident who sawed off a corpse's leg. If this implant design turns out to be a breakthrough in orthopedics, I'm going to make sure he gets the credit. He deserves that much and more."

"And Dr. King?"

"He can rot away forever as far as I'm concerned." Even though they were alone in the small waiting room, Ben lowered his voice. "Detective Becker spoke with police from London. King's name was linked to three unexpected patient deaths at the hospital there too, but, like in Madison, there was no evidence that he'd purposely caused them. He resigned and moved back to the States. Whether those deaths were due to incompetence—which I find hard to believe since he's such a meticulous guy—or actual mercy killings, I'm not sure. Becker hasn't passed that on to me. My guess is they'll never know."

"Those poor people." Laurette shook her head.

"And five here: Mrs. Templeton, Mr. Paulson, Ms. Simmons, Lenny…and now Sophia." Ben's voice hitched. "Cops found the three ortho patients buried in the woods in King's yard, but only superficially, given the frozen ground. Bite marks on all of them, missing flesh here and there, some exposed bone, but they certainly weren't eaten like King seemed to think he was doing. You probably read in the news that he had a bunch of silver buried in his back yard too. Silver cutlery, silver platter, maybe other stuff from his apartment. Seems he really thought it could hurt him, like Kryptonite or something. And yet he chose patients with the implants as his victims. That's messed up."

"Derek thinks Dr. King believed the indirect exposure to silver would make him immune to it one day, like a vaccine. So as long as he didn't touch the metal with his bare hands, he thought he could grow stronger from it."

"Whatever," Ben muttered. "Guess he didn't know you had a silver watch on under your sleeve."

"The man is severely ill. You cannot rationalize his thoughts.

Derek still believes a part of Dr. King wanted to get caught. That's why he didn't bury the limbs."

"Maybe. Maybe not. The case could also be made that he left the limbs in the parks to throw suspicion Lock's way. They were his implants, after all. I asked Patel when I spoke to him the other day, but he just blinked his tired eyes at me and shrugged." Ben sighed. "Guess Derek gets another feather in his cap. Not to mention the best case-study publication any physician—psychiatrist or otherwise—has scored in a while."

"He's a brilliant psychiatrist. Plus, he has made sure all the plane survivors will get the therapy they need."

Ben fiddled with the teabag thread dangling from his paper cup. "I wasn't very nice to him. I'm sorry about that. I should've apologized to him before he went home. When you're back in Atlanta next week, will you tell him for me?"

"Of course. He holds no grudge. You saved his life."

"It's just…I guess I saw him as…competition." Embarrassed to have finally admitted that, he took another drink.

"He understands. And don't worry. You two are both wonderful doctors. He is not your competition." She lifted an arched eyebrow. "In anything."

Ben averted his gaze but nudged her knee with his own. She nudged back, and it was the lightest he'd felt all week. But then he checked the clock, and his pain flooded back. A few more minutes. He continued to try to distract himself. "Thank you for helping Mrs. Sinclair. She's living through hell with her eyesight, and she doesn't have anyone but me and Soph—" He swallowed. "Well, I guess just me now." Laurette squeezed his hand, and he lowered his eyes. "I'm going to really miss you, Bovo."

"And I you. But it's only until the end of June. Just over four months."

"But then are you…are you going back to…" Ben couldn't bring himself to say it. He always knew the time would come when Laurette might return to her country, but it was too painful to dwell on.

"To Philadelphia, yes."

He whipped his head toward her. "You're going to take the epidemiology job here?"

She smiled. "I am."

"Please don't do it because of me. Because you think I'm too fragile right now. I don't want you to change your plans for me."

"You think too highly of yourself." She winked. "But I'm doing this for me. It's a wonderful opportunity."

Ben leaned back and closed his eyes, his enormous relief momentarily quelling his anguish.

"It's what I want. It's what my heart wants."

He opened his eyes and caught her gaze. There was so much he wanted to say to her. "Laurette, I—"

Sophia's nurse stepped into the waiting room and cut him off. "It's time," she said gently.

He nodded, handed his cup of tea to Laurette, and, as an afterthought, his phone too. He didn't need it going off at such a somber time. With a baseball in his throat and wet noodles for legs, he stood and somehow made it back to Sophia's room, trailing behind the nurse and her soft-soled shoes.

Rita and her parents sat around Sophia's bed, holding hands with her and each other and praying silently in their circle of grief. When Ben entered, Rita motioned for him to join her on her side. She took his hand, and he reached across the bed for Mrs. Diaz's. In that somber, horrible, awful moment, all past anger and regrets were suspended.

Mr. Diaz cleared his throat and prayed out loud, his words speaking of God's love and eternity and peace. Ben longed to believe them. After a few minutes the nurse returned with the ICU doctor. Both women were of similar ages, not much older than Sophia.

"Whenever you're ready," the doctor said, her tone soft and respectful.

The family members dropped each other's hands and stood. Rita bent to kiss her sister on the forehead, and her parents followed suit, tears flowing freely. When it was Ben's turn, he pressed his lips against her soft flesh, his tears blending with those of her family's, and said, "Rest in peace, my Sophe. Thank you for believing in me, even when I didn't believe in myself, and thank you for our beautiful son."

When he stood, he wasn't sure he'd ever breathe again. He nodded, and the doctor and nurse performed their duties of removing Sophia from all life support. Quiet sobs emanated from Sophia's family until the cardiac monitor finally flat-lined, and then their grief exploded. A strange noise erupted from Ben's own throat, and he felt like he might faint. All he could see was Maxwell and the toddler's mother who would be no more.

He clawed at his neck. He needed air. He had to get out of there.

He shot out of the room and bolted down the hall toward the stairwell, not passing the waiting room to see if Laurette was still there, not stopping to call anyone, not pausing to even question his actions.

He simply needed escape.

## 53

Unsure where else to go in his dizzying dichotomy of needing to be with someone but also needing to be alone with his grief, Ben drove to the Sethfield Long-Term Care Facility, his torso pitched forward and his fingers a vise-grip on the chilly steering wheel. In her coma his mother would be unable to respond, but if Willy were to be believed, she would listen. Ben would get his head in a better place and then go to his father's, scoop up his son, and never let go.

Once again he'd fled the hospital without a coat—didn't even have his phone; Laurette still had it—but at least his sweatshirt was thick and the shirt underneath long-sleeved. When he could breathe again, he would call Laurette from the desk phone at the center so she wouldn't worry.

He arrived at the drab brick complex, parked in the nearest spot, and trudged up to the second floor, all but ignoring the mid-February weather. The door to his mother's room was open, and a physical therapist named Arun was exercising her muscles. Since Ben's last visit, which, given all that had happened, was over ten days earlier, he saw Willy had replaced the flowers with a fresh bouquet, and a new paperback sat on her end table. Ben had been reading *The Kite Runner* to her. Willy must've finished it.

"I can take over from here," he told Arun. Although he tried to keep his voice from trembling, he imagined his eyes looked like two swollen beets from all the crying.

"You sure?" Arun, a lanky man with a gentle manner, lowered Harmony's left leg back onto the bed.

"Yes." Ben hadn't meant to sound so abrupt, but it was all he had to offer. He needed to be alone with his mom.

"Oh. Okay. Finished her left side and was just about to start on the right."

After Arun left, Ben studied his mother. Though hollow, her lightly freckled face usually seemed at peace. Today, however, she looked strangely weary, and her auburn hair splayed rather wildly over the pillow. Like two flesh-colored chopsticks, her pale arms were crossed over her chest on top of the blanket.

He covered her left leg with the starched blanket and flipped the right side up, tucking it between her legs for modesty. After rolling her nightgown up to her thigh, he began range of motion exercises, starting with her ankle. It felt good to be doing something.

"It's Ben, Mom. Sophia's gone." His words got stuck in his throat, and his eyes threatened to leak again. "I'm sure Dad filled you in on what happened. We just…" He swallowed. "We just took her off life support."

Working her calf and tibialis anterior muscles, he flexed and extended her foot. "It was awful, just awful. She didn't deserve this. Letting her go was the hardest thing I've ever done. I now understand what it took for Dad to do what he did with Max. I told him that last night. Told him I was sorry for judging him." Ben knew he was babbling but was unable to stop. "He's been so helpful to me—with Maxwell, with Sophia. Laurette has been too. I better call her soon. She'll be wondering where I am."

He lowered his mother's foot to the bed and flexed her knee joint. "Dad says you talk to him. Says you told him to protect me." He massaged her hamstring, the muscle atrophied but the skin over it warm and soft. "You know me. Hard to believe what I can't see. Even after all I've been through. But last week?" He puffed out his cheeks. "Last week, if I didn't know better, I'd swear it was you who guided me to Dr. King's place, helped me find Sophia. My common sense tells me it was simple logic, but I guess it doesn't hurt to say thank you."

He glanced up at his mother's face, unsure what he expected to see, but certainly not the worry frown all over it. He'd have to ask the nurse if she'd been ill. Something seemed off with her.

As they sometimes did, her eyes moved beneath her closed lids, but there was no sign of responsiveness beyond that. Unlike Willy, Ben had no expectations Harmony would ever wake up, and the doctors agreed. Still, she wasn't brain dead like Sophia had been, and she required nothing but enteral feeds through a G-tube.

Once he was practicing as an orthopedic surgeon, he'd take over the payments from her absentee parents. Maybe even move her someplace swankier. How they could hold such a grudge, he had no idea. How could they not want to see their grandson or great grandson? As Ben had just witnessed with Sophia, life was too short for that.

He realized he was still massaging his mother's calf muscle. "Sorry, Mom. Not myself right now. Let's do your hip." He started internally and externally rotating the joint. "I was just thinking about your parents and how life is too short not to heal old wounds. Maybe I should track them down again. I could have Sethfield call them."

An unmistakable look of pain darkened his mother's already bothered face.

Ben lowered her leg to the bed. "Am I hurting you?" he asked stupidly, as if she might answer. When her face contorted even more, he scooted to the head of the bed and rested the back of his hand on her forehead. He had no idea what was going on. It was as if the mention of her parents had upset her. But that's crazy, he thought. "I'll get the nurse—"

Someone burst into the room. It was Laurette, dressed in a new cherry-red coat, the old one ruined by blood and battle with Dr. King. She was panting, as if she'd just run all the way from her car, and her expression was so urgent it filled Ben with a sudden panic. "What's wrong?"

"Thank God you're here," she said breathlessly. "We've been looking all over, and I have your phone."

Ben stepped away from his mother's side. "You're scaring me. Is it Maxwell? Is he—"

"It's Sophia. She's awake, Ben, she's awake!"

"What…how…" Ben blinked in utter confusion, mouth agape, gaze traveling back and forth between Laurette and his mother. "I don't…I don't understand."

"It's a true miracle. It was only moments after you left. Her heart started beating, her lungs pulled air, her eyes opened. I…I…" Laurette seemed close to shock herself. "I can't understand it either. Like you, I am first and foremost about science. But this? This I cannot explain."

For a moment Ben wondered if Laurette was playing an awful trick on him, a horrible and vile trick, but she would never do such a thing. He started for the door. "I have to get back there. I have to—"

He froze. The hair on the back of his neck stood up. Something —no, *someone*—was speaking inside his head. It was Harmony's voice, as clear and melodic as he'd ever heard it. It said: *Hear me, my sweet Benjamin.*

Slowly, disbelievingly, he turned around to face his mother, weirdly frightened by what he might find. She was unchanged, leg still uncovered from their therapy, arms still folded over her chest, hair still splayed on the pillow. But her facial expression seemed less distressed. In fact, if Ben didn't find the whole notion preposterous, he'd say she looked…relieved.

Although her mouth showed not a hint of motion, she spoke to him again. *It's not Sophia's time.*

And then, just when he thought he was losing his mind for sure, she added, *I'm going to need her.*


## THE END

# AUTHOR'S NOTE

At the time I started writing *The Bone Hunger*, silver was not a part of orthopedic medical implants, although research was underway in that area because the element does indeed have antibacterial properties. As far as I know, implants remain silver-free, but as always with science in fiction, what's imagined sometimes becomes reality. If that's since the case, allow me this fictional liberty. On a similar vein, I strived to be as accurate as I could with the story details, but sometimes writers embellish. It makes for a juicier tale.

Montgomery Hospital is fictional, as are the other businesses named in the novel, including Keplen Biomedics. As I've mentioned before though, if Willy's Chocolate Chalet existed, I would be one of their most loyal customers.

# ACKNOWLEDGMENTS

As always, seeing a book to fruition involves many people along the way. I want to thank my keen-eyed editor, Kevin Brennan, and my invaluable beta reader, Kate Johnston, as well as Alec for his early read and insights. My sincere gratitude also extends to Officer Johnsen for giving me a cop's eye view of the police details and scrub nurse Sarah for reviewing the orthopedic surgery scenes. Any errors in the depiction of either profession are entirely on me. Furthermore, I wish to thank my wonderful and supportive online community. Your social media shares, comments, and kindness prove the internet can be a sweet and wonderful place. Another big thank you to my husband and sons for letting me bounce ideas off them and never being afraid to say, "That's dumb."

Finally, as always, I want to thank you, the reader, for giving me your time in a world that's already too scarce of it. Without you, writing wouldn't be nearly as much fun.

# ABOUT THE AUTHOR

Carrie Rubin is a physician-turned author who writes genre-bending medical thrillers. She is a member of the International Thriller Writers association and lives in Northeast Ohio.

To hear about Book 3 in the Benjamin Oris series or other upcoming releases, visit:

www.carrierubin.com

# ALSO BY CARRIE RUBIN

The Bone Curse

Eating Bull

The Seneca Scourge

CPSIA information can be obtained
at www.ICGtesting.com
Printed in the USA
LVHW042308310720
662090LV00005B/599